I0803010

PRAISE FOR
PHEASANTS NEST

'Louise Milligan brings her trademark clarity and compassion to a page-turning novel that examines the ripple effects of a devastating crime in real time. In *Pheasants Nest*, Milligan takes the reader on an unflinching journey beyond the headlines to the heart of the crime, where Kate Delaney, along with those desperate to save her, has her own poignant (and often darkly funny) story to tell. A lively, assured debut that is a welcome addition to the Australian crime fiction canon.' **JACQUELINE BUBLITZ, author of *Leave the Girls Behind***

'Milligan is a gifted writer, immersing us into a story as addictive as *Gone Girl* but with a distinctive Australian voice.' **PATRICIA KARVELAS, journalist and broadcaster**

'I loved the book. It's complex, and beautifully structured, and delivers intelligent insights into the worlds of policing and media without ever seeming to try too hard.

I consumed this novel in one sitting. In the character of Kate Delaney, Louise Milligan has given voice—and humour, and deep respect—to the ranks of women reduced every year to the stark, monochrome chalk outline that is "Victim of Crime".

It's a compelling story, written with tautness and wit. But its greatest achievement is to remind the reader that when human beings do dreadful things to each other, the pain and grief and horror do not happen in a vacuum; there is also love, and courage, and someone who will do the right thing even when it's terrifying.

Louise Milligan has spent most of her journalistic career refusing to turn away from pain. And in *Pheasants Nest*, she demonstrates with elegance and generosity what else can be seen when one squarely faces suffering, and human depravity. Namely: courage, love, black humour. All the things that are variously present in humans before they become victims of crime, but sometimes are forgotten after, in that terrible, flattening isolation of being a person to whom something unthinkable has been done.

In the characters of *Pheasants Nest*, one can clearly perceive some of the people who have most stayed with Milligan over her reporting career. In giving them depth and warmth and life beyond the chalk outline that reads "Victim of Crime, she does them—and us—a great service.' **ANNABEL CRABB, journalist, broadcaster and author of *The Wife Drought***

'Louise Milligan's journalism has always championed those who have been abused and victimised. Now she takes that same perspective into fiction, in this gripping, sinister—yet also wryly funny and realistic—crime thriller.' **JANE CARO, author of *Lyrebird***

'A gripping and devastating all-too-real thriller that had me on the edge of my seat, desperate to know how it was going to end.' **SARAH BAILEY, author of *Body of Lies***

'Anyone familiar with Louise Milligan's work will not be surprised to find her first novel is nuanced, considered and deeply concerned with the darkest places a human soul can go. But it's the style, pluck and heart in these pages that make what should be an unbearable story unputdownable. *Pheasants Nest* is simply unmissable.' **HAYLEY SCRIVENOR, author of *Girl Falling***

'When writers of truth write fiction, a profound understanding of the world echoes on every page. Louise Milligan's extensive experience as an investigative journalist provides an insightful backdrop to the story of the kidnapping of Kate Delaney after a night out with friends. Milligan's use of shifting perspectives allows the reader to see how the crime plays out through the eyes of everyone involved. Laced with clever insights and wisdom, *Pheasants Nest* propels the reader on a rollercoaster ride of peril and nail-biting tension. At the same time, the characters seem so real, you want them for your friends. Some of them, at least. It feels like everything Louise Milligan has learnt, has led to this novel.' **VIKKI PETRAITIS, author of *The Stolen***

'A crime novel that could only be written by a fine journalist—so original, funny and true. *Pheasants Nest* is a pleasure all the way.' **DAVID MARR, journalist and author of *Killing for Country***

'A blockbuster of a story . . . Louise Milligan has written a superb and disturbing page-turner.' **READINGS**

'Witty, suspenseful and compelling, Louise Milligan brings a fresh perspective to crime fiction . . . A thought-provoking and beautifully told story.' **SISTERS IN CRIME**

'Gripping . . . A compulsive, character driven thriller, *Pheasants Nest* is an excellent novel that I devoured in a single sitting.' **BOOK'D OUT**

Louise Milligan is a multi-award-winning investigative journalist for ABC TV's *Four Corners*, the Australian national broadcaster's flagship current affairs documentary program. Louise's first novel, *Pheasants Nest*, was published in 2024 to wide acclaim, and was shortlisted for the 2025 Best Debut Fiction, Indie Book Awards and the Best Crime Fiction, Danger Awards. She also is the author of two bestselling non-fiction books: *Cardinal, The Rise and Fall of George Pell* and *Witness, An Investigation into the Brutal Cost of Seeking Justice*. Her books have been awarded multiple prizes, including the Walkley Book Award, the Davitt Awards Best Non-Fiction Crime Book, the Melbourne Prize for Literature People's Choice Award, the Victorian Premier's Literary Award's People's Choice prize, the Sir Owen Dixon Chambers Law Reporter of the Year Award, a Press Freedom Medal and a shortlisting for the Stella Prize. Louise's journalism, particularly her coverage of historical institutional child abuse and the experience of women in the criminal justice system and parliament, has broken national and international news, sparked government inquiries and led to profound cultural change and law reform. She started her career in newspapers and is a former High Court correspondent and political reporter. Born in Ireland to an Irish mother and Scottish father, Louise moved to Australia as a child. She lives in Melbourne with her husband and two children. *Shellybanks* is her second novel.

LOUISE MILLIGAN

SHELLYBANKS

ALLEN&UNWIN
SYDNEY • MELBOURNE • AUCKLAND • LONDON

This is a work of fiction. Names, characters and incidents are products of the author's imagination or are used fictitiously. Any resemblance to actual events or persons, living or dead, is entirely coincidental.

First published in 2026

Allen & Unwin
Cammeraygal Country
83 Alexander Street
Crows Nest NSW 2065
Australia
Phone: (61 2) 8425 0100
Email: info@allenandunwin.com
Web: www.allenandunwin.com

Allen & Unwin acknowledges the Traditional Owners of the Country on which we live and work. We pay our respects to all Aboriginal and Torres Strait Islander Elders, past and present.

NATIONAL LIBRARY OF AUSTRALIA

A catalogue record for this book is available from the National Library of Australia

ISBN 978 1 76147 035 6

Cover design by Christabella Designs
Cover images by Riccardo Rea (Poolbeg Lighthouse and ocean); Shutterstock (rock wall)
Typeset in 12/19.2 pt Minion Pro by Bookhouse, Sydney

10 9 8 7 6 5 4 3 2 1

MIX
Paper | Supporting responsible forestry
FSC® C001695
FSC www.fsc.org

The paper in this book is FSC® certified. FSC® promotes environmentally responsible, socially beneficial and economically viable management of the world's forests.

FOR ALL OF THE GREGGS

'They thought they had only a girl to deal with and that, therefore, they could ride roughshod over her. But she would show them their mistake. They wouldn't have dared to have treated her like that if she had been a man.'

JAMES JOYCE, *DUBLINERS*

PART ONE
KATE

1

COCKLE LAKE

THE TIDE IS out. The shallows resemble vast silver mirrors spread over the endless brown silt, dotted with cockle shells and cuttlebone shards and smoothed out bits of green glass that used to be bottles. The air smells of kelp and sewage and industry. Two stained red-and-white ESB chimney stacks tower above the landscape. A tiny crimson lighthouse sits at the end of a snaking sea wall.

Kate Delaney's feet sink as she plods across the sand and it almost swallows her little patent leather shoes, staining her white frilly anklets.

She's come here with Nana and funny Auntie Dolores, who works at the bottle factory behind the chimneys and is on her lunch break. Dolores always holds Kate's hand the tightest. Dolores looks at Kate like she could eat her with love. When Dolores kisses Kate on the cheek, she sometimes wipes away a tear.

Kate's mother's mouth will harden into that straight white line when she realises Nana and Dolores have brought Kate to Shellybanks in her new shoes. The brown stains in her socks won't come out in the white wash.

Kate Delaney doesn't care. She's inspecting the shells she's collected on the way out to the cockle lake that shimmers in the middle of Dublin Bay, right off the shore of Shellybanks. She's going to ask her daddy to drill holes in the shells so she can fashion them into a necklace. She inspects the pink and brown stripes on the white ridges, turning over her favourites in her little hand.

She sees a compass jellyfish on the sand and it's so beautiful she longs to hold it, but she's afraid of it, too. She picks up a stick and is poking at it, overcome with repulsion attraction, when she is startled by a rushing of water. The tide is coming in, waves are lapping. First waves: toes. Second waves: ankles. Third waves: knees. She looks around for Nana and sees her standing on the wall; Kate recognises her purple dress, patterned with hyacinths, and brown coat. Nana is waving her arms furiously.

The water begins to swirl. Kate's stick legs feel unsteady.

Don't get caught in the currents, Kate Delaney. Run for the wall.

Straining against the pull of the water, she tries to run, but her feet sink into the silt.

Beside Nana, Dolores is screaming, her arms reaching for Kate, ready to run to her. Nana is holding Dolores back.

Don't get caught in the currents, Kate Delaney. Children have drowned.

The tide is moving quickly now, and the limestone wall feels so far away. It feels as if she'll never reach it. Blooms of moon jellyfish pulse by. Tears sting her eyes and her heart is beginning to race.

Don't get caught in the currents, Kate Delaney. Don't get caught.

For years afterwards, she relives that panicked dash to the wall at Shellybanks in her dreams. She never seems to reach that wall.

Don't get caught in the currents, Kate Delaney. Run for the wall.

2
ISLAND

KATE DELANEY IS floating.

The Ionian Sea looks like a rippled sheet of teal glass. It's so salty she hardly has to move to stay afloat. It's the clearest sea she's ever seen, and the water on her skin feels somehow more unctuous and milky than the ocean in Australia.

Her white limbs are spread out like the slender arms of burnt-orange sea stars resting on smoothed rocks on the ocean floor.

The sun warms her Celtic body, so liberally slathered with sunscreen, she looks a little blue. Huge dark glasses shield her eyes from the blazing sun. She can hear the screams of teenagers jumping off the rocks into the water not too far away. Beyond that is the wonky sound of church bells ringing, slightly off key.

Kate Delaney is trying to just be. It seems the only place where her mind is truly still is when she's allowing herself to be gently carried by this glassy sea.

But her reverie is broken when someone grasps her abruptly around her waist.

The old terror immediately floods her body. Fight or flight? Kate chooses flight, breaking away from the hold and diving towards the sea floor. She holds her breath, sunglasses still on and eyes closed, the sound of church bells replaced by her pulse pounding in her ears. She opens her eyes for a small peek and sees a luminescent fish. She's a siren under here. Maybe if she stays under for long enough, he'll leave her alone.

When she is forced to rise to the surface to breathe, she can hear a faint, distorted voice calling her.

'Kate! Kate, it's okay—it's just *me*.'

Gasping and blinking, she splutters. Kate can make out a hand with two distinctive freckles in the crevice next to his thumb. Nails bitten down. Soft skin untroubled by manual labour. Liam Carroll's hand. She knows she's not some sort of Raquel Welch, emerging from the ocean as a vision of glistening swept-back hair and lithe limbs. The seawater makes her cough and stings her eyes. She senses she resembles a drowning marmalade kitten in oversized Prada sunglasses and a dotted retro maillot.

'Fuck you, Liam Carroll! Don't ever fucking do that to me again.'

'I'm sorry,' Liam says. 'I'm so sorry.' He cups her face in his hands and gives her a salty kiss. 'You really shouldn't swim in those sunglasses, though. You'll wreck them.'

Her limbs soften. She starts to cry. She wonders when the rush of fear at the tiniest things will end.

'I'm sorry, too,' she manages.

'Come on,' Liam says, putting his arms around her. 'Let's get you dry.'

They towel off and walk back to the little villa Kate chose because the magenta bougainvillea in its whitewashed courtyard reminded her of her flat at home. She dries her hair and puts on a fifties sundress patterned with cherries and a pair of espadrille wedges, then dabs a slick of crimson onto her lips.

Kate has always thought you should dress well when you feel like shit. It can't help but drag you out of glum.

Liam is sitting at the little wooden table as she walks in. He looks at her and smiles. 'I love you,' he says, his brown eyes warm.

Liam is now in the habit of saying all the things he couldn't manage to say before, all the things he regretted not saying during those dark times when he'd thought he'd lost her. He used to be more circumspect. Cooler. He's not anymore. She doesn't care. She understands.

He pulls her towards him and peels the cherry dress off her again. She's standing tall in her wedges, and he puts his mouth on her thighs.

It had been a huge relief to Kate to realise that the sex with Liam was still a going concern.

It had taken time. She was terrified at first. Not so much of the act itself, but that the trauma would somehow make her love him less. But it didn't. Nothing about the way Liam held her resembled the violence of what had happened to her that night in the alley with that awful human.

She kicks off her espadrilles and they stumble across the cool tiles towards their roughly made bed.

—

Kate has joked to Liam that she has plagiarised this life from George Johnston and Charmian Clift. She had fantasised about escaping to an idyllic Greek island, surrounded by artists and intellectuals. She'd pose for their black-and-white portraits, and they'd be characters in her novel. They'd have rollicking parties, thumping their fists on the table as they argued about politics. She'd exchange knowing glances with Liam across the table.

In reality, she's still struggling to focus on stringing a sentence together.

So, she's relieved that Liam has taken long service leave from the firm. Neither of them has a solid plan about the length of time they'll be away. Just as long as it takes. They go for walks and swim in the shimmering sea. She loves how he takes pride in finding the best tavernas, where they eat sea bass practically still jumping from the ocean, with oregano and lemon juice and olive oil and tamarix greens and octopus carpaccio and saganaki. They wash it down with minerally Assyrtiko wine from Santorini.

They sit at the tables patrolled by neighbourhood cats waiting for scraps and invent stories about the locals.

When they settle the bills, the cats leap onto the table, scurrying away with a head of sea-bream and the tail of a red snapper.

—

Each morning, Kate walks down a rocky path to a tiny pebble-strewn inlet. The other beaches on the island are decked out with beach umbrellas and serve Aperol spritzes and endless portions of tzatziki and fried whitebait. Beaches crammed with over-tanned, ageing Sloane Rangers, lolling in the sun in micro bikinis, making future melanomas. But this cove is almost always deserted. Usually, that would put her girl hackles on edge, set her anxiety thrumming, but it is so beautiful she makes the effort to tamp down her fear.

Liam is looking younger and fitter and, to Kate's eyes, even more handsome. His almost-black hair seems thicker in the salty air. His eyelashes become clotted in the ocean. He wears linen shirts and navy shorts, and his arms glow with a golden tan. No defence counsel yells at him, ever. He doesn't get passive-aggressive text messages about costs. He hasn't used the words 'catastrophic injury' or 'contumelious disregard' for two months.

Back home in Australia, before they left, Kate's newspaper editor, Cameron Patrick, seemed almost a little afraid of her.

Camo didn't know what to do with his pity. He couldn't give her eye contact. It was as if her trauma was somehow catching.

After some time recovering in hospital and then at home, she initially attempted to return to work, but she'd frequently have to go and sit on the toilet, shaking. She'd sit and stare at the bathroom tiles, study the little chrome lock on the door, wonder how long the coat hook had been missing. While she did it, panic would tumble over her, in waves. She'd finally go back to her desk and hope no one spoke to her. She couldn't form words. She mainlined antacids and sprayed her face with rosewater mist and felt like she might self-combust from heat. Her colleagues gave her sideways glances, sometimes sympathetic, sometimes a little afraid.

Liam had had to take the car keys from her, as she had made the mistake of telling a few people that, at times, she was overwhelmed with the sense of wanting to drive into a tree. She wasn't going to drive into a tree, of course; it was just a feeling. A feeling of blotting it out. She felt like she was in that nineties movie, *Fearless*, with Jeff Bridges, where he is a middle-class white guy who has PTSD after surviving a plane crash, and strikes up an unlikely fierce bond with a Latina woman with whom he has, ostensibly, nothing in common beyond the fact that they were both survivors of the crash. Kate remembers that scene where the pair of them drive towards a wall at speed. She remembers seeing it, many years after it first came out, and thinking that the Jeff Bridges character was being indulgent and childish, and feeling sorry for his wife. But now she gets it. Now she sometimes feels like driving towards a wall, at speed.

She was grateful that Liam had, at least in some ways, shared her trauma, and so she could just be this person with the jangled nerves around him, because he had the jangled nerves, too.

She managed to bash out a first-person piece about her ordeal, just before the Walkley Awards' deadline closed. The paper ran it as a breakout page-one splash and an accompanying feature in the weekend magazine. It was good, and she knew it, and everyone knew it. But it was also abundantly clear that they couldn't exactly give that prize to anyone else.

Was there any other journo in Australia, ever, who had been raped, then kidnapped, then left for dead and somehow, miraculously, survived? Kate didn't suppose so. She could have offered up some pretty sloppy prose and, as Camo would have said, they'd have turned that shit into strawberry jam. But she didn't. Her prose was tight. And bright. And unflinching. It hurt to read it. She wanted it to hurt.

People told her how *Incredibly Brave* she was. She just tried to change the subject. What do you say to that? What choice did she have? Anally raped in a dark alleyway. Kidnapped by the loser who did it. Locked in a freezing cage under a highway bridge, with only the ghosts of suicides to keep her company. Left to contemplate her death while he threw himself to his. She just tried to survive. And almost didn't. Until they found her.

'How are you faring, Ms Katie D?' Camo asked, using the annoyingly jovial nickname she tried to ignore. They were sitting at the newspaper's top table in a casino ballroom, lights casting a fuchsia glare on their skin. She'd just floated onto the stage and accepted the Gold Walkley.

Her peers rose to a standing ovation, because, of course, *they had to*. Liam linked her arm to get her up there, because she mightn't make it on her own.

'I don't feel brave,' she told her editor, staring ahead, blinking and holding a champagne flute to her lips. 'I can't feel my skin.'

'You just do whatever you need to do, Kate,' Camo told her. 'I think you might need some more leave to get better.'

She sardonically noted—through her trauma—that he had waited for her to write the piece that had the most online clicks in the newspaper's history before delivering this information.

But still.

'The company will cover you for as long as it takes,' he said, squeezing her hand.

One of the nuances about Cameron Patrick had always been that while he was an insufferable womaniser and could at times be a total jerk, he was utterly capable of ultimately doing the right thing. He could reach into himself and find sensitivity and empathy. His face would soften in this very kind way. Perhaps that was why he was a successful womaniser in the first place.

He spoke to the newspaper's proprietor, and it was agreed that they would pay Kate Delaney her full salary on leave until she could work again. They wouldn't worry about any sort of work insurance regimes or whatever. Kate would just say the word when she was ready to come back.

It was the sort of old-fashioned gentlemen's agreement that the proprietor and his senior editors would execute from time to time.

Kate Delaney was being paid to go to the other side of the world, to try to recover from a crime that had fixated the nation and left her hyper-vigilant and afraid. Her employers could be arseholes at times. But when they wanted to, they knew how to find their core of decency. And for that she was grateful.

Kate dipped into her inheritance. Her parents, Mary and Billy, had been, to their credit, financially responsible. They had healthy life insurance policies, and the mortgage had been paid off. She wouldn't be rich, but if she was careful, she would never have to worry too much about money. She paid for the flights to Greece and an upfront lump sum for the accommodation, and off to Athens she and Liam flew. She knew she couldn't go without him.

From there, they had ferried to the island with the magenta bougainvillea, the burnt-orange sea stars, the pebbles that gleamed like gemstones, the church bells that clanged slightly off-key, the cats that queued up outside the fishmonger every morning, the whitewashed walls and the teal glassy ocean.

So, now, she's had the edges knocked off her, but here she is, wearing fifties sundresses on a tiny Greek island, just like

Charmian Clift. She'll never have a better opportunity to produce the Great Australian Novel.

If only she can stop shaking and figure out what the hell to write.

3

PHONE CALL

KATE IS LYING on their bed under a thin waffle blanket, her head on Liam's arm, watching the sun glinting through the olive grove behind their house. She can feel his breath on her back, his body curled around hers. A rooster crows and she can hear the splashing of someone doing laps in the pool next door. When she lies really still and closes her eyes, she hears the waves.

Her phone buzzes on the bedside table and she reaches for it reluctantly.

It's a message from her aunt, Dolores Murphy, who is getting married in Killarney in eight weeks' time. Kate and Liam have already booked their flights. They'll go to the wedding, then stay on for a few weeks. Kate wants to show Liam around the country of her birth and his ancestors before they return to their island.

Ah, Kate, terrible news. Call when can. Dolores.

Kate adores Dolores. Her aunt prides herself on being 'bold', the Irish word for naughty. 'I'm a very bold girl,' she'll deadpan, with a glint in her eye. 'I speak three languages: English, a little bit of Irish, and Bad.' She swears like a trooper, smokes a solid pack a day, and does as she pleases. She's stubborn and honest and loves Kate with an intelligent ferocity. She had never made any secret of the fact that Kate was her favourite. There is something particularly special about being loved by an auntie, Kate thinks. When Dolores hugs her it's like sunshine on her skin.

She scrambles out of bed.

'What's up, Kater?' Liam asks sleepily.

'I'm not sure yet. Need to ring Dolores.'

When her aunt picks up the phone, she's sobbing.

'Jesus, Dolores, what's happened?'

'You need to come, Kate,' her aunt manages.

'But what's happened?'

'It's Kevin. I'm losing him.' Dolores starts to wail. She sounds like a little girl.

'What did he do to you?' Kate asks, anger rising. If Kevin has dumped her beloved aunt just before the wedding, she'll kill him.

'Jaysus, he did nothing,' Dolores says between sobs, 'except love me. He had chest pains the other night and didn't he go to the doctor to have it checked out, and didn't your one tell him to go to the hospital, and didn't they then tell him they needed to open him up?'

'What did they find, Dolores?'

Dolores sucks in some nicotine then says in a quavering voice, 'Only that he's fucked. *Fucked.* Mush, they found. They found mush.'

Dolores explains that Kevin's liver was cirrhotic and his pancreas cancerous. Like so many men of his generation, Kevin has always been on friendly terms with the drink and hardly ever went to his GP. But he just kept powering on, pretending there was no bother at all, until the morning when he collapsed on the kitchen floor with those chest pains.

'He hasn't woken up,' she says. 'And they tell me he won't.'

'Oh, Dolores. I'm coming.'

'Thanks, pet.'

'Love you.'

'Do you really think you should go?' Liam asks when Kate tells him what's happened.

'What kind of question is that?' she snaps, irritated. 'It's family. It's Dolores. Of course I should go. Why wouldn't I?' Sometimes he has this tendency to baby her in a way he never did in the before times.

'I just don't want you to be exposed to any more trauma,' he says quietly.

'This isn't exactly trauma, as such,' Kate says. 'It's just really, really sad. And life's fucking trauma, isn't it? Besides, Dolores would come if it was me.'

'I know. But Dolores hasn't been through what you've been through.'

'You've got no idea what Dolores has been through,' she retorts.

If she is honest with herself, Kate isn't entirely sure what Dolores has been through herself. There has always been something, a big gaping something, at the heart of Dolores Murphy. Though an often ebullient sort of woman, she would sometimes suddenly go quiet or even get angry. Kate's mother, Mary, told her how Dolores had lived away for a time when she was in her teens, and then came back. But the subject was a no-go zone in the family. No one talked about Dolores's past. Except to say that she was 'a bit of a soul'. And, if Kate expressed any curiosity, 'Don't you be asking all your questions, Kate Delaney.'

What Kate does know is that after years of being single, never showing any interest in men, Dolores had met Kevin in her early fifties and was as smitten as a schoolgirl. Everyone in the family was delighted for her and she had been planning their wedding for months.

'Anyway, I'm not going to discuss it,' Kate says to Liam. 'Could you please just go and change my flight? And yours, too, if you're coming.'

'Of course I'm coming, Kater.' He squeezes her hand.

'Good.' She pulls her hand away and bites the quick around her thumbnail.

It's bleeding again, Liam notices.

He walks into the front room and stares out the window at the cobbled streets and whitewashed buildings with blue-painted window frames. A donkey is clopping its way up the lane. He can smell spanakopita and coffee. Their peaceful reverie is coming to an end, he senses. He sighs and opens his laptop and logs in to the Aer Lingus website.

They pack hurriedly and board the ferry for the mainland. She presses her face against the dirty acrylic of the ferry window and thinks of Dolores. Slowly, Athens emerges, stretching out over the brown landscape like clusters of quartz, glistening in the pink dust. Kate tries to ignore the knot of anxiety in her solar plexus and breathes.

As they are boarding the plane that night at Athens' international airport, Dolores texts again.

He's gone.

4

DUBLIN

KATE DOZES THROUGH the four-and-a-half-hour flight, waking in time to see glimpses of startling emerald through the grey clouds.

'Look,' she whispers to Liam. 'Home.'

She lapses into a melancholy silence, reminded of her mother, Mary, whose ashes Kate scattered among the seals in the waters off Port Fairy. Mammy always referred to Ireland as 'home', but she never made it home in the end.

Fuck life to hell that someone like Mammy died so young, Kate thinks. Fuck life to hell that Dolores has lost her love. Fuck life to hell.

It's Saturday.

When Kate was a child in Dublin, Saturdays meant children collecting their grushys from wedding buses. Do they still do the grushys? she wonders. It's been decades since she actually attended a wedding in Ireland. Back then, there'd be killings made as wedding guests en route from church to the reception flung coins at the neighbourhood kids, who scurried for every last punt like sewer rats.

Kate's younger cousin, Richie Daly, was the King of the Grushys, elbowing others out of the way, as he dived for the coins and stuffed them in his pockets.

Richie Daly was the sort of 'right young gurrier' who would lift up sofa cushions to find change that had fallen out of his dad's pocket. Who'd save up his Easter eggs till all the other kids had eaten theirs and then he'd pull out the chocolate and slowly peel off the coloured foil.

'Wha'?' he'd say, as his younger cousins salivated at the sight of the eggs they'd long since eaten.

At his first holy communion party, Richie approached every ageing uncle with his hand out for a tenner.

Of course, every ageing uncle (and aunt) would undoubtedly give you a tenner at your first holy communion anyway. That was kind of a legislative requirement. But you weren't meant to ask. You were meant to seem surprised that money was being lavished on you in this way. You were supposed to act as if you weren't expecting it at *all*.

When Richie Daly and Kate Delaney had their Blessed Holy Day, the oul' ones couldn't help but admire Richie's pluck, though.

'Ah, go on, Richie Daly—the *hide* of him,' they said to each other, winking, taking a sup of their pints and pressing the wrinkled notes into his hand. Richie would hold the cash up to his face. It shone slightly and smelled like leather.

Looking up from the corner where she sat in her own first communion finery, reading *What Katy Did Next*, Kate clicked her white patent leather-clad heels together and clucked her tongue. 'You're very bold, Richie Daly,' she said, adjusting the prickly combs that held the scratchy veil onto her lacquered cloud of auburn hair, as she watched him collect the cash.

'Bold, yes, and richer than you,' Richie shot back.

Richie Daly didn't need grushys or first communion tenners anymore. He had recently completed renovations on a five-bedroom house with a terraced garden in Foxrock. He had offices in the vast tech precinct that had now risen alongside The Dodder behind Auntie Maggie's flat. He was great fun and Kate was looking forward to seeing him.

Maybe if Kate Delaney had cared more about grushys and less about books, she muses, things would have turned out differently. Maybe if Kate Delaney had cared more about grushys, she would never have become a newspaper journo. Maybe she'd never have been on the tear with a gaggle of girlfriends, also journos, who'd egged her on when she sassed The Guy.

Maybe. Maybe not. These are the sorts of maddening rabbit holes her brain takes her down all the time. It's pointless, and she knows it's pointless, but she does it anyway.

Her pulse quickens as she thinks of The Guy.

Fuck life for The Guy being born. Fuck life for The Guy doing what he did to her. Fuck life.

She snaps open a yellow Rescue Remedy tin and pops two in her mouth for good measure. Are these things merely placebos? Possibly. She's been mainlining them for months.

She reaches for Liam's hand and entwines her fingers in his.

'What's up?' he asks.

'Just thinking about grushys,' she replies, gazing out the window and shifting in her seat.

'Grushys?'

'Never mind.'

The plane wheels bump bump through misty rain onto Dublin tarmac.

They collect their bags from the luggage carousel and, through the crowd of people, Kate spies Dolores Murphy standing alone and somehow shrunken.

Kate drops her bags and runs over to her aunt.

'Ah, c'mere to me,' Dolores says, enveloping her in a tight hug. Then, weeping, she takes Kate's face in her hands and smiles through her tears. 'Still the most beautiful girl in the world.'

Dolores has been saying this to Kate since she was a baby. Kate gets that it's not true and that Dolores is horribly biased, but it always makes her feel safe in the way those well-worn childhood scripts do.

Dolores always signs her cards to Kate from 'your good-looking auntie'. Kate loves that. Dolores is an attractive woman, but she's not a pin-up girl. Her eyes have naturally comically long lashes and always seem somehow to be winking at you. Her heavily veined hands have long fingers, bedazzled with the clusters of semi-precious jewels that are her weakness. Kate remembers her once sporting what appeared to be an enormous emerald-cut diamond atop a gold ring.

'Jesus, Dolores,' she had said. 'How did you afford that?!'

'It's a cubic zirconia, you eejit,' Dolores had said, with a raspy laugh.

Kate's mother, Mary Delaney (née Murphy), was an altogether softer looking woman. But Dolores's unswerving dedication to nicotine has started to have its way with her.

'I'm going to see Nico,' she'd always say before she ducked outside for a fag.

Kate knows how guilty Dolores feels that Mary Delaney, a teetotaller and non-smoker, was taken so early, while she, who could smoke and drink anyone under any table, has remained in rude good health.

But Dolores is one of the best people Kate has ever met in a way that's hard to convey to anyone who doesn't know her. She never had any children herself, but she's mothered Kate all her life. Some of Kate's earliest memories are of being pushed in the buggy by Dolores, or sitting on the bed with Dolores's jewellery box and picking out which earrings matched her outfit for the day. Dolores was a rebel and a risk taker, but she was always incredibly protective of Kate, even more so since her sister died and Kate was left alone.

'I'll never replace your mammy, but you can think of me as a second mammy,' Dolores had said when she flew over to Melbourne for Mary's funeral. Coming from anyone else, that would have pissed Kate Delaney right off. But coming from Dolores, it was a comfort.

And that's why seeing Dolores now, shrunken and pale and wearing grief like a drab anorak, is so hard for Kate to take.

Dolores notices the way Kate is looking at her.

'Ah, don't,' she says. 'I don't want to hear it. I don't want to talk about it.' She holds up her hand as Kate goes to speak. 'I just want you here. That's enough.'

Kate nods.

'Now,' her aunt says, exhaling, 'where is the famous Liam Carroll?'

Kate motions to Liam, who has kept a respectful distance during this scene. He approaches, laden with all of the luggage.

'Ah, Kate, he's gorgeous!' Dolores says.

Liam blushes. 'Nice to meet you, Dolores. I'm so terribly, terribly—'

Dolores holds up her hand again. 'No. Don't. I don't want to start fecking crying again. I'll be no use to anyone.'

'You don't need to be of use to anyone,' Kate says as she relieves Liam of her bags. 'It's your duty to be a bloody mess. And there's nothing wrong with crying. It's healthy. I've cried for Australia this past year.'

'And so you should, so you should,' Dolores says, squeezing her again. 'I just wish that bastard hadn't killed himself because I would have flown over there and made *him* cry, so I would. And then I would have killed him myself. And I'd've found a cruel and unusual way to do it, too.'

'Let's not talk about him,' Kate says, swallowing.

'Oh God, Kate, I'm sorry,' Dolores says. 'I'm just so tired. I'm so, so tired of crying. You know what I mean? It hurts—physically and mentally. My bones hurt. My brain hurts. I don't want it anymore. Or at least, not for now. I wish it would fuck right off till the funeral. I'll cry then. Now I've got too much to do.'

'That's why Kate and I are here, Dolores,' Liam says softly. 'We're here to help you. Lawyers aren't everyone's favourite class of human, but we're good at times like this.'

'Ah, you're a good boy,' Dolores says.

'He's a keeper,' says Kate.

'He is that,' says Dolores.

—

Leaving the terminal, they make their way to Dolores's small car for the drive to her tiny terrace in Ringsend.

Dolores is quiet. Her bedazzled fingers grip the wheel. She usually has a pathological need to fill silences, as if silences are somehow inhospitable, but now she is all out of words. And so is Kate.

While the approach to Dublin from the air is green, at ground level it is mostly brown and grey. Stained grey statues of the Blessed Virgin peering with oddly stern serenity from the roofs of austere mission-brown seventies-era schools with treeless playgrounds. *Hallowed be thy name.* Eighteenth-century churches. *Peace be with you. And also with you.* Sparsely patronised pubs with faintly chartreuse lighting. Áth Cliath double deckers rumbling down streets littered with Taytos packets and cigarette butts. Swans gliding through polluted canals. Kate loves it all.

Her pores seem to tingle when she arrives. *This is where I am meant to be. These are my people.* But then she opens her mouth and speaks, and it turns out she's not one of them at all. 'I'm not like all those Americans searching for their roots,' she wants to protest. 'I'm part of this.' But she has had to accept that she'll always be looking through a windowpane, tapping on the glass.

When they get to Dolores's tiny terrace, Dolores fixes Kate and Liam some brown bread and Kerrygold butter and ham and Irish tomatoes. Dolores stews tea in a slender silver pot that belonged to her great-granny and pours the brew in an elegant brown stream.

'Now,' she says.

Kate squeezes her hand.

When Liam doesn't quite know what to say in a crisis, he makes himself indispensable. So, the next morning, he starts on the many phone calls that need to be made. Undertakers, banks, distant relatives, catering, coffin, urn.

Kate and Dolores, meanwhile, alternate between conversations and crying jags.

'I think I'll have soup at the wake,' Dolores says at one point. 'Everyone likes soup. And brown bread. Sheila up the road can get the best soda bread.'

Sheila delivers some soup to taste and it's delicious.

'Ah, it's not right,' says Sheila, looking at a photo of Kevin on the sideboard.

'It's not,' says Dolores blankly. 'Nothing's right. Nothing will ever be right again.'

Sheila fixes her gaze on Kate. 'And what about you, Kate? Howarye?' In her voice is the familiar blend of sympathy, discomfort and curiosity.

'Howarye? *Howarye?*' Dolores answers on Kate's behalf. 'Well, of course she's fecking shite. She's doing the best she can, Sheila. And she's very good to come here for me.'

'Sorry, sorry, sorry, right so,' Sheila says, and gathers her bag and her raincoat. 'I'll leave you to it.'

'We really appreciate you making the soup,' Kate says. 'You're very kind.'

'Ah, it's nothing,' Sheila says. 'Mind yourself, Kate. Mind yourself, Dolores.' And she bustles out.

Dolores is still muttering indignantly.

'Dolores, she's helping you . . . and us,' Kate reminds her. 'And anyway, I'm used to people looking at me like that.'

'You're an awful good girl, Kate Delaney,' Dolores says, and pours them another cup of tea.

5
THE REMOVAL

KEVIN O'BRIEN WAS a kind man, but he generally kept himself to himself and he could count his real friends on a hand and a half. He and Dolores had been happy together. They would have a pint at the pub a few nights a week and chat away to the locals, but they did not cast a large shadow over their community. They didn't go to bingo, which Dolores thought was for eejits who threw their money down the drain. And they didn't go to mass, which Kevin wouldn't have minded so much, but Dolores thought was for eejits who believed in the sky fairy. She hadn't entered a church since 1979, save for a wedding or a funeral. But that was another story altogether.

So, the matter of Kevin's removal was something that was causing Dolores some anxiety. Typically, a removal, which involved a loved one's body being laid out in the home or the funeral parlour, would see a line of well-wishers queuing up the street to come and pay their last respects. Dubliners did a very good line in death. But Kevin just didn't know that many people.

Dolores wanted to do the right thing by him. And a removal was expected. She would just have to make do; whoever would come, would come, and feck the others to hell. The next day they would have the funeral, then go to the wake at the GAA, where they'd eat soup.

Dolores goes ahead to the funeral parlour to meet the director and spend some time alone with the body. Kate and Liam linger in town for a while before going to meet her. The funeral parlour is an ordinary shopfront on an ordinary street in south-west Dublin, where Kevin had lived before he moved in with Dolores. Inside, though, it's all pastel plush carpet and hushed tones and *I'm very sorry for your loss.*

The undertaker is called Brenda, and she wears a maroon skirt suit with a ruffled blouse, her hair in a heavily lacquered chignon.

When Kate sees Dolores sitting on her own on a pink stuffed armchair in the foyer, hot tears spring to her eyes. Dolores Murphy doesn't have much money, but she's good at putting an outfit together and she looks very chic. Kate has always thought there is something devastating about seeing someone who has lost their beloved dressed beautifully for the funeral. Especially in this case. Dolores Murphy had waited all her life for love.

Liam gives Dolores a peck on the cheek before going to wait in the foyer. Australians don't do removals and the idea of seeing a dead body is horrifying to him. The last body he'd seen was his mum. Dolores understands.

Brenda wafts over. She smells overpoweringly of Elizabeth Arden's Red Door and hairspray. She speaks to Dolores in a tone that one might employ with a child who has learning difficulties. She seems perturbed by the fact that she can't call Dolores 'Mrs' and often goes to say 'Mrs' and then stops herself. Every time she does it, Kate—aware of the horrible irony in the fact that Dolores and Kevin had been only a few weeks off being married—feels like stabbing her.

'I'm very sorry for your loss,' Brenda says to Kate.

Kate wants to retort that it's not *her* loss, it's Dolores's loss. But then, she doesn't want to insult Dolores by intimating that Kevin O'Brien, whom Kate barely knew, was not a loss. So she just nods awkwardly.

'Now, Mrs . . . Dolores,' Brenda says, turning to Kate's aunt, 'Kevin is in here. It's cold tonight so we've got the heater on. But I want you to tell me if it gets too hot in there, because won't his make-up run? We can't have that.'

Dolores is grasping on to Kate's hand for dear life and, underneath the lipstick she's applied for this odd occasion, her chapped lips are pressed firmly together. She doesn't say anything.

'Right, so,' says Brenda, and opens the door.

The room is suffocatingly small. It has the look of the room in a middle-class house that no one ever enters, the room where they keep the figurines and the Good China. In the centre of the ceiling is a glass chandelier that is far too large for the space. The carpet is pale green with little pink rosebuds scattered on a diamond-shaped trellis. The heavy curtains are tied back with gold sashes, and lace netting covers a fake window glassed over the bricks.

At the end of the room is a faux open fire with a manufactured stone mantelpiece. Debussy's 'Clair de Lune' is tinkling out of the speakers.

In the middle of the room, laid out among the pearlescent satin folds of an ornate coffin, is Kevin.

Kate's heart skips an unpleasant beat. The sort of beat that hurts. She doesn't really cope with corpses and this one is no exception.

Kevin had always had a goatee, but the hospital had shaved it for hygiene reasons or something. He looks absolutely nothing like he did in real life. The undertakers have slicked back his thick curly hair like he's some sort of gangster. His face is thick with some sort of unspeakable funereal foundation. His pallor is stone grey but for a couple of daubs of pink blush which make him look like he's in a pantomime.

Dolores goes and clasps Kevin's hand, which doesn't look like a human hand anymore, but rather like the hand of a cheap doll whose roughly stitched fingers are stuffed with spongy polyester and covered in flesh-coloured pantihose. The tops of his hands have an orange hue, while his palms are the colour of marble. Have they used freaking bronzer on his hands? Kate wonders. Is this meant to make them feel better? Undertakers are so odd.

Kate starts to feel waves of nausea. She's imagining having to do this for Liam. Imagining Liam's cheeks roughly rouged, and Liam's lovably messy hair all combed and Brylcreemed by some lady called Brenda. She looks away.

—

In the hallway, Liam is worried about Kate. He knows she wants to support her aunt, but he also knows that this place is not at all good for her in her current state.

He himself is feeling sick about being here, thinking of his mum, Pauline, and the last time he saw her: at the private family viewing, lying in one of these coffins, her hands clasped absurdly as if in prayer. It was the sort of image that never really leaves a teenage son's mind. The sort that has never ceased to haunt him.

He approaches the door of the parlour and sees Kate, her face white, her eyes darting around in an effort to avoid the elephant, or coffin, in the centre of the room. Glancing at it himself, he is reminded vividly of his mum, and he starts to feel a bit breathless and clammy.

And so, he turns on his heel and walks out of the funeral parlour. He strides down the road to the near-empty pub with the chartreuse lighting and orders a Guinness with a whiskey chaser. And then another. And another.

—

Despite Dolores's fear that no one would show up, the chairs around the perimeter of the parlour have been occupied by a small but respectable crowd of neighbours and family wanting to pay their respects to Kevin. After standing for a while with her arm around her aunt, nodding and exchanging the stiff pleasantries one does at a time like this, Kate feels a need to sit down, but the only chair available is right next to Kevin's head.

Don't look at his head.

She tries to make small talk with the Syrian family who are sitting next to her. They lived in a council house next to Dolores's place and Kevin would help them out occasionally with odd jobs. The woman is weeping as she recalls how kind he was, and Kate is making empathetic little sounds but all she can think of is the fireplace and Kevin's make-up.

Don't look at his face.

Two friends of Dolores's from up the street bustle in.

'This is Bernie and Bernie,' Dolores announces to the room.

One Bernie is waif-like, and the other Bernie is plump. They wave hello.

'Ah, would you look at him,' thin Bernie says, clucking her tongue. 'Doesn't he look gorgeous? Wouldn't you think he was only asleep?'

Kate calls absolute bullshit on this in her mind. Kevin doesn't look gorgeous, and he doesn't look asleep. He looks unrecognisable and dead.

Plump Bernie walks over to the coffin and kisses Kevin on the forehead. 'Rest in peace, chicken,' she says. 'Sleep the sleep of the just.'

As the room fills, the heat becomes stifling. A split-system unit pumps out hot air from the corner of the ceiling, and below it the faux fire burns away merrily.

'Kate Delaney, would ye look at you,' a distant uncle says breezily from the other side of the room. 'I don't think I've seen you since you were fourteen.'

'Ah, she's the image of her mammy,' his wife says, raising her voice slightly to carry over the corpse separating them. 'The image. Poor Mary. Gone too soon.'

Kate nods stiffly.

Don't get caught in the undertow, Kate Delaney.

Don't look at his face.

Brenda is nowhere to be seen and Kate wonders if she should go and tell her to turn down the heat. She can't help but glance from the fire to Kevin and, sure enough, something is trickling down the side of his face. He's melting like a waxwork figure on a hot day at Madame Tussauds. *For the love of God.*

Kate's auntie, Annie Daly, has taken the seat alongside her. Annie is a good and warm woman—her mother's younger sister. She takes Kate in her arms.

Kate starts sobbing silently, trying not to show that she is beginning to hyperventilate. 'I'm not used to these things,' she whispers. 'I'm not coping.'

'Want to come out into the corridor for a minute, pet?' Annie says.

Kate looks over at Dolores, who is busily receiving people for Kevin. She nods and they go outside.

'I'm sorry, Annie,' she gasps. 'You must think me terrible.'

'Ah, go on with ye,' Annie says. 'These things are bullshit. I'm here for Dolores, but I hate these fecking removals.'

'I'm so hot,' Kate says, trying to catch her breath as the anxiety rolls over her. 'His make-up was running, Annie.'

'Oh Jaysus, tonight,' says Annie.

Kate looks around for Liam, wanting to introduce him to Annie, but she can't see him anywhere.

'Listen, Kate, I know you're trying to be a good girl for Dolores, and she really appreciates your support, but this is not good for you,' Annie says, her eyes shining with meaning. 'Richie's in his car waiting for me. Do you want to go and sit with him?'

Richie Daly, King of the Grushys.

Kate nods.

'Grand,' Annie says. 'Off you go.'

Stepping outside, Kate takes big gulps of freezing air. She glances around but Liam is still nowhere to be seen. Where the fuck is he? Why would he leave her at a time like this?

Over in the corner of the car park, she spies Richie Daly's latest-model Range Rover. She walks over and slides into the passenger seat.

'Kate Delaney,' Richie Daly says, his big round face beaming.

Kate smiles back at her naughty cousin.

'Fancy car, Richie Daly,' she says. 'Long time no see. Thank God for you.'

'Only the best, cousin. Only the best. And yeah, there's no way I'm going in there.'

'I thought removals were still normal here?' Kate says.

'Well, they are for the likes of Mam and Dad's age, but I think they're bollocks. Why would you want to go and look at an oul' corpse?'

'I guess it's a sense of closure,' Kate says. 'And at least the Irish confront death.'

'We never fuckin' shut up about it,' Richie says.

'True,' Kate continues, 'but Australians look the other way. Button it up. Get all uptight about it. All that WASPy shite. But God, that room is so tiny. And they've got the *heater* on, Richie. The heater. I kid you not, Kevin's make-up was starting to run.'

'Christ,' Richie says, 'that's desperate.'

He lights up a cigarette and, seeing the look of horror on her face, asks if she wants him to roll down the window.

It's going to be either freezing Dublin air or cigarette smoke in an airless car. She opts for the former.

'You're a bold boy, Richie Daly,' she says, sighing.

'I am that,' says Richie, blowing a smoke ring out through the Range Rover window. 'But it's part of my appeal. You know what your problem is, Kate Delaney?'

'I suppose you're going to tell me.'

'You think too much and too hard. It's not good for you.'

'Should've worked on maximising first communion tenners and scouring the floor of wedding receptions for loose change.'

'Ah, for fuck's sake, you'll never let me live that down, Kate. But maybe you should've.'

—

The removal is finally over and Dolores and the mourners file out of the funeral parlour. Kate is by now nauseous, not from anxiety, but from passive nicotine inhalation.

'See ya, Richie,' she says, giving her cousin a quick peck on the cheek. 'Thanks for coming to the rescue.'

'At your service,' Richie says with a wink. 'You look after yourself.'

Kate gets out of the car and walks over to Dolores.

'I'm starving,' Dolores says. 'Let's walk down to O'Grady's.'

O'Grady's turns out to be the pub just down the road.

In the corner of the room, sitting alone, is Liam Carroll. There are four empty pint glasses on the table and a shot glass. He's asleep. Kate walks over and nudges him awake.

'Not the time, Liam.'

'Oh, sweetheart, I'm so sorry. I just can't do death at all.'

'Yeah, look, I'm not wild about it either. But sometimes we have to step up.'

'I feel like I'm stepping up all the time. I feel like all I do is step up. Trying to work out what is the best way to step up. How not to trip up on the way up to stepping up.'

She softens. 'You're right. I'm sorry. Your entire life at the moment is stepping up. It's just that I had a panic attack and couldn't find you. They had the heating up so high that Kevin's make-up started running.'

'Oh Christ,' says Liam.

'Yep,' says Kate. 'There was a split system heater *and* a faux fire. In a funeral parlour. For a removal.'

'Good grief,' says Liam. 'Want a chardonnay?'

'I do,' says Kate. 'I really, really do.'

He kisses her then pulls away. 'You smell like Marlboro reds,' he says.

She shrugs. 'Richie Daly,' she says nodding in her garrulous cousin's direction. Richie is in the corner, gesticulating. 'Don't ask.'

—

The next day is the funeral. They send off Kevin O'Brien in the style he deserves. Kate tries not to cry too much, but it's hard. She just doesn't cope with things the way she used to, and she resents that.

After the service they have a pint at The Gravediggers pub, because it seems wrong not to, and then they head to the wake at the GAA.

At the wake, Sheila's soup and soda bread goes down famously. The soda bread has walnuts in it, and herbs, and is far fancier than any soda bread Mammy used to buy.

Then everyone settles in on the drink.

Dolores Murphy seems to have had about twelve gin and tonics and appears well on the way to getting trolleyed.

If only Kevin were here to get her home. Right now, he'd be belting out 'Dirty Old Town', which was his song. He had a decent set of pipes on him, and he loved a singsong.

There was something about the combination of the gasworks wall, the old canal and the smoky wind that always got Kate right in the solar plexus. Dublin.

In the corner, Uncle Padser has started singing 'Annie's Song' by John Denver, which is his staple. Mountains in springtime, storms in deserts, sleepy blue oceans. Nothing to do with Dublin at all.

The chorus sets Dolores off again. 'I can't get my head around the fact that he's not here,' Dolores tells Kate, slurring her words slightly. 'You know yourself?'

'I do,' Kate says.

'I keep waiting for him to walk in,' Dolores continues. 'He'd love this night. But wasn't that funeral nice? And the soup.'

'The soup was great, Dolores. And the funeral was perfect. And there wasn't a dry eye in the chapel. And there shouldn't have been. Kevin was a good man.'

'The only man,' Dolores says. 'The only man. Well, almost the only man.'

There was another man, as it happens. But Dolores has never mentioned him. Not to anyone.

'Can I ask you something, Dolores?' says Kate. 'Why did you wait so long to partner with someone?'

'*I* didn't wait,' Dolores says. '*They* made me wait. *They* ruined my life.' Her face has hardened.

'Who?' asks Kate. 'Who ruined your life?'

'I don't want to talk about it tonight. I don't want to spoil Kevin's night talking about those bastards. But I need your help, Kate. You take Liam off tomorrow for a few days to see some of the country and, when you come back, I'll tell you.' She looks away and turns to Kate again: 'I need your help.'

If Kate Delaney is running away from trauma, Dolores Murphy has accepted she has to run towards it.

6

WET RAIN

THE RAIN IS coming down sideways outside their little rental car. Wet rain. All around her, the countryside has disappeared under sheets of water. Kate had been reluctant to leave Dolores, but her aunt insisted that she needed time to herself to recover from the funeral.

Neil Finn's jangly piano ballad 'Message to My Girl' is blaring through the car speakers. Liam puts his hand on her leg and, even now, Kate winces.

'I played this over and over when I was in that horrible motel room off the Hume Freeway when you were missing,' he says. 'To bloody torture myself. It did the job nicely.'

'If it weren't for the extreme circumstances, I'd say that was very undergraduate of you,' she says with a smile.

'Oh, it's far too mainstream a song to be undergraduate,' he says. 'Undergrads would one hundred per cent turn their noses up at Split Enz.'

'More fool them, Liam Carroll—it's a bloody great song.'

'It is.'

'It makes me happy.'

'Me too.'

They sit in silence for a while, feeling somehow warmed by the rising melody of the eighties electric piano.

They crest a hill, and a sign announces that they're in County Offaly: IRELAND'S ANCIENT EAST.

Her face has gone grey.

To the right of the car, dotted along the horizon, are giant windmills, their blades seeming to struggle to beat through the sideways rain. Kate starts to shake.

'Stop the car!' she chokes out.

'In this rain?' replies Liam. 'You'll get bloody soaked.'

'Stop the fucking car, Liam! Stop the fucking car!'

He pulls over onto the narrow shoulder, and the small hire car is buffeted with the force of passing vehicles.

'Sweetheart, why don't you just open the door and lean out if you need to be sick? It'll save you getting wet.'

'I don't fucking care.'

She's crying now. The familiar tightness is rising in her chest. Her arms are tingling. Her ears are ringing. Her brain feels like an old seventies TV set on static.

Kate stumbles out of the car, drops to her knees in the grass and vomits as she looks at the windmills, the first sight she saw when she regained consciousness after her rape and found herself in the back of a shitty used car being driven by a shitty human through the New South Wales Southern Highlands.

The grass is long but has been pelted so hard by rain, it looks like a little kid whose mother has washed his hair and combed it down to the side, all 'nice' for mass.

The sight of her sick all over it is making her sicker. Her face feels wet and freezing and her hair is sticking to her head. But she's almost oblivious to it.

The thing that always strikes her in these moments is how, when you relive trauma, it's not as if you are consciously thinking about the bad things that happened; it's your body that does the thinking, or the remembering, for you. Your mind is too agitated to reflect on details. It just sails along on a tide of anxiety.

She vomits up the black pudding she had for breakfast (man, she is regretting that fry-up now) and keeps vomiting until there's nothing left but bile.

'Don't come out here,' she says when she notices Liam unbuckling his seatbelt. 'It's too late for anyone to hold back my hair. You don't need to get wet as well just because you feel sorry for me.'

'Sweetheart, you'll get ill.'

'I am ill, Liam. I am bloody ill. Look at me. I'm ill. I'll always be ill.'

She howls in a way that hollows out Liam's insides. He doesn't know what to say. She knows he doesn't know what to say. She feels sorry for him for not knowing what to say, but she also feels angry at him because she is full of rage and he's the only one there. She can't be bothered tempering her tone.

As she finally stops heaving, the rain eases off.

Liam gets out of the car, opens the boot and rummages in their luggage for the beach towels they'd packed. He drapes one over Kate's shoulders and starts towelling her hair dry with the other. He wraps his arms around her and holds her tight.

'It's going to be okay, Kate.'

'No, it's not, but anyway . . .'

She rests her head on his shoulder and cries softly and then he leads her back to the car.

'I don't have a blanket,' he says as he starts the car, 'but there's a servo up ahead and they might have one.'

A mile or so down the road they veer off to the left, following the sign that reads SERVICES. Kate has her head down.

'Um, Kate?' Liam says, his voice changing.

'This is not the time for dad jokes,' she tells him.

'Kate, you have to look up. Like, you really, really have to.'

She sighs and looks up to see a huge sign looming over them. WELCOME TO MONEYGALL, COUNTY OFFALY. ANCESTRAL HOME OF BARACK OBAMA. She looks at Liam.

'Um, welcome to Barack Obama Plaza,' Liam says, pointing to another sign.

'Oh my God, this is excellent,' she manages, and takes a tissue from her pocket and blows her nose loudly.

They pull in at the back of the 'plaza' (it's a servo, but you've got to love the pluck) and walk inside to see a giant picture of Barack Obama and his wife, Michelle, presumably arriving in County Offaly to his 'ancestral home'. Another sign reliably informs that just five minutes away is the 'actual' pub where the President imbibed a pint. In the photo of said historic moment, the First Lady is looking somewhat bemused. Obama looks like he's loving it. Or O'Bama, as they like to refer to him around here.

A vending machine dispenses commemorative Barack Obama Plaza coins.

'Christ, I love this country so much,' Kate says.

Liam motions to the gift shop, where they are selling t-shirts emblazoned with *What's the craic, Barack?*

He buys one for each of them and they immediately put them on. The woman on the till tells them how she had yelled out, 'You're *gorgeous*, Michelle!' to the First Lady as she passed.

'The tragedy of this situation is that we can't take a selfie in the t-shirts here,' Kate says, 'because I look so terrible.'

'You don't look terrible to me, Kate Delaney. You're wearing a *What's the craic, Barack?* t-shirt. You're the hottest woman alive.'

She kisses him. Then they get back in the car and continue on down the road.

—

They spend a few blissful days lazing in their spa hotel. They take up residence in a tiny cottage on The Burren, and at night eat lobsters fished that morning from Galway Bay. They walk all the way along the Flaggy Shore, pausing to pick up smooth stones patterned with fossils that bring to mind an Aboriginal dot painting. They stand with their faces to the wind on the Cliffs of Moher. The grass on the top of the cliffs is like an emerald carpet in a seventies conversation pit. Kate tries to ignore the signs urging prospective suicides to call the Samaritans. Tries not to think of the ghosts of the jumpers who lived in the trees and were her only company during those bleak days she spent in a cage under the Pheasants Nest Bridge. Instead she looks out to the pounding waves of the North Atlantic. Liam sees the tears streaming from her eyes and wipes them away for her.

Don't get caught in the currents, Kate Delaney.

'Did I ever tell you my dream about Shellybanks?' she asks him.

'I don't think you did.'

'I mean, it really happened, when I was a child. But then it happened over and over again, all my life, when I went to sleep. So, if you're in Dublin and you walk to Sandymount Strand from Ringsend, there's a beach path that takes you all the way to the Poolbeg Lighthouse. It's that lovely little red lighthouse right out in the middle of Dublin Bay. Well, twice a day, all the water disappears from the bay and it's kind of grey sand as far as the eye can see. And there's a beach called Shellybanks. It's not a beach like we think of beaches. I mean, I'd be surprised if anyone ever wore a bikini at Shellybanks. But it's absolutely blanketed with cockle shells.'

She fishes into her pocket and pulls one out and shows Liam.

'This is my lucky cockle shell. I always carry it in this coat pocket.' She runs her fingers over the ridges of the shell. 'It's from Shellybanks. I always think that if I lose this, or break it, I'll run out of luck.'

'Did you have it when you . . .'

'When I was abducted? No. I was wearing another coat that night. Maybe that's why he took me.'

'That's uncharacteristically superstitious of you.'

'Maybe. Anyway, when I was little, I went to Shellybanks with Nana and Dolores. People in Ringsend often call it *the* Shellybanks. It was a cold day, so there was no thought of swimming. But the tide was well out and so I wanted to walk on the squelchy sand. Nana didn't like it, because she was always nervy about water. Most kids couldn't swim in her day, and she was always talking about this one who drowned in the canal and that one who fell into the Dodder "*and wasn't his poor mother broken-hearted*", and that sort of thing.

'But the tide was out so far that it seemed safe enough and I begged Nana and so she let me go, and she and Dolores waited back behind the wall.

'Anyway, so there's this pool of water in the middle of Dublin Bay out from Shellybanks called the Cockle Lake. And kids would often go swimming in the Cockle Lake in the summer. But there had been drownings, too, especially back in the days before anyone had swimming lessons. The thing about the tide in Dublin Bay is that it just comes whooshing back at a ferocious speed from out of nowhere.

'So, I'm out there, plodding along in my little patent leather shoes and frilly socks, collecting shells and looking for crabs and examining jellyfish, and then I start to feel the water lapping around my feet. I look up, and see that I'm surrounded by water. In no time the water is up to my knees, and it's getting higher and higher, and I start screaming. And I can see Nana back at the wall, waving her arms. And Dolores is *freaking* out and screaming at me to run for the wall and not to get caught in the current. And by this time, I am really struggling to run. My dress and coat are weighing me down. My feet are sinking into the sand. And I'm wailing. And look, in my memory, there are jellyfish everywhere, but maybe my memory has exaggerated that, but I'm just beside myself that I'm going to get stung by jellyfish. And I'm certain that I'm going to get swept away to my death.'

'God, that sounds terrifying,' says Liam.

'It was. And the worst bit was how I was trying so desperately to reach the wall but it never seemed to get any closer.

'Anyway, eventually this man came along. I can still picture him. He was wearing one of those tweed flat caps and walking a red setter. And he runs into the water and hauls me out, and he dumps me on the sand at Shellybanks. I'm so cold that I'm practically blue. And poor Dolores is weeping uncontrollably and giving out to Nana for letting me play there in the first place, and then Dolores squeezes me so tight and just storms off, leaving Nana shaking her head.'

'I can see why you've never forgotten it,' says Liam.

'God, I must have had that dream hundreds of times. I have it when I'm anxious. For me, Shellybanks is anxiety. Anxiety is running for the wall. Anxiety is jellyfish and whooshing water and sodden patent leather shoes.'

'And yet you've kept a cockle shell from this place for good luck?' Liam furrows his brow.

'Yeah. I have. Well, I made it out.'

'You made it out of Shellybanks, and you made it out of Pheasants Nest.'

'Yeah, I suppose I did.'

'Does Dolores remember that day?'

'I don't know; I've never spoken to her about it. I was so little, but I clearly remember that day and how upset she was, and how there was something going on between her and Nana, and I just sort of knew intuitively not to bring it up again.'

'Do you know if Dolores ever went back there?'

'Of course! She loved going to Shellybanks. She worked for years at the bottle factory up behind it. And I know she used to go walking there with Kevin. She sent me photos of the two of them at sunset.'

'How about we go there when we're back in Dublin,' Liam suggests. 'We can take Dolores for a long bracing walk; it'll be good for her. And maybe you can, I don't know, face your fear?'

'Okay, Oprah Winfrey,' Kate says, smirking.

'Well, sorry. But you know what I mean. I'm trying to help. I get that it's not always my strong suit.'

'Oh, it is, Liam Carroll. It is.'

She kisses him and they walk back along the cliffs to the car.

7

TO THE LIGHTHOUSE

LIAM WAKES UP in Dolores's spare room and looks out the double-glazed window to her garden. There's a cobbled path and, along it, lines of Kate's and Liam's washing flapping against the grey sky. Dolores adores doing laundry and shares with all the women in Kate's family an obsession with 'good drying days'. The sun might only peep from behind the clouds and the requisite good drying weather only lasts an hour or two, but it is to be seized and never wasted. The minute they arrived back in Dublin, she had insisted they empty their suitcases and dump their bag of dirty washing on her kitchen floor. Liam is a bit sheepish about this woman who he has only just met flinging his unmentionables into the front loader, but Kate, who has inherited the laundry bug despite her otherwise dim view of housework, assures him it's best he let Dolores get on it. When the weather turns later today, she'll bring it in and finish it off in the hot press, which, Liam has discovered, is the Irish name for the cupboard housing the water heater, and doubles as a drying room for laundry spoiled by endless misty rain.

At the end of the path that Kevin laid is a little hut where he kept his tools. Dolores, who has never picked up a hammer or pair of pliers in her life, can't bear to go out to the hut now. She's asked Liam what on earth she should do with it all, but he's at a loss. Liam isn't very handy himself. His hands have the softness of a solicitor who spends his weekends thumbing through vintage vinyl at record shops and turning the pages of the latest issue of the *New Yorker.* He has never known exactly what to do with a spirit level, and he feels like he should win a Nobel Prize when he successfully constructs flat-pack furniture.

'I don't know, Dolores,' he told her. 'I think you should leave it well alone for now.'

There are crows lined up along the wall at the end of the garden. Over the back wall is the bleak courtyard belonging to the Christian Brothers, next to the red-brick lodging for the ageing clerics who used to terrorise kids at the local primary school.

Liam turns over to Kate. She's facing the other way, a tangled mess of red hair, emitting polite little snores. He lifts her navy pinstripe pyjama top and gently traces his hand along her waist. She always feels so pleasingly warm. She flinches in her sleep. He buries his head in her hair. It smells like lemon verbena.

On the bedside table next to him is an almost empty blister pack of antidepressants. She doesn't ask about those. They haven't even discussed the fact that he's on them; he doesn't want to burden her with his problems when she has so many of her own. He has sometimes reflected that there is an inevitable selfishness in the profound post-traumatic stress disorder she lives with, but how could it be any other way? And how can he possibly say as much? He can't.

He's started trying to wean himself off the tablets because he hates the thought of chemically regulating his emotions. He finds even the act of putting them in his mouth depressing—ironically—even though he knows that they help. It's not something he's sought his doctor's advice about, and he suspects his doctor back home wouldn't be best pleased. And it creates spikes of erratic behaviour. Bursts of anger that he buries. Feelings of helplessness and futility. A sudden, overwhelming need to be alone—like when he ran away from Kevin's removal and installed himself at the pub with his pints of Guinness and chasers of whiskey.

But apart from this push-pull with his medication, Liam is also starting to feel pangs of resentment. Ireland represents his family's distant heritage but, unlike Kate, this is not his home. If he is absolutely honest with himself, he doesn't love it here. While in theory, he's grown up with the romanticism of kissing your girl by the gasworks wall, the reality of this dirty old town leaves him a bit cold. The Dodder is filthy. His fingernails get dirty each day from the pollution. He's completely fucking horrified by the obsession with death. The statues of Our Lady dotted across town have started to give him the creeps. He finds Taytos crisps comically overrated. And while he appreciates the Irish are cheerful and funny, they speak so fast he can't really understand what they're saying to him half the time. He's longing for the beautiful Greek island.

Kate wakes up and turns around and runs her hand across his brow. 'I love you,' she says. Her green eyes are bleary, and her face is a bit puffy and creased, but she's beautiful to him.

'I love you, too,' he says.

'I'm so glad you are here with me,' she says. 'So, so bloody glad.'

He presses his lips together and swallows. 'Me too,' he says.

He gets up then goes and stands under Dolores's shower, which, like seemingly almost every shower in the northern hemisphere, has low water pressure. He lets the warm water trickle over him like an afterthought, and he wonders what to do.

He comes out of the bathroom to see Kate knocking gently on her aunt's door.

'Dolores, we've had an idea. Do you want to come to the Shellybanks with us? We'll walk all the way down to the Poolbeg Lighthouse.'

'You go on without me,' Dolores's voice says flatly from behind the door.

Kate motions to Liam to make himself scarce. He throws on some clothes and pads downstairs to make a cup of tea. He's dying for a long macchiato.

—

Kate opens the door to Dolores's room. Her aunt is lying on the bed with one of Kevin's jumpers over her face.

'I suppose you think I'm an eejit,' Dolores says after a minute or two, pulling the jumper off her face and staring at the ceiling. 'Acting like a teenager.'

'Dolores, come on. You loved him. He died suddenly. You were supposed to have a life together. You're not acting like a teenager. You're acting like a human.'

'He used to smell so good,' Dolores says. 'Do you know what's driving me mental? Kevin was such a private man. He didn't even have the Facebook.'

Kate stifles a smile at her aunt's boomer reference to social media.

'It used to annoy me, because he was too proud to have it himself, saying, "*I don't want feckers knowing my business*", but then he was always logging on to my account to see what the world was up to. "*Oh, would you believe it, Sheila Byrne has up and left Tommy! Didn't I tell you she had notions?*"'

She starts to laugh through her tears.

'Oul' hypocrite he was. But now, I wish that he did have the Facebook. Because there's just no trace of him online. When I pull out my phone on the bus, I want to google him and find him. I want to find moving pictures of him. We didn't ever go for the videos. And somehow, he's just becoming, I don't know, like a vapour or something. I can't make out the lines of his face in my mind.

'But do you know what I mean? I keep googling him, Kate. I keep googling him. And he's not there. He's nowhere. It's like he just disappeared. Well, of course, he *did* disappear. Because he's dead. Now he's just fecking ashes on my mantelpiece in that stupid urn. And I'm starting to lose his voice, Kate. I'm losing the shape of him. I'm losing his voice. I feel, how would you say? I feel like I'm being disloyal, because *I can't remember him.*'

Dolores picks up the jumper and puts it over her face again and inhales deeply. 'The smell of this helps. The lines start to get less fuzzy. The shapes are sort of forming, do you know? And I can hear the faint echo of his voice.'

'Oh, Dolores, I know what you mean. I do.' Kate rubs her aunt's arm vigorously. 'I'm just wondering if it might help for you to come with Liam and me to the Poolbeg Lighthouse. Didn't you and Kevin used to go for walks there?'

Dolores takes the jumper off her face. 'We did.'

'Well.'

'Well.'

'It might help you form the shapes?'

'I suppose it might.'

'I'm going to jump in the shower, and then we'll be ready to go when you are.'

'Oh, I had a shower at six o'clock this morning. I'm not sleeping at all, and I thought I might as well get up. Right, so. You get ready and we'll go. You're a bloody-minded woman, Kate Delaney.'

'Come from generations of them, Dolores.'

'Right you are.'

—

The taxi drops them off at Sandymount Strand where they meet Kate's uncle and Dolores's brother, Gerry Murphy. Dolores had called him, saying her brother knew someone who'd be able to get them inside the Poolbeg Lighthouse.

'Howarye, Dolores? That funeral was beautiful, so it was,' Gerry says, giving his sister's shoulder a squeeze. 'And Kate, good to see you again, beautiful girl. Your ma will never be gone, never be gone, so she won't,' he says.

'I know,' Kate says. 'I'm the *image* of her.'

'I hate to sound like your Auntie Maggie, but it's true. "*The image. Janey tonight.*"' He breaks into a big smile, revealing a gap between his front teeth; Kate supposes she got hers from him.

'And you too, Liam,' Gerry says. 'You all right?'

Liam nods. 'I am, thanks, Gerry.'

'Fair play to you, coming all this way for Kevin's funeral,' Gerry says. 'Fair play.'

'Thanks, mate,' Liam says. 'And also for bringing us to the lighthouse.'

'Ah, no bother, it's grand,' Gerry says. 'Do you see it? Right down there at the very end of that wall?'

'It's so pretty,' says Kate, gazing at the little crimson tower at the end of the long stone wall. From here it looks like a tiny red pawn from a chess board in a doll's house.

'It is that,' says Gerry.

It seems artificial at this point to call Gerry Murphy 'Gerry'. He's known in Ringsend as Happy and that's what everyone has called him for years. The nickname is well earned: he isn't just happy himself; he spreads it around. 'He'd give you the shirt off his back, so he would,' they'd chime as Happy Murphy walked down Bridge Street.

Happy used to put on shows for the entire extended family when Kate was a child. The eleven Murphy siblings, the first grandchildren and Kate's grandparents would pile into the tiny front room and Happy would have created some wacky costume out of his father's old clothes. He'd have them all in stitches.

Happy passed on to Kate a love of The Smiths, James Joyce and Oscar Wilde. She remembers him spinning The La's 'There She Goes' on his record player a good five hundred times one summer and that song always makes her feel hopeful now. He keeps old copies of *NME* in the attic, and he was famously on the barge on Grand Canal Dock where U2 filmed the video for 'Gloria'. He still to this day has a Morrissey quiff, with razor-sharp side-burns, and on nights out he wears rolled-up 501s, creepers and tartan jackets. He's hard to miss, he never stops talking, and Liam likes him a lot.

'Now, is everyone up for the long walk?' Happy asks. 'You know it's eleven kilometres? Dolores, will you be okay?'

'Go on with you, Happy Murphy,' Dolores says. 'I may be a good few years older than you, but I'm fit. I walk seventeen thousand steps a day, so I do.'

'Answer me this now,' Happy says. 'Why do you not give up those fags? You'd be fitter still.'

'Don't be a gobshite,' says Dolores. 'Which reminds me. I need to have a word with Nico.' She pulls a packet of cigarettes from her crossbody bag and lights one up.

'I really wish you wouldn't, Dolores,' says Kate.

'Not you too,' says Dolores.

'Sorry to be on your case. It's only because I love you. Would you not think of vanity, if not your health?'

'I'm afraid that horse has bolted,' Dolores says. 'Not even that oul' Botox can help me now. I'm a lost cause.'

'Okay, walkers,' says Happy. 'To the lighthouse.'

'To the lighthouse.'

And they set on up the path.

8

POOLBEG

WALKING THROUGH THE Irishtown Nature Park, there's reclaimed land and brambles and salty silt and creeping thistle and glistening grey water to their right, and unlovely industry to their left. The stained red-and-white Poolbeg chimneys that welcome ships to Dublin tower above them. The smell of the 'shitter', as Happy calls it (known in polite company as a 'waste treatment facility'), wafts through the air. By the end of the day, Kate will feel slightly light-headed, oddly queasy.

As they go, Happy regales them with stories of hungry Ringsend kids 'boxing the fox', or stealing apples, from the trees of the well-to-do homes with gardens in Sandymount (hardly anyone has a garden big enough for an apple tree in Ringsend) on the way to their picnics at Shellybanks.

'On one occasion, the owner pulled a gun on me and says, "*Ye little maggot!*" Happy laughs.

Liam is laughing along as he feels his phone vibrate in his pocket. He pulls it out and sees another message to add to the list of those he's been ignoring for days. They're from his boss, Sebastian Le Carre.

> Hello mate! How's Greece? We need to talk . . .

> Liam, could you give me a bell?
> We're really under the pump here and I'm wondering if
> and when we could have you back?

> We've got a group of clients about that cosmetic
> 'surgeon' on Insta who was fitting leaky implants.

> Mate, where are you? Is everything okay?

Et cetera, et cetera. He has started to answer them so many times, only to put the phone away when Kate comes into the room. Hanging back from the others now, he quickly types out a response.

> Promise I'll call you tonight.

Then he puts his phone back in his pocket, and strides ahead to catch up with Kate and reach for her hand.

Happy, who could talk under wet cement, is still at it. There's the story of the Pigeon House Road that runs down to Shellybanks beach (no pigeons involved). The story of the dog that got caught in the rocks (Happy to the rescue).

They reach the end of the nature park.

'You three okay if we keep going on down to the lighthouse and walk down the Shellybanks on the way back?' Happy asks.

'For sure,' says Kate.

'All right, no bother.

They wander past Shellybanks beach and among the ruins of the old sewage pumping station that lies at the start of the sea wall.

'Back in the day,' Happy says, 'this would've been like a holiday resort, because people had no money. We'd come down here and we'd sit on the wall. People would have their flasks of tea and their chairs and their picnic blankets. And we'd be starving, with only apples we'd robbed from boxing the fox.'

On the bluestone walls of the ruins, which locals have lovingly patched up with cement, are commemorative plaques for the dead. For a forty-five-year-old man, a wooden sign: *Ashes cast on the tide. Near this place that he loved. Tread softly.* Gold letters on wood for: *Docker and artist. This was his oasis.* A rain-beaten teddy bear lies next to a broken ceramic pillow: *Rest in peace, Dear Grandad.* Condolences for: *A real Ringsender, loved spending time down the Shellybanks with his wife.* And Kate's absolute favourite—a small, slim, simple plaque, with the man's name and dates of birth and death and the words: *That's gorgeous.*

Dolores runs her hands over it. 'That's exactly the sort of thing Kevin would have said.' She wipes away the tears that are now streaming across her face in the wind.

'He was an awful good man,' Happy says, putting his arm around her shoulders. 'Never a word of trouble.'

Kate wonders whether *'That's gorgeous'* is really the sort of thing that Kevin would have said at all. He was a quiet and kind man, but there was a shrewdness about him. He didn't suffer fools. But Dolores is just doing that thing that people do when someone dies. It's too painful for her to countenance anything other than that he was more or less perfect.

The sea wall snakes for four kilometres. On either side, the water is still. But Happy tells them that at times it gets so choppy that the wall almost disappears.

They pass the Half Moon Swimming Club, which used to be nudist and men only, Happy tells them.

Dolores shakes her head. 'Men only. In the fucking sea! How can they own the sea? Who gave them the right?'

Then she sees a woman bobbing past in a one-piece.

'Good for you, love!' Dolores shouts to her.

A man who works for the port pulls up in a little run-around. 'Y'all right, Happy?' he asks, winding down his window. He winks at Kate. 'And who might this be?'

Dolores nudges in front of Kate. 'I'm Dolores Murphy—I think I was in school with your brother Joe,' she says. 'Are you Pat Purtill?'

'Ah, I'd say you were,' he says. 'And I am him. I've come to help you into the lighthouse. Happy, you owe me one. Lucky you brought your good-looking niece from Australia.'

'Easy, tiger,' says Liam with a chuckle. 'That's my good-looking girlfriend from Australia.'

'Right you are,' Pat Purtill says.

Pat drives up to the lighthouse and they follow on foot. As they approach the courtyard leading to the lighthouse door, they can hear him cursing and blinding.

'Would you fuckin' look at that? Can you bleedin' believe that shite?' Pat's saying.

While it's only been about a year since Happy last brought some friends to the lighthouse, the door has rusted shut since.

Pat bangs with a hammer, jimmies with a screwdriver, kicks the door with some force and no small degree of melodrama. Nothing works.

'I must say, I love his commitment to the task,' Liam whispers to Kate. 'Isn't he meant to be working?'

Kate is trying not to laugh. 'He is meant to be working, yes.'

A father who is out for a day trip with his two little boys watches with interest. 'Can I bring my kids in, too?' he asks.

'Jaysus, no,' says Pat. 'Health and safety. These here are VIPs from Australia.'

'Very important,' whispers Kate to Liam, suppressing a giggle. 'Don't you know who we are?'

The door is proving difficult, but Pat Purtill is not wont to give up.

'Right,' he says, turning to Happy. 'I've got some rope in me car. I'm going to tie it to the handle, and then tie the other end to my towbar, and then I'm going to drive that fuckin' door open!'

'You are not,' says Happy.

'I am that,' says Pat.

'Are you sure?' asks Kate. 'That's a lot of effort to go to.'

'Of course I'm sure,' says Pat. He winks at her and his gold tooth glints in the pale sun. 'Right so.'

The rope slips from the handle at the first few attempts, to disappointed groans from the onlookers. But eventually the car edges forward and the door to the lighthouse springs open with such force that they all gasp and give Pat a huge round of applause.

'Jaysus, that was something else, Pat,' says Happy.

'Not Jaysus at all. Good rope. Now'—he turns to Kate and Liam—'do ye want to come in?'

'We'd love to,' says Liam.

Inside the lighthouse, it is dark and musty. The black and red chequerboard tiles on the floor are so dusty that they look pink and grey. There's a big mint-green ridged strut all the way up the middle. Small arched windows with stone sills at least four feet thick look out to the glassy grey sea. Down below, a golden retriever is peeing on the rocks, a toddler is screaming at having lost his ice cream to the waves, and Lycra-clad joggers are making their way along the sea wall, causing Liam to comment on how incongruous they look, when surely they should be wearing tweed and Aran jumpers and galoshes.

'It's not 1943,' Kate says, laughing.

Their little party heads up the narrow staircase, clasping the slim black balustrade.

'Mind yourselves,' says Happy. 'Don't fall.'

They reach the top, push open a heavy green door leading to a small red iron balcony and look out at Dublin Bay.

The air is thick with moisture and has a bite to it. Periodically, a soft mist of rain blows over. In the near distance, a vast area of cotton wool envelops the horizon. It's moving towards them at quite a pace.

'There's a fog approaching,' says Happy. 'We'll need to get back before that sets in.'

'This is sort of magic,' says Liam.

'I love you,' says Kate.

'I love you, too,' he says.

'Enough of that, lovebirds,' whispers Happy, nudging them. 'You'll be upsetting Dolores.'

Dolores is facing out to sea, her hair blown back by the wind. She's looking out to Howth at the tip of Dublin Bay, where she and Kevin used to go for walks along the headland to another lighthouse.

'I think I've had enough,' she says, and heads towards the spindly staircase.

Kate and Liam have one last look at the view then follow.

Kate notices writing on the wall. 'What's this?' she asks.

Dolores, Liam and Happy come over to see.

Written in large red letters, in what seems like nail varnish, are the words: *Where is my MAMMY?*

Dolores gasps like someone's just given her a sharp elbow in the kidneys. She bolts down the stairs and charges out of the lighthouse.

9
SHELLYBANKS

STARTLED BY HER aunt's reaction, Kate looks at Happy. 'What's that about?' she asks.

'I've no clue,' says Happy. 'I've been up here a good few times, but I've never noticed that writing.'

'But why is Dolores so upset?'

'I really couldn't tell you, Kate.'

The fog has set in, a proper pea souper. They cannot see a thing in front of them, nor behind.

Dolores Murphy has vanished somewhere into the mist.

'Dolores!' Kate calls. 'Dolores, where are you?'

Nothing.

Kate, Liam and Happy hasten down the path along the top of the sea wall, calling her name repeatedly, but there is no answer.

They run down to Shellybanks to see if Dolores is there.

The stone wall Kate was so desperate to reach in her childhood and her dreams fell down years ago, but the beach itself is more or less the same. Dirty grey sand that matches the fog, with a thick carpet of cockles and cuttlefish shards. A white octopus with dappled puce spots and bedraggled tentacles has been washed up on the sand. The eyes on either side of its head look up at them with befuddled resignation.

A red sign says NO DUMPING, and beneath it are four blue plastic bags full of rubbish, but it's the next sign that draws Kate's attention.

RABHADH

WARNING

In the middle of a yellow triangle is a lone figure with his arms in the air, a black wave threatening to overwhelm him.

PERSONS GOING 200 METRES BEYOND THIS NOTICE ARE IN DANGER OF BEING STRANDED BY INCOMING TIDES

Kate gulps and looks out at the sea.

The rippled surface of the sand is being rapidly swallowed by a sneaking, snaking tide. There are no big blue breakers of the type that might dump you onto an Australian beach, but there are hidden currents beneath the seemingly innocuous grey waves. Untrustworthy waves with secret agendas. Waves that might drown you.

Don't get caught in the undertow.

It's hard to see beyond a few paces, because the fog is so thick, but Kate walks out onto the sand.

'Dolores!' she calls.

'Kate, please don't,' Liam says.

She ignores him.

'Dolores, *please*!' she shouts into the mist.

Happy has his phone out and is trying to ring for help, but the reception here is terrible, even though it's fewer than six kilometres to O'Connell Street.

Liam clambers over to the top of the rocks for a better view and notices a smudge of red maybe one hundred and fifty metres out.

'I think I've found her,' he calls down to Kate, adding, 'Jesus Christ, Kate, please come away from the water.'

As she reluctantly retreats to the rocks, Liam takes off his shoes and awkwardly rolls up his jeans. He jumps down on to the sand, squelching as he does, and sets off towards Dolores. The water lapping at his feet feels icy. It's not long before it creeps up to his ankles and then his calves. As he wades further in, he's almost pulled off his feet by the strength of the current.

'Dolores!' he shouts.

In the distance, the red-raincoated figure drops to its knees.

Liam tries to move towards her but the rushing tide is urging him sideways. He thinks he's moving in a straight line, but the sea won't have it. His toes feel numb, and his hands are getting bluish. He turns back to look for Kate but can't see the beach behind him; faces forward again but can't see anything in front, except for the faint patch of red in the distance.

It starts to rain: not the soft Irish rain he'd grown accustomed to, but icy rivets that seem to pierce his skin.

He's beginning to feel scared now. Over the whoosh of the sea, he can hear Kate screaming his name from the shore, but her voice is growing increasingly faint.

Don't get caught in the undertow.

'I'm coming, Dolores,' he calls, trying to sound confident and manly, but if he is honest with himself, Liam Carroll is starting to regret this foolish rescue attempt. The water is now up past his waist. Swimming feels more perilous than walking. But walking is so hard. Suddenly the current changes direction and comes towards him with a force that knocks him off his feet.

Ahead, he can see Dolores being swept towards him by the tide, and then suddenly she is passing him, gurgling and coughing, and the tide is sweeping him along, too—and then, abruptly, they are both deposited unceremoniously on the muddy shore. Happy and Kate come running and drag them out of the water before the current can change its mind.

Kate is kneeling beside Dolores. Her aunt's body seems so tiny with her clothes clinging to her.

Dolores vomits sea water onto the grey sand.

'Oh, Dolores,' Kate says.

'Jaysus, Dolores, what's wrong with you?' Happy starts, but Kate gives him a stern look and he falls silent.

Kate looks up at Liam, who is bent over with his hands on his knees, coughing and panting. He puts his hand up. 'No, don't,' he says. 'Don't.'

She knows not to push him. She nods and goes back to Dolores, who is still lying motionless on the sand, staring listlessly out ahead. Happy has finally managed to get through to Pat Purtill, who comes running with some towels and hands one to Liam as Kate and Happy set about trying to dry and warm Dolores.

Liam goes over and sits on the rocks, shivering and shaking his head. *What the fuck is this all about*? he wonders. *What the fuck am I doing here?*

He sighs and pulls his phone from the bag he'd dropped on the rocks before dashing into the water. He texts his boss, Sebastian.

I'm booking a flight home.

It's the small hours of the morning in Melbourne, but Sebastian Le Carre replies immediately.

Good man.

Dolores is pale and still and soaking wet, but they can hear the raspy wheezes of her breath.

'Maybe shouldn't have had so many meetings with Nico,' she says dully as Kate and Happy help her to her feet.

Pat offers to drive them to the hospital. 'Ye really should get yourself seen to, love,' he tells Dolores kindly, and to Kate's relief Dolores doesn't object.

Kate and Liam take the back seat with Dolores between them while Happy sits in the front with Pat.

'Kevin wouldn't want this,' Kate says to Dolores.

'This has nothing to do with Kevin,' says Dolores. 'Kevin's not here.'

'What did you think you were doing out there?'

'I don't know. I just wanted to walk into the fog. I just wanted to disappear.'

'Please tell me what this is about, Dolores.'

'I will. I just need to catch my breath.'

'This is too much, Dolores. Too much.'

'I'm sorry, pet.'

'I don't have a mammy anymore, Dolores. I have you. I *need* you.'

'I know, pet.'

'Then how could you do this?'

Her aunt is silent for a couple of minutes. Then she says, 'I was a mammy.'

Kate Delaney turns to look at her aunt. 'What?'

'I was a mammy,' Dolores repeats. 'And then I wasn't.'

PART TWO

DOLORES

10
FOURTEEN

DOLORES WAS SPANISH for 'sorrows', but at fourteen, Dolores Murphy had not entirely earned her name nor understood its etymology.

Dolores was fourth of five girls in Mammy's brood of eleven. Girls are many things at once, but Mammy often referred to them by their archetypes. Patricia was pretty and dutiful. Mary was serious and studious, eschewing the typing pool to go back to night school and university. Annie was a dreamer who married early. Carmel was the indulged baby who later bolted to Canada.

Dolores Murphy was bright and fizzy and mouthy.

There was a black-and-white photograph of Dolores with Annie and Mary when Annie was a baby and Dolores and Mary were girls. Dolores was only about four, with dark gold hair tied in the giant bows that were the style of the time, and dark, fierce eyes. She looked off to the side with an expression that said, 'Oh, for fuck's *sake*.' That was more or less her resting face from that time on.

Mammy never understood why Dolores could never keep clean. She'd send her down the Shellybanks with her siblings to play for the day with hair neatly combed and pinned with clasps, dressed in a freshly ironed sundress and cardigan, and she'd return looking like she had been moonlighting in a coalmine. 'Jesus, Mary and Holy Saint Joseph, Dolores, it's like the dirt jumps on you,' Mammy would sigh. Dolores seemed to possess a complete inability to detect stray crumbs on her lips. Annie would look at her through narrowed eyes and think that, surely, she must know. The gaps between her teeth seemed perpetually lodged with whatever they'd had for dinner. Her shoes were always scuffed and her hair hopelessly tangled. She never walked anywhere, and why would you if you could run? Her knees were always crusted with scabs, and she'd broken six toes, two thumbs, her left arm and her right ankle.

But what Mammy found most exasperating about her fourth daughter was her mouth.

'This,' Mammy would say, chasing the child around the house with a brush, pointing to Dolores's mouth with a jab, 'will get you into trouble.'

It wasn't that Mammy never told Dolores that she loved her. She never told any of her children that she loved them; mothers weren't demonstrative like that back then. But with some of them, she showed it. She was constantly telling Patricia what a good girl she was. She scraped together what little money she had to buy Joe, the youngest of the eleven, music lessons and a ticket to America. She doted on Happy, because everyone in Ringsend loved Happy. Plus he was the oldest boy, and that meant something.

Dolores was one of the in-betweeners. Mammy didn't just fail to say she loved Dolores—she acted like she didn't love her. Or at least, that's what Dolores thought. Mammy considered her bold, and a nuisance, and a mouth.

Mammy had taken Dolores out of school at fourteen, like she did all of the Murphy girls, because she needed the money they could bring in from going out to work. Dolores was enrolled in a tech course and gave half of her money from her part-time job to Mammy. She would arrive home, and dinner would already have been served and eaten.

'Ah, sure, I didn't know what time you'd be home,' Mammy would say with a shrug, though Dolores usually arrived home at the same time every day. 'Fix yourself some bread and jam.'

Dolores would go to bed hungry, vowing that she would leave this fecking house and this fecking woman at the earliest opportunity.

Mammy was certainly a difficult woman, but circumstances had made her so. Daddy was more generous with rounds at the pub and the racecourse than he was with his wife and children. Dolores had once found Mammy crying because she didn't have enough money for food. 'Go and ask Himself for money for the messages,' Mammy told Dolores.

But Daddy baulked at the idea of putting his hand in his pocket. 'Go and ask your mam,' he said, running his hand through his thick black hair, smoothing the moustache that Dolores always thought made him look like Stalin, if Stalin had been ineffectual and passive aggressive and half-sozzled on Guinness every night. He sloped over to the large brown television set to turn the dial and changed the channel.

Dolores watched her mother go to Daddy's coat, hanging up under the stairs. She fished in the pockets and pulled out a thick wad of cash. Mammy sank down on a chair in the kitchen and stared at the money on her apron. Daddy hadn't mentioned to her—he never did—that he'd had a lucky day at Leopardstown. Daddy loved the horses, and a plucky dark bay called Sheila May (Not) that he'd had his eye on for a while had come in at ten to one. Both Dolores and her mammy knew that he was most likely planning to spend his winnings on the fancy woman who lived around the corner at number eighteen: the woman with the gold hoops in her ears and the red lips and the six children from three daddies and the parade of late-night visitors. Dolores and Mammy had seen Daddy going into her house once, but Mammy had simply turned her head and made a sign of the cross, and she and Dolores never spoke a word of Daddy's visit to the fancy woman.

'That bastard,' Dolores said. 'Give me that money and I'll run down to Mrs Byrne on the corner before she closes.'

'Jesus, Mary and Holy Saint Joseph, Dolores Murphy!' her mother screeched. 'Don't you be talking about your daddy like that. You wash out your mouth.' Mammy put the entire roll of notes right back into Daddy's coat pocket, walked out to the scullery and slammed the door. That night they ate tinned beans that Mammy had found at the back of the cupboard. Two tins thirteen ways and the heel of some brown bread did not a dinner make. Daddy said nothing, though, and ducked out for a pint as soon as they'd finished.

Dolores Murphy got a job on the switchboard of a city bank. Dolores Murphy saved her money. She combed out her tangles, lined her eyes with kohl, spent her money on well-cut skirts and monochrome blouses and expensive shoes and exuded an air of insouciant nonchalance. She took up smoking Gauloises. She saved up for a record player and made her siblings listen to David Bowie's 'Heroes' on constant rotation.

After work, she would dart around the corner to the *leabharlann phuiblidhe*, the local public library.

The library was a squat Art Deco building striped with white paint and bricks the colour of a dormouse. There, Dolores spent her free hours continuing the education she'd been denied. She'd look up words she didn't understand, like *hyperbole* and *ennui* and *serendipity* and *quixotic* and, to her abiding teenage horror, *fellatio*.

She looked up *representative democracy* and *first-past-the-post* and the *Long March* and the *First Amendment* and *Let them eat cake!*, which was really brioche. So, she looked up *brioche*, too, while she was at it. She read 'The Love Song of J. Alfred Prufrock' and *The Importance of Being Earnest*. She hated *Sons and Lovers* but loved *Brideshead Revisited*. She read a lot of fairly schlocky novels, not knowing, nor caring, that they were schlocky. She even read *Fear of Flying*, hiding it inside a vest in her chest of drawers so Mammy wouldn't see it and go off her rocker.

'Janey tonight!' she'd mutter under her breath, with her torch under the blankets, reading Erica Jong's racy prose.

'What are you doing over there in that library, Dolores Murphy?' Mammy would ask, looking at her through narrowed eyes.

'Reading books,' said Dolores. 'And looking up words I hear at work that I don't understand. And learning about history.'

'You'll be getting notions, Dolores.'

'And what if I do?'

'No one likes that.'

'Well, I like it. I like how it makes me feel.'

Mammy just shook her head.

Dolores's older sister Mary—who'd had the sense to get out early to explore her own ambitions, was now married and pregnant with the child who would grow up to be Kate Delaney—would come and sit on her bed. Mary was the only one, at that time, who got her bookish ways. 'You'll never change the way Mammy thinks, Dolores,' Mary would say.

'I don't want to change the way she thinks. I just want her to accept who I am.'

And Mary could offer her no reassurance, because acceptance was never Mammy's strong suit. Instead she'd squeeze Dolores's hand and then they'd both put their hands on Mary's belly and feel the baby kicking as Mary recited some poetry, and everything would be right in the world until Mary had to get the bus home again.

'Don't go,' Dolores would whisper.

'Ah, Dolores, mind yourself,' Mary would say, and ease her way down the narrow staircase, hand on the small of her back, to steady herself.

One day, Dolores got home from work after her usual nip over to the library. It was six o'clock. She walked into the kitchen and Annie was clearing up the dinner plates.

Annie looked at Dolores, and her face reddened. 'Ah, now, Dolores, I didn't know when you'd be in,' said Mammy.

Dolores was home about the same time every day.

It happened again. And again. Dolores would burst in the door and hear the scraping of forks shovelling scraps and bones into the bin.

'Been at the library again?' Mammy would ask, not looking up from the sink.

Dolores would thump up the stairs and throw herself on the bed and cry herself to sleep, hungry.

Fuck them all.

The morning that Dolores Murphy turned fifteen, she found a card sitting on her bedside table.

Happy birthday Dolores.

Your Mam and Dad.

Mammy was never one for making a show of herself. But inside the card was something Dolores had never before received for a birthday: ten pounds. She put the punt up to her nose and smelled it, wondering what this was about.

When she walked through the front door that evening, instead of finding the others had already eaten, she heard the sound of dishes being put on the table. The smell of sweet, salty brine filled the house. Mammy had made her favourite—boiled bacon with cabbage and floury mashed potatoes laden with butter, and bread and butter pudding for afters.

'Now, Dolores,' Mammy said. She slid a newspaper cutting across the table. It was an advertisement: *Cookery School for Young Ladies.*

Dolores looked up at Mammy.

'This would be perfect for you, Dolores.'

'But I hate cooking, Mammy.'

'All the more reason. What husband will ever want to marry you?'

'Maybe I don't want to get married.'

'Are you wanting to consider a vocation as a sister?'

'I'd rather eat shite. I don't want to be a nun, Mammy. I'm just not sure I want a husband either.'

'Ah, for God's sake.'

'You're not exactly selling the marriage proposition to me, Mam,' Dolores said, gesturing to Daddy, who had already finished his dinner and collapsed on the brown and white settee, slipper-clad feet propped up on the coffee table, dirty glasses falling down his pock-marked red nose, snoring in truncated fits and starts, a little river of drool seeping from the corner of his open mouth.

'Where did you get a word like "proposition"?'

'In a book.'

Mammy chose not to take the bait. 'All's I'm saying is that you could learn a skill. A skill for work—and if, please God, you meet someone, for your home, too.'

Dolores suspected Mammy didn't care less whether she had a skill or not. She just wanted her out. Dolores had no interest in a life of catering and matrimonial slavery, but she did want to escape this house, with its children and its glowing Sacred Heart statue and its dirty linoleum and its yellowing lace curtains and its smell of stale sweat and old turnips. Dolores was sick of her sister's clammy feet in her face in the bed at night. Sick of going to sleep hungry because her mother resented her. Sick of her father barely acknowledging her presence. Sick of Mammy's drab shame, which she wore constantly, like one of her polyester floral dresses.

'Let me have a look at it,' she said, and peered at the newspaper clipping. *Silver service dining. Cooking skills. Full-time work in the catering field. Conference centres. Learn on the job. A Nationally Recognised Diploma.* At the bottom, *Please do not hesitate to call the Directress*, a telephone number and a tiny crucifix logo.

Directress. That seemed strange and formal.

But still.

Mammy nodded at her encouragingly.

Dolores went to the upstairs bedroom and took out the little steel box in which she kept her Gauloises. She sat on the sill and blew smoke rings out the window and thought.

Directress.

Two weeks later, Dolores Murphy packed her bags and left Ringsend.

And that was how it all started, she tells Kate Delaney in her kitchen decades later, as she recovers from being swallowed by a foggy sea at Shellybanks. That was how Dolores Murphy's life came undone.

11

THE BIG HOUSE

THE BIG HOUSE was two and a half hours from Ringsend, in the countryside outside of Galway. Trundling along the narrow lanes in the bus provided by the cookery school, Dolores Murphy gazed out at the soft landscape, almost startled by the green. She had barely left inner Dublin since she was a small child, and though she knew in theory there were places with stone cottages and tractors and brambles and crab apples, she had almost no practical experience of them.

Sitting at the front of the bus were two women, Nuala and Róisín, who had introduced themselves to Dolores and a gaggle of seven other spotty, unremarkable girls as their supervisors. They instructed the girls to address them as 'Miss'. Miss Nuala had fair hair, parted to the side and pulled back behind her ears with tortoiseshell combs. She wore a Laura Ashley dress with a large, frilled collar and pale pink lipstick and, Dolores recognised from her wistful visits to the Switzers perfume counter, a floral scent considered the first word in understated chic. Miss Róisín wore a grey Donegal tweed skirt, a lemon angora cardigan and a necklace of seed pearls.

Miss Nuala and Miss Róisín smiled at the girls, but not with their eyes. Their eyes had an oddly fixed quality about them. When they looked at you, they looked for a beat too long. When they tapped you on the shoulder, their hand rested there in a way that sent a chill down your spine. They spoke in cold and slightly affected Dublin 4 accents and had gemstone rings but no boyfriends. They later explained that they had taken a vow of celibacy. They said things like they were 'terribly pleased' to have you on the bus. Dolores later discovered that Miss Nuala had a doctorate in theology from University College Dublin and Miss Róisín said she was an accountant. She found them both oddly magnificent and slightly frightening.

Not as frightening, nor as haughtily magnificent, as the Directress, though. They alighted from the bus at the gate to the Big House to be greeted by a pigeon-chested woman with hair piled on top of her head and a faintly Edwardian air about her.

'And who might you be?' she asked, peering down her nose at Dolores.

'Dolores Murphy,' Dolores said. 'I'm from Ringsend.'

'How darling,' said the Directress, though they both knew it wasn't.

In a wheedling soprano, the Directress trilled:

'And there she goes, my Ringsend Rose,

In God's garden, there's none ra-rer . . .'

She placed her hand on Dolores's blushing cheek and left it resting there for a beat too long.

The Big House was a grey and white Georgian manor on the Abbert River set on thirty-three acres of poplars, beech, sycamores, oaks and hornbeams.

As they walked towards the front door, Dolores gasped. 'It has a moat,' she whispered to one of the other girls.

'And a tower,' said the girl.

'Yes, the moat and tower are the Victorian part of the property,' the Directress said. 'They were added in the 1820s. It's very grand, isn't it, girls?'

The girls just bit their lips. Miss Nuala and Miss Róisín exchanged a glance.

'Now, let me show you where you'll be staying,' Miss Róisín said briskly.

The girls were shepherded to a squat, bluestone annexe that must have once been servants' quarters or part of the stables. There was a separate entrance through a rusty red iron gate with a giant padlock. While the main entrance was manicured, the lawn looking like it had been weeded with tweezers, here, the grounds were curiously unkempt. No one had bothered to clear the dandelions and thistles along this rocky unsealed driveway. No one had swept up the gathering piles of russet leaves.

Dolores would come to know these driveways well. Where women in frayed pinafores lugged laundry bags and polished steps with their heads bowed. Silent women. Women who weren't asked for opinions, and whom no one was supposed to see. Women who were told how grateful they should be. They were referred to as the Help. Dolores Murphy, despite herself, despite her pluck and her inner rebel and her fuck-them-all attitude, would become one of these women. Dolores Murphy would become the Help.

Some of the girls around Ringsend would whisper about the laundries run by nuns where friends who had 'gotten themselves into trouble' would be sent to have their babies. But no one had mentioned this place, nor these people, and there were no nuns and babies here.

Dolores and the six other fifteen-year-olds, as well as a girl from the north side who was only thirteen, knew only that they were here to study for a nationally recognised qualification under the supervision of professionally trained instructors. They knew nothing about the Group—the organisation that ran the course—beyond the fact that it was somehow connected to, at that point, an obscure and very pious branch of the Catholic Church.

'When did you get your catering qualification?' Dolores asked Miss Nuala in those early days. 'Was that after you did the PhD on St Augustine?'

Miss Nuala just pressed her lips together and motioned for Dolores to keep filling the teapots for the breakfast at the conference centre.

'Why did you give up accounting?' she quizzed Miss Róisín. 'Didn't you prefer that to teaching girls how to iron shirts and bake apple tarts?'

But Miss Róisín only answered, 'Hush, Dolores,' and changed the subject.

The girls rose at 4.30 am and they finished at 9 pm. Dolores, who was not a morning person, would tumble out of bed, brush her teeth still blinking in the dark, then tiptoe down to the chapel in her slippers for morning prayers. Dolores didn't quite know why there had to be morning prayers at a catering course designed to prepare the girls for a career in hospitality, but when she asked the question of Miss Nuala one day, Nuala had given her such a hard look that Dolores thought it best not to ask again. Dolores Murphy was trying to be good.

They learned how to fold bedsheets into hospital corners and towels into swans, to starch men's socks, to place silver cutlery from the outside in, how to make bechamel that wasn't lumpy and steak that was medium rare. Dolores developed calluses on her knees from all the scrubbing of linoleum and blisters on her hands from smoothing the table linen over the Elnapress. They worked seven days, and the only respite was mass or bed.

The Group held prayer meetings and retreats and special conferences and ran marriage courses for couples on how to ensure their union remained holy. Dolores and the girls were not permitted to stay in any of the rooms where these were being held.

They were to serve meals and tea and coffee to the participants and clear up after them. They were to be seen and not heard.

Each morning, some of the girls would be driven to the college for young men. Miss Nuala and Miss Róisín explained that they were never, on pain of death, to speak to the young men, nor even look at them. It was a mortal sin to be coveted. At the men's college, they would be handed laundry bags of each student's dirty washing for the week. Seven pairs of socks, seven pairs of underwear, seven shirts, seven vests, seven pairs of trousers and seven handkerchiefs. Any thoughts of lust Dolores might have felt for the young men was well and truly quashed by their laundry. She would try not to vomit as she rinsed bulbs of mucous from the hankies or skid marks from the pants. She thought of how first their mothers had done this and how now they had her. She didn't like it, but she was trying to be good.

The girls were instructed never to entertain any notions of entering through the front driveway of the young men's college, which, again, like the Big House, had its own sense of pristine order. Daffodils, crocuses, perfectly clipped grass, strangely symmetrical hedges. They were to silently make their way to the entrance down the road where a metal plaque on the stone post said CATERING. They'd swing open the iron gates and there, again, was the unsealed rocky road, which no one had weeded in years.

She hadn't heard a whisper from her own mam since she arrived, nor from her dad or her brothers and sisters, but she figured they'd write soon enough.

Some of the other girls were already tiring of the endless work and were starting to get restless. Two of them told the Directress they wanted to leave. There were loud voices one night, and Dolores heard a bang and one of them shouting that she hated this miserable place. Before the sun rose the next day, there was much slamming of doors, scratching of suitcases on linoleum, the wheeze of the bus door opening. And when Dolores got up for morning mass, she noticed that two of the girls' beds were empty.

None of the remaining girls said anything about it. The girls at the Big House were not encouraged to speak to one another. They barely knew each other's names. Dolores was working alongside them every day, but it was like a form of parallel play—doing the same things, but not doing them together. They were not encouraged to be friends and Miss Nuala and Miss Róisín subtly pitted them against one another. Miss Nuala would roll her eyes conspiratorially at Dolores when one of the other girls messed up—dropping a soup spoon on the floor, for instance, or breaking a glass. *You're not like them, Dolores,* her look would say. *You're better.*

Dolores didn't see many of the other girls sticking it out. But she was a good worker, and the Directress and Miss Nuala and Miss Róisín seemed pleased with her. And she wanted to prove to Mammy that she could do something well. Maybe for Daddy to notice how well she'd done. Or to notice her at all. No, she wouldn't be going back to Ringsend without a qualification in her hand. She couldn't bear the thought of the disappointment and resentment she'd almost certainly see on Mammy's face, if she did. So she stayed.

She did notice that she was being marked out for what the Directress referred to as 'special attention'.

One morning, as Dolores was trying to wake up, blankly watching the milk soak into her Rice Krispies, Miss Nuala came into the kitchen and sat down beside her. She smoothed her skirt and clasped her hands on top of the table.

'Morning, Dolores,' she said, smiling warmly, but not with her eyes.

'Howarye, Miss Nuala?'

'I'm grand, thanks, Dolores. Has the Directress told you that I'm going to be your tutor? I'm so pleased.' Miss Nuala put her hand on Dolores's hand and left it for a beat too long.

'Tutor in what?' asked Dolores, easing her hand out from underneath Miss Nuala's.

'In life, Dolores. In the spirit. I'm going to help you be a better person. You can come to me about absolutely anything. We're going to go for walks and have our chats every day. You're special, Dolores. I can see that you're not like the other girls. You're industrious and you're a serious girl. I want to tell you about the Father.'

'The Father? You mean God?'

'Well, yes, God is our father in heaven. But the Father was our father on earth.' She pulled a little mass card from her pocket and put it on the table between them. It had a picture of a Latin-looking priest with a kindly expression on his face and his arms outstretched in joy. 'The Father learned to find special people like you, Dolores. People who have a vocation.'

'I have absolutely no interest in being a nun,' Dolores said, 'if that's what you're getting at, Miss Nuala.'

'Oh, no, this is something different altogether,' Nuala said. 'This is a vocation to a life of service. We think you would be brilliant Help.'

Dolores Murphy was bright enough to hear the contradiction in those two words. If she was so brilliant, why should she be the Help?

By now, Dolores had realised what the Help did. They did all the cooking and cleaning and washing and ironing. They were not married and were expected to be celibate. They were expected to meekly serve the guests who attended the conference centre, but were instructed to not otherwise be seen, and they were never to speak unless spoken to. They entered the building through separate back doors.

'The Father knew what was best for all of us, and he would know what was best for you. You are a great worker, Dolores.'

Dolores smiled weakly.

'In two weeks' time, Miss Róisín and the Directress and myself are going to a conference in Rome for young ladies from universities all over the world. And we'd like you to come with us.'

'Rome?' echoed Dolores.

'Rome. Isn't that just wonderful, Dolores?'

'I've never been to Italy,' said Dolores. 'Well, to be fair, I've never been to Belfast.'

Miss Nuala nodded. 'I thought as much. It'll just be you and Mairéad coming with us.'

Mairéad was a very earnest girl from a tiny village outside Charleville who had mousy hair cut in a sensible style and lots of freckles. Mairéad was the sort of girl whose ears blushed hotly if she was asked a question. But she was very strong and got all her chores done ages before any of the other girls. She didn't back-chat and she didn't complain. She was at morning mass before most of them had even rolled out of bed. The Directress told Mairéad she had the Right Kind of Attitude.

Dolores reflected for a moment that the Dolores Murphy of a few weeks ago would have had withering views on Mairéad. The Dolores Murphy of a few weeks ago would have thought Mairéad a bit of a boring culchie who was probably into Cliff Richard. But the Dolores Murphy of a few weeks ago was disappearing into herself. Dolores hadn't picked up a book or listened to David Bowie in weeks. She was mostly too busy—and when she wasn't, she was too tired to think much.

And look: Rome. Dolores Murphy was going to Rome.

'But why am I going to a conference for university students? I'm going to get a job in catering.'

'Because you're special,' Miss Nuala said, the 'sh' in special whistling through her front teeth. She clutched Dolores's hand.

'What do you think, Dolores?' she asked, smiling, but not with her eyes. 'Imagine it: we can eat square pizza and drink espresso. We can visit the Forum and go to the ancient village of Ostia Antica. We can gaze up at the ceiling of the Sistine Chapel and we can buy rosary beads in St Peter's Square.'

'The Trevi Fountain and the Spanish Steps?' Dolores had seen pictures of them in a travel magazine in the *leabharlann*.

'The Trevi Fountain and the Spanish Steps. All of it. All of it! What do you say, Dolores?'

'Well, I say yes, Miss Nuala. Of course I bleeding say yes.'

Miss Nuala put her finger to her mouth to indicate that ladies didn't say 'bleeding'. And she gave Dolores's hand a squeeze and held it a little too long.

—

The next two weeks were a blur of preparations for the big trip. The other girls looked at Dolores and Mairéad through narrowed eyes. Most of them intended to leave the Big House, and for those who had not yet given up, this was the final push towards the door.

Dolores felt sorry for them, but she couldn't help but feel pleased to be singled out in this way. If only Mammy could see her now! That said, she knew in her heart that the biggest reason she couldn't go home was she had nothing to go home to but Mammy's brutal disappointment.

So Dolores and Miss Nuala had their chats each afternoon. They'd walk down the path, over a little stone bridge and into the meadow. They'd sit among the buttercups and eat blackberries they'd collected from the brambles along the way.

Any doubts Dolores might have had about the incongruity of being brilliant Help were ebbing away. Dolores blushed hard when she overheard Miss Nuala telling Miss Róisín that Dolores Murphy was a very handsome girl, and that she had a way about her. Miss Róisín agreed. They'd never said as much directly to Dolores, lest she get carried away with herself. Pride was a sin. But Dolores could tell they'd meant for her to hear it, and it made her heart swell a little.

'Don't tell Mairéad or any of the others I said this, but you're the standout,' Miss Nuala said once as she pierced the stems she was fashioning into a daisy chain. 'Mairéad's awfully dedicated and a good worker, but she's not you, Dolores. You're our little star.' Miss Nuala had a slightly sibilant tone to her voice, and so her 's' sounds had that little whistle. 'As for that other lot, Dolores, I'm afraid to say, God forgive me, they're really not up to scratch.'

'How do you mean?' Dolores asked.

'Oh, I shouldn't be telling tales,' Miss Nuala said primly, but there was a faint smile on her lips.

'Now,' she said, 'what do you think?' She placed a crown of daisies onto Dolores's head and smoothed her hair. 'I wish I had my camera, Dolores. You look a picture.'

Miss Nuala fumbled open the clasp of her stiff handbag and pulled out a little silver compact mirror. 'Here. Have a look.'

Dolores prised open the compact, which was engraved with *Nuala* in fancy cursive, and as she looked at herself, sitting among the buttercups with a daisy crown. And she felt warm.

Sometimes Miss Nuala would come and sit on her bed late at night and stroke her arm.

'Tell me about your life, Dolores. You know you can tell me anything.'

And so she began to tell Miss Nuala that she had never felt special in her life before. How Mammy had made her feel small when she deliberately didn't leave enough dinner for her. How Daddy made her feel invisible.

'But I'm not invisible. And I'm not small.'

'I know, dear, I know,' Miss Nuala said. 'That's why you're in the right place here.' And she stroked Dolores's arm some more.

Dolores felt ashamed of the electricity that danced up her arm when Nuala did this. But not so ashamed that she asked her to stop.

Miss Nuala carefully took out her tortoiseshell combs, shook out her wheat-coloured hair, combing through it repeatedly. The paddle brush's silver handle was inlaid with mother-of-pearl.

She took Dolores's finger and ran it along the brush handle. Dolores felt a pain in her chest.

'Do you think that they really love you, Dolores?' Miss Nuala whispered in her sibilant way, her pale cornflower-blue eyes fixed on Dolores. 'I mean, I am sure they think they do but, you know, not everyone's cut out to be a parent, even though they want to be.'

Dolores thought of Mammy in her polyester dress, standing at the sink, clucking her tongue at her as she came in from the *leabharlann*, her green eyes burning.

'I've never said this to anyone, but I'm not altogether sure they do at all,' Dolores said, feeling instantly ashamed and disloyal to Mammy, who after all had been pregnant on and off for a good twenty years.

Nuala nodded sympathetically. 'We love you, though. You know that, don't you, Dolores?'

Dolores didn't, quite. But no one in her life had ever said those words to her before, and to hear them spoken aloud sent a rush of warmth tumbling through her body.

Dolores Murphy didn't recognise, then, what love-bombing was. She just knew that it felt good. She began to feel addicted to the little rushes of oxytocin that she'd feel tumbling through her body when Nuala paid her attention.

She often had trouble sleeping. She would wake in the night in fright as the wind whipped across the fields. She missed the sound of the buses thundering around the corner—that was comfort to Dolores Murphy. One night she woke from a nightmare in which Mammy had fallen into the Dodder and drowned. The children were all wailing. Daddy had taken himself to Clarkes and, when he came home, he was stocious and he just shouted at them.

Miss Nuala, whose room was a few doors down, must have heard Dolores crying, because Dolores awoke to find her standing beside the bed in her mint-green broderie anglaise nightdress.

'Dolores, what's wrong?' she whispered.

'I had a nightmare,' Dolores sobbed. 'Mammy died.'

'Now, Dolores, don't you be thinking those thoughts,' Miss Nuala said. 'Why don't you drag your mattress and blankets down to my room and you can sleep on my floor?'

'Will the Directress mind?' Dolores asked.

'It'll be our little secret, so it will,' Miss Nuala said.

So, Dolores carried her mattress down the hall and laid it on the floor next to Miss Nuala's bed.

'Now,' the supervisor said, sitting on the bed, 'mind yourself. You'll feel much safer here.'

Dolores looked at Miss Nuala's bed. It was very narrow and there was no mattress at all, just a wooden board on top of the wire springs.

On the wall above it was a photograph of the Father, his arms outstretched. On the far wall, a crucifix. On the chair, some missals and Miss Nuala's prayer journal.

Dolores slid under the covers of her bed on the floor, and Miss Nuala put her hand on Dolores's head and stroked her hair. 'There now,' she said. 'You're safe here.'

Then Miss Nuala stretched out on her strange hard bed and eventually fell asleep. Dolores lay on the mattress and stared at the ceiling rose. She didn't really feel safer here, but didn't want to insult Miss Nuala. The moon was full and it was shining through the curtains, which Miss Nuala explained she kept open. A daddy-long-legs was making its way across the wall, the moonlight distorting it so that it looked comically frightening. Dolores turned over and noticed a wooden box about a foot long under Miss Nuala's bed. The box was carved with crucifixes.

Miss Nuala was snoring. Dolores marvelled at how she could sleep on that awful hard board. Mammy had always accused Dolores of being nosy and perhaps Mammy was right. She kept looking at the box, wondering what was inside. She waited a couple of minutes and carefully pulled the box towards her and opened it. Inside was a mass card depicting the Father, and a small whip made out of rough corded rope, with seven knotted ends. On some of the knots, she noticed what appeared to be dried blood. Dolores put the whip down as if it had stung her. Also in the box was a small purple velvet pouch. She opened it and found a strange and elaborate metal chain about the diameter of a choker necklace. But what a strange necklace. On the side of it that would face the skin were what appeared to be squared-off barbed-wire ends.

Dolores heard someone opening the toilet door down the hall and quickly returned the pouch to the box and slid the box back under the bed.

'Jaysus,' she said to herself, and turned over to face the wall. She lay there, unable to move or to sleep, until Miss Nuala shook her at 4 am and told her she'd better go back to her own room before the Directress woke them for morning mass.

12

ROME

THE WEEKS FLEW by and suddenly Dolores Murphy found herself hitting the tarmac at Fiumicino Airport.

'It means "little river",' she whispered as she gazed out the window.

'What does?' asked Miss Nuala.

'*Fiumicino*,' Dolores said in her best Italian pronunciation. 'Isn't it a beautiful word?'

The Directress didn't normally allow books—and Dolores was usually too tired to read them after working all day, in any case—but she had made an exception and allowed Miss Nuala to go to town to fetch Dolores a copy of *Italian for Beginners*. Dolores had practised every night.

'I suppose it is,' said Miss Nuala. 'Although personally I have always preferred French to Italian.' She placed her hand on

Dolores's thigh. 'We're here,' she whispered in her ear. 'Isn't it exciting? We're going to meet the Pope.'

'*Il Papa*,' said Dolores, ignoring the little voice in her head telling her that the Dolores of old would have scoffed at people like her Auntie Maggie, who went on pilgrimages to Rome and Lourdes and believed cripples could rise from their wheelchairs and walk again and stigmata actually happened.

She yawned. They had been up since long before dawn to drive the two hours to Shannon for their flight. She had been too excited to eat more than a slice of toast washed down with a cup of tea.

'*Signore e signori, benvenuti a Roma!*' said the purser in a nasal voice.

A gaggle of earnest-looking young women ahead of them burst into applause.

The Directress, who had been snoring in the row in front of them was awake now, and she turned to Miss Nuala and Dolores and beamed beatifically. 'Isn't this marvellous?' she said. 'They're all coming to the conference.'

'Can I meet them?' Dolores asked.

The Directress pressed her lips together, and Miss Nuala gave a little laugh. 'Funny Dolores—you are such a little dote, so you are.'

Dolores didn't know what she meant. She looked across the aisle to Mairéad and Miss Róisín. She noticed that Miss Róisín was whispering to Mairéad, her hand on Mairéad's thigh, and that

Mairéad's ears were crimson. Mairéad glanced over at Dolores then pushed Miss Róisín's hand off her lap before turning her head to look out the window. Dolores felt a little sick.

—

They stayed in a suburb of Rome north of the Vatican in a large but fairly drab apartment with high ceilings, cold travertine tiles and crucifixes on the walls. Dolores and Mairéad were to sleep in a bunkbed in a room at the end of the hall, and the Directress, Miss Nuala and Miss Róisín each had their own rooms. As Dolores walked down the hall to put away her luggage, she noticed that the beds in the other rooms were like Miss Nuala's at home. Instead of mattresses, just, again, hard boards. She turned to Mairéad, but Mairéad just looked at her and said nothing.

That day they went to St Peter's Square. The Italian sun beat down on stalls selling plastic rosary beads and little rippled glass bottles of *limonata* and *chinotto*. Handsome young priests glided by in soutanes. Flocks of nuns wore white habits, horn-rimmed glasses and scratchy-looking grey tights that must have been murder in the heat. American tourists in flip-flops, t-shirts and short shorts compared notes about overpriced *trattorie* and complained loudly about how hard it was to find someone who spoke good English. Pigeons bobbed down to steal what remained of boxed panini, and rats scurried behind rubbish bins in hope of tasty morsels. And thousands of earnest young university students from all over the world clasped their hands in delight at the prospect of an audience with *il Papa*.

Dolores and Mairéad gasped at St Peter's Basilica, awed by the scale of it.

'This is the most beautiful place I've ever been, so it is,' said Mairéad.

'Not that there's much for us to compare it to,' said Dolores. It made Dublin seem like a grubby afterthought.

'Can we go in?' she asked Miss Nuala.

'Of course,' replied Miss Nuala. 'But we can't stay long, as His Holiness will be appearing within the hour.'

Inside the basilica, Dolores gazed in wonder. How could she even begin to comprehend the beauty of the place? It could be described as too much, were it not on such an epic scale. It was cold and smelled of incense and candle wax and she had never felt so tiny. The organ played one note continuously. She understood for the first time what the phrase 'religious experience' meant. Miss Nuala, standing next to her, placed a hand on her shoulder and left it there for many beats too long but Dolores barely noticed as the music coursed through her body, cementing her feet in place. It wasn't even music, per se, just an all-encompassing wall of rapturous sound. She felt it in her sternum and her toes and her groin. The Directress turned to them and nodded with a fixed look in her eye. Miss Nuala nodded back. She took Dolores by the hand and led her through the cathedral. They lit candles and Dolores said a prayer for Mammy and the children.

When she stumbled out into the sunlight, she was blinking and slightly dizzy. The sensory overload of the heat and crowd was too much. His Holiness appeared on the balcony and the crowd roared. All around her, the earnest university students were crying. The PA system was echoing, and the Pope was saying something, but Dolores Murphy couldn't quite make out what. Some of it was in Latin, some in Italian, some in English, but her ears were ringing too loudly for her to decipher any of it. Pigeons circled overhead. It grew steadily hotter and hotter. There was a persistent hum of Vespas and sirens and cars honking. Near her, an official was saying to a young moustachioed tourist, '*Attenzione! Attenzione! É vietato fumare.*' The moustachioed tourist was rolling his eyes and blowing smoke rings in the official's face. The Directress clucked her tongue. The smoke made Dolores nauseous. She hadn't eaten since that toast all those hours ago at Shannon and it was now late afternoon. All of a sudden, everything went black.

—

She woke up in the bottom bunk, the evening sun streaming through net curtains. Miss Nuala was sitting on the side of the bed, stroking her forehead with a damp cloth.

'Darling Dolores, I think you must have got a touch of heat stroke,' she said.

'Where is everyone?' Dolores asked, her mouth feeling like it was full of sand.

'They've gone out for supper,' said Miss Nuala. 'Let me fetch the Help and ask her to bring you some *zuppa*.'

Miss Nuala went to the hallway and rang a little brass bell with a ceramic handle.

A woman appeared at the door, holding a large wooden laundry basket in one arm. She had thick black eyebrows, chocolate eyes, shiny hair scraped back in a bun and cheeks so red they seemed stained. She was wearing an old-fashioned maid's outfit.

'*Signorina*, you awake! *Santa Maria*,' she said, crossing herself.

'This is Rosaria,' Miss Nuala said to Dolores. 'She's here to provide anything we need. She's the gentlest, holiest person, and service is her vocation, isn't it, Rosaria?' She spoke in the sort of voice she might use to address a twelve-year-old child with special needs.

'*Si, signorina*,' said Rosaria to Miss Nuala in a weary voice. She turned to Dolores. 'I will bring you some *minestra. Va bene, piccolina?*'

'Yes, thank you,' Dolores said.

'*Va bene*.' Rosaria bowed her head and disappeared down the hall.

She returned a few minutes later with the most delicious soup Dolores had ever tasted, with a slice of crusty bread on the side.

Miss Nuala sat on the edge of the bed and insisted on spooning the *minestra* into Dolores's mouth, despite her protests that she could feed herself.

'I'm sorry if today was too much, Dolores.'

'It was magic, Miss Nuala. I think I must have gotten too hot. And hungry—I was too excited to eat earlier. I'm not good when I don't eat. We're good eaters in my family.'

'That's our fault, I'm afraid, Dolores. I'm so sorry.'

'Ah, sure, don't be.'

'Tomorrow will be a great day, please God. And we'll mind you, Dolores, I promise.'

Dolores Murphy ate all the soup, and she felt much better. She fell asleep with Miss Nuala stroking her cheek long before Mairéad returned and clambered into the bunk above.

The next few days were very busy. Masses and visits to holy crypts and lectures from sensible-looking women with lots of children at home about how to be faithful and pure servants of God.

At one point, the Directress pressed a mass card into Dolores's hand with a picture of a young female saint.

'Pray for Saint Maria Goretti,' the Directress said. 'A teenage saint.'

Dolores didn't remember much about Saint Maria Goretti as her eyes had always glazed over when the nuns at school began to bang on about the saints. But she nodded and told the Directress she would.

Despite Miss Nuala's promise, they didn't eat much, and they walked miles on cobblestones every day and Dolores felt permanently light-headed.

'When are we going to the Spanish Steps?' Dolores asked Miss Nuala as they were walking from one lecture to the next.

'Oh, in good time.'

'What about the Trevi Fountain?'

Nuala frowned.

'Dolores,' she said, a little hiss on the 's', 'do you know how terribly lucky you are to be here? Do you think many other girls from Ringsend get to travel to Rome on an all-expenses-paid trip? When I say, "in good time", I mean it.'

Dolores blushed hotly. Miss Nuala had never scolded her before.

The Directress, who was walking ahead with Mairéad and Miss Róisín, turned to look at them. She gave Miss Nuala a little nod and kept walking.

'Can you tell me about Saint Maria Goretti?' Dolores asked Miss Nuala as they walked back to the apartment, hoping this might get her back in Miss Nuala's good books.

'Oh, she was wonderful,' Miss Nuala said softly. 'A virgin martyr. Maria chose not to be violated. She was only eleven and a horrible man tried to rape her. Maria told him that it was a sin, and she would rather die than give up her purity to a man. Our purity is so precious, Dolores. It should be guarded at all times.

And so, he stabbed her fourteen times. But she died pure. Maria is the patron saint of rape victims.'

Dolores looked at Miss Nuala. 'I don't understand,' she said. 'How would it have been her fault if she was raped? Why is it a good thing that she died?' Dolores had always got into trouble with the nuns at school for asking these sorts of 'impertinent' questions.

'Imagine being stained like that, Dolores, and the shame it would have brought her,' Miss Nuala said. 'What a brave thing to do. You should say a prayer to Saint Maria Goretti every night.'

Miss Nuala's explanation made Dolores feel distinctly uncomfortable, but she didn't question her further.

That night, as she drifted off to sleep, she heard Mairéad weeping quietly in the bunk above.

Dolores sat up in bed. 'Mairéad, what's wrong?' she asked.

'I can't say,' Mairéad said.

'Can I help?'

'Nobody can,' said Mairéad. 'I rang me mammy and me daddy and I told them about Miss Róisín, and they're raging, so they are.'

'What about Miss Róisín?' Dolores asked, feeling tight in her chest.

'You know, Dolores. You know that you know. Don't think I can't see that. Why don't you just go to sleep? What does it even matter?'

Dolores Murphy did feel that she knew, but didn't know how to put it into words. She also realised that this was almost the longest conversation that she and Mairéad had had. And that there was something inherently wrong about that, for reasons she could not quite articulate.

—

The next morning, they were all still in their nightdresses when Mairéad's burly, bearded father rapped the brass lion's-head door knocker. Rosaria opened the door.

'*Buongiorno, signore, come sta?*'

'I've come for my Mairéad,' he said tersely. 'I want you to take me to her right now.'

The Directress came to the door, wrapping her dressing-gown around her.

'Now, Mr O'Riordan, this is not on.'

'I'm here to collect my daughter,' Mr O'Riordan said, pushing past Rosaria. 'Get out of my way.'

He pushed his way in and shook his fist at the Directress.

'Well, I never,' said the Directress.

'I sent my girl for a cookery class. She did not sign up for any of this. I'm taking her home.'

'Sign up for any of what?' replied the Directress.

Mr O'Riordan's face was so red he looked like he was going

to spontaneously combust. He just shook his head. 'May God forgive you all.'

Miss Róisín, standing at her bedroom door, glanced across the hall at Miss Nuala, who was standing at hers. Their eyes looked glassy. Dolores noticed that Miss Róisín had some thread that she was tightening around her pinky, until it went purplish. Around the collar of her nightdress was what appeared to be a bloodstain.

'This is a wonderful opportunity for a girl from Charleville,' the Directress said firmly.

Mr O'Riordan shook his head. 'We're not from Charleville, we're from Effin,' he said, referring to a tiny village just outside the town.

The Directress rolled her eyes a little. 'Well, *Effin*, then,' she said with a slightly contemptuous smirk. 'Dairy country, as I understand it? Do you keep cows, Mr O'Riordan?'

'I tell you what, if I don't clap eyes on my Mairéad very soon, things will start to get pretty effin' difficult for you,' he said, jabbing his finger into the Directress's breastbone.

'Well, I *never*,' repeated the Directress, outraged.

He marched down the hall. 'Where is she?' he demanded.

Mairéad, who at the sound of the knock on the door had returned to the room she shared with Dolores, emerged now fully dressed and clutching her suitcase. 'I'm here, Daddy,' she said, and she ran into her father's arms.

Mairéad O'Riordan and her daddy left without another word to anyone.

Miss Róisín and Miss Nuala silently closed the doors to their rooms. The Directress smoothed her blush jacquard housecoat, patted her brow and rang the bell for Rosaria to make tea.

'What a hideous man,' said the Directress to Dolores, who was still standing, staring at her. 'What are you looking at, Dolores? Off you go.'

A little later, Miss Nuala came down the hallway and knocked on Dolores's door. Dolores was lying on the bottom bunk, bewildered.

'It's for the best,' Miss Nuala said. She took her paddle brush out of her dressing-gown pocket and began to run it through Dolores's hair in long, even strokes.

'Now,' she said, 'everything's going to be all right.'

'I'm so tired,' Dolores whispered. 'And so confused.'

Miss Nuala didn't respond, and just kept brushing Dolores's hair.

'How old are you, Miss Nuala?' Dolores asked.

'What kind of a question is that to ask a lady?' Miss Nuala said. 'But since you ask, I'm thirty-two.'

'I'm not yet sixt—' Dolores began to say, but Miss Nuala hushed her, placing her finger on Dolores's mouth, as if to shut it. She left it there, salty on the tip of Dolores's tongue for so many beats that Dolores lost count of the beats. The nauseating electricity pulsed from Miss Nuala's fingertip right through her and yet she didn't move.

Outside, Dolores could make out the sound of fighting cats and church bells.

Miss Nuala put her lips very close to Dolores's ear. 'It's our secret,' she whispered, placing her hand on the softest inner part of Dolores's thigh and leaving it there. 'Your skin is so smooth. Do you know how special that is?' Miss Nuala's hand was cold.

With her other hand, Miss Nuala then grasped Dolores's own hand and started to recite the rosary. Dolores could see, through the Liberty-print poplin of Nuala's dress, the spiky chain that she had found under Miss Nuala's bed, fastened around Miss Nuala's thigh.

'Hail Mary, full of grace, the Lord is with thee,' she began. 'Will you say it with me, Dolores? Will you? Close your eyes.'

Dolores Murphy remained silent. How had this all come from a cooking class? Where was it all leading? Dolores was too tired and hungry to think through to the end of the questions that danced in her mind.

Miss Nuala recited four decades of the rosary with her eyes closed. Her voice rose in intensity as she continued, and she removed her hand from the uppermost part of Dolores's thigh and placed it on her own. Through her half-closed eyes, Dolores noticed that Miss Nuala was rhythmically pushing the little barbs attached to the chain into her thigh and wincing slightly as she did it. Tiny pinpricks of blood stained the fabric.

When she unclasped Dolores's hand, her fingernails had left sharp little half-moon imprints on Dolores's skin.

Miss Nuala opened her eyes and saw Dolores staring at the blood on her dress.

'Self-mortification,' she whispered, in a voice that was jarringly soothing. 'You're going to learn all about it. It's a way of offering up your sufferings to Our Lord. It's pain, but it's good pain.'

Dolores felt a spike of fear at this, and Miss Nuala seemed to sense it, as she stood up and changed the subject.

'Why don't you get up and run a bath? We need to start our day and forget that any of this ever happened.'

Dolores went and ran a very deep bath—the sort of bath that Mammy would have given out to her about. She scattered in orange-scented bath salts. At home, as fourth girl, her bath was always after her sisters' and the water was usually tepid and cloudy. Sometimes it made her gag, and she would empty it and refill it, and then Mammy would chase her around the house with a wooden spoon, threatening not to turn on the immersion for a week.

She lay back in the bath until her hair fanned out around her and the water covered her ears. She felt like she could bathe for days. In the crack between the door and the floor, she could see the shadows of people walking up and down. There was terse whispering, slamming of doors, some agitated sentences in Italian from Rosaria. What would Daddy do if she were to ring home? Would he even get out of his chair? Dolores submerged herself completely. And underneath the water, she cried.

The Directress and Miss Róisín and Miss Nuala never uttered a word about Mairéad O'Riordan again. It was as if she had died, but no one grieved her passing. No one lined up for her removal or sang at her wake. She just ceased to exist.

Dolores Murphy was not yet sixteen.

She hadn't heard from Mammy and Daddy at all.

In Ringsend, Mammy was standing at the kitchen sink, washing up the children's breakfast dishes. Behind her, Happy was sitting at the table, finishing some toast and doing his homework—late, as usual. Joe was in his wooden highchair, tossing handfuls of Rice Krispies on the floor. Mary, who had come down to visit, was madly trying to clean them up with the brush and shovel. Annie was blowing raspberries on three-year-old Mickie's belly. Mickie was squealing, 'Again! Again!' In the middle of the table was a pile of letters, addressed in Mammy's spidery capitals to *DOLORES MURPHY.* They had been carefully opened with a paper knife and were sealed with yellowing sellotape across the top fold. Each of them was stamped in big red letters: RETURN TO SENDER.

It was the next day that Dolores Murphy whistled.

13

THE HELP

TO WHISTLE WASN'T like blowing the whistle. In fact, it was the opposite. To whistle was to acquiesce, to renounce that part of yourself that had ever put up a fight. To whistle was to sign up to be a permanent member of the Group.

The morning that it happened, they were eating breakfast and the Directress announced to everyone that this was to be Dolores's special day. Dolores noticed that Rosaria, who was clearing the dishes, stopped abruptly and looked at her. Her eyes widened. And then she bustled into the kitchen.

Dolores carried her cereal bowl out to the sink.

'*Signorina*, please, no—don't,' said Rosaria, the deep crimson of her cheeks spreading to her neck in angry blotches.

'Don't what?' trilled the Directress behind them. The Directress never went into the kitchen.

'Don't clear up the plate,' Rosaria said quickly. 'It's Signorina Dolores's special day, no empty the plates,' she said, and gave Dolores a look that the Directress couldn't see.

The Directress gazed at Rosaria for a moment, narrowing her eyes, but said nothing. She turned to Dolores.

'Come on, little Ringsend Rose, it's time to get ready,' she said breezily. 'I bought you a dress on the Via dei Condotti. I'd rather like you to wear it.'

With a last, hard glare at Rosaria, she ushered Dolores out of the kitchen and as she left, pushed the door back so hard that it slammed sharply and the whole kitchen shuddered. Dolores turned to Rosaria, who was standing, looking after them, wiping her hands on her apron, chewing on her lip until it bled a little.

The dress came in a big box with a white velvet sash.

'Open it!' said Miss Nuala beaming at Dolores, but not with her eyes.

Dolores untied the ribbon tentatively, lifted the lid of the box and stared, lost for words. It was in the style of a prairie dress, with the sort of bell sleeves, fitted at the wrist, that were popular at the time. It was made of a synthetic, gauzy fabric printed with tiny lilies of the valley and finished with a lace trim under the bust and on the cuffs. It was the shade of runny egg yolk. If she'd seen a girl dressed like that in Ringsend, she'd have called her a fecking eejit.

Dolores Murphy felt ill.

'Well, go on, dear, do try it on,' said the Directress, her tone implying a benign command rather than a request.

The three of them stood there, waiting for Dolores to do as she was told.

She went to her bedroom and slowly pulled the dress over her head, straining to do up the long row of closely spaced covered buttons that lined the back of the dress and to ease them into their loops. Standing in front of the mirror, she noticed that it fit her perfectly. Her breasts looked high and round and her waist looked small. And despite it being the last thing she would ever choose, she looked quite pretty, in a docile, simpering sort of way.

Miss Nuala came in and looked her up and down.

'Well, would you look at you,' she said quietly, placing her hands on either side of Dolores's waist.

She pulled her silver-handled brush from her pocket and quickly arranged Dolores's hair so that it was half up, half down, held with a pearlescent clasp. Next, she handed Dolores a glossy apricot lipstick, compact and a mascara wand. Dolores dutifully applied the make-up. Miss Nuala dabbed a small amount of clear gloss in the middle of Dolores's lips, pushing her finger slightly into her mouth at the end and giving her a wink. Then she helped Dolores step into a pair of white high heels. She looked like she was going to a dance in North Carolina.

'Now,' said Miss Nuala, guiding her to the door, her hand on Dolores's waist.

Dolores hobbled out to the Directress and Miss Róisín.

'A vision!' exclaimed the Directress. 'It's a shame we didn't work on deportment, but never mind, there's always time.'

'Quite,' said Miss Róisín, smiling, but not with her eyes.

Dolores didn't know what deportment was. She missed being able to look up words in the library. There were no dictionaries, nor any other books, in the Roman apartment except a book in Italian about the Father, prayer missals and several copies of the Bible.

'A teenage vision,' said Miss Nuala, stroking Dolores's arm. 'Shall we say a prayer of thanks to a young saint?'

'What a marvellous idea,' said the Directress. No one ever said 'marvellous' in Ringsend. 'Let's say a prayer to Saint Maria Goretti.' She bowed her head and brought Nuala, Róisín and Dolores into a little circle, indicating that they should bow their heads, too.

'Oh Saint Maria Goretti who, strengthened by God's grace, did not hesitate even at the age of eleven to shed your blood and sacrifice life itself to defend your virginal purity.

'Look graciously on the unhappy human race which has strayed far from the path of eternal salvation . . .'

Even as far down the rabbit hole as Dolores Murphy found herself, even though times were different then, she still knew this was a profoundly odd thing to pray about on what was supposed to be her special day. She glanced surreptitiously at Miss Nuala and Miss Róisín, but their eyes were closed, their heads bowed in prayer.

'*Teach us all, especially the youth,*' the Directress said, lifting her gaze to look directly at Dolores, '*to flee from anything that could offend Jesus and stain our souls with sin . . .*'

Dolores racked her brain to think of what possible sin her soul had to this point been stained with. Wanting to marry David Bowie? Stealing her sisters' make-up? Never listening to a single word Father Moore said in mass? Wishing Himself would just take a heart attack from the drink and die and leave some money to Mammy so she could live a decent life?

'*Obtain for us from our Lord victory in temptation, comfort in the sorrows of life, and the grace which we now earnestly beg of thee . . .*

'*Saint Maria, pray that we may one day enjoy with you the eternal glory of Heaven. Amen.*'

Miss Nuala and Miss Róisín chimed in, '*Amen.*'

'*Saint Maria Goretti, pray for us,*' the three women intoned in unison.

Dolores mouthed the words with them, but no sound came out.

Rosaria was standing in the doorway, holding a feather duster. Dolores could see that her eyes were brimming with tears.

It would be the last time during those years that Dolores Murphy would wear anything new, that was hers and not Miss Nuala's and Miss Róisín's hand-me-downs or a maid's uniform.

For the past few days, Miss Nuala had been preparing Dolores with scripts. About what it meant to whistle. About her vocation. About how she, Miss Nuala, had a vocation, too.

As they sat in a taxi on the way to the chapel where the ceremony was to take place, Miss Nuala kept speaking about the first-ever Help, who lived with the Father, and how she was one of the most godly, obedient creatures who ever walked the earth, and how serving the Father and Holy God gave her life meaning.

'Are you ready to whistle, Dolores?' Miss Nuala asked, taking Dolores's hand.

'You keep talking about the Help, Miss Nuala. I understand about devoting my life to Holy God. But what if I want to have a boyfriend? Or even lose my mind altogether and get married? Or, you know, become a librarian or go to a David Bowie concert?'

'Oh, darling, that's not your vocation,' Miss Nuala said. 'Do you think that we'd ever suggest something for you that was not what God planned? And think of all the skills you've gained in your cookery course.'

'I could still use those skills as a married woman, Miss Nuala.' Dolores kept thinking of Rosaria, standing there with her tear-filled eyes, her feather duster and her bleeding lip.

'Ours is not to question, Dolores,' said Miss Nuala, placing her hand on Dolores's knee and leaving it there. It didn't sound like an answer. But Dolores Murphy felt like she was on a train that she couldn't get off, not until it reached its final destination.

They arrived at the chapel and Miss Nuala brought her into the chilly Holy Crypt to see where the remains of the Father were kept. Dolores felt scared, but knew Miss Nuala would give her one of her hard looks if she said so.

An older Spanish woman came to greet them.

'This is Elena,' whispered Miss Nuala. 'One of the very first ladies to become the Help. She's here to help you whistle, Dolores.'

'Hello, my darling. It is time,' said Elena, and took Dolores by both of her hands.

She led her to a corner of the chapel, where there was a desk.

'Here,' she said, and handed Dolores a fountain pen and a sheet of lined paper. 'You must write to the Father that you have a vocation to become the Help.'

'But what if I ever want to get married?' Dolores asked. Panic was rising in her chest.

'But, my dear, that is not your vocation. Think of all the work you've done.'

The Directress, Miss Nuala and Miss Róisín stood behind Elena, arms linked, nodding firmly. The idea of defying them made Dolores feel small and helpless.

She sank into the seat at the desk and Elena handed her a template.

And Dolores, copying the words provided, began to write.

Dear Father,

My name is Dolores Murphy. It is my belief that I have a vocation to be the Help. I humbly ask for your holy blessing.

And that was that. Dolores Murphy had whistled.

Elena led her out into the sunshine, and the Directress, Miss Nuala, Miss Róisín and other women she had met at the conference began hugging her and congratulating her.

'Oh, darling Dolores,' said the Directress, 'we are just so pleased. Shall we take a Roman constitutional back to the *appartamento*?'

Miss Nuala and Miss Róisín smiled and walked ahead up the street, arm in arm, whispering to each other. At one point, Dolores noticed Miss Róisín getting something out of Miss Nuala's hair and Miss Nuala colouring and them both giggling conspiratorially. At another, Miss Róisín's palm was in the small of Miss Nuala's back as she pointed out a palazzo or some such to Miss Nuala. Her fingers at times almost stretched down to Miss Nuala's coccyx. Miss Nuala's cheeks were flushed. She never looked back once at Dolores all the way to the apartment.

'Well, Dolores,' said the Directress, noticing her watching this, 'we'll be heading back to the Big House tomorrow. That's where your vocation begins.'

Dolores smiled weakly and began to wonder what exactly she had done. She had this overwhelming need for her mammy. But Mammy wasn't there.

—

When they arrived back at the Big House, the affection with which Dolores had been showered ceased so abruptly she could almost physically feel the whiplash. Dolores was shown to her new quarters in a different wing and introduced to two other Help living there, Betty and Michelle. Neither was particularly friendly. Betty, who was in her early forties, seemed ancient to Dolores. Michelle was in her mid-twenties and had been living at the Big House since her teens.

'I hope you haven't come back from Rome with notions,' Betty said. 'The work will sort you out.'

After mass, Dolores Murphy watched from her window as a busload of fresh teenagers arrived for the cookery school. She saw Miss Nuala, dressed in a cream angora sweater and duck-egg blue tweedy skirt, ushering a pretty redhead off the bus, pointing out the architecture. Miss Róisín was attached to another girl. Dolores saw her stroke the girl's hair.

Miss Nuala glanced up to see her standing in the window and Dolores waved at her. Miss Nuala gave a stiff little smile and resumed her conversation with the redhead.

She was obviously just very busy getting the new girls settled, Dolores told herself.

Betty walked into her room.

'Here,' she said, throwing a pile of old pinafores at Dolores. 'Some of these ought to fit you. Take three. They'll be your work uniform from now on.'

—

The new regime was even more strict than when she was in the cookery school. She still rose at 4.30 am for mass and then scrubbed the floors. Still spent endless hours at the Elnapress, still cleaned mucous and shite from seven pairs of pants, folded hospital corners and steamed towel swans. She was to work seven days a week, sixteen hours a day. There was no lock on the door of her room, and she had no keys to the rest of the house. If she went anywhere, she had to be escorted by Betty or, occasionally, by Miss Nuala and Miss Róisín or the Directress. She had no purse. She was warned never to go near the front entrance of the property. She was never to make eye contact with any man, ever.

'If you are serving a man in the conference centre,' the Directress said, 'do your work quickly and efficiently. Maintain a pleasant demeanour, but do not smile. You do not want to tempt him. Remember, purity is your responsibility. Pray to Saint Maria Goretti.'

As the Directress was saying this, she was flanked by Miss Nuala and Miss Róisín, who were nodding vigorously. Dolores caught Miss Nuala's eye. Miss Nuala looked away.

She was to eat meals only in the kitchen in the Helps' quarters, and these meals comprised leftovers from the catering at the Big House. The food was often cold, and the bread had often gone stale.

Who was this Dolores Murphy? She hardly knew. Somewhere inside her, the old Dolores Murphy was telling them all to feck off. But she was buried further and deeper every day. Could she explain why she did this if anyone had asked? Probably not. Every now and then she caught sight of herself in one of the gilt-framed mirrors in the parlour or the dining room. Her white face. Her skinny body in the shapeless pinafore. Dolores Murphy had disappeared into herself. She hated it, but she couldn't find a way to properly express it.

She was told to write to Mammy and Daddy and tell them that she wouldn't be home for holidays, because she was required to go to other big houses to help with the work. The Directress came and dictated the form of words to her.

A couple of weeks after the letter was sent, the Directress came to tell her that Mammy was on the phone. To Dolores's knowledge, it was the first time that Mammy had called her the whole time she'd been at the Big House. Mammy didn't have a phone, so she'd have to go to Mrs Behan next door or, if she wanted some privacy, down to the phone box on the corner. She was obviously in the phone box, because Dolores could hear the sound of cars moving through lashing rain. She felt a little pang of longing for Ringsend.

'Dolores, are you not getting my letters?'

'What? Mammy, you never sent any.'

'I did that. Sure, didn't I send Paul's first communion photo? Ah, Dolores, you should have seen the little dote. Didn't I send the mass card for Sean O'Doherty's funeral? Ah, it was beautiful. They were lined all the way down Pearce Street for the removal. Did you know he was drownded in the lock? Brutal, it was. Sheila O'Doherty was broken-hearted, so she was. Wasn't Father Moore's homily the loveliest thing I ever heard? Your Auntie Maggie was in floods of tears, *floods*, because didn't she go to school with Sheila O'Doherty? They went to Lourdes three times. And Sheila's Philly had his first communion with Paul just the day before his daddy died. And Sean O'Doherty sang at the mass for the first communion. And everyone said he was the most beautiful singer. It was brutal, Dolores. *Brutal*.'

There was nothing in this world that Mammy liked to discuss more than death.

'But listen, there must be a problem with the postal, Dolores. I'll have a word with the TD, and he can have a word, please God.'

Mammy was always down in the local politician's office, complaining about issues in the neighbourhood.

'Ah, Mrs Murphy, how lovely to see you. What can I do for you now?' was Brendan O'Donnell's regular, if slightly weary, refrain. Mammy was quite the micro lobbyist. She had got ramps into the GAA for Mrs Behan's disabled son. She had picketed out the front of O'Donnell's office for weeks over pollution from the power station. What Mammy lacked in palpable affection for her children, she made up for in community spirit.

'So howarye, anyway, Dolores?'

'Well, I got to go to Rome, Mammy. I went into St Peter's.'

'You did not?!'

'I did—it was part of my course.'

'Well, you lucky girl.'

'Now I'm working here full-time. I'm tired, Mammy, they have me working very hard.' Dolores heard a little catch of breath on the phone, but it wasn't Mammy; it sounded as if a person had been going to say something, but then caught themselves and didn't.

'Why can't you come home for Christmas?' Mammy asked.

'Oh, it's very busy here and I'll be required to help with the other houses,' Dolores said, wary now of who else might be on the call. 'The work can't get done on its own, Mammy.'

Mammy wasn't so sure about that, but she was prepared to give the Directress the benefit of the doubt. When Mammy had mentioned to the local TD Brendan O'Donnell that Dolores was attending the cookery school, Mr O'Donnell had nodded approvingly and said, 'She'll be in very good hands down there, Mrs Murphy. I've attended conferences there and the Directress is a very impressive and well-connected lady. Our Lord must have good plans for your Dolores.'

'How are the children, Mammy?'

'They're good. Didn't Gerry make his confirmation?'

'Oh, what did Happy choose for his confirmation name?'

'Christopher.'

'Well, that's pretty boring, Mammy. I would have chosen Augustine or Benedict.'

'Well, you know how Saint Christopher is the patron saint of travellers. And Gerry loves cars. We're still getting over you insisting on Honorata instead of Bernadette or Frances.'

Mammy giggled. Dolores hadn't heard her laugh in years.

'Well, all that time over at the library had to have some benefit, Mammy. Did you know Saint Honorata was kidnapped?'

'I did not know that, Dolores.'

'How're the girls?'

'Well, I could have murdered that Carmel Murphy last week, so I could. She brought the little ones down to the Shellybanks without proper warm clothes. And then didn't she let Mickie pick up a jellyfish with his bare hands and put it in his bucket and bring it home? And I had to put vinegar on his hands because he had a brutal rash.'

'Poor Mickie!'

'Oh, don't you be feeling too sorry for him. Mickie's still a little imp. He'll be the death of me. And didn't Joe take his first steps? He walked right across the floor in front of your daddy, and Daddy gave out because he walked in front of *The Late Late* and he was grabbing on to the television at Gay Byrne.'

'Oh, the wee dote,' said Dolores, tears springing to her eyes as she pictured her little golden-haired brother toddling across the front room. 'I miss you all, Mammy,' she said.

As she said it, Betty walked up to the phone on the landing and waved to Dolores.

'Dolores,' she mouthed, 'you need to go and sweep out the fireplace. It's filthy. The Directress will be raging when she gets back tomorrow.'

'I'm sorry, Mammy, I have to go,' Dolores said.

'Well, it's nice at least to hear your voice, Dolores.'

'It's nice to hear yours, Mammy.'

'I'll have a chat to the TD.'

'Good idea, Mammy.'

'Your daddy sends his best.'

Dolores knew he didn't, but she appreciated her mother's white lie.

'Remember to say a prayer for Sheila O'Doherty and little Philly.'

'I will, Mammy.'

Mammy hung up, and Dolores felt queasy as she heard a little sigh and a second click as if a phone were being put down somewhere else, too. She felt a little chill. As she replaced the receiver in its cradle, she remembered that today was her sixteenth birthday. Mammy hadn't mentioned it.

'Does anyone else have problems with the post here?' Dolores asked Betty, who'd been waiting impatiently for her to end the call.

'What do you mean, like?'

'Do they have trouble getting their mail?'

'Well, not that I know of. But you needn't be worrying about mail. We're your family now, Dolores. Focus on your work and Holy God. Now, off to that fireplace.'

—

Dolores was bone-tired. It was half past eight. Her knees hurt from scrubbing floors. Her fingers were callused. As she was sweeping out the fireplace, Miss Nuala tapped on the door.

'Miss Nuala!' said Dolores, trying not to sound as pleased as she felt, even as she wondered why on earth the sight of this strange woman should make her so happy.

Without speaking, Miss Nuala switched off the light, so that only a small lamp remained burning in the corner.

She walked over and sat down on the stiff armchair beside the fireplace, smoothing her hands over her kilt and folding her ankles to the side. Dolores had barely seen Miss Nuala in weeks. She ached for affection, even Miss Nuala's odd affection, which made her feel both nauseous and warm. She was embarrassed that Miss Nuala was seeing her like this, in her sooty pinafore.

'Hello, Dolores, pet,' said Miss Nuala, smiling, but not with her eyes. 'A little bird told me it was your sixteenth birthday today. I trust that your vocation is treating you well.'

'Well, I—' Dolores began to answer, and hoped to do so truthfully, but Miss Nuala clearly wasn't here to listen.

'Good. Now, I want to have a chat to you about your spiritual journey, Dolores.'

'Sure,' said Dolores, bowing her head.

'It's very, very important that Our Lord is the foremost thing in your mind, Dolores,' she said, that little hiss on her 's'. 'Do you know, he's everything to me? Everything, Dolores. That's why I'm here and not teaching at college. That's why I'm spreading his word and the Father's word to the next generation. I could be selfishly living my own life. I could be going to dances with young men. I could be having eleven children like your mammy and look, for some that is a holy path. But it's not *my* path, Dolores, because I have a vocation. And it's here.' She reached out her hand and ran a freezing finger along Dolores's cheekbone. 'And do you know how we can keep Our Lord foremost in our thoughts and banish all the other selfish thoughts?'

'How?' asked Dolores.

'Do you remember we spoke in Rome of self-mortification?'

Dolores remembered the tiny bloodstains on Miss Nuala's nightdress and the half-moon imprints of her fingernails in Dolores's hand. She nodded slowly.

Miss Nuala took out an elaborately decorated wooden box and placed it in front of Dolores.

'Open it, Dolores.'

Dolores opened the box and found two velvet pouches inside—one small, like a jewellery pouch, the other large.

Miss Nuala took the small pouch from the box and pulled out a spiky chain like the one Dolores had found under the supervisor's bed.

'Sit up here,' she said, rising to make room for Dolores on the armchair. 'Just make sure you don't get soot on this chair. The Directress bought it in an antique auction, and it cost a fortune. But look, it's our little secret, because she and Miss Róisín are down in Cork at a retreat for a few days. I'm holding the fort.'

Dolores nodded. She could hear a ringing in her ears. She sat on the chair in the dim light and looked at Miss Nuala.

Miss Nuala slowly lifted the hem of Dolores's pinafore. Her leg shone blue in the moonlight streaming in from the window. She rested her hand on Dolores's knee for a few moments, and then she fastened the chain around Dolores's thigh and held it there.

Dolores winced with the pain. But she also felt the nauseating electricity going through her, as Miss Nuala's fingers touched the inside of her thigh underneath the chain.

'Now, Dolores, the Father wants you to wear this at least once a day, for at least an hour, while you are doing your work. Do you think you could do that for me? For the Father?'

'Won't it hurt?' asked Dolores.

'Oh, funny Dolores. Only a little. Look . . .' And Miss Nuala raised her kilt to reveal the barbed chain around her own leg, over the top of her nylons. Dolores thought it was an awful waste of a good pair of tights, but she said nothing. She noticed a patchwork of blue bruises underneath the nylons.

'Darling, a little pain is the whole point. We have to offer up suffering for Our Lord. And it's only once a day. Just for a little bit. I would have thought it's the least you could do.' She looked searchingly into Dolores's eyes then reached into the box for the second pouch. 'You'll need this, too,' she said. Miss Nuala pulled a whip from the pouch—the same as the whip Dolores had found under the supervisor's bed.

Dolores opened her mouth to speak—she wanted to say that this was too much.

Miss Nuala put a finger on Dolores's mouth to hush her. 'You know what to do, Dolores. Our Lord will thank you.'

Then she got up and walked out the door, leaving Dolores to the fireplace.

Dolores sat in the freezing semi-darkness with the barbed chain still wrapped around her thigh. It hurt. But it was supposed to, she reminded herself. She returned to her position in front of the fireplace, the barbs digging into her leg with every movement. A tear rolled down her cheek and into her mouth.

She licked it away, finished the job, and then unfastened the chain and put it back in its pouch.

In bed that night, she inspected the little marks on her thigh.

Sixteen, she thought.

She remembered that song by Ringo Starr, which had come out when she was still in primary school, 'You're Sixteen, You're Beautiful and You're Mine'.

When Joe was a tiny baby, and Mammy was still recovering from what had been a terrible birth and shocking mastitis, Dolores used to cradle Joe in her arms and pretend he was her baby.

'*You're six weeks, you're beautiful and you're mine,*' she would sing to the gurgling infant, clutching him to her and dancing gently around the kitchen.

She sang the words softly to herself now and, only because she was shattered, she eventually fell asleep.

14

SIXTEEN

AS THE WEEKS and then the months wore on and the leaves tumbled off the hornbeams and the sycamores and the oaks, it occurred to Dolores Murphy that she had completed her cookery course and had for some months now been full-time Help, yet she had still received no wages. At first she thought that perhaps she had miscalculated the time since she started. But then one month went by, and another, and another, and she realised that it was now far too long and there must be some sort of mistake.

She didn't know how to raise this—Dolores was intimidated by the Directress and had been brought up by Mammy to believe that it was somehow shameful to ask for money. Mammy rarely even asked Daddy for money.

It was only just before she left Ringsend that Dolores discovered just how much money Daddy was taking home from the co-op. One of her friends, Barbara, was working there in accounts and was disgusted to learn that many of the men there had an agreement with management that they would be paid part of the salary in cash so that their wives did not know how much they earned and so they could spend money on themselves and, frankly, the drink and the horses. Management liked the flexibility, and the men were generously paid.

'Is Daddy one of them?' Dolores had asked, already knowing the answer.

Barbara only gave her a fixed look.

'Mammy has always thought he was on low pay,' Dolores said, shaking her head at the memory of Mammy putting the money back in Daddy's jacket.

'Well, I can tell you he isn't. Your Daddy is doing pretty well for himself.'

'Himself being the operative word,' Dolores had sighed.

She decided to talk to Michelle.

Dolores raised the subject one evening as she was scrubbing pots and Michelle was drying; Betty was in the dining room, resetting the tables for the next morning.

'Michelle,' she whispered, 'when do we get paid?'

'We don't,' said Michelle, looking straight ahead.

'What? Why?'

'Because this is a vocation, Dolores. It's not a job. And it's not like we need money. Everything is provided. The Directress is very generous to us. We don't pay rent, they give us clothes, they feed us—what else could we want for?'

'But it is a job. Jesus Christ, Michelle, it's nine o'-fucking-clock. And what are we doing? We're working. And we're not being paid. We have to write to the Directress to ask her to buy us a toothbrush or pads, for Christ's sake.'

Michelle's eyes widened at the very mention of sanitary pads.

'Our clothes are old uniforms and Nuala's and Róisín's hand-me-downs.'

Michelle turned and looked at her. 'Cursing doesn't improve your argument, Dolores,' she said. 'You sound very common.'

Dolores coloured and knew that this would not go unremarked.

—

The next morning, the Directress came into the kitchen. She had barely spoken to Dolores in weeks.

'Dolores, I am going to have to issue you with a fraternal correction,' the Directress said. 'You have been bad in spirit and in words.'

'But I have been so good in spirit, all I ever do is work,' Dolores protested.

'Well, my dear, that is your vocation. It is your vocation to be kind and gentle and hardworking and to give yourself over to the work and the spirit. To carry yourself like a lady, but to be child-like in your devotion. Do you know that the Father saw the Help as almost like children in their very holy innocence and simple piety? What a lucky thing for you, to have such an uncomplicated life. The Lord has blessed you with that. It is most certainly not part of that vocation to use the language of the sewer or to take Our Lord's name in vain. Think, if you can be so gracious, for one minute'—the Directress's eyes became sharp and her voice very low—'of the opportunities that have been afforded you. Of the sheer generosity. The time. My God *tonight*, Dolores, the selfishness is just appalling.'

Dolores looked at the floor. She felt like she would burn alive with the shame.

'You can be better than this, Dolores. And you know that you can. Now, here is what is going to happen. Tomorrow, Miss Nuala will drive you to another conference centre in Meath. We have had an unfortunate circumstance there—two of the supervisors, Miss Margaret and Miss Helen, have suddenly left.'

Dolores looked up. 'Why did they leave?'

The Directress sighed. 'Dolores, that is none of your business. But they have really created a problem for us. Poor Miss Nuala will have to divide her time between the two houses and I will be going back and forth, too. It's most inconvenient, but we do what we can in the service of Our Lord and we put Him before ourselves.'

Dolores looked at her shoes, which were coming away from the soles, and silently wondered about Miss Margaret and Miss Helen.

'You will spend some weeks working there to give you a sense of perspective and to renew your commitment to Our Lord and the Father and your vocation and what we call The Work. Miss Nuala and myself will attend periodically, and I hope that it will give you a sense of independence and pride in what you are doing here.'

'But what about Christmas? I don't want to be away from Mammy.'

'Your mammy is a sensible enough woman,' the Directress said. 'I'm sure she would agree that this is for the best.'

When the Directress had left, Dolores went up to her bedroom and put the spiky chain around her leg. She pulled the whip out of its large velvet pouch and did what Miss Nuala had told her to do. She went into the bathroom. She turned around and craned her neck to see her back in the small mirror above the handbasin. There were no large mirrors anywhere in the Helps' quarters because vanity was a mortal sin. And what would they be needing a full-length mirror for anyway? She whipped herself, flinching, until long red welts appeared on her back. Then she turned around to face the mirror and looked at herself properly for the first time since she had left Rome. Her eyes were blood-shot and there were big, puffy circles under them. She looked so much older and more tired than any sixteen-year-old should. Dolores Murphy burst into tears.

Dolores and Miss Nuala drove the roughly two-hour drive to Meath the following day. Dolores looked at the signs for Dublin wistfully, but they drove north and didn't go into town. While the Big House was a rambling Georgian manor set in lush grounds, the Meath house was newer. Though built in a mock-Georgian style, its grass was too even, its hedges too precisely clipped. It felt like one of those painted-on background scenes in an old film rather than a real house with real people.

'Right so,' said Miss Nuala, slamming shut the trunk on the Hunter after Dolores had taken out her case. 'This will be home for the time being.'

Miss Nuala had barely spoken to Dolores during the two-hour trip. When Dolores had tried to make conversation, Miss Nuala's answers had been mostly monosyllabic and terse. It lashed rain the whole way and Miss Nuala mumbled to herself. Dolores had seen her the previous day coming back over the little stone bridge from the meadow with the pretty redhead. The pretty redhead had been wearing a daisy-chain crown.

'Howarye, Miss Nuala?' Dolores had said, and Miss Nuala and the pretty redhead had given her a slightly pitying smile.

'Oh, grand, thanks all the same, Dolores,' Miss Nuala had said, and as she and the pretty redhead skipped away, Dolores could hear them giggling.

Skipped. They'd skipped. And they'd giggled. Even through her twinges of jealousy, Dolores Murphy had found herself thinking, not for the first time, that Miss Nuala's behaviour was decidedly odd for a woman in her thirties. Dolores was reminded of the girls who lived just south of Ringsend, where Irishtown bled into Sandymount and the houses had bay windows and gardens with fruit trees and beds filled with standard roses and poppies and dahlias. And elaborate door knockers. Those girls thought themselves better. They'd whisper in the schoolyard about Dolores and her friends, calling them knackers.

But they were just schoolgirls. Miss Nuala had a doctorate. Miss Nuala had a position of authority. Why was she making daisy crowns for girls half her age? Why did she rest her hand on their faces and their legs for just a little too long? Why did she ration her attentions and pick new favourites and make the old ones feel small?

And yet. And yet. She still craved and missed Miss Nuala's attention.

But Miss Nuala was not giving it.

Her posture seemed even more rigid than usual. Her smile, when she was forced to give it to Clodagh, the Help who greeted them at the door, seemed forced.

When they got to Dolores's quarters, Miss Nuala whispered that she trusted that Dolores was doing her corporal mortification.

Dolores nodded vigorously. 'I am, Miss Nuala.'

The supervisor pressed her lips together. 'It's now more important than ever, Dolores. Give yourself over to the Lord.'

Dolores hated herself for wanting it, but she wished Miss Nuala would place a cold hand on her cheek. She was so starved of affection and love, that this strange, inappropriate woman was the only person from whom she could hope to receive it.

Instead, Miss Nuala told Dolores that she had puffy eyes, and it wouldn't do for even the Help to let themselves go.

Even the Help.

'Brush your hair before you go downstairs, Dolores. And they have a vegetable garden here. Why don't you head down there when you have your break and harvest some cucumbers? Slice them up and put them on your eyelids before you go to sleep. They have a marvellous cooling quality. You won't know yourself. We must look presentable, even if it is only for Our Lord.' Miss Nuala gave Dolores a long, unblinking stare. 'Don't let the Directress down, Dolores,' she said. 'Be a pet.'

Dolores watched Miss Nuala's slim ankles walk away down the hall, heels clacking on the highly polished boards. When she had disappeared from view, Dolores crossed the icy room and lay face down on the single bed with its grey woollen blanket. The blanket was unpleasantly scratchy on her face, but she supposed that she could chalk it up as a corporal mortification and maybe skip on whipping herself as hard this week.

As she was lying there, Clodagh popped her head around the door. She had thick, glossy black hair, kind green eyes, olive skin and a wide mouth that seemed permanently on the verge of a smile.

'Ah, for God's sake. You look wrecked, Dolores, so you do,' she said.

Dolores recognised the accent. She sat up.

'Are you from Ringsend?' she asked eagerly.

Clodagh nodded. 'Down the Pigeon House Road,' she said. 'Do you know it?'

'Of course I bleedin' do! I'm from Bridge Street—near the church.'

'Go 'way with you!' said Clodagh, giving her a playful push. 'I can't believe we've never met. But I'd be a good few years older than you.'

Clodagh looked to be in her mid-twenties.

'I'm sure we have people in common,' Dolores said. 'I'm a Murphy.'

'Oh, for God's sake, I think I know your mammy.'

'I hope she didn't give out to you. She's always giving out.'

'Ah, she's not so bad. I'm an O'Reilly. But the youngest, Christina, is only five years younger than me, so would've been a good few years ahead of you at school. Listen, c'mere to me, Dolores, have you been crying?'

Dolores said nothing.

'Ah, Jaysus, these fuckers will do it to you. I fucking hate them, so I do. Pompous eejits.'

Dolores gasped. 'You can't say that—my God, if the Directress finds out . . . That's why I'm here. I've been punished for my foul mouth. Fraternal correction.'

'What they don't know won't hurt them, and I won't tell if you don't,' Clodagh said with a conspiratorial smile. But it wasn't the sort of conspiratorial smile she'd get from Miss Nuala, that sort that sent a chill down her spine and put her teeth on edge. Clodagh smiled with her eyes and she laughed heartily.

'Why are you here, then?' Dolores asked her.

Clodagh's smile dropped and she stared out the window for a time.

'Me Daddy ran off to Birmingham with some girl he met at a dance at Dun Laoghaire. They used to do it in the car park and he, well, you know, he got her pregnant. It was a right scandal at the time. He doesn't send much in the way of money, and he hardly ever comes back to see us. Me mammy doesn't cope. Sometimes she has to go into the hospital with her nerves. Auntie Mary had to take some of us when that happened, though Mary's got six of her own and really can't afford it. It was just easier if I wasn't in the picture. One less mouth to feed. And then I got stuck here in this shite hole.'

'I'm sorry,' said Dolores quietly.

'Don't be. Everyone has a reason for being here. I'm sure you have yours, too. Now listen, Dolores, them oul' sheets aren't going to wash themselves. Come on, let's get to it.'

Dolores Murphy realised it was the first time since she had left Ringsend that she had met a real person who could perhaps be a real friend.

They went down to the laundry and started on the seemingly endless pile of washing. After a while, Clodagh said, 'Open up that press there, will you?'

Dolores opened the two cupboard doors and inside it was a little table on wheels. On top of the table was an old record player.

'I found this in the hut at the back of the garden,' Clodagh said. 'And I assumed it would be broken, but it works perfectly, so it does. No one else knows I have it. We've had a few Help move to other centres, so I've been on my own down here for a while.'

Clodagh dragged a little three-legged stool to the cupboard, stepped on top of it and reached up to a high shelf. She pulled down an album and removed it from its sleeve. She lowered the needle onto the LP and the building wail of Brian Eno's synthesiser echoed through the scullery. 'Heroes'.

Dolores clutched the sheet she had been ironing to her chest. It felt warm and smelled of lavender. She began to cry again.

'How did you know, Clodagh?'

'I didn't. You've just got good taste, too,' said Clodagh, fashioning a floral sheet into a cape and spinning around the room. She pulled out the album cover and ran her hand over David Bowie's face. 'Isn't he dreamy?'

'This song is everything to me, Clodagh.'

'How could it not be?'

'Won't we get into trouble?'

'No one is here until tomorrow. We're footloose and fancy free until then, Dolores Murphy. Help, break free!'

'Jaysus, I could kiss you.'

'For feck's sake, please don't.'

'I won't,' Dolores assured her. 'It's just, I'm just so happy. I've been so sad and so fucking lonely. And how good it feels to say *fucking* and not worry I'm going to get a fraternal correction.'

The two girls twirled around the room, singing loudly.

'You know what else?' asked Clodagh as the song faded out.

'What?'

'I've got fags.'

'You have not?'

'I have that.'

They went out to the little stoop behind the laundry that led to the washing line and Clodagh pulled out a packet of menthols.

'Not Gauloises?' asked Dolores.

'Well, hello, Lady Muck. Aren't you dead fancy? No, not Gauloises. But you know, beggars can't be choosers, like.'

Dolores inhaled the stale mint smoke into her lungs, and it had been so long since she'd had a cigarette it made her head spin. She lay back on the stoop and gazed at the sky through the branches of a chestnut tree.

'It's good to meet you, Dolores Murphy,' said Clodagh. 'You're all right for a kid.'

'You're all right yourself, Clodagh O'Reilly.'

Dolores took another drag of the cigarette then said, 'Clodagh?'

'Mmm?'

'Does your mam send letters?'

'Oh, Dolores, do you not know? The Directress takes them all. She thinks families are a distraction from our vocation. And the odd time that she does let you have a letter, it's always been opened first.'

'I thought there was a problem with the mail.'

'God, no. They don't want us talking to our families is all. They want us here to be their fecking slaves.'

'Why do you stay?'

'Where would I go, Dolores? I have no money. I have no keys. I haven't caught a bus in years. I did try it, once, and the minute I got down the road I just stood there, not knowing where to go. I tried to hitch a ride for a while, but no one picked me up. And then the Directress got wind of it, and they came and collected me. And I'm standing like a right eejit in the rain with no coat and no money.'

'How did you get the Bowie LP?'

'Not long after I found the record player in the hut was one of the few times they actually allowed me to go back to Ringsend for Christmas. I had no money, but I begged my older brother Brendan to buy me some LPs and I brought them back here in the lining of my suitcase, along with a few packets of fags. I just missed the music so much. I've had to be really careful to make sure I only play them when there's no one around.'

'Do they make you do the corporal mortification?' Dolores asked in a tiny voice.

Clodagh laughed sourly. 'They don't *make* you do the corporal mortification,' she said in her poshest D4 accent. 'You *want* to do it, to offer your suffering up to Our Lord.'

She rolled her eyes and lifted up her pinafore to show permanent scars where the chain had been.

'Even when I don't wear it now, I'm in pain. I have to beg them for Disprin. I asked to go to the doctor once and they sent one of their doctors all the way from Merrion. I remember he had dandruff on his collar and a gold signet ring with a little black diamond in the centre. Your one kneels down and insists on rubbing my thighs. He was a right old lech. Then he stands up and tells me that I'm a hypochondriac, and did I know what a hypochondriac was? Patronising shite, he was. I said I did. And you know what, Dolores? I shut my mouth and put up with the pain and tried to ration out the Disprins, because the thought of seeing himself again made me fecking homicidal.'

Dolores shook her head as she looked at the whitish scars and purple bruises on Clodagh's leg.

'That said, he was nowhere near as bad as Miss Róisín.'

Dolores shot her a questioning look and Clodagh looked back at her meaningfully. And then she changed the subject.

'And do you know what? I've been needing new shoes for months now. See?'

Dolores looked down at Clodagh's brown lace-ups. The stitching between the upper leather and the sole was coming apart and they flapped when Clodagh walked.

Clodagh unlaced her right shoe and carefully eased it off, wincing as she did. Her sock was stained with blood, Dolores noted, and beneath it her foot was covered in a patchwork of nasty blisters and sores.

'They're killing me. But the Directress told me there's no money for new shoes. Mind, there's still money for the two dozen bottles of Pol Roger Winston Churchill that I was instructed to bring down to the dining room last week. Now, I don't know much about champagne, but I'm sure that's a fancy one.'

'Oh God, I'm so sorry, Clodagh,' Dolores said. 'Did you show her your feet?'

'Of course I did. She told me she was God's representative, and He was giving me spiritual direction, through her, that I was to suffer the pain of the sore feet and offer it up to Him.'

'That is seriously mental.'

'Of course it is. It all is. But they make you so tired and so isolated that you feel like it's normal. And it takes every single ounce of energy you have to realise that it's completely bonkers. But you know what? I'm hatching a plan, Dolores. I'm going to be free. Now, shall we get this shite finished?'

'I suppose we have to.'

They took a last drag on their cigarettes, then stubbed them out in a little jar Clodagh kept under the sink.

'Once we're done, let's get an early night, because we'll have to be up at the crack of dawn to get a start cooking the lunch for the people from the retreat who are arriving tomorrow,' said Clodagh. 'The Directress wants smoked salmon blinis and so I'm going to have to make hundreds of the little fuckers. Blini, piped Philadelphia, little curl of smoked salmon, chives. Blini, piped Philadelphia, little curl of smoked salmon, chives. Rinse and fucking repeat.'

'Sounds delightful,' said Dolores. 'But can we come out for a fag again sometime soon? Maybe we could rob a bottle of Winston Churchill.'

'Only if we want to be crucified! But listen, I'm going home for Christmas. The Directress has given me leave because me granny's terminal. She's only got weeks to live. You wouldn't believe the holy show it's been getting the approval to go.'

Dolores tried not to betray the fact that she was far more upset that Clodagh was leaving than she was sad for her granny.

'I'm going to be leaving Tuesday morning.'

'But that's only three days away! What am I going to do?'

'Survive, Dolores. That's what you're going to do. Survive.' Clodagh stood up and dusted off her hands on her apron. 'Now.'

15

THE MEATH HOUSE

WHEN CLODAGH O'REILLY was driven away in Miss Nuala's green Hunter, Dolores Murphy thought her heart would shut down. The past three days had been hard work, but the companionship of a person who had normal emotions and made her laugh had felt like medicine. The monotony of her existence meant that time had an imprecise quality. Three days could feel like three months. An hour could feel like a week.

Clodagh told her that she'd once had a boyfriend called Danny, and she'd called him the Champion of the World.

'What happened to Danny?' asked Dolores, who had never had a boyfriend and always wanted one. It sickened her slightly to contemplate that the closest thing she had experienced to the sort of electricity she'd read about in books she snuck home from the library was the strange, sad and, the more she thought on it, predatory attention of Miss Nuala.

'I heard he got married to some girl from East Wall when I left for the cookery school,' Clodagh said. 'I know he must have sent me letters, but of course I never got them. He probably thought I wasn't interested. And at that stage, I was so brainwashed by all their holier than Hosanna in the highest shite, that I really thought I had this stupid vocation, and I went along with it.'

'So, this isn't a vocation for you?' Dolores asked.

Clodagh laughed and shook her head. 'Not in the fucking slightest.'

'Do you miss him?'

'Of course. Look, was he "the one"? I don't really know. I never really had the time to properly find out. He was pure gas, though. He took me to see *Love Story*.'

'Oh, our Mary brought me to that when they played it again at the Carlton in O'Connell Street. Ali MacGraw was pure gorgeous. I was broken-hearted at the end.'

'She was. We held hands all the way through. I let him put his hand under my blouse.'

Dolores's eyes widened. 'How did that feel?'

'Like I'd just necked a pint of cider. Brilliant, of course. And he was a fucking *ride*, Dolores. He had the bluest eyes and the blackest hair. Champion of the World.'

Dolores smiled at the use of the term 'ride' to describe a handsome boy. It made her ache for home.

'But listen, Mammy was just keen that I come and get a qualification from the cookery school. She pushed me into it.'

'That sounds just like my mammy,' said Dolores.

Clodagh laughed sourly. 'I think they go in search of desperate mammies.'

'Really?'

'Well, I don't exactly know but, let's face it, there are enough desperate mammies in Ireland to keep the cookery school in business for a very long time.'

'True, that. There are enough desperate mammies in Ringsend, let alone Ireland. Ah, Clodagh. I'm going to miss you.'

'You're going to be fine,' Clodagh had said as Dolores stood in her bedroom doorway, watching her pack that morning. 'You just focus on the work now.'

'I'm so lonely, Clodagh.'

'I know you are, chicken. Don't be talking. I'll be back soon enough.'

But as Dolores waved the green Hunter goodbye, she wasn't convinced.

And her instinct was right. She waited and waited for her friend to return, but Clodagh O'Reilly never darkened the doorstep of the Meath house again.

—

A slow fortnight after Clodagh left, the Directress arrived unannounced to find Dolores swaying in the laundry to the sax solo in Bryan Ferry's 'Let's Stick Together', which was rotating on the little record player. Dolores was, she could not lie, being quite sexy with the Hoover. It was 9 pm and she was finishing her work for the day. She'd been up since five that morning, working alone. The Directress took one look at her, walked over to the power plug and yanked it from the wall. Then she wheeled the old record player out of the room.

The next morning, Dolores went downstairs to see the Directress dumping the record player and Clodagh's LPs onto the back of a lorry. One by one, she tossed each record onto the lorry tray like it was a discus: Bryan Ferry, Slade, T. Rex, the Velvet Underground, and there, flying through the air, was David Bowie. Wide-eyed, palm outstretched, seeming mock-horrified that this strange, old-fashioned lady didn't recognise his genius.

'No!' said Dolores, forcing it out at what felt like the top of her lungs, but it was really a whimper.

'This doesn't just call for a fraternal correction, Dolores. This . . . music, if that's what I can even call it, represents mortal sin after mortal sin after mortal sin. Illegal drugs. Intercourse out of wedlock. The taking of Our Lord's name in vain. *Sodomy.* Good God in heaven, girl.'

'It's just music,' said Dolores. 'And it belongs to Clodagh. It's not yours to take.' Dolores couldn't believe she was being this bold with the Directress.

'You needn't worry about Clodagh,' said the Directress, with an icy smile. 'Don't ever speak of her again.'

—

Years later, Dolores Murphy would discover that when Clodagh O'Reilly got back to Dublin, she had run away to South Australia with the Champion of the World. She'd gone back to school and on to teachers' college and she'd become a primary-school music teacher in the suburbs of Adelaide. The grannies at the bingo spoke in dark terms about how *that Clodagh O'Reilly* had taken Danny from his wife and children to Australia to live in sin. Clodagh's mammy was mortified that her own daughter had followed her father's example to live a life of infidelity. Dolores's mammy had offered up rosaries for Danny's wife and children and Poor Mrs O'Reilly. She muttered that *that Clodagh O'Reilly* was an 'awful woman'.

'What would you know, Mammy? You don't ever know what's really happened to a person until you walk in their shoes,' Dolores had snapped. 'I knew her once and she was good to me.'

Mammy had just clucked her tongue.

Dolores Murphy had ached for her friend of three days for years.

—

Clodagh's departure induced in Dolores a deadening anxiety. She would wake up in the morning and, as she knelt on her callused knees in the chapel, her stomach would churn and her head would feel light. She was filled with a kind of dread that she couldn't explain. She dreamed of snakes. She had started standing at her windowpane and contemplating throwing herself to the ground below. But was it high enough? Would she just break her back and then have to live as a cripple with these awful people? Would they send her back to Ringsend? What sort of life would she have there?

She remembered reading aloud as she sat out the back of Mammy's kitchen, smoking one of her Gauloises while Mammy was in town, laughing to herself and thinking herself a frightfully sophisticated fourteen-year-old. She didn't feel sophisticated now. She just felt cold. And lonely. And alone. The initial plan to keep her here for a few weeks as a fraternal correction seemed to have been abandoned. She once asked Miss Nuala on one of her visits when she would be going back to the Big House.

'Hush now, Dolores,' Miss Nuala had said, and placed her finger on Dolores's mouth before turning on her heel.

Betty was sent from the Big House to be head cook. Dolores was responsible for the cleaning. Betty barely spoke to her except to bark instructions. The Directress had cut back on the number of visitors on account of the staffing shortage, but they were still brutally overworked. Betty looked tired and old and angry all the time. Whenever Dolores asked if anyone else would be coming to help them, Betty lost it at her altogether and told her she should pray to Our Lord instead of complaining.

She wondered about the people who came here. Women with tinkling laughs and lacquered blow-waves and outfits from

Switzers. Men with horn-rimmed glasses who looked important and smoked pipes. People who never made eye contact with her, who never thanked her when she placed their soup in front of them or fetched them a spoon when theirs fell on the floor, but who were there to discuss Holy God. She sometimes wondered what exactly they were doing, what was the whole point of it all. No one told her much. She was just the Help. But mostly, she was just so bone-tired that she didn't have time to think at all.

'Blessed are the meek, because they shall inherit the earth,' the Directress would sometimes say to her. But Dolores didn't feel blessed. She felt invisible.

—

A few weeks after the Directress threw Clodagh's record player on the lorry, Dolores went out one Monday morning to collect a box of vegetables that was being delivered to the back entrance of the Meath house. She always looked forward to this weekly task as Mr Mackie, the grocer who brought them in his van, was an amiable man, and her only regular contact with a person who didn't treat her with disdain.

'Top of the morning, Dolores!' he would sing out as he swung open the van doors. Mr Mackie was a fan of Tom Jones and would belt out 'It's Not Unusual' as he rolled up the driveway.

'Da, da-da, Da, da-da, da-dah daaaahhh,' he'd sing, clicking his fingers and giving her a wink. 'Do they never give you a holiday?'

'I'll get a holiday soon enough, Mr Mackie,' she'd lie.

But this morning, when the van rolled up, it wasn't Mr Mackie who got out.

Her first glimpse of him was his smile. The whitest teeth she had ever seen, gleaming against his dark skin. At a time when many men had unwieldy sideburns, shaggy beards, his tight curls were clipped neat and short, and his gleaming skin was clean-shaven.

'Hello there,' he said in a voice like a French horn, looking at her very steadily with his large brown eyes. She guessed he was about nineteen or twenty. 'I'm Marcus Akenyemi.'

'Hello, Marcus Akenyemi,' she said. 'I'm Dolores Murphy.'

'Dolores,' he said thoughtfully. 'Did you know that your name means "sorrow"?'

She nodded. 'Yes,' she said. 'I did.'

'I'm sure you are too young to have experienced much of that, though.'

Dolores felt a sudden and mortifying urge to cry. 'No, not too young at all,' she said.

It hurt to look at him, he was so beautiful. Every time she glanced back up at him, it was like staring at the sun, and she had to look away. She knew her face must be scarlet. She smoothed her hands over her shabby pinafore and looked down at her scuffed shoes. She looked a state.

'Where's Mr Mackie?' she asked.

'He's taken ill, I'm afraid. He has a weak heart. I've been working for him back at the shop for a while and he's got me looking after things for now.'

She noted a slight Dublin twang in his accent, which was otherwise very proper and hard to place. She nodded and looked at the ground. 'Poor Mr Mackie. He's a good man. How did you end up in Meath?'

He laughed. 'You mean where do I come from?'

She blushed at how provincial she must have sounded, asking the question that everyone asked, no doubt.

'I'm from Lagos. Well, originally. But I am studying at Trinity. My parents saw that I was running with the wrong crowd back home in Nigeria and packed me off here. I've taken a semester off to travel around Ireland and do odd jobs to pay my way. That's how I met Mr Mackie.'

'Your parents paid for you to go to college in Dublin when you live in Nigeria?' she asked. 'They must be much, much fancier than my parents.'

He shrugged. 'Now,' he said, straining slightly with the large box of vegetables he'd been holding as they chatted, 'where do we put these?'

'Oh, sorry, sorry, sorry,' Dolores said. She was so dazzled by Marcus that she could barely focus on what they were supposed to be doing. It felt as if every single one of her pores was somehow singing at once.

As they were unloading the boxes filled with turnips, potatoes and cabbages from the van, his hand momentarily brushed hers and Dolores Murphy jumped back like she had been given an electric shock.

When they were done, he smiled broadly. 'It was a pleasure to meet you, Dolores Murphy,' he said, taking a perfectly pressed checked handkerchief out of his pocket and wiping his brow. He shook her hand and smiled broadly again as he went to leave.

'It was a pleasure to meet you, too, Marcus Akenyemi,' she said.

As he turned to walk back to the van, she whispered, 'Don't go.'

'Pardon?' he said, turning around. 'Did you say something?'

'No, never mind,' she said quickly.

He chuckled and, with a last wave, got into the van and drove off, leaving Dolores Murphy staring down at the palm of the hand he'd just touched.

Dolores's weeks were short and long. Short in the sense that she worked so hard that the days bled into one another. Long in the sense that the hands of the clock ticked over slowly as she waited for the little things that made her life less intolerable—Guinness pie on Friday night, and the infrequent visits from Miss Nuala. She would drive Dolores into town to buy her the necessities she had run out of like sanitary pads or shampoo that she'd written down in the leatherbound notebook, which was kept in the hall. Not for Miss Nuala's company, mind, but for the brief change in scenery.

On those odd occasions, Miss Nuala had little to say to her beyond a set of instructions. Dolores seemed surplus to needs or wants as far as Miss Nuala was now concerned, and her only points of conversation were to remind her to polish her shoes or file her nails, or to tell her she'd heard that there were smudges on the cutlery or the dinner service or that the tea for the breakfast had been lukewarm and that 'Really, Dolores, you could do better'. And occasionally, she'd whisper that she hoped, please God, Dolores was still doing her corporal mortifications.

And in her mind, Dolores would answer, 'Yes, I am still whipping myself. I don't know why and, yes, I am a fucking eejit for doing it. Yes, I am still wearing a horrible spiky chain around my thigh as I work for no pay for the shower of snobbish hypocrites who come here for a spiritual retreat. Yes, I'm still not allowed to speak to these people nor even look them in the eye. Yes, I'm pretty sure that the smarmy TD who comes with his secretary is having it on with her while his wife is at home in Ballsbridge with thirteen children, thinking that he's here getting closer to Holy God. Yes, I'm watching him. I don't look him in the eye, but I see him, and I hear the way he speaks to the secretary. Yes, I have caught the eyes of the secretary and, yes, she knows that I know, and she blushed and looked away. Yes, I'm fairly certain that all the other judges and accountants and Directresses and whatnot who come here know all about it, too, and yet still bang on about mortal sin and Christian values and how glad they are that he's spread God's message in the Dáil. Yes, I'm lonely. Yes, I wish I had listened to that Help in the kitchen in Rome. Yes, I wish I'd called my daddy like Mairéad did, to come and collect me, and I wish that my daddy would ever bother to do such a thing, or to ever remember my birthday, or to even glance up at me when I walked in the door back in Ringsend. Yes, I feel sick and confused and chilled to my fecking bones that I ever let you put your cold hands on me or listened to a single word that you said. And yes, I hate this place and, yes, more and more, I hate you, Miss Nuala.'

Dolores Murphy would sit in the Hunter and stare straight out at the countryside and craft ever more scathing retorts to Miss Nuala. Her mind would whir with fury, but her mouth would remain closed. And she'd remind herself, over and over, that there was nothing for it, and that she was trapped.

She did have a conversation, once, where Miss Nuala told her that should her parents ever try to come and collect her to bring her home, that it was, by them, a mortal sin to take her away from her Holy Vocation. And that she was to scream loudly and tell them not to take her. And her Family here, her real family now, would keep her here, in this safe and Holy place, where she belonged.

Dolores was by now, long past believing any of this. She bristled every time she heard the word 'Holy' or 'Family', always emphasised in that capitalised way that Miss Nuala and the Directress had. But she was long past thinking she had any choice but to silently acquiesce. She only hoped that at some point she would be allowed to go home. If she did, she would hatch a plan to stay in Dublin and she would never see these hideous people again.

—

Another of those short-long weeks had passed and it was, miraculously, Monday morning again. Dolores had put cucumbers on her eyes the night before as Miss Nuala had recommended she do, and she brushed her hair, sweeping it to one side in a pretty turquoise clasp Miss Nuala had dropped in the kitchen. She used some beetroot juice from a can to subtly stain her cheeks and her lips, hoping she wouldn't smell like root vegetable or vinegar, and rubbed a rose from the back garden on her wrists and neck just in case. Then she daubed some Vaseline on her lips.

She looked at herself in the mirror and, if she did say so herself, she looked something approaching pretty. She was still wearing the hideous pinafore they made her wear every day, but she chose the smaller one that hugged her hips and her bust.

She was embarrassed to think of Marcus seeing her looking like an old-fashioned servant, but her feelings of shame were eclipsed by feelings of . . . what? Dolores Murphy had to admit it was desire.

She stood at the back of the kitchen and watched Mr Mackie's rust-coloured van roll up the long road that led to the Meath house and follow the driveway around to the back entrance that was reserved for Help and deliveries.

'Hello, Dolores Murphy,' Marcus said as he swung out of the driver's cab.

'Hello, Marcus Akenyemi,' she said, and she knew now that perhaps the beetroot stain was a step too far, as her blush had done the work for her.

'You look somehow different,' he said, and smiled.

'I look like a right gobshite in this pinafore,' she said, rolling her eyes.

'Well, a very pretty gobshite, if you don't mind me being a little bold, Dolores.'

She thought she would die on the spot.

'Have you seen *Annie Hall*? They're replaying it in town. I never saw it when it came out and I was wondering, well, if you might join me.'

She looked around to make sure no one was in earshot.

'I haven't seen *anything*, Marcus,' she whispered. 'I'm not *allowed* to see anything. I'm not allowed books, I'm not allowed to see films and I'm not allowed to leave.'

He gaped at her. 'What do you mean, you're not allowed to leave?'

'Even if I wanted to go I don't have any money for a bus or a train, because they don't pay me. I don't have a purse. I don't have a key to this house.' She walked into the kitchen and grabbed the leatherbound notebook. 'See this book? This is where I'm to write down things I might need—like you know, shampoo or soap, and, when they're feeling charitable, they collect them for me—but only the cheapest ones, mind. On the odd occasion, they run me into town to get a few messages. And when they do, one of them accompanies me at all times, in case I leg it or something. But how could I leg it, Marcus? Where could I leg it to? I have no money and wouldn't even know where to start.'

'Pardon my language, Dolores, but Jesus Christ.'

'I know,' she said. She couldn't stop talking now, it was all pouring out of her. 'See this entrance we're standing in? This is the only one I'm allowed to come in and out of. I'm not allowed in through the front door, Marcus. I'm not worthy of the front door. I'm not allowed to give eye contact to any of the men I serve. I'm to be seen and not heard. They feed me leftovers and they clothe me in hand-me-downs from these two posh D4 girls, well, women, actually, who sucked me into this strange world. I'm to call these two "Miss" and I don't even know the name of the woman who is responsible for me. I'm just to call her the bleeding Directress.'

'The Directress? That's quaint,' said Marcus. 'But seriously, Dolores, this is terrible.'

'I *know.* But I have no way of getting out. They stole all of my mammy's letters and then I thought she just stopped writing. They listen in to my phone calls. I have no friends and no one to talk to. I rise before dawn and work till late.'

Marcus was shaking his head. 'Dolores, what you are describing sounds like slavery.'

'It is that,' Dolores agreed. 'I'm hungry all the time. And I'm tired, Marcus, so tired, but if I complain the Directress tells me any suffering of mine is nothing compared to Our Lord's suffering on the Holy Cross.'

'Good grief, Dolores. I'm so sorry.'

She looked around again. 'If they saw me talking to you, the Directress would be raging. I'd have fraternal corrections from here to kingdom come.' She shivered.

'Fraternal corrections? Who are these people?'

Tears stung her eyes. 'They're the worst people in the world, Marcus.'

Even as she said it, she heard a door bang somewhere behind her.

'Here,' she said. 'Let's have those boxes. I can't be seen talking to you.'

'So, am I to take it that it's a no to *Annie Hall*?' he said as he helped her set the boxes of vegetables onto the kitchen table.

'You're gas, Marcus Akenyemi,' she said. 'Of course it's a no. It's a "no" to everything, here.'

'Is there something I can do to help, Dolores?' he asked, looking her in the eye. He put his hand on her shoulder, and she felt waves of warmth wash through her.

'I don't know,' she said. 'I am going to be on my own on Thursday for a night.'

'Great,' he said, smiling. 'I'll collect you at half five.'

'That would be deadly,' she said. 'But I'm really serious, no one can know this is happening. No one.'

'I'm a vault, Dolores.' He gave her hand a little squeeze and smiled.

16

TARA

THE BIGGEST CONCERN for Dolores Murphy between now and Thursday was the fact that she had absolutely nothing to wear. But not in the sense that most girls thought they had nothing to wear. Dolores just didn't have any clothes that were even remotely presentable. Her clothes weren't just hand-me-downs from Miss Nuala and Miss Róisín; they were the jumpers that had pilled, blouses missing a button, skirts that had faded in the wash. There was the dress the Directress had given her in Rome, but Dolores wouldn't be caught dead going out with a boy in that. She would look a right sight. And Meath was chilly at this time of year.

She walked down the hall to the room that Miss Nuala occupied on her rare visits. Hanging up in the press was a selection of outfits that Miss Nuala would lose her mind about if she thought Dolores was wearing them. She pulled out a fitted angora sweater that still had a faint waft of perfume and a kilt-like skirt that finished mid-calf. In the small chest of drawers, she found a pair of tights. Miss Nuala's feet were about half a size smaller than Dolores's, but needs must. She pulled out a pair of oxblood Mary Jane brogues and crammed her feet into them, pleased that she had always had well-turned ankles, and thinking she must remember to apply plasters to her toes and heels before she went out.

She ran down to her bedroom and tried on the rest of the outfit. She looked quite lovely; perhaps not in the way she would have liked to look—not, for instance, like a sophisticated Bowie fan—but certainly better than she could ever manage in the old clothes they gave her.

She fixed the turquoise clasp in her hair. And she sat on the side of the bed and prayed that Miss Nuala would not turn up between now and Thursday and realise her clothes were missing.

The next few days, she rose at 4 am and worked till 11 pm, determined to get all of her chores done so that she could afford to lose a few hours on Thursday night.

On Thursday afternoon, she watched the Directress see off the last of the visitors to the retreat and then usher Betty into her own Morris Minor and trundle away down the road.

She did the dishes as quickly as humanly possible and cleaned the tables and polished the cutlery and wiped the burners on the cooker till they shone. She made sure nothing looked even remotely amiss, and when she was done, she stood and looked at her work and felt pride. Not because she gave a shite about this job or these people, but because she had got it all done so quickly and so well, and now she could pretend, at least for a few hours, that neither this place nor those people existed, and that she was free. That she was someone who wore oxblood Mary Janes and angora jumpers as a matter of course.

She found some old mascara in Miss Nuala's dresser. It was a bit dry, but it still did the trick. She lined her eyes with a small stub of kohl and found a half-empty pan of blue shimmery eye-shadow and applied it with her finger. She unbuttoned the angora jumper. She looked down at her bra, which was beige and mortifyingly unsexy. But still.

She ran downstairs and found some sherry in the liquor cabinet in the dining room and took a couple of swigs. She saw headlights shining through the kitchen window and felt a rush of warm blood to her head. She didn't need beetroot stain on her cheeks this time. They were flushed all on their own.

'Dolores Murphy,' he said, when she opened the door to greet him.

'Marcus Akenyemi,' she replied.

As he helped her into the cab of Mr Mackie's van, he said, 'I wiped it down—I didn't want to ruin your clothes.'

'That's awful good of you,' she said, staring at the road because how could she possibly look at him?

As they pulled up in the car park at the back of the cinema and Dolores saw the small crowd milling around, she gasped and slid down in her seat.

'What's wrong?' Marcus asked.

'All those people,' she said. 'I hadn't thought . . .' She felt a tremor of fear. 'What if someone recognises me? What if they tell the Directress?'

'I'm sure no one will notice you,' Marcus reassured her.

She looked at him. 'They might not at first, but they'll notice you,' she said. 'And if someone who knows the Directress then notices me'—she swallowed—'there'll be murder.'

'What do you want to do?' Marcus asked, looking at her.

'Well, I don't want to go back to that oul' place,' she whispered, and looked out the window.

'I suppose you've been to the Hill of Tara?'

She had to admit that she had not. The Hill of Tara was not far from the Meath house and she had heard visitors talk about it. But she hadn't been anywhere.

'There won't be anyone there now,' he said. 'It's quite magical.'

'Should I be trusting you, Marcus?'

'Well, I think you should.'

She looked at him and nodded, wondering if she was taking leave of her senses.

So, they drove to the Hill of Tara.

'Come on,' he said, and she got out of the van and followed him up a narrow path through an ancient graveyard with lichen-covered Celtic cross headstones, so old they were no longer standing up straight.

'Jesus, this is a bit creepy, Marcus.'

'Sorry, I didn't mean to frighten you. The hill itself is this way.'

They walked around the back of the churchyard, past the statue of St Patrick who, according to legend, had come to this place to meet the pagan kings and announce the arrival of Christianity in Ireland, and there was the hill, just as Marcus had promised. The undulating grass slopes shone in the last rays of sun.

He took her hand, and together they climbed up to the top.

'Did you know that the people of ancient Ireland thought this was an entrance to the otherworld?' he said. 'This was the seat of the kings.'

She admitted she didn't know. She knew almost nothing about the Hill of Tara and very little about any Irish history for that matter. She was ashamed to tell him how basic her convent schooling had been.

'This is the Mound of the Hostages,' he whispered, showing her an entrance to an ancient tomb. 'There are the cremated bones of hundreds of people beneath us.'

'You take a girl to all the nice places,' she joked. 'But seriously, it does feel magical.'

They sat on the grass and looked up at the stars.

'Listen,' she said, 'did you ever play Nick Drake's "Northern Sky"?'

He nodded.

'I love that song.'

He smiled and took her hand. 'Aren't you the romantic?' he said. 'When I'm bored,' he continued, 'I like to come here and roll down these hills. Did you like rolling down grassy hills as a child?'

'My God, I loved it,' she said. 'But I'm not exactly dressed for the occasion.'

'Here,' he said, and took off his coat. 'Put this on so you don't spoil your clothes.'

She pulled off Miss Nuala's Mary Janes, glad to have them off her feet, and took off the tights.

'This is very bold, Marcus,' she said, but he just smiled.

They lay down on the grass and rolled down the hill. Dolores laughed the whole way, until they fell on top of each other at the bottom. She lay in his arms, giggling, and realised that she could not remember laughing this much for the entire time that she had been away from Ringsend. She could barely remember laughing at all, apart from those brief days she had spent with Clodagh. And the thought of that made her cry. She put her head on his chest and sobbed a little.

He put his arms around her. 'Dolores, I didn't mean to make you cry.'

'You didn't. You didn't make me cry at all,' she said, but she couldn't stop.

He pushed her hair out of her eyes and with his thumb wiped away the two little blue-black rivers streaming down her cheeks from the shimmery eyeshadow and eyeliner. And then he kissed her mouth.

She kissed him back. It was the most wonderful thing that had ever happened in her life.

'Dolores, have you ever . . .?'

Her face burned. 'Of course I haven't.'

'I'm so sorry,' he said. 'That was thoughtless of me. I shouldn't have asked.'

'But I want to,' she whispered.

'You do? Are you sure?'

'Definitely,' she said.

'*Definitely* definitely?'

'*Definitely* definitely.'

And so, they did. And it hurt a bit, of course it did. As it always does, the first time. But Dolores Murphy was used to pain. This wasn't that sort of pain. While it was happening, she blotted out the other sort of pain. And Marcus was the kindest, most beautiful human she had ever met in all her sixteen years. In a moment of bravery, she told him as much.

He kissed her and told her everything was going to be all right. And for some reason, she believed him.

Afterwards, they lay in the moonlight.

'Dolores, what's this?' he asked, tracing his finger over a little purple patchwork of bruises and pinprick scabs on her thigh.

She swallowed and lifted up the angora jumper and rolled over to show him the red welts on her back.

'Jesus Christ, who did this to you?'

She turned to face him again. 'I did it to myself,' she whispered and put her hands over her eyes.

'What? Why?!' He tried to prise her hands from her eyes. 'Dolores!'

So she told him about self-mortification. She told him about creepy Miss Nuala. Her odd and predatory and affectionless attentions. It all started spilling out of her before she could even think about the fact that she might be oversharing. About how she was so love-starved that she even craved seeing Miss Nuala. She told him about the teenage martyr Saint Maria Goretti and how they glorified her. She told him everything. How lonely she had been. How she hated them. If Clodagh O'Reilly had been her gateway drug to rejecting it all, Marcus Akenyemi was her heroin. She assumed, as the words fell out of her, that he would think her a complete lunatic. Perverted and demented and sad. That he would never want to see her again. But it was worth it somehow, to unburden herself, to share the weight of her unhappiness.

He listened in silence, stroking her forehead.

'Dolores,' he said when she had finished, 'this cannot continue. This is abuse. Exploitation. We need to get you away from this place as soon as possible.'

'But how?' she whispered.

Marcus thought for a moment then said, 'I'm going to get you out of here.'

'You've only known me, like, five minutes, Marcus.'

'I know, but I can't see a person be treated like this. I need to get you away. We can work out what to do when you're safe.'

And because she had no other choice, she trusted him.

He drove her back to the Meath house and walked her to the door. He put his arms around her waist. She put her head on his shoulder and kissed it.

'I know that was probably proper weird for you, but it was magic for me,' she said, looking up at him.

He pushed her hair out of her eyes and bent to kiss the tip of her nose. 'I'll be back for you, Dolores. I'll let you know the plan when I come with next week's delivery.'

'Do you promise?'

'I promise.'

Dolores closed the door behind her and put her arms around her waist the way he had. She could still smell him in her hair. She put her hair over her face and breathed deeply. She reminded herself to get Miss Nuala's clothes handwashed and dried first thing in the morning.

Marcus Akenyemi got back into Mr Mackie's van to drive home to the little cottage he was staying in behind the Mackie property. He liked that girl an awful lot. She was quirky and determined and not like any of the girls he had known. Intuitively smarter than a lot of them at college. He was worried about her, and worried about how they were going to get her out of that miserable place, but he didn't want to think on that right now. He was still in the afterglow, and all he wanted to think about was how it felt to have that funny girl in his arms. The night sky was blanketed with stars. And was that a shooting star? Or was it a satellite? He started singing Lou Reed's 'Satellite of Love', accelerating around the bends in the narrow country road. *Sat-ell-ite of . . . Love.*

He was still singing as he crested a hill and saw the flash of two eyes and a tangle of antlers as a deer leaped out from behind a hedgerow and straight in front of him. As Marcus swerved to avoid it, the van skidded and flipped right over. And then everything was black. And silent. The deer skipped off, unharmed.

—

On delivery day the following week, Dolores Murphy heard the crunching of tyres on stones around the circular driveway. She felt as if she would burst with excitement. But instead of a rust-coloured van, this one was white. And instead of Marcus Akenyemi getting out of the cab, it was Mr Mackie himself, looking pale and puffing a little with the effort of walking.

'Mr Mackie! Howarye?' Dolores asked, trying to hide her disappointment. 'Let me help you get the things out of the van.'

'Thank you, Dolores. You're a good girl, all the same.' Mr Mackie didn't look his usual cheery self at all.

'Go on with you. But listen, you shouldn't be doing this work with your heart. Where's Mr Akenyemi?'

Mr Mackie's face was ashen. 'Oh, Dolores, did you not hear?'

'Hear what?'

'There was a terrible accident last week. He borrowed my van to go out one night and something happened on the way home, and wasn't he run off the road?'

The world went still around her as she looked at him. 'And what?' she whispered.

'Ah, Dolores. We lost him. He was gone long before the ambulance arrived. He was an awful good boy, Dolores. Never a moment of trouble. His daddy's flying out from Lagos to collect his body this week, please God. I feel terrible for that poor family, losing that young man, so I do . . .'

Mr Mackie kept speaking, but Dolores couldn't hear him over the ringing in her ears. She dropped the box of vegetables and ran inside the house and up to the toilet. And she was sick, over and over again.

Dolores Murphy started being sick every day. She refused to leave her room; she stopped speaking and she barely ate. When she did eat, the feelings of nausea overwhelmed her, and she was sick again. Her entire body ached with grief. She didn't cry, though. It seemed somehow too big for tears. Every time she heard the crunch of tyres rolling over the stones on the driveway, she dragged herself to the window and looked down, half-expecting him to be there with his boxes of vegetables and his enormous smile. But then she would see it was just a Mercedes carrying that smarmy TD and his secretary, or Father Domenico in his soutane, or the Directress, or Mr Mackie. Because Marcus Akenyemi was never coming back. Marcus Akenyemi was in a grave in Lagos, covered with wilted marigolds and his mother's tears.

They had to fetch another one of the Help from the Big House to cover her duties. The Directress came to her door several times, with a pained expression on her face.

'Good Lord, Dolores, whatever is the matter?' she asked.

But Dolores refused to speak and eventually the Directress shut the door, clucking her tongue.

Miss Nuala was sent to try to coax her out of the room. She came and put a freezing hand on Dolores's brow.

'Dolores, darling, please—you need to tell us what's wrong,' she said.

Dolores pulled up the covers and turned to face the window.

'I'll say a rosary for you,' Miss Nuala said, and tiptoed out. Dolores heard her whispering in the corridor with the Directress.

The Help from the Big House would bring her meals, but she'd look at the mince and potatoes or boiled cabbage and bacon and run into the toilet to be sick again. The only food she managed to keep down was lightly buttered toast.

After some weeks with no change, a doctor was dispatched. As he opened her bedroom door, she recognised the gold signet ring with the black diamond, but she was too sick to care if he was the same one who had molested Clodagh.

He took her vital signs and then listened to her chest.

'Dolores, I think we're going to have to get a urine sample and take a blood test,' the doctor said.

She just nodded.

He took some blood, and then she went into the toilet with the little canister and peed into it.

'Let's see what this comes back with. In the meantime, you need to keep up your fluids and you really do need to see if you can keep some food down,' he said.

She looked at him blankly.

'Is there something you want to talk about, Dolores?'

She shook her head. Not with him.

He put his stethoscope back in his bag and clasped it shut. He left the room. The Directress was waiting outside.

'Well, Dr Lonergan, what do you think?'

The doctor gave her a meaningful look. 'Let's see,' he said, and left.

—

The next morning, Dolores woke from another fitful sleep to hear the Directress shrieking in the hall.

'My God in Heaven, that *wicked* girl.'

The Directress burst into the room as Dolores was leaning into a bucket she had next to the bed, trying to vomit.

'Dolores Murphy, get out of that bed. Kneel next to it and offer up your sins to Our Lord.'

Dolores gave her a quizzical look.

'Don't look at me like that, you sinful little wretch. After all we have done for you, and this is the way you repay us. Merciful God in Heaven.'

The Directress stood there, her arms folded across her pigeon chest, glaring. Dolores realised the Directress was staring at her belly. She looked down and noticed that, despite the fact she'd barely eaten for many weeks, her tummy was protruding ever so slightly in a way it never had before.

'Yes, that's right, you disgusting girl,' the Directress thundered. 'I don't know who, what or why, and frankly, Dolores, I do not want to know. I'm disgusted with you. You are soiled. You have lost your vocation. Your soul is forever stained, and you will *never* make it up to Our Lord. Your purity is gone. You can never get that back, Dolores.'

Miss Nuala came and stood in the door.

'I just cannot believe that you would be so unbelievably ungrateful, Dolores,' she whispered.

'Grateful for what?' retorted the voice in Dolores's head. But her chapped lips said nothing.

They stared at Dolores's belly in the most horrible, intrusive way, like she was some sort of exotic python at the zoo, and they couldn't peel their eyes away from it. Neither of them said what was so disgusting and sinful, but from the way they stared at her belly Dolores could guess. She started to sob.

She remembered a lecture they had once given the girls at the cookery school about how your purity was like Sellotape. Miss Róisín had cut a piece of the tape with the scissors and fashioned it into a little curl. They had made them pass the curl around the circle until it got to the last girl. The Directress then asked the girl to show it to them all. 'Is it sticky anymore?' she had asked, and the girl shook her head. 'Think of yourself as this Sellotape if you sleep around,' she said, triumphantly. 'You're just as worthless.' Miss Róisín had taken the little roll of Sellotape and dramatically thrown it in the bin.

It was clear to Dolores that in their eyes, she was now that Sellotape.

'That's right: cry, Dolores,' said the Directress. 'Weep for your mortal sins. Ask Our Lady for forgiveness, because I can tell you now, *I* will never forgive you.' The Directress marched out the door.

Miss Nuala shook her head. 'I'm very disappointed in you, Dolores,' she said, and she too left.

Dolores ran into the toilet to be sick again. After she had finished, she wiped her mouth, lowered the seat and sat down. She looked down at her little protruding belly and put her hand on it. Inside her was a little piece of Marcus Akenyemi, the best human she had ever known. A tiny little person was forming. And as heartbroken as she was to know that she would never see Marcus again, the idea that his child was growing inside her was the first thing in weeks that made her feel calm.

The next day, the vomiting stopped.

17

WITH CHILD

DOLORES MURPHY WAS now to be completely invisible to any visitor to the Meath house. They set up an ironing station in the bedroom next to hers so that she could undertake some light duties without being seen by the guests. She was given cutlery to polish, napkins to fold and shoes to shine. The Father, Miss Nuala had often reminded her, had seen the Help as being almost child-like in their purity and devotion to their celibate vocation. The idea that the Help could be with child was anathema to everything they stood for, so it was vital that no one ever saw her in her maternity pinafore.

Dolores expected that at some point she would be shipped off to a home for unmarried mothers but, for now, the Directress seemed to have other plans.

The calluses on her knees began to fade and the circles under her eyes disappeared. Her hair became thicker and glossier and her skin glowed.

She noticed that the previously frosty attitude of Miss Nuala had changed. As she had moved into her second trimester and the vomiting ceased, she began to feel ravenously hungry. The thing she craved more than anything else was rice pudding. Miss Nuala arranged for it to be brought to her regularly. She even brought chocolates one day.

'I'm going to mind you, Dolores,' Miss Nuala said, placing her cold hand on Dolores's warm belly in a way that was typically proprietary. 'We have to make sure baby is strong.'

Dolores began to wonder why she hadn't thought to get pregnant before.

'Sometimes, Dolores, when life gives us lemons, we must make lemonade,' Miss Nuala would chirp. 'And you know, I often have to remind myself that Our Lord always knows best.'

If Dolores Murphy had paused to think of it, this appeared to herald a complete change in Miss Nuala's rather dogmatic life philosophy, but Dolores was tired, and pregnant, and sixteen. She shuddered to think how Mammy would receive the news that she was expecting a black baby out of wedlock. She was still in a state of deep denial about how and where she was going to raise said baby.

She had not, of course, revealed the identity of the baby's father and, when she paused to think of it, she found it rather tellingly strange that none of them asked. Had other Help got pregnant in the past? Who were the fathers? The hypocritical TD, perhaps? The doctor with the black diamond in his gold signet ring? An errant brother or priest?

One night, Miss Nuala came up to see her after dinner. She seemed to have had one too many sherries, as the apples of her cheeks were ruddy and she stumbled slightly as she entered the room.

'What was it like, Dolores?' she asked, perching on the end of Dolores's bed.

'What was what like?' Dolores replied.

'You know. *It*. I assume it was your first time. Did it hurt?'

'Oh, well, a little, yes. But everything else was magical.'

'I must say, it never seemed magical to me,' Miss Nuala said. She stroked Dolores's brow. 'I never much liked men.'

'I got that impression,' said Dolores flatly.

'Did you?' Miss Nuala giggled. 'Dolores, how you're growing.'

Dolores looked down at her little bump, but realised as she caught Miss Nuala's eye that Miss Nuala hadn't been looking at that.

'I don't like you looking at me like that, Miss Nuala,' she said. 'And I don't like you touching me. And I don't want you to ever do it again.' Dolores had no idea where the courage to speak like this had come from.

Miss Nuala's eyes widened. And then they narrowed. She pressed her lips together. 'I don't know what you mean, Dolores,' she said, flicking her hair, straightening her kilt and standing up. 'I have heard that girls can become irrational when with child.'

Dolores expected that that would be the end of Miss Nuala's visits, but it wasn't. She continued to bring rice pudding, and she insisted on delivering hot milk to help Dolores sleep at night. She told Dolores that the Directress had ordered her to stay at the Meath house for the duration of Dolores's confinement. Sometimes she'd come and read her passages from the Gospels. Dolores found it, and her, stultifyingly boring, but it was better than working sixteen-hour days. Miss Nuala never touched Dolores again.

—

While the vomiting had ended, Dolores had pains in her pelvis and back as the baby got bigger. Like all the women in her family, she had narrow hips, and when Dr Lonergan came to see her again, he remarked on that, saying that she could be 'in for a time' as the baby appeared to be big. She didn't really know what that meant. She looked at herself in the mirror and saw that, while she had put on very little weight, her stomach was enormous. It felt tight like a drum. She knew Mammy had had a hard time with some of the babies, but neither Mammy nor anyone else had ever explained to her what that meant. Mammy would just come home from the hospital looking grey, and Auntie Maggie would be summoned to help with the children. Daddy would sit in his chair like he always did.

Dolores could sometimes feel the baby kicking. Would the baby look like her or Marcus? Thinking of Marcus would make her feel warm. And then it would make her feel cold.

As the months dragged on, it became more and more difficult to move around.

'Mother of God, Dolores, that baby will be huge,' the Directress said.

Dolores Murphy's slim ankles were now swollen with fluid and her face was constantly flushed with the effort it took just to breathe. She remembered Mammy talking about walking on uneven surfaces to try to bring on the birth. She couldn't quite compute in her mind how it could. But she couldn't quite compute in her mind anything about having a baby. They would allow her to go for walks from time to time out the back of the house, as long as there were no guests staying, and she would walk up and down brick steps and wonder whether this might be the day. She was so uncomfortable and just wanted this baby out of her. She remembered hearing one of her aunties saying something about tinned pineapple. She wondered if she could ask Miss Nuala to bring her some, pretending that it was a craving.

One day Mammy called and they put her through to the phone in the hall. Miss Nuala gave her a hard look before she went to pick up the phone, as if warning her not to dare mention her condition. As if she would. The Murphy girls were working class but they had been brought up to be 'ladies'. Mammy would never be able to show her face at the Legion of Mary again.

'You sound out of breath, Dolores,' Mammy said down the line, her voice sounding so tiny and faraway.

'Ah, it's just the hard work, Mammy,' Dolores said. 'No rest for the wicked.'

'Well, don't you be giving the Directress any lip.'

'Mammy, please,' Dolores said, turning her ankles in circles in the vain hope of shifting the fluid pooling around them.

'You're all right.'

'I miss you, Mammy.'

'You'll see me soon enough.'

A tear trickled down Dolores's cheek. 'I hope so, Mammy.'

'I'm proud of you, Dolores.'

It was one of the nicest things Mammy had ever said to her. Which is why it kicked her in the solar plexus to think that if only Mammy knew the truth, she'd die altogether.

Dr Lonergan had told her that the baby would be born in mid-September. But mid-September came and there was still no baby. The uneven surfaces only made her back hurt more. The tinned pineapple Ms Nuala dutifully delivered made her heartburn worse.

Then one morning she woke up and the bed was soaked. The pain was excruciating. She screamed out for Miss Nuala, but the Directress came running instead.

'It's happening, please God,' the Directress said. 'I'll call Dr Lonergan.'

'Aren't I going to hospital?' Dolores asked. 'I feel like I'm going to die.'

'You won't die. This is natural. You're not the first woman and you won't be the last. Look at the crucifix on the wall and offer up your suffering to Our Lord.'

'I need some medicine!' Dolores cried. 'Please.'

'You do not,' said the Directress flatly. 'You need to suffer for your sins.'

She felt like her insides were tearing apart.

Instead of Dr Lonergan, another woman arrived first, one whom the Directress told Dolores was to be addressed as Nurse Matron. She wore a habit and appeared to be a nun.

The nurse matron ordered Dolores to lie on her back on the bed and then she pulled a sheet over her and told her to spread her legs and push.

Dolores screamed. 'Please, make the pain stop!'

'Be quiet, child,' the nurse matron said. 'You should have thought of that before you got yourself in this situation.'

The labour went for fourteen hours and, towards the end, the nurse matron seemed concerned. Dr Lonergan finally arrived, with a large pair of what Dolores would later discover were forceps. Dolores tore from front to back. Eventually, though, she heard a little cry.

In the nurse matron's arms was a chubby baby girl with large brown eyes and chocolate skin; she looked far bigger than the brothers and sisters Dolores remembered Mammy bringing home. Dolores's eyes filled with tears as she gazed at the child. She had a birthmark in the shape of a strawberry above the folds of her little elbow, Dolores noticed. Her tiny feet kicked.

The Directress walked in and, seeing the baby, looked like she would keel over. 'She's—'

'That she is,' said the nurse matron grimly. 'Lord in Heaven save us.'

'You wicked, *wicked* girl,' the Directress spat at Dolores.

Miss Nuala walked in, and the Directress motioned silently to the wailing infant and made a sign of the cross.

'Mother of God,' said Miss Nuala. 'I'll have to explain to the O'Farrells.' She looked at Dolores and shook her head. 'This could complicate things.'

Dolores felt light-headed and weak; she was having trouble following the conversation.

Dr Lonergan, who had been standing in the corner smoking a pipe, came over and injected something into her arm.

'Who are the O'Farrells?' she asked Miss Nuala.

'Well, they're to be the parents, of course,' Miss Nuala said.

'But I'm this baby's mammy,' Dolores said.

'That's a ridiculous notion,' said the Directress, her voice rising sharply. She was shaking. 'You're sixteen, you're unmarried, and this baby is . . .' She couldn't bring herself to say the word. She turned to Miss Nuala. 'You'd better get them on the line. We'll have to handle this sensitively.'

Dolores struggled to keep her eyes open. The room was becoming blurry. The Directress and Miss Nuala were talking in agitated voices, but they sounded far away. She could hear the sound of the wind, and when she looked out the window, a flock of starlings circled in the grey sky. She turned to the nurse matron, who was bathing the baby in a small basin.

'Let me hold my baby,' she whispered.

'That's not advisable,' the nurse matron said. 'We can't have you getting attached.'

Dolores tried to get out of the bed, but then she fell to the floor. The lights went out, the noise faded, and she never got to hold her baby.

Dolores Murphy never saw the infant again.

Each day for two weeks, the nurse matron would come and give her another needle, and then Dolores Murphy would feel like she was under water. It didn't dull the pain so much as dull her mind. It hurt to go to the toilet. Her breasts were tender and sore and leaking, and the nurse matron gave her a tablet to stop the milk. Her stomach looked like a miserable deflated balloon.

'Please,' she'd beg the nurse matron, 'let me see my baby.'

'Your babby's in a better place now,' the nurse matron would only say. 'And a very lucky babby indeed given the surprise you gave us all. The O'Farrells weren't keen, but we've found another very happy couple who were desperate for a family and were willing to look past it. The child will have a very fortunate life, please God.'

The nurse matron never said who that happy couple was.

It began to dawn on Dolores Murphy that she was never going to be Marcus Akenyemi's baby's mammy. The Directress started talking about her returning to duties.

And so, several weeks after the baby was born, Dolores Murphy finally ran.

18
HELP

KATE DELANEY DRAWS a large breath. She's been sitting in Dolores's kitchen since they got home from a brief spell at the hospital after the incident at Shellybanks that afternoon, and it's now 3 am. The doctor in the A and E told Dolores she was a very lucky lady. Liam Carroll was physically fine, but moody. He had gone straight to bed at 8 pm.

Dolores Murphy is made of hardy stuff, though. And now that her aunt has told her the true story of what happened during those missing years, Kate understands that she has had to be.

'How did I not know any of this?' Kate asks, taking Dolores's hand in hers.

'No one knew, Kate,' says Dolores blankly.

'What happened to the baby?'

'I have no clue. But I think about her every single day. Every time I'm in town and I see a young woman who has curly hair, or looks like she might be mixed race, my heart starts pounding. And I'll stand there and stare at her, trying to work out if she's my girl. Then the young woman will open her mouth and she's speaking Italian or something, and I feel like a right fool. I don't even know her name, Kate.'

'I wonder if she's still in Ireland? And what she knows about her history?'

'I'm sure she went to one of their families, so knowing them, I suspect she wasn't told much.'

'She probably thinks she was adopted from another country. Did you ever tell anyone about Marcus?'

'No, I didn't.'

'Not even Kevin?'

'I told Kevin that I had been in love with someone before and that he had died. Kevin wasn't one for sentimentality and I don't think he wanted to contemplate me with someone else. He could be a bit jealous at times. I didn't tell him any detail and I certainly didn't tell him about the baby.'

'Dolores, everything you've described about the Father and the Directress and the Help—it sounds like a cult.'

'I know. I know. I can see that now. But back then, I didn't even know what a cult was. I was a child, really. After I left, I went to work in the bottle factory back in Dublin, and I never told a soul what I had been through. I thought that no one would believe me that such a place was even operating just twenty-five miles up the road.'

'The Directress sounds like a right witch.'

'She was.'

'Where is she now?'

'No idea. She must be ninety if she's even alive.'

'And what about Miss Nuala?'

'I assume she's still with them in some capacity. Do you know, I never even knew her full name? I never knew any part of the Directress's name. Kate, it's so strange. I buried it all for so long, but they stole my baby.'

'They stole your baby. They imprisoned and abused you. They stole your wages. Miss Nuala abused you. My God, Dolores'—Kate grasps her aunt's hand a little more tightly—'they stole your *life*. And you really never breathed a word about it?'

Dolores shook her head. 'Not to anyone. Not to your mam. Not any of the others. Not to Mammy or Daddy. None of my friends in Ringsend. I was desperate not to draw attention to myself. For years I thought they would come looking for me. I was so afraid of them. On the one hand, I was so ashamed that I had allowed myself to surrender to all of it, and on the other I was so ashamed about the birth and the damage it did to me. Them forceps. Oh, Kate, I was so ashamed. That's why I never met anyone for a long time. And I was grieving Marcus.'

Dolores rubs her eyes and goes to the cupboard to pull out a couple of mohair blankets for them. The second hand on the oversized railway clock ticks loudly on the wall.

'How did you get away?' Kate asks.

'I got up very early one morning determined to leave, but I had no idea where to go. So I ran over to the Hill of Tara. I just wanted to be where Marcus had been. I rolled down the hill on my own. I must have looked a right dope, Kate, but I was in such a state that I didn't care. And I went into that little tomb in the Mound of the Hostages. I started to feel very afraid. It was so creepy in there. All those souls of the dead people below. And then I went and rolled down the hill again, and I lay in the grass for a while and I remembered him.'

Kate feels heartbroken thinking of her aunt. It also reminds her of her own ordeal, trapped under the Pheasants Nest Bridge, with only ghosts of the suicides to keep her company. She tightens the blanket around her shoulders and grinds her teeth.

'Oh, Dolores.'

'I know. I have never felt so alone in my life. But look, I understood I needed to get away because I knew they'd come looking for me. I went back out to the main road, and I was terrified, Kate, because it was so close to the house. I tried to hitch a ride, but no one would pick me up. I was breaking my heart crying, so I was. Just walking along. I kept walking and walking. And then I came to a phone box. And something came over me, I decided to ring triple nine.'

'Wow, Dolores, that was brave.'

'Well, as it turned out, not so much. I rang triple nine and they asked me if I wanted Gardaí, fire or ambulance. And I said Gardaí. And they asked me where I was, and I said I was in County Meath. I was still too scared to say exactly where. So anyway, I was put through to a gard and I was so scared, Kate. All I could say was, "They took my baby; they stole my baby."'

'And what did the gard say, Dolores?'

'Well, of course he said something like, "Who took your baby? Who are you? Is your baby all right, love?", that sort of thing. And I just panicked and kept breaking my heart crying. And the gard was saying, "You're all right, you're all right, we can help you." And then, Kate, I just hung up the phone and I kept running along the road. And then, would you believe it, Mr Mackie came along in his van. He slowed down and asked if I was all right. I said I wasn't. And he drove me to his house and gave me a cup of tea and asked me what he could do. Do you know, Kate, that he was one of the only people who ever asked me what *I* wanted to do? And so, I told him that I had to get away. That the Directress was a very bad woman, and she was not paying me for my work.'

Mr Mackie was very upset at what she told him, Dolores explains, but he was not the type to make a scene.

'I doubt he would have ever raised it again with the Directress,' she says. 'They were a good source of income for him, and Mr Mackie had mouths to feed. But he was very kind. He gave me fifty pounds, which was a lot of money in those days. More than he could afford, I'm sure. He drove me into town, and I went and got some clothes and other bits. I got changed in the toilets in Clerys in O'Connell Street and threw that horrible pinafore in the bin. I would've burned it if I could. And then I got the bus down to Ringsend. And to be honest, Kate, it played right into Mammy's notions of me being a bold and unreliable girl. But she didn't push it. I think perhaps she had known in her heart that something was off with the letters not reaching me and so on. And I suspect she probably felt a bit guilty for having completely neglected me for a couple of years. You know, she never inquired. She never came to visit. She was my mammy, and she never asked any questions or really troubled herself to find out who these people were and what sort of operation they were actually running there. But she was too busy with the kids, you know? She didn't have the time to think about me. And Daddy was useless. I did get the sense that she had missed me, though. She was much nicer to me after that.'

Dolores is speaking almost without stopping for breath. It's all pouring out of her so rapidly, she looks like she might be sick.

'There was no way I was going to jeopardise our relationship by telling her that I'd had a baby to a black man who wasn't Catholic. She'd've died.'

'I daresay she would have,' Kate said.

'It was another time,' Dolores continued. 'And Mam was a prisoner herself, in many ways, of the Church. All them children, for so many years. And Daddy—I mean, for fuck's sake, Kate, he was hopeless. He was just like a piece of furniture rather than a flesh-and-blood father.'

'And there were so many more women like her, too,' Kate said. 'Fuck this country. I love it so much, but all of the needless pain that has been caused to women does my head in, Dolores. Sometimes I feel like I could scream with it. But you know, I think Nana softened as she got older.'

'She did. Well, I think the country changed around that generation. All the things they were clinging on to sort of fell away. And you know, Mammy had secrets herself.'

'What sort of secrets?' Kate asked.

'Well, sometimes I would be lying awake when Daddy came home from the pub, stocious drunk. He'd be cursing and blinding at her. And sometimes he'd chase her up the stairs. And she would tell him he was an awful man, and it would start as a bit of a game, sometimes, but then it wasn't a game. And look, I would hear them, and she would be screaming out in pain.'

Kate felt herself go hot and cold and her pulse started to race.

Her aunt must have seen something in her face because she said, 'Oh God, Kate, I didn't mean . . . I'm so sorry, I do be forgetting . . . Here's me, blethering on about my own problems. I'm sorry I'm so insensitive.'

Kate drew a deep breath and held up her hand. 'It's okay, Dolores. I can't live in a bubble. It just makes me so sad for Nana.'

'Yes, when I thought about it in later life, it made me able to make peace with her and the way she had treated me. She was a victim.'

'But her neglect of you had such terrible consequences, too, Dolores. You're right to feel angry at her for that.'

'Am I, though? She did the best she could in the circumstances. I think I annoyed her because I reminded her of what she could never be. I mean, she never had time for going to the library. She was just permanently knackered. And what happened to me was a consequence of that. So, she didn't ask any questions. And I didn't give her any answers. I remember the last time I ever spoke to her, when she had gone into the care home with the early Alzheimer's.'

Dolores starts to cry softly.

'After such a hard life, she deserved a better end once the kids had grown up. But anyway, I remember going in there, and she looked up at me, and most times you'd visit and she wouldn't know who you were at all. But this time, Kate, she started weeping. And I was saying, "You're all right, there, there, Mammy," because it was terrible to see her crying like a child. And she just kept saying, "I'm sorry, Dolores; I'm sorry, Dolores; I'm sorry, Dolores." And I started crying, too.'

Kate pulls her chair next to Dolores and puts her arms around her aunt. 'I'm glad you had that moment with her,' Kate says. She's so tired, but she knows Dolores needs to tell her whole story. 'Dolores, I don't remember you ever having a boyfriend,' Kate says.

'No. I was traumatised. I was also left with problems down below after what they did to me with those forceps. I had to go to the north to visit a Protestant gynaecologist. Couldn't risk going to one here, back then. I didn't want anyone to see me. I had to have surgery to fix it. And I didn't want to risk falling in love with some fella and then losing him like I lost Marcus. Plus, I was absolutely terrified of getting pregnant again. Do you remember Ann Lovett, the fifteen-year-old who died in the grotto?'

Kate does remember being told the horrific story of the girl who died giving birth to a stillborn baby in a grotto dedicated to the Virgin Mary back in the mid-eighties, and how some local schoolkids had found her body. It had caused the whole country to reflect on the way it treated young women who had babies out of wedlock. No one who was in Ireland at the time could ever forget it. Kate was only a very small child when it happened, but people had spoken of it for years afterwards.

'Oh my God, yes. Poor Ann Lovett.'

'It was desperate. Desperate. Well, that was only about five years after the Directress and that lot took my baby away. I remember I was broken-hearted when I heard about it. I could relate so much to what she went through. I cried and cried and cried. And I think, in a way, it set me back a bit. It brought back the old fear.'

Kate's own eyes fill with tears. 'That was one of the saddest stories I ever heard. But your story is so sad, too, Dolores. I feel terrible that you went through this alone. You know, you could always have talked to me about it.'

'Ah, pet. The wound was too deep. I felt like if I opened it up, I'd never close it again.'

'I get that, now.'

'I'm sure you would. And you know, I'd meet lads down at the GAA or whatever, and they'd be talking about Liverpool beating Man United. And how could anyone ever compare to Marcus? They couldn't. So, I kept myself to myself. Also, I didn't want to repeat Mammy's mistake of having all those children. I didn't want to ever be a prisoner of any kind again—even if it was by circumstance or choice. I wanted to go on holidays to Corfu or the Algarve when I felt like it, buy nice things for myself, have an easy life. And I got a lot of auntie love from the likes of you. From time to time, when I got into my thirties and I was all fixed and I started to come to terms with the shame, I would have a holiday fling, and that would keep me going for a while. But nothing remotely serious. Then, after years and years of keeping myself to myself, I met Kevin. I was pushing fifty and I had come to think I was completely past it. But he didn't think so. And he just charmed me, despite myself. And I figured enough time had passed. I could risk putting myself out there a bit. So much for that, Kate.'

Sitting at the kitchen table, with dawn stirring through the window, Dolores looks tiny.

'We have to make this right, Dolores. How can I help?'

'I'll tell you how, Kate: I'd like you to help me find her. I don't think I can go on until I at least try. The loss of Kevin has just brought back the loss of my baby and the loss of Marcus before her so sharply. I can't bring back Kevin, and even if I could bring back Marcus now, it was so long ago—what would I even be saying to him? But I want to at least try to find my child. I buried the regret inside me for so long. I walk out of my house now and I feel like howling with it, Kate. I see a baby and I'm almost wanting to snatch it out of the buggy. But she wouldn't be a baby. She's a young woman in her thirties and she's out there somewhere. My girl. I need my girl. I need to know who she is. What she loves, what she hates. Who does she take after? I haven't a clue where to start. But you, with your journalism and so on, you'd probably have a better idea than me about how to find someone. And maybe Liam can help with his law.'

'You know, Dolores, I think there's an important story to be told here. I mean, there must be lots of other Help out there who were treated the same. It's slavery. There is no other word for it. I can't believe I've never heard of this before.'

'There would be loads. I can't remember most of their names, though. I have no idea where I'd start looking for them.'

'Okay, well Clodagh O'Reilly is a start. I can find an address and hopefully a phone number for her in Adelaide. I can get my friend

Sylvia to do an electoral roll search. And what about Mairéad? She was clearly unhappy; she might have a story to tell, too.'

'She was from Effin. Jaysus, it's a tiny place. There can't be too many Mairéad O'Riordans in Effin. She wasn't very friendly to me, though.'

'Maybe she thought the same about you, Dolores. You know, maybe she thought you weren't that friendly to her. But you're both in your fifties now.'

'That's true.'

'But listen, the first point of call for us is the police. You need to report a crime, Dolores. Let's face it. There's more than one crime here. Abuse. Slavery. And they stole your baby. That's a crime. You didn't consent to that.'

'I know.'

Kate Delaney and Dolores Murphy tiptoe up to bed. They're exhausted and emotionally spent. But for the first time since Kevin died, Dolores feels something that feels like hope.

Kate climbs in next to Liam, who is snoring a little, and snuggles under his arm. She has never felt so grateful for him. He smells like toasted cinnamon.

The room lights up with a silent message notification flashing on Liam's phone on the bedside table. Kate leans over him to read it and sees it's from his boss, Sebastian, in Australia.

When will you fly?

—

They sleep in the next morning till long after the sun has burned the frost off the grass in Dolores Murphy's little garden. Kate had woken every couple of hours before finally dropping into a deep sleep at 8 am. She opens her eyes after hearing the front door shut behind Dolores, who has gone down to the shops for her messages. She tiptoes into the bathroom and has a quick shower and brushes her teeth. Then she slips back into bed beside Liam, without her clothes.

'That's cheating,' he says, feeling her soft, clean, lemony skin beside him as she runs her hand along his arm.

'No one has ever made me feel like you do,' she says.

'Ditto,' he whispers.

She climbs on top of him and kisses him on the mouth. He smiles sleepily and puts his hands around her waist. She tries not to cry out in case Dolores bursts in the front door.

'Don't leave me, Liam,' she says.

'Oh, sweetheart. You're still mine and I'm still yours. I won't ever *leave you* leave you.'

'I can't be on my own.' She rolls off him and puts her head in the crook of his shoulder.

'One of the reasons I fell in love with you is that you're the toughest and smartest girl in any room,' he says. 'You can do anything. And that fucking creep hasn't taken that away from you. You're still here. He's gone. But you know, I can't just put my life on hold indefinitely. I still need to work—and I *like* my work. And I don't know, Kate, yesterday was a lot. I want to support you and your family, but that was really bloody grim.'

'I know it was. I'm so sorry. And thank you for what you did.'

He squeezes her hand.

'Dolores told me her whole story last night, Liam. It's unbelievably chilling. She was part of this weird cult-like organisation called the Group who pretty much enslaved her and then stole her baby. She was only a teenager, and she got pregnant to this Nigerian guy and then he died, and they took the baby to give to some couple she didn't know. And she never wanted to give her baby away. She doesn't even know the baby's name.'

'God, that is insane. Poor Dolores.'

'I don't want you to think badly of her. She's amazing.'

'I don't think badly of her, sweetheart. I like her a lot.'

'She survived all of that and never said a word to anyone about it because of the shame and the fear. She wants to find the baby, who would be in her thirties now. My cousin. I have to help her, Liam.'

'And that's what you do best, Kater. Listen, why don't you stay here for a while and help Dolores? It will give you a project. I really don't think you're up to full-time work yet, but this could sort of ease you into focusing on something other than recovery. Were there other women like her? I don't want to sound mercenary, but it sounds like it's a story, if she'd be up for it. I mean, it sounds like this cult should be exposed.'

'Yeah, that was my thought exactly.'

'I'm so bloody proud of you, Kate. You're going to be okay. *We're* going to be okay. I've never really talked about this with you, given that the burden you're carrying is so much bigger than mine, but I think going back to work might be good for my own mental health. I need to think about other things for a while.'

She props herself up on her elbow. 'Like contumelious disregard?'

'Yes. Who among us doesn't pine for some contumelious disregard in their life?'

'I get that I've been selfish.'

'Jesus, Kate. No, you haven't. You've been surviving. And you are doing an incredible job of that.'

'I don't feel like I am. Promise me you won't find some other easier girl.'

'Kate.'

'Liam.'

'You're my best girl.'

—

Liam Carroll phones the owner of their villa on the Greek island to tell them they won't be coming back after all. He flies home to Melbourne two days later. As he reclines in his seat in the A380, he is consumed with guilt and relief in equal measure, missing Kate already and hoping that he hasn't made a terrible mistake.

Kate Delaney is frightened of being alone, but doesn't want to show it. She's frightened of the dreams—the flashbacks to being locked in a cage under a bridge, freezing and hungry. The flashbacks to being raped in an alleyway, her face pressed into the cobblestones. The flashbacks to thinking no one was going to find her. And that she would never see Liam again.

The first night without Liam, she creeps into Dolores's bedroom.

Dolores is wearing a fluffy pink robe and a face mask and is reading a novel Kate gave her to take her mind off the grief.

'Dolores, can I sleep in here, just for tonight? I don't know how to be alone yet.'

'Ah, Kate, of course.'

When they switch off the light, Kate is overwhelmed by the sense that her aunt is not Liam. She smells like hairspray and cigarettes, not cinnamon. Her small frame doesn't take up enough of the bed. Kate lies awake in the darkness, confronted by the fact that she is going to have to learn how to be on her own. There will be many nights from here on that she will be spend staring at the wall, wishing she could fold herself into the crook of his arm.

The only thing for it, she realises, is to keep herself focused on the huge task in front of Dolores. The task of finding that baby.

'Let's go to Pearse Street tomorrow,' Kate says to Dolores. 'It's time.'

19
GARDAÍ

PEARSE STREET GARDA STATION is a snecked-granite baronial pile of a place across the road from the bus stops outside Trinity College in town. On either side of the arched main doorway are stone sculptures of two Dublin Metropolitan Police in conical helmets, peering down censoriously at those who enter.

It's heaving the morning that Kate and Dolores go to report a historical crime. There is no one at the scratched, circular front desk and so they sit down on the white plastic chairs and wait. Next to them, a woman in a cobalt shell suit is talking to herself and anyone who will listen.

'Who wants to join me over at the pub for a Coca-Cola?' she yells.

Kate and Dolores smile thinly and talk about the weather. The sun is streaming through the dirty windows, falling on three little boys with neatly combed hair and navy school uniforms and Coke bottle glasses, standing with one foot propped against the wall and eating packets of cheese-and-onion Taytos.

'What are you lookin' at?' demands their mother, who is well dressed but has a black eye.

'Oh, nothing,' Kate says quickly. 'I was just thinking that your boys are very sweet.'

The woman gives Kate a suspicious nod and Kate switches her focus to something else. A large sepia-toned photograph of Pádraig Pearse's profile hangs above the row of white plastic seats.

'He looks so serious,' Kate whispers to Dolores.

'Well, he had a lot on his mind,' says Dolores.

Stained bulletin boards advertise what to do when you are reporting a lost or stolen mobile phone and advice lines for European visitors in financial difficulty. Anto and David and Rat and Deano have all graffitied their names on the felt with biro.

Eventually, a garda comes out and sits behind the desk, and one by one those assembled approach.

It takes at least an hour for the garda to get through all of the people waiting. The woman with the black eye and the three little boys disappear through the navy arches. The woman with the cobalt shell suit is given some pamphlets and a reassuring pat on the shoulder. 'I'm not sure I like the look of you,' she says to Kate as she heads out the door.

'Man, these gardaí earn their wages,' Kate says to Dolores.

'They do that,' Dolores replies. 'I feel sick,' she says, as the garda attends to the person in line before them.

'You needn't,' says Kate, and squeezes her aunt's hand. 'Okay, let's do this.'

'I'm here to make a report about a missing baby,' says Dolores when they are standing in front of the scratchy wooden desk. 'Or a stolen baby, actually.'

'Your baby?' the garda asks Kate.

'No, no, not mine.'

'Your grandchild?' he says, motioning to Dolores.

'No,' says Dolores. 'My baby.'

The garda looks confused.

'But she's not a baby anymore. She'd be thirty-five now.'

'Oh, so this is a historical matter?' the garda says.

'I suppose it is.'

'Who was the father of this baby?'

'He died before she was born. He was from Nigeria.'

'How did he die?'

'In an accident—he was driving a van.'

'I'm sorry for your loss.'

'It was a very long time ago.'

'Can I ask, did you report the, ah, theft to the Gardaí when it happened?'

'Well, no, I didn't—at least, not immediately.'

'Can I ask why?'

'I was afraid.'

'Were you in one of them mother and baby homes?'

'No, I wasn't. I was in, well, I suppose you could describe it as a sort of a cult. But I did call the Gardaí eventually. From a phone box somewhere down the road from the Hill of Tara in County Meath. On that same road. I don't even know the name of the road. I couldn't ever bring myself to go back there. I was too afraid. I just know that's where I was.'

'And what happened when you made the call?'

'Well, I started to explain they had taken my baby, but I didn't say who or why or anything but then I got very afraid, and I hung up the phone. All I told the switchboard lady was that I was in County Meath.'

'I see. That's helpful. There might be a record of the call.'

'I was afraid for years that they would realise I'd made it, and someone would come and find me. I don't know what I thought was going to happen, but it scared the living daylights out of me.'

The garda looks at Kate. 'And what's your relationship to Ms . . .'

'Murphy,' says Kate. 'My aunt's name is Dolores Murphy. My name is Kate Delaney.'

'Right, so. Well, Ms Murphy, are you here to make a formal statement about this missing baby who is now an adult?'

'I suppose I am,' says Dolores.

'This will be complicated,' the garda says, tapping his pen on his notepad. 'I haven't done one of these before. I'm not sure if it's even a criminal matter.'

Kate wishes that Liam were with them now. He'd know exactly what to say.

'I think you'll find that it is a criminal matter,' she says. 'For a start, Dolores was never paid in the two years she spent working as a servant in the houses run by these people. She had no keys and no money. She was given hand-me-down clothes, and she had to work up to sixteen-hour days. She had no days off. And when she got pregnant, as a very naive teenager, they basically kept her prisoner until she had the baby, then they drugged her and took the baby away. She never got to name her baby, or to even hold her. She had to run away to escape.'

'Were there locks on the doors?' asks the garda.

'No,' says Dolores, 'but they didn't exactly need them. It's hard to explain, but I had nowhere to go and no money to get anywhere. I was constantly reminded that it was a mortal sin to disobey them. Oh, and I was encouraged to whip myself and wear a kind of barbed-wire chain around my thigh while I worked.'

'Janey Mack,' said the garda. 'It does sound very bad. But see, the problem, like, is that it's historical, which means it's not straightforward. It's way above my pay grade, I must say. I think you'll need to make a formal statement with a sergeant. I promise that someone will look after you, but we may need for you to make an appointment. Give me a moment and I'll go and have a chat out the back there.'

Dolores nods and Kate puts her arm around her.

After a few minutes, the garda returns.

'Right so, I've got a solution for you, Ms Murphy. We have a new inspector here who moved to Dublin a few months ago. He's a very good man, in my experience, and I'd really trust him, like. I asked when he'd be available to take a long statement—because Dolores, this will take you a few hours at least. So, you need to prepare yourself for that. He said next Wednesday. Would that suit your schedule?'

Dolores smiles weakly. 'I don't have much of a schedule at the moment,' she says. 'I've just suffered a bereavement and I'm on leave from work. So, I can fit in with him.'

'I'm sorry for your loss, Dolores. Let's say Wednesday, half ten, then. If you come here to the front desk and ask for Inspector Christy Redmond, someone will bring you through.'

Dolores's eyes are shining with tears. 'Thanks very, very much'—she looks at the garda's name tag—'John Barry. This is a very big step for me. I appreciate your kindness.'

'I'd say it is,' says John Barry. 'Now. Mind yourself. Inspector Redmond will take very good care of you.'

PART THREE

SINÉAD

20
DAUGHTER

ACROSS TOWN, IN a semi-detached white house over the road from Marlay Park in Rathfarnham, a woman is packing a suitcase. Downstairs, her mother is pacing the kitchen while her father rustles his newspaper, pushes his spectacles up his nose and tries to pretend nothing is amiss.

Sinéad Mulroney is an only child. And although she is thirty-five years of age, she seems younger than she is, having been babied all her life. She's about to make that right.

Her parents, Donal and Maureen Mulroney, both have mousy-brown hair and pale eyelashes and a freckly translucent skin tone with hints of blue. Both of them have legs like sticks and, even if they eat like horses, their ribs stick out. They've both had terrible eyesight since they were children and can't see much without their glasses. Donal and Maureen are so alike they could have been siblings.

'Did you never consider getting one of them DNA tests just to be sure you didn't come out of the same box?' one of their friends once joked at a dinner party, implying that Maureen and Donal look so alike they must be related to each other and should have checked.

'Well, for a start, they weren't available in the seventies,' Maureen had scolded, retreating to the kitchen to noisily scrape the remains of the vol au vents from the plates into the bin and putting the Jameson back in the press.

But it has always been clear that Sinéad Mulroney could never have come out of that box, nor even one remotely like it.

Sinéad's hair frames her face in tiny dark ringlets, highlighted with gold. Her skin is caramel, her eyes are brown and large, and she has long, dark lashes.

She rarely makes eye contact with others, but stares into the middle distance almost as if in a trance. She sometimes takes several beats to answer a question, and people make the mistake of thinking her rude. But Maureen can almost see the slower cogs in the wheel of her daughter's cognitive processing. And when she does reply, Sinéad's answers can verge on the devastating—something to which her parents became accustomed when she was a child.

'How are you today, Sinéad?' Father Cleary had asked the ten-year-old girl when he was over for supper at Maureen and Donal's after mass.

Sinéad had looked out the window for a long moment and then looked at him, but not in the eye, and deadpanned, 'I'm fine, Father. Why do you wear a dress?'

'Well, dear, it's not exactly a dress,' Father Cleary said with a chuckle.

'And further,' said Sinéad, 'if Our Lord died on a cross, and so a cross was an instrument of torture for the Romans, why do people wear crosses around their necks? Isn't that disrespectful to Jesus's memory?'

'Well, that's a very good question,' Father Cleary said, laughing nervously.

'Then why won't you answer it?' Sinéad replied and walked out of the room because she knew that he wouldn't.

'That's some child,' Father Cleary said to Maureen Mulroney.

Maureen and Donal were used to their daughter's at-times confronting combination of blunt precocity and what used to be called seeming 'a bit slow'. *That's just Our Sinéad*, they'd tell the likes of Father Cleary. *She's not one for tact. But her heart's in the right place.*

Sinéad Mulroney wanted to know why they were spreading this ridiculous lie at mass that they were eating the body and drinking the blood of Christ when it was quite clearly a wafer and sherry. She wanted to know why nuns couldn't be priests and why women couldn't be priests and, as she got older, how the Virgin could, in fact, be a virgin and why anyone cared that she was.

Maureen's and Donal's answers were never satisfactory.

But Sinéad Mulroney's thorniest questions related to her heritage: *Why did my mammy in Africa give me up? (Mammy is your mammy. We think your birth mother must have died.) What of? (We don't know—maybe malaria.) Why malaria? (Well, it's a problem in Africa.) And why am I not as black as the other children in Africa? (That would be a question for your birth mother but, unfortunately, she's not here to ask.) And where in Africa am I from? (The adoption agency wasn't sure. The main thing is that your mammy and daddy love you very much, Sinéad, and you are very, very much wanted by us.)*

There was no adoption agency, of course, and the lie sometimes felt corrosive and wrong. But it was a more palatable explanation, and one which wouldn't invite more unanswerable questions. And Maureen and Donal Mulroney had lived their lives in a not-insubstantial amount of fear that the secret of Sinéad's adoption, such as it was, might be discovered.

Adopted children, the Mulroneys would tell their daughter, *are the luckiest children in the world, because their mammies and daddies wanted them the most. Their mammies and daddies couldn't have babies, and so did everything in their power to give a good home to a baby who didn't have one. Whose mammy had died or couldn't manage. Just imagine what would have happened to those poor babies otherwise.*

'God is gracious' was the meaning of her name, Sinéad was told. God had, in His mysterious way, been gracious to the

Mulroneys. For years they had prayed to Our Lord for a baby, but no baby had come. Maureen had severe endometriosis that saw her twisted in pain most months. On top of this, Dr Lonergan told a mortified Donal, he had a low sperm count. Donal was an accountant and the sort of man that had never used the word 'sperm' in a sentence. The likelihood of them falling pregnant was remote. They had begun to accept that adoption was the only answer, but they had been on a waiting list for eighteen months and were told it could still be years before they were granted a child. The introduction of the Unmarried Mother's Allowance in 1973 had seen the numbers of women going into mother and baby homes decline rapidly during the latter part of the 1970s and it had become increasingly difficult, in Ireland, to adopt. Maureen Mulroney offered up prayers every morning and every night, but by 1979 she was starting to feel like she would never be blessed with motherhood. It was then that she had heard of the Situation the women in mass were whispering about unkindly: *Margaret O'Farrell's black baby.*

Margaret O'Farrell had an adoption agreement, it was said, with a God-fearing teenager who had lost her way and fallen pregnant. The girl was desperate to make amends for her loss of purity and was in no position to look after the child. The father was not in the picture and the girl's employer was helping her find a suitable home for the baby. Margaret O'Farrell was an extremely observant Catholic and belonged to an obscure wing of the church that was secretive and cliquey and seemed to have a lot of very wealthy members. She had a five-year-old child, but had not been able to fall pregnant again. She was desperate for siblings for her little boy. Everyone in that group seemed to have at least seven babies and Maureen Mulroney intuited that Margaret O'Farrell felt on the outer.

But when the time arrived for Margaret O'Farrell to pick up her baby, the teenager's employer had regretfully informed Margaret that there was a problem: hadn't they discovered once the infant was born that the father seemed to have been—she mouthed the word silently—*African*? And so, while the baby was not black as the ace of spades *as such*, she was undoubtedly, well, there was no delicate way to put it, *chocolate*.

Margaret O'Farrell had received this news with floods of tears, the ladies in mass informed Maureen Mulroney. It wouldn't be *right* to bring up a baby like that in a parish like theirs, she declared. Wouldn't the children make fun of her at school? Wouldn't she be socially ostracised? It just wouldn't be *fair*. To the baby, that was. And Margaret O'Farrell had made a sign of the cross and said seven decades of the rosary. The baby would not be hers.

But on discovering this, Maureen Mulroney had looked at Donal and said that she was willing to take the risk. She wanted a baby so desperately, and that poor little soul deserved a good home. They would give her everything they possibly could: the best education, a lovely house, pretty clothes. That child would never want for anything. Margaret O'Farrell's attitudes aside,

Ireland was slowly becoming more progressive, they told each other. They could make it work.

And so, Maureen Mulroney approached Margaret O'Farrell after mass the following week and asked if Margaret would put in a good word.

And that's how Maureen Mulroney met the Directress.

—

The Directress raised Maureen Mulroney's hackles from the moment she met her. That is to say, she made Maureen instantly feel as if she was skating on the sort of ice that might shatter beneath her at any moment. The Directress's emotions seemed to Maureen to be performative and strained. As if she was ticking the boxes of how one was *supposed* to behave when demonstrating empathy rather than actually feeling it. She lurched between imperious and cold and overtly saccharine in a way that made Maureen feel giddy. Not giddy in the way of young lovers; giddy like she'd been on one of those rides at a fair where you want to be sick afterwards and seem to have a headache for a week.

'Maureen Mulroney, what a dear name,' cooed the Directress when they met at Bewley's on Grafton Street for an introductory coffee. 'I can't wait to make you a mammy.'

Maureen knew instinctively that this was a strange thing to say. That this woman should not have the power to make anyone a mammy. It made her wonder about the poor girl who was giving up the baby, and what her circumstances might be.

And yet.

And yet, Maureen Mulroney was desperate for a baby. Walking on the way to Bewley's that morning, her ovaries had hurt at the sight of toddlers in prams. She wanted to pick them up and squeeze them. To eat them, almost. Their apple cheeks and their little fat fingers, with the little dimples where the knuckles should be. When she heard them cry, she wanted to pick them up if their mammies didn't do it quickly enough. She looked at their mammies through narrowed eyes and wondered if anyone could want a child as much as she did. These lucky women, who only had to have intercourse with their husbands to conceive. Whose husbands weren't accountants with low sperm counts who had never used the word sperm in a sentence.

And then she mentally scolded herself. Because Donal was a good man. And she loved him. And he couldn't help it if he had a low sperm count. Just like he couldn't help it if she had the endometriosis.

But still.

But still, she wanted that baby so much that she was willing to look past the alarm bells that were sounding inside her head like a factory was on fire.

'Now I do have to raise a slightly *sensitive* issue with you, Maureen,' the Directress said, sliding in front of Maureen a slice of apple tart with custard that she had insisted on ordering and which Maureen didn't feel like eating. 'It's the small matter of the baby's—'

'Race?' answered Maureen. 'I have heard about that, and I have to say that I don't mind at all.'

'Well, now, that is an enormous relief,' said the Directress, clasping her hands. 'For reasons I can't quite comprehend'—her lack of comprehension was patently a lie—'Margaret O'Farrell seemed troubled by it, but I see that you are a bigger person than that.'

'I don't want to be criticising or commenting on Margaret,' said Maureen, sensing a trap. 'But the colour of that baby's skin is of no matter to me. I just want to give a child a good home. I will love that baby with all my heart as if she were my own.'

'And what are your circumstances?' asked the Directress, although she had made it her business to find this out already.

'Well, my husband, Donal, is an accountant. We've been married six years. We're looking to buy a house in the Rathfarnham area.'

'Oh, a lovely neighbourhood,' said the Directress.

'Yes. I have notions of pushing a buggy around Marlay Park.'

'Ah. Wouldn't that be nice, now?'

'It would.'

'And do you work, Maureen?'

'I'm a librarian by training, but I wouldn't work, no, if we were to raise a child. It's been so hard for us to get to this point, I wouldn't waste a single second away from that baby.'

'I can't imagine how any mother could,' said the Directress, pursing her lips, which, Maureen couldn't help but notice, were drawn in a cupid's bow more excessively harsh than the natural line of her mouth. With her papery white skin and hair piled up in that old-fashioned Edwardian style, it gave her the appearance of an ageing porcelain doll. 'I do often wonder whether these women's libbers ought not be allowed to have babies at all. Give them to mammies who really want them, I say.'

Maureen hated to hear other women judged. And she hated the thought of anyone being deprived of motherhood. But while she loved her own job as a librarian, a part of her she did not entirely care for had felt similar pangs of resentment about mothers who went off to work. How could they waste their time away from their dear little ones? Hers was not to judge. And yet.

And yet.

'The baby in question is now ten days old,' the Directress informed her. 'She's being kept at a house in Donnybrook belonging to a family friend of our dear Dr Lonergan. Her mother had a difficult birth, but she is very young, of course, and so will bounce back, I'd say, with no trouble. The baby is in rude good health. Indeed—' the Directress gave a haughty laugh—'she has a rather substantial set of lungs on her.'

'Oh, I'm sure I'll manage. I had much younger brothers and sisters.'

'Well, then. There's nothing like a big family to prepare you for the reality of a sleepless babby.'

'And the mother,' Maureen said slowly. 'Is she, er, all right with this whole process?'

'Oh, she's getting used to it,' said the Directress. 'She's aware that she cannot care for the poor child. She does not have the money and there is no father in the picture.'

'What happened to him?'

'It appears he died in a car crash.'

'Oh dear, that is sad,' said Maureen.

'Well, everything happens for a reason, as they say,' said the Directress.

Maureen wondered about that. She did.

But still.

But still. If that man had not died in a crash, would Maureen Mulroney be about to become a mammy? Perhaps not.

'When may I meet the mother?' Maureen asked.

'Oh, my dear, Dr Lonergan says that would not be at all advisable,' the Directress said. 'The last thing we need is for her to get attached to any notion of her baby or who the child is going to. It's best—*for her*, mind—that she knows nothing about you. The healthiest thing for her is just to move on. She's only sixteen and has her whole life ahead of her. She must treat all of this as just, well, a bad dream. And pray to Our Lord that she never strays in such a *monumental* way again.'

'Poor girl,' said Maureen. 'It can't be easy all the same.'

'Well,' said the Directress, with, again, what Maureen could only think was a horrible little laugh, 'one supposes that she ought to have thought of that before she did what she did. I mean, can you imagine if it was your daughter, and you discovered such a thing had taken place?'

'I'd love her no matter what,' said Maureen firmly. 'Who was the father, anyway? What about his people?'

'As I understand it, because I did some delicate "investigating" after we got this terrible shock, he was a student who was working temporarily for our local grocer, who had taken ill. He had started delivering groceries to our property in County Meath.' (Who was 'our'? Maureen wondered.) 'And the girl must have met him. Though they can't have met too many times at all, because the grocer's heart had only given out a matter of weeks before. I have to say'—the Directress took a deep breath and stirred her coffee dramatically—'the whole thing is absolutely scandalous, and she's only lucky that she has good God-fearing people around her to set her back on the straight and narrow, so she is.'

Maureen thought of the sixteen-year-old and shuddered to herself. How lonely she must be. How hard it would be, to give up a baby. To lose someone to a car accident who must have meant something to her if she was prepared to give herself over to him like that. Maureen Mulroney had never been one for big shows of emotion, and she and Donal had never been big on passion, but she appreciated that not everyone was the same. And she remembered what it was like to be sixteen. That poor girl.

And yet.

And yet, Maureen Mulroney desperately wanted that baby.

'What about the paperwork?' Maureen asked.

'Oh, Dr Lonergan is arranging that with our TD,' said the Directress vaguely.

Maureen gulped at what she sensed was not exactly in keeping with the hoops that the adoption authorities were currently asking the Mulroneys to jump through. But still.

But still.

'When can I meet the baby?' she asked in a small voice, pushing the apple tart through the custard on her plate.

'Oh, I'm certain that can be arranged as soon as possible,' said the Directress gaily, and she clicked her fingers for the waitress to bring the bill.

21

BABY

MAUREEN MULRONEY WOULD never forget that day in a front room of a Georgian terrace in Donnybrook. The friend of Dr Lonergan, a plump lady with a pained expression on her face, was sitting in the parlour with the Directress and another woman who had light blonde hair swept up in tortoiseshell combs. The blonde was wearing a pastel tartan kilt and white tights. Her eyes were the palest blue and she smiled, but not with her eyes.

'Maureen Mulroney, this is Nuala,' said the Directress. 'She'll show you in to meet baby.'

Nuala took Maureen by her hand; the woman had the coldest hand Maureen had ever felt. It sent a shiver down her spine.

'I'm so pleased to meet you, Maureen,' said Nuala. 'You must be terribly excited.'

'Oh, I am, Nuala,' Maureen replied. 'Really.'

Nuala opened the door to a room with burgundy flocked wallpaper and an elaborate crystal candelabra. On a shelf on the wall was a very expensive-looking statue of Our Lady. In another corner was a picture of a man who looked to be a priest of some sort with outstretched hands and a beatific smile on his face.

And in the corner, in a pink bassinette, was Sinéad.

Maureen Mulroney's eyes filled with tears as soon as she saw her. Her chubby little arms looked fitted on at the wrists. Her cheeks were round. Her eyes were closed and her long lashes fell on her cheeks. She opened her eyes and appeared to smile with her little gummy rosebud mouth, and Maureen Mulroney told herself it wasn't wind. The baby was smiling at her: at her mammy.

'Oh, Nuala, may I pick her up?'

'Of course you may,' said Nuala.

Maureen took the infant in her arms and pressed her face to the baby's head, breathing in the scent of her fontanelle. Her hair felt like velvet against Maureen's cheek.

'Oh, my darling, darling girl,' Maureen said.

'She's sweet, isn't she?' said Nuala. She sounded like she was talking about a baby giraffe at the zoo.

'She's absolutely perfect,' said Maureen.

The Directress came in then and beamed the way one is supposed to beam if one is absolutely delighted.

'Isn't this just marvellous?' she gushed. 'Meant to be, one might think.'

Maureen carefully eased Sinéad back into the bassinette and the Directress told her she could bring *your new baby girl* to the car, where Donal was waiting.

And the two of them drove home, speechless, hardly able to believe their extraordinary good fortune.

Sinéad was an easy baby who met all her first milestones. She was turning over at eight weeks, crawling at six months, an early walker. She said her first words at seven or eight months. Da-da, much to Maureen's consternation. Then na-na, for mashed banana, which she loved, then finally Ma-ma. Maureen bought all her baby clothes from a French designer catalogue. She was, she joked to the other mothers at baby playgroup, that silly mother who fell for the cream angora and cashmere babygro, which Sinéad was sick on once, never to be worn again. Sinéad's hair was thick and grew quicker than that of the other babies, and Maureen delighted in pinning it back in little round clasps. Every single moment of her daughter's life was documented in photographs, which Maureen had developed immediately and then pasted in leatherbound photo albums.

As she began to walk, Maureen bought her little shell-pink patent leather shoes that looked gorgeous, Maureen thought, against her lovely skin. Sometimes people stared when Maureen was wheeling Sinéad in the buggy, but Maureen generally didn't care.

'Is her daddy a foreigner?' an old lady once asked her at Tesco, but Maureen just smiled.

There were no signs initially that there was anything different about Sinéad, none that Maureen could discern, except that sometimes, for absolutely no reason, she would unleash the most bloodcurdling, high-pitched wail. She wasn't hungry, she didn't have a temperature, she didn't need her nappy changed and she'd been for a good long walk. She wasn't cold and she had plenty of toys to keep her occupied. She was cuddled as if her life depended on it. On several occasions, it got so bad that Maureen had to get the bus to the hospital, only for Sinéad to calm down altogether the moment they crossed the threshold. The doctor would check all her vital signs, but nothing whatsoever was found to be wrong with the child.

Donal began to tease Maureen that she was an overanxious mother; babies would cry, he'd remind her, and she couldn't be off to the A and E every time Sinéad had a bad afternoon.

'I know babies cry, Donal. And our Sinéad is actually not much of a crier,' Maureen would snap. But honestly, these incidents only occurred once every few months, and for the most part Sinéad was an easy baby. Eventually Maureen had to concede that Donal had a point. Babies would be babies. There was no point trying to make sense of them. Just let them be.

What Maureen found most distressing were the supermarket tantrums. Or at least, they would have seemed like tantrums to the casual observer. They started long before the Terrible Twos were supposed to commence. Sinéad couldn't have been more than fourteen months. But she would scream as if her life was ending right there in Superquinn, as if her mother was torturing her on a self-styled rack. Maureen had neither the language nor the experience to comprehend what exactly was going on, but she intuited one thing: Sinéad was not being a bold girl. She was not demanding a toy or sweets. And she wasn't in danger. She was just overwhelmed. Maureen would quickly wheel her buggy out into the fresh air, where the little girl would calm down and drift off to sleep.

When she did reach the Terrible Twos, she was not a particularly difficult child in many ways, but from time to time she would do things that were absolutely mortifying. She was a biter. But it seemed not to be about hurting the other child; she wasn't retaliating because, for instance, they had taken her favourite teddy away. She just seemed to like the feeling of flesh as she bit into it. On more than one occasion, mothers of more frail-looking children (Sinéad always seemed to pick the weaklings) would cluck their tongues and say, 'It's always the parents,' and Maureen would want to protest that she could not possibly work harder than she did to be a perfect mother, whatever that was.

It was at this point that Maureen began to see the hard stares and, to be frank, the racism.

'Who's the daddy?' she heard one mother whisper to another at the local swing park one day.

'Sure, the official answer is an accountant called Donal, who, as I understand it, hails originally from Donegal,' whispered the other mother. 'As for the postman, well that's another story altogether.'

Maureen would burn with anger, but she said nothing, just wheeled away a chirping Sinéad, who was completely oblivious of her crime.

As her baby became a toddler, Maureen noticed that Sinéad wasn't speaking. The other children in playgroup were starting to form short sentences, but Sinéad said very little. And when she did speak, she seemed to mangle her words. And while the other little girls had tea parties and played dollies, Sinéad seemed uninterested in joining their games. She played alongside the other children, not with them. She seemed perfectly content, but she was not engaged.

If Maureen was honest with herself, she had to admit that little Sinéad was not especially social with other children. But she did not seem bothered that they didn't include her in their games. She was content to be pushed on the swing, for hours if Maureen would only oblige. Or to spin the roundabout round and round and round and round and never get sick. She needed to be run ragged and, if she was, she was calmer. She was a good sleeper at night, but during the day never slept in her cot or, as she got older, her little sleigh-shaped bed. And Maureen would have to take her for long walks in the buggy to get her to nap.

Maureen didn't mind so much. She'd get the bus to Dun Laoghaire and walk all the way down to the James Joyce Museum in the Martello tower at Sandycove. As a librarian, Maureen had always been a prodigious reader and, while her little one slept, she'd chat away to the ladies in the museum and read through James Joyce's letters. And sometimes she'd leave a sleeping Sinéad with the ladies downstairs, who would sip tea and coo at the gurgling toddler, while she climbed the narrow stone staircase up to the rooftop where Stephen Dedalus meets Buck Mulligan at the start of *Ulysses*. There, she'd gaze out at people bobbing up and down in the water in the Forty Foot and watch the tides go in or out. And she'd feel grateful for her uncomplicated life with her little beauty.

On other days, she'd head to Sandymount Strand and wheel Sinéad all the way down the headland, all the way out to the Poolbeg Lighthouse. And on the way back, she'd buy Sinéad an ice cream and let her paddle in the shallows at Shellybanks, keeping an eye out for the returning tide.

And all the while, Maureen Mulroney was unaware that just past the stained red-and-white ESB towers, in the typing pool at the bottle factory, was Sinéad's mother, Dolores Murphy, who thought about her lost baby every single day.

Sinéad Mulroney finally found her voice at about four years old. And suddenly, Maureen's fear that her daughter was 'slow' dissolved. The little girl went from hardly saying anything at all to speaking full sentences in an oddly formal voice, with an accent that wasn't exactly Dublin but couldn't be readily placed. At school, she went from sounding out every single word to chapter books in what seemed like the space of a year. Her teachers were happy enough, if a little perplexed by this child who seemed, and looked, like she came from another place and time.

Maureen had read to her daughter every night since she had brought her home from Donnybrook, and the shelves of the wooden bookcase in her nursery were filled with all the books that had fired Maureen's own imagination as a child: *The Wind in the Willows*, *Alice in Wonderland*, the Narnia series, *The Magic Faraway Tree*. But Sinéad seemed happiest when she was reading books about snakes. She could tell you all about alligator snapping turtles and wolf spiders and what mammals you might find in the jungles of furthest Peru. Her mind was a mental map of the world.

'Where would you like to go on your holidays?' Donal would often ask at the start of the school year, meaning Portugal, or Mallorca.

'Costa Rica,' would be Sinéad's firm reply. 'Or Java. Or Suriname. Or the Japanese mountains, to see the snow monkeys.'

The Mulroneys never went to any of those places, but it didn't stop Sinéad from asking.

Maureen and Donal would do the quiz in the weekend paper each week, and one Saturday morning they were completely stumped. 'Four countries bordering Guatemala' was the question.

Donal prided himself on his geography, but Central America was not, he had to admit, his strong suit.

'Sure, why don't you ask Sinéad?' suggested Maureen.

Their daughter was nine and a half.

Sinéad looked at them unblinkingly. 'Mexico, El Salvador, Honduras and'—she looked at the ceiling for a moment—'ah yes, Mammy: Belize.'

Maureen and Donal swelled with pride. 'You're a little *genius*, so you are,' proclaimed Donal.

She was a champion speller and won the district spelling bee with 'chiaroscurist' at age eleven. But she couldn't tie her shoelaces until she was thirteen.

The country was, at that time, an extremely monocultural society. When Sinéad was finishing primary school, Maureen read in the newspaper that almost 94 per cent of the Irish population had been born in the republic. And of the 3.5 million people who lived in Ireland, there were fewer than four thousand Muslims in the whole country, only fifteen hundred Jews and fewer than a thousand Hindus. There was never anyone in Sinéad's class who looked remotely like her.

Maureen and Donal had moved away from the parish where Margaret O'Farrell sat in the front pew with the other ladies who looked down their noses at Sinéad, and where the chilly Directress gave communion with an air that suggested she was giving out winning lotto tickets.

It became immediately clear once the adoption transaction, such as it was, had taken place, that the family were not welcome. That the little brown girl and her earnest parents were a source of embarrassment to the Directress and her pals at the church in Merrion. That the Directress's smiles were more forced each time Maureen Mulroney saw her.

Sinéad, in that way that she had, seemed to instinctively know that the Directress was bad news. And in one of her more mortifying moments, she pointed to the Directress in the pew across the aisle from them and said, in a very loud preschooler voice, 'I don't like that lady, Mammy!' As they were walking out of the church, for what would be the last time, a sympathetic man who ran the local chipper whispered to Sinéad, 'Me either! You tell her!'

While their new parish was far more progressive, Sinéad didn't have many friends. But it wasn't so much her race—ignorant as she was of its origins—that marked her out as different. Sinéad Mulroney was considered by her classmates to be 'odd'. It caused Maureen and Donal a great deal of worry, but it never seemed to bother their daughter much. 'I don't need ten friends,' she'd say, 'I just need one who understands me.' Maureen and Donal could not deny the wisdom of this.

Her one friend, Karen, was a serious little girl with dark blonde hair who also lived in a house facing the Marlay Park. Karen wore green ribbons in her pigtails and her clothes always matched those of her younger sister. She was terribly good at mathematics, stuck googly eyes on conkers and made necklaces out of painted Polo mints. Karen had an impressive butterfly collection that Sinéad never tired of sorting through. The two little girls would spend hours sitting cross-legged on the floor of Karen's attic bedroom separating their peacocks from their red admirals and painted ladies.

Karen's mammy was one of thirteen from Ringsend. On those rare Dublin days when the sun peeked from behind the soft rain clouds, Karen's mammy would sometimes bring the girls to Shellybanks for a swim. They'd poke at compass jellyfish and collect cockle shells and search for elusive periwinkles.

'And where are you from?' a man walking his wolfhound might ask.

'Rathfarnham,' Sinéad would deadpan, and keep walking.

'Well, you've been told,' Karen's mammy would say with a giggle, and they'd go to the chipper on the way home.

At the Irish Glass Bottle Company, known to everyone in Ringsend as the Bottle House, Dolores Murphy, whose shorthand was now a good one hundred and fifty words a minute, would be taking dictation.

Sinéad Mulroney never went inside the little red lighthouse at the end of the snaking sea wall. She never wrote *Where is my MAMMY?* on the wall. That was someone else's child. So many babies were separated from their mammies, over so many years.

Their worlds were parallel, but they never collided. Dolores Murphy never bumped into the serious girl with the ringlets and the salted caramel skin at Shellybanks. Sinéad Mulroney never clapped eyes on the chain-smoking typist who sang David Bowie in the shower. Kate Delaney, the cousin Sinéad never knew of and never met, moved to Australia and spent baking afternoons sitting under she-oaks, dodging spitfires and trying to get out of kiss chasey. The pea soup fogs rolled in, the tides ebbed and flowed, and their lives carried on.

And all those years pass and Ireland changes. Music tastes veer from Duran Duran to Blur to Snow Patrol to Pharrell Williams. Gay Byrne leaves the *Late Late*. Mass attendance plummets. Pubs close. Bernadettes and Patricias become Aoifes and Niamhs. A referendum is called on the subject of same-sex marriage and, eventually, a huge majority will vote to support it. Immigration soars. Neurodiversity finds its way into pedagogy. And a young, autistic, mixed-race woman who had spent her life being asked, '*And where are you from?*' becomes, suddenly, cool—not just in what might have been described euphemistically as an *exotic* way, but just in a regular nonchalant way. She's working her way, slowly, through her second degree. She has managed, for some time, to hold down a job showing hordes of Americans around the GPO, trying to ignore the high pitch and volume of their voices when they tell her their great-granddaddy was from Tipperary.

'He was *not*?!' she has learned to script in a good-natured way.

'He was an O'Meara,' they'll explain. And then the Americans will pull out their phones to show her a picture of themselves drinking a Guinness at Nellie O'Brien's with a Mayfair or Nashville

Instagram filter applied. In the photograph will be a long-lost O'Meara with a pained expression on their face, saying *Slaínte.*

Now, it's Sinéad Mulroney's turn to ask, 'Where am *I* from?' And she doesn't know the answer. Inside of her, this question has been burning quietly for years. She's never wanted to upset Maureen and Donal. But it's just got to the point where she can't mask it anymore. She's thirty-five. A young thirty-five, granted, but thirty-five nonetheless. Most of the girls she went to school with are now mothers. She attends their baby showers and coos into their designer prams at their little bundles. She rolls her eyes when, right in the middle of a deep and meaningful on the phone, they break off to shout, 'Niamh, not in your mouth!' Then she'll hold the phone out from her ear as little Niamh wails like an air-raid siren because the offending article has been yanked from her fist.

She'd rather pluck her eyes out with a rusty spoon than have one of her own, but that said, all these babies and toddlers get her thinking. Thinking about the parts of her story, or the story she's been told, that have just never added up. She's beset with the sense that her earnest, well-meaning, middle-class parents have been lying to her all her life. And Sinéad Mulroney knows it in her bones and is incandescent with rage.

Today, she's packing her bags and demanding that her parents tell her the *truth*, and a weeping Maureen and Donal don't even know where to start.

Maureen stands at the kitchen window looking out to the hydrangeas she's planted in the garden and tries to think of where she would begin the story. There are the lies to their own daughter, the fact that they never bothered to check on the birth mother. But apart from everything else, Maureen Mulroney fears that what took place was not exactly legal. And she just isn't sure where that leaves her and Donal.

'Would you not sit down, Sinéad?' asks Donal.

'You can't be serious,' says his daughter.

Sinéad has no fixed plan, no real idea what she'll do or where she'll end up, she just feels an overwhelming urge to get out. So, she marches out of the semi-detached house across the road from Marlay Park, takes a cab to Dublin Airport, gets on an EasyJet flight to Gatwick, a train to Euston, and then the Eurostar to Gare du Nord.

22
A HISTORICAL CASE

SINÉAD MULRONEY LEAVES Dublin a month before the Wednesday morning when Kate Delaney and Dolores Murphy take a taxi back to Pearse Street.

A female garda ushers them through a door behind the reception desk into a rabbit warren of corridors and they're brought into a little interview room. 'Would you like a cup of tea?' the woman asks.

'That would be lovely, pet,' says Dolores, and then regrets calling the garda 'pet', because she suspects that no one does that to any of the men. 'Sorry for calling you pet,' she says, colouring. 'I'm very anxious today.'

'Ah, go on with you—I think it's lovely,' says the garda, and she smiles.

As she hurries off to fetch the tea, Inspector Christy Redmond tap-taps on the door. He is a man nearing retirement, with snowy hair, a fit, slim build and pale green eyes permanently on the brink of smiling. For someone who has spent much of his professional life charting different types of human misery, he is remarkably cheerful and radiates a calmness that puts Dolores at ease. He's what used to be called a thorough gentleman.

'Dolores Murphy?' he says, clasping her hand, his eyes crinkling up in the corners in an agreeable way.

'That's me,' says Dolores. 'And this is my niece, Kate Delaney. She's here for support.'

'Well, we all need that,' he says, 'and especially in a situation like yours, Dolores—may I call you Dolores? I'm very pleased to meet you both. Now, I know that this is going to be very, very difficult. And since you're about to tell me a lot about yourself, I think it's only fair I tell you a bit about me, so it's not a one-way street.'

'I'd appreciate that very much, Inspector,' says Dolores.

'Ah, Dolores, you can call me Christy.'

Christy Redmond has, he tells her, just finished up several years as chief inspector of the Aran Islands, a job he loved not just for the beauty of the place, but for the friendliness of the people. That said, the job had its moments. He was once walloped by a drunk in Joe Watty's pub. And he was called to break up a fight at the dance hall which resembled a fish-filleting stall, after a man pulled out his knife and stabbed a local in the scrotum and the thigh. Dolores's eyes widened in alarm, but Christy assured her that while the victim had lost a good deal of blood, he had survived to dance another jig and drink another pint.

'On the whole,' Christy assures them, 'it was a pretty quiet job, and I was very happy to do it. In a post like that you are essentially in charge of everything. If you mess it up, there's no one else to blame, Dolores. And you see the full gamut of humanity in all of its good and its bad.'

What Christy Redmond did not reveal was that his main task while stationed on the islands was by any ordinary measure a grisly one. Every couple of months or so, he might be called to a beach on Inisheer because someone had seen a murder of hooded crows or an unkindness of ravens picking at a hand or a foot that had washed up on the rocks. In the old days, the body parts would have come from fishermen who had been blown off those same rocks, or drowned when their boats had been caught in the inhospitable seas of the North Atlantic. But in more recent times, the scavenger birds were more likely to have found the remains of jumpers who had ended their lives at the Cliffs of Moher. The signs for the Samaritans that Kate Delaney and Liam Carroll had seen when visiting in recent weeks were not, as Christy Redmond well knew, merely precautionary. When the stray hands or feet couldn't be identified, Christy would at times be dispatched to DNA labs in the UK to try to find a match. And then he'd fly home and head over to some little town in Clare from which someone had gone missing and inform whoever loved them that they'd been found.

It was a duty that Christy Redmond took very seriously, and one he was glad to be the one to do. He always treated those mothers and wives and husbands and friends and neighbours with the decency that he hoped he'd be given, if it were his son or daughter or spouse or great-uncle who had decided it was all too much.

Of course, he doesn't tell Dolores and Kate about the body parts, as he is a sensitive man, and he never does know what has come to pass in the lives of the people who sit before him. Which is just as well, as the story of the Cliffs of Moher would be chillingly resonant for Kate Delaney.

Christy then gets down to business. He explains that, unfortunately, Kate will have to leave the room while Dolores gives her formal statement, as it's important that Dolores's recollections are not in any way polluted by other people's interpretations or accounts.

'Did Garda John Barry mention that it will likely take a few hours for you to make this statement?'

'He did that,' says Dolores, taking a deep breath.

'If you don't mind, I'll be asking Garda Barry to take the notes while I conduct the interview.'

Dolores nods her assent.

'Will you be okay?' Kate asks her aunt.

'I'll be fine,' says Dolores.

'You're a bloody marvel.'

'It runs in the family.'

—

John Barry had not exaggerated in his estimate. The formal interview takes four hours in all, and Dolores is absolutely beaten at the end of it.

They take a short break, then Kate, who has filled the time doing damage to her credit card at Brown Thomas, rejoins them in the interview room.

'Now the good thing is,' Christy assures them, 'we have several clues here. We have some names, and we don't have others. But we have points from which to start an investigation, and that is a very positive thing. I must say, I've seen a lot, lot worse.'

'You have? Thank you Inspector . . . Christy,' Dolores says.

'Not at all,' says Christy. He motions them to allow Kate, apologetically laden with shopping bags, to come in and support Dolores again.

'Now, let's run through these names and locations, shall we? So, we have Mr Mackie. He's in Meath, somewhere near Navan.'

'That's correct, sir,' says John Barry.

'Well, if he's still around, he can confirm that he picked up Dolores on the road. And maybe he'd still be in contact with the Akenyemi family and we can ask them for a DNA sample. That will help if your daughter has for some reason been in contact with the Gardaí herself. We've got a phone box somewhere near the Hill of Tara and a phone call made in . . . let's see, the autumn of 1979? And that was put through to the station at Navan.'

'That's right,' says Dolores.

'Okay, one of us can head to the district office in Navan to check that out tomorrow. We've got a woman referred to as the Directress. Do you know anything about her?'

'I never even heard her name,' said Dolores. 'She was tall, with a sort of pigeon chest and a weirdly drawn on mouth and she'd pile her hair all up on top like some sort of Edwardian lady. I mean, that was one of the styles at the time. She may have changed that. She had very pale skin and her hair was a mid-brown, as I recall it. Dyed, like. She'd've likely gone grey by now.'

'All right. We've got two other Help: Clodagh O'Reilly and Mairéad O'Riordan. Now, where are they from, can you remember?'

'Mairéad was from Effin, near Charleville.'

'Well, that's a small place, which will be a help to us.'

'Yes. And Clodagh moved to Adelaide, to become a primary-school teacher. Alls I know is she married a man from somewhere around Ringsend-Irishtown called Danny. She called him the Champion of the World.'

'Well, that's a good nickname, Dolores.'

'She was smashing. Lovely, you know?'

Kate pipes up. 'I think I could help here. I could have someone check the electoral rolls in Adelaide.'

The inspector nods. 'Thank you, Kate.'

Kate nods, glad to be of help.

'She may also be on the Facebook,' Dolores suggests. 'There are lots of O'Reillys from Ringsend on there and she's liable to be connected to them. She might even know the Directress's name.'

'And what about Miss Nuala and Miss Róisín?' asks Christy. 'I assume we don't know their surnames?'

'No,' says Dolores. 'I suspect we were deliberately told as little as possible about them.'

'Could well be, could well be,' muses Christy. 'So, Miss Nuala was thirty-two when you first met her, you mentioned in your statement. So, she'd be pushing seventy now, I suppose. And the Directress—how old would you say she was?'

'She was dead old-fashioned in her ways, and back then I thought she was a hundred, but you know, I think she was probably in her fifties.'

'Right, so she'd be in her late eighties, up to ninety, then. Then, listen, we've got the O'Farrells, who were going to take the baby but didn't.'

'Yes,' says Dolores. 'But I don't know their first names and I had the impression that they were very much involved in the Group. I don't know how much help they'd be.'

'And the other one we've got is a Dr Lonergan. How old would you say he'd've been, Dolores?'

'I remember I thought he was very old at the time, too,' she replies. 'But he was probably my age now—you know, in his mid-fifties. I was sixteen. Everyone seemed old to me then.'

'I know what you mean,' says Christy Redmond. 'I remember thinking my mother ancient when she turned forty. Now, listen, Dolores. I think before we do anything else at all, we need to put some advertisements in the media, like an appeal—do you know what I mean?'

Dolores nods cautiously.

'There will be a young person out there who might well be wondering. I suspect the adoptive parents, such as they are, do not know the full story. How do you feel about that?'

'That sounds very overwhelming, if I'm absolutely honest,' says Dolores.

'The thing is, Dolores, apart from people who have guilty consciences—the Directress and Miss Nuala and the like—no one else will actually know that this relates to you.'

Dolores sits silently for a few moments. 'What if they come after me, Christy?' she asks in a tiny voice.

'Dolores, if these people were going to come after you, they would have done it by now,' he says, giving her hand a pat. 'They've known all along where your parents live in Ringsend. There are a lot of powerful people connected to the Group—I know, because we've had pressure from them right up to the Commissioner about other matters. And I can tell you without a word of a lie, Dolores, that he has stood firm. But right now, the easiest way for us to get information is for us to put some notices in the newspaper and then sit back and see what filters in. And meanwhile, we'll contact who we can contact. But I do agree with the assessment of your niece here. This was child stealing, Dolores, and it was abuse. And I won't stand for it.'

Kate likes this man. 'What do you think, Dolores?'

'Okay, let's fucking do it. Pardon my language, Inspector.'

'Desperate times call for desperate language, Dolores. I'd curse, too.'

'Me too, like, for what it's worth,' says John Barry.

Dolores feels safer than she's ever felt. And more vulnerable than she's ever felt. And more hopeful than she's ever felt.

—

They publish full-page ads in the *Irish Times* and the *Irish Independent*, and put up posters around town, seeking information in relation to a half-Nigerian baby girl who was born in 1979 in County Meath and stolen from her sixteen-year-old Irish mother. Christy Redmond feels absolutely certain that the parents who took the baby will see the ad and know it refers to their daughter. Whether or not they will come forward is another matter entirely. He suspects the Directress and Miss Nuala will go to ground, but he's not too bothered about them at this stage—though things could get pretty ugly for them down the track. He's absolutely certain that the Directress at least will have access to the finest barristers in the country and that she will not give herself up easily. He's seen her like before. They employ the help of politicians and priests. They start culture wars. They fight dirty. They embark on expensive, covert PR campaigns—including against the Gardaí themselves and the victims of their crimes. They cry witch hunt. They are usually men and their friends say, 'This is not the man I know.' When it is a woman, it's even more devastating, because their femininity disarms the public. They try to wear down prosecutors and complainants. They're brutal.

—

Two days later, Donal Mulroney is reading the *Irish Times* with his rashers and eggs when he sees something that makes him spill his hot tea all over the newspaper.

'Maureen! Come quick, love,' Donal calls.

Maureen, who hasn't slept more than an hour or two a night in the weeks since Sinéad went off in a taxi, runs into the dining room.

'What is it?' she asks, wiping her hands on her apron, fearing the worst.

Donal straightens his tea-stained newspaper and shows her the full-page ad about the historical case of the stolen Nigerian baby girl. It's underneath the latest revelations about the dead babies at the Tuam mother and baby home.

Maureen Mulroney's heart feels like it has stopped. 'Oh, Donal,' she says finally. 'What should we do?'

'I don't know, love. Perhaps we'd be best to sit tight.'

'Well, we could call the Gards, like it asks.'

'And then what, Maureen? Then what? Who knows what kind of trouble we might find ourselves in? At least we know that Sinéad is unlikely to see it, since she's left the country and switched off that infernal phone. If we just keep quiet, it might all blow over.'

'But Donal, how many people know? How many people know that we got this baby at that time? There can't have been very many baby girls fitting that description born in 1979. We know there weren't. I mean, Margaret O'Farrell and the ladies in the parish knew, and they knew the circumstances in which it was done. You know those adoption papers we have aren't legitimate. We never even met the mammy. This must have been started by her somehow. Oh, holy mother of God, Donal. This cannot come to any good.'

'I think we need to make contact with the people who organised the adoption,' Donal says.

'Sure, what can they do, Donal?'

'I don't know, Maureen, but we need to speak to them. I'll think on it today and make a phone call tomorrow.'

Donal and Maureen Mulroney drift around the house all day, not knowing what to say to each other. They feel paralysed by fear. That night, they go to bed but they don't sleep at all. They lie next to each other as stiff as boards, their matching pale eyelashes framing matching red-rimmed eyes.

That night, Sinéad Mulroney is on a Tinder date in Prague. She's been out for sushi and is about seven sakes down. She's working part-time for now, teaching evening English classes to college students. She doesn't think she'll hang around, but it doesn't really matter. She dates girls some nights and boys others. She has a brilliant time with both. She thinks about telling tonight's date about her history, but fuck it, she thinks, you only live once. He won't want to know. Her Irish SIM card is tucked away in a zipped-up compartment of her wallet. She's loving the freedom she now has, on a European burner mobile phone. Completely uncontactable. She hasn't looked at her Facebook page. She doesn't watch the Irish news or read the papers. Sure, she'll go back home eventually. In a few weeks. Or months. Or whenever. But for now that life seems so far away, and it feels fucking great.

She rides her date like a pony.

Two days later, Donal and Maureen Mulroney disappear. They are in their late seventies by then, retired and leading very quiet lives. No one is expecting them. They don't belong to clubs and while they do go to mass, it's folly for priests to monitor attendance in the way they once did. It doesn't do to know how many people are dropping off each month, even if they are fairly observant parishioners like Donal and Maureen. The prayers of the faithful will have to be read by someone else. The Mulroneys' parents are long dead and those of their siblings who are still alive are in care homes or, in one case, Canada.

With Sinéad off the grid, no one notices that they are missing until much later, when their Volkswagen is found abandoned in a field in the Wicklow Mountains. Donal and Maureen are not in the car. The boot is open and waterlogged with rain. Local deer have been drinking from it. All that's left in the car is a statue of Our Lady, white robes, blue crown, containing holy water, swinging from the rear-view mirror.

—

Christy Redmond decides he'll start with the low-hanging fruit—the people he knows live or lived in Ireland for whom he has surnames. Mr Mackie, the grocer near Navan in County Meath, shouldn't be hard to find. Nor will Mairéad O'Riordan. In the basement at Pearse Street they have phone books going back to the 1950s and he finds a yellowing one from the late seventies, choking on the cloud of dust that bursts into the air as he pulls it down from a high shelf.

He runs his finger down the list of grocers in Meath.

Dermot Mackie's Fresh Fruit and Vegetables. Oldtown Road. He returns to his desk and looks up the address on his computer.

It draws a blank. The business doesn't seem to exist anymore—which isn't a surprise given the state of Mr Mackie's health thirty-five years ago. He looks up the Register of Electors. No Dermot Mackie. There would have been a police report for Marcus Akenyemi's accident. He asks John Barry to call the Navan police station and get them to look for it, and while they're at it to check their call logs from 1979 to see if there is a record of a young woman phoning about a stolen baby.

'And you might pay a visit to the Mackie property on Oldtown Road and see if there's anyone still living there. Perhaps there's a Mrs Mackie? If so, ask her if Dermot mentioned picking up this girl, and whether she stayed in contact with the Akenyemi family and has their contact details.'

'Yes, sir,' says John.

'Sure, it's a start. I'm going to see if I can find this Mairéad O'Riordan.' He wonders if she is still in the tiny town outside of Charleville. He googles 'Mairéad' and 'Effin', and the first hit is a PDF of a school newsletter. On page three is a picture of a woman with a ruddy complexion and a no-nonsense expression on her face, standing at a cake stall.

—

'Effin National School, this is Mairéad,' says a singsong voice on the other end of the phone.

He knows it is fiendishly juvenile, but Christy struggles to stifle a giggle. He clears his throat.

'Yes, yes, hilarious,' Mairéad says. 'Have you already taken your Instagram selfie out the front? Just make sure that there aren't any children in the photos, please.'

'I'm terribly sorry,' he says. 'It's Inspector Christy Redmond here from the Pearse Street Gardaí in Dublin.'

'Oh, Inspector, I'm the one who's sorry. I was only messing with you. We just get a lot of them oul' prank calls.'

'I can imagine you do,' he says.

'Do you know Facebook wouldn't even let us post? They kept banning us because they said our name was offensive. It made the papers a few years ago and now we do be getting all these people ringing up who think it's absolute gas, Inspector.'

'That must be wearying, Mairéad.'

'It is. Now, how can I help you?'

'I just wanted to check that you are indeed Mairéad O'Riordan?'

'I am,' she says. 'Or at least, I was until I got married. I'm an O'Malley now. But what do you want from me, Inspector?'

'Oh, you're not at all in trouble, Mairéad. I am just hoping you might be able to help me with a historical case I'm investigating.'

The phone goes silent for a few beats.

'I see. Well, I'll do the best I can. Can you tell me what it's about?' she asks in a low voice.

'I'd rather talk to you in person, Mairéad, if it's all the same to you.'

'Sure, sure. No bother.'

'I'll head down there tomorrow, if you don't mind. What time do you finish work?'

'I'm done at half three. Listen, Inspector, I'll meet you at Jimmy's Bar at quarter to four.'

'Grand.'

'Right, so.'

Mairéad places the receiver down and stares at her grey Laminex desk for a good minute. She wraps her cardigan around herself, feeling cold suddenly. *A historical case.*

23

EFFIN

CHRISTY REDMOND IS a punctual man and so he leaves Dublin early for the drive down to Effin, a tiny dairy farming town where County Limerick bleeds into County Cork. Jimmy's Bar is a small, grey, unremarkable pub at the top of a hill, with low ceilings and very few visitors from anywhere else. When Christy walks in the door at twenty-five to four, all six of the locals sitting in one corner crane their necks and look at him for a good thirty seconds.

'Afternoon,' says Christy, tipping his hat.

'Afternoon, Garda,' says the barman, even though Christy isn't wearing a uniform.

Am I that obvious? he wonders.

He orders a packet of salt and vinegar crisps and a half-pint of low-alcohol beer, then carries them to the furthest corner from the locals who are pretending to watch the football on the telly while surreptitiously watching him.

Mairéad O'Malley arrives punctually at quarter to four.

'How's it going, Mairéad?' asks the barman as she enters.

'Can't complain,' she answers. She glances around the pub, sees Christy in the corner and gives him a stiff nod. 'Could I have a gin and tonic, Aidan?' she asks the barman.

She brings her drink over to Christy's table and slides into the seat opposite.

'Listen,' he says quietly, 'why don't we finish these drinks quickly and then head somewhere a bit more private for you. Is home far away? Could we go there?'

'I'd rather not, all the same,' says Mairéad.

'I understand,' says Christy. 'Okay, let's just talk about ordinary things and then we can head out to my car to have a proper conversation.'

'That sounds fine to me,' she says. 'I just want to say to you, Inspector, that I'm not at all comfortable talking about the past, if that's what you're here for.' She sits with her arms folded across her chest. Mairéad O'Malley's once-mousy hair is now grey and cut short. She's quite stout and wearing a fawn Fair Isle jumper, sensible trousers and sensible shoes. She looks, Christy thinks, like the sort of woman you could rely on to run a raffle. She does not look remotely like the sort of woman who would ever want to draw attention to herself, or to be seen with a visiting policeman investigating a case. She's blushing, her freckles disappearing into the crimson of her cheeks, as the locals in the corner try to see what's going on.

'I know these things can be difficult, Mairéad.'

'I'm not one for a fuss, Inspector.'

They down their drinks as quickly as is respectable and then head out to Christy Redmond's car. They drive in silence to a remote road and Christy pulls over.

'It's to do with Rome, isn't it?' she asks, folding her arms tightly across her chest again and gazing out the windscreen.

'What makes you say that, Mairéad?'

'Well, Inspector, for the most part,' she says, pulling at one of her gold huggie earrings, 'I've led a very quiet life. I've never had any trouble and I've never been any trouble. I answer the phones at a lovely little school with an admittedly funny name. I live in a town where everyone knows everyone and year in, year out, there's hardly a spot of bother. There is nothing else in my life that would ever cause any garda to be asking me questions. It can only be that shower from County Galway and their so-called cookery classes and Daddy fetching me home from Rome.'

Mairéad looks like she wants to be sick.

'And to be honest, Inspector, I have absolutely no interest in speaking about what happened to me, only that once I'd had kids of my own, I began to think that if anyone did . . .' She trails off and looks out the window at the cows in the field. 'If anyone ever did anything to them, I'd knock their block off, God forgive me.

And I can only assume that the reason you're wanting to talk to me is because there's been a problem with another girl. So, I'll help you. Off the record, like. If there is such a thing.' Her palms become sticky, and she wipes them on her fawn trousers. 'But other than that, I really don't know why I agreed to come.'

'That's very good of you, Mairéad,' says Christy Redmond. 'I wanted to ask you if you remember Dolores Murphy.'

She exhales slowly. 'Of course I do. How could I forget her?'

'Would you describe her as a truth-teller?'

'Now, Inspector, that's a very long time ago. And even though we were both stuck in that awful place, and then the only ones who went to Rome, I hardly got to know her. And I think that was deliberate, on their part. They didn't encourage us to become friends. In some ways, when I reflect on it now, they almost set us against each other.'

'Dolores said the same,' Christy Redmond replied.

'Well, she would. But if you are asking me if I thought she was a liar, I don't remember anything that would suggest she was. She was a different sort of person from me. More of a dreamer, I suppose. A bit mouthier, in as much as anyone could be mouthy in that environment. I hope she is all right, though. I've always wondered how she got on.'

'Do you remember Miss Nuala and Miss Róisín?' he asks quietly.

Mairéad takes off her seatbelt and opens the car door. She gets out and stands up, arms crossed, looking out across the fields.

Christy gets out to join her.

There is a single tear running down her cheek, he notices. He puts a hand on her shoulder, and she flinches slightly.

'I've tried all my life to stop thinking about them. I was a child, Inspector. I mean, I know I was a teenager, but a fifteen-year-old from a farm in Effin in the seventies was the equivalent of a twelve-year-old from Dublin now, when it comes to that sort of thing. And a pretty unsophisticated twelve-year-old at that. She made me so confused. She made me hate myself for years.'

'So, Miss Róisín . . . how should I put this? She interfered with you?'

'Yes. But it is very, very hard for me to put into words. My husband, Gerry, knows nothing of this. My mam and dad knew, of course, but not the details. In retrospect, I feel very proud of the girl I was, Inspector, that I had the courage to tell them as much as I did. And I love my daddy, God rest his soul, for coming to get me away. And I know by the looks on Dolores's face back then that something was happening there, too. So, I'm guessing you're here because something similar happened to Dolores.'

'I'm very sorry to hear what you went through, Mairéad, and that is something I will want to look into, but it's not the primary reason I'm here today.'

She stares at him. 'Then why are you here?' She is trying not to betray her anger: at him for dragging out of her something that she had long kept buried; at herself for speaking up when there was no need.

'Well, I wanted to ask if you knew Miss Róisín's or Miss Nuala's surnames, or if you remember the name of the Directress.'

'Ah, now, I've often thought about that. They never told us. Which, as I got older and the enormity of what they had done to us dawned on me. I mean, beyond the, well, sexual interference, there was the slavery. There's no other word for it, Inspector. They treated the Help like slaves.' She shakes her head in disgust. 'And I could see it in that Help in Rome. I am trying to remember her name. Was it Rosamaria?'

'Dolores told me Rosaria.'

'No, that's right. It was Rosaria. She kept trying to pull me aside when she had tiny little moments to warn me. It was only ever snippets. She knew. She could see the misery and the shame in me. And she also wanted me to know that they weren't paying her. And I asked her about the whipping. Did Dolores tell you about that?' Mairéad's face is almost purple now.

'She did, aye.'

'Dolores and me never discussed it, but I assumed they were introducing her to it, too. And the chain? The spiky chain. Oh, God forgive me, my language, but it was so incredibly fucked up, Inspector. There's no other way to say it. That they were encouraging teenagers to hurt themselves, supposedly as a penance, or mortification, or whatever they called it, for Our Lord. As if Jesus, a gentle man, would want teenage girls to be harming themselves. Well, that's not the Jesus we learned about in mass down here. It's not the Jesus they're teaching the children about in our school. And then . . . touching us while they talked about it. Disgusting, so it was. And then pretending they were all holier than thou and leading a life of celibacy for Our Lord and the Father, and all that. Oh, Inspector, it makes me so, so angry.'

'I'd say it does, Mairéad,' he says, sighing. 'I'd say it does.'

'But no, I don't know their surnames, and I don't know the Directress's name. I hope they're all burning in hell. Do you know, I used to lie awake and dream of burning that place down with them all in it?'

'I'd say you did, Mairéad,' the inspector says gently. 'But I'm awful glad that you didn't. When you left, did you ever hear from any of them again?'

'Not a word. It was like I had never existed as far as they were concerned. And for so many years, it felt like a bad, bad dream. Mam and Dad didn't want to talk about it—I think back then, they felt that it was better just to brush it all under the carpet and move on. And I was mortified, like, Inspector. Absolutely mortified. So, there was no way I was talking about it. There was no language to use. So here we are, and the first person I'm talking to about this in thirty-odd years is a gard I've never met before. Life is a funny old thing.'

'It is that, Mairéad. I'm sorry.'

'Ah, don't be. It's hurting me to talk about it, but in some ways it's like the release of a pressure valve, Inspector.'

'Call me Christy, Mairéad.'

'It doesn't seem right.'

They were silent for a spell.

'So, what is it that you're investigating?'

'Well, I can't say too much, I'm afraid, and I appreciate that must seem hypocritical, since you've just told me things you haven't told a soul in thirty-five years.'

'I understand how criminal investigations work, Inspector.'

'Sorry, I don't mean to patronise you. But I am investigating the matter of a stolen baby. Well, she's no longer a baby, of course.'

She turns and looks at him. 'Dolores's baby?'

'Aye.'

'They took it?'

'That's what she alleges.'

'Those monsters.'

'They don't sound like the best people, all the same.'

'It doesn't surprise me for one second. Not one. Poor Dolores. You know, Inspector'—Mairéad wipes her eyes—'I have felt bad about Dolores. I felt guilty for leaving her there. That I didn't open up to her. That I didn't ask her what she was going through. I let my daddy come and take me home and I left her with those witches.'

'Listen, Mairéad, that's a lot to put on yourself. You were still a child, remember. And a victim.'

'I know that now, but it didn't stop me feeling terrible in my heart for years.'

'Well, if you don't mind me saying, Mairéad, you're making up for it now.'

'How so?'

'By talking to me. And if you'd be good enough to be a witness in this case, that would be another way. But I don't want to put that on you now, either. And I know it's a big decision.'

'It is,' she says. 'This is a small place, Inspector.'

'Yes.'

'And that'd mean having to talk to my Gerry. And the kids.'

'I'm sure it would mean a good few difficult conversations. But I'm also sure you'd agree that these people need to be stopped.'

'They do,' she says immediately. 'They definitely do. Listen here, Inspector. Give me a day or two to think on it.'

'I will that, Mairéad. Sometimes we have to take the right path, instead of the easy path.'

She nods. 'In the meantime, I'm going to put on my thinking cap and see if there isn't anything I can remember that might help you find these people.'

'I'd appreciate that. And one last thing, Mairéad: am I right in assuming your daddy has passed away? What about your mammy?'

'Mammy's in a care home with the dementia,' she says, 'and, yes, Daddy died a good ten years ago.'

'Sorry for your loss.'

'He was a good man, Inspector.'

'It sounds like he did the right thing when it was called for.'

'That he did.'

'That's all we can ask from a father.'

Christy Redmond and Mairéad O'Malley get back into the car and he drives her along the narrow, hedge-lined road and back up the hill to Jimmy's Bar, where her car is parked outside.

'Thank you, Inspector,' she says, looking straight ahead through the windscreen. It has started lashing rain, and the light of the pub windows glows orange through the droplets as the wipers swing back and forth.

'Well, the thanks are all mine, Mairéad.'

'No, they're not, all the same. Thank you for being kind. It feels good to have spoken.'

'Well, it's a privilege to be the one to hear it, Mairéad, as much as I wish it never happened.'

'You're a good man, I see that.'

'I try. Mind yourself, Mairéad.'

'Mind yourself, Inspector.'

She gets out and runs through the rain to her car.

Christy Redmond watches her drive away into the sodden Effin darkness.

And Christy has that feeling one so often has in policing that someone has said so much, that it was such an effort for them, and yet in reality they have said so little. You have gone on a huge emotional journey with them and yet you've only inched ever so slightly forward in your investigation.

—

Mairéad O'Malley née O'Riordan can't stop thinking. Her mind whirs and whirs.

She pulls up to the cottage she and Gerry had built on the edge of Daddy's land and opens the front door.

'Gerry, love, you need to sit down.'

—

Two days later, Christy Redmond gets a call from a County Limerick landline.

'Right so, Inspector. I'm in. And you need to go to the church at Merrion, in case Dolores didn't mention it. That's where a few of them would go. And Miss Róisín—ah, feck it, I'm not calling her Miss now—she was an accountant, by training at least. She told me she went to UCD. And she had worked at a small firm in Ranelagh for a time, I remember. I'd say she was thirtyish when I met her. I don't know if that helps much. But I'll keep racking my brain, so I will.'

So little information, but again, Christy Redmond knows, to her, so much.

'You're a very good woman, Mairéad O'Malley. Thank you.'

Mairéad is smiling as she puts the phone back in its cradle on her grey Laminex desk. It immediately starts to ring.

'Effin National School, this is Mairéad.'

And the caller, who sounds like a fourteen-year-old boy, laughs out loud and says, 'Effin great!'

'Hilarious, go on and get your selfie out the front,' she says. But as she hangs up the phone again, she laughs out loud, for a long time. *Effin great.*

'You all right there, Mairéad?' asks Tommy Curran, the janitor, who is passing by her desk in reception.

'Never better, Tommy. Never better.'

And Mairéad O'Malley folds her cardigan around herself and gets on with counting the money from the hurling fundraiser.

—

On the drive back to Dublin after speaking to Mairéad, Christy Redmond calls John Barry.

'John, I need a list of all of the Nualas and Róisíns who did accountancy and theology at UCD in the late sixties or early seventies. And maybe a year or two after. Frankly, there can't have been that many even in a ten-year period. So few women graduating from anything back then. And then when you take out all the other names, you should be grand.'

'Right, Inspector, consider it done.'

John calls back a few hours later.

'Found them, Inspector. Nuala Christine O'Rourke got her PhD in 1972. Róisín Margaret Downes graduated in economics the same year then went and got herself a postgraduate qualification in accounting. They were both at a university residence. So, it seems they knew each other before they went to work for the Directress in County Galway.'

'Brilliant work—you know what to do next.'

'Register of Electors, check on those two names? On it, Inspector. I'll check all our data files, too. Assuming you'll pay the visit to the residence?'

'Right you are, John.'

'By the way, I had the district office in Navan check the phone records. There was a call from a phone box in 1979 about a missing baby that matches Dolores's recollection of what she said. The file says they would keep a watching brief but there's nothing more. I haven't got to the Mackie place yet, either, so I'll head up there and see what's what.'

24

DUBLIN 4

CHRISTY REDMOND KNOCKS on the door of a white mock-Georgian terrace that somehow brings to mind a Barbie Dreamhouse if Barbie lived in Dublin 4 instead of southern California. The gardens are too pristine, the furnishings too chintzy. The floors too clean, the knocker too shiny, the front step too polished. It seems far too sterile for a place where university students loll about. The young women he does see are not the rainbow flag-waving, piercing-laden, navel-baring young women you often saw on campuses these days. They remind him of the paparazzi pictures of Kate Middleton when she was at St Andrew's College with Prince William. Hair that's been carefully fashioned into bouncy ponytails. Barely there make-up. Chocolate knee-high boots that have an equestrian air. Knits made of angora and cashmere. Double-breasted cream coats. That sort of thing. It all spells money.

He gives his details to a receptionist, whose eyes widen ever so slightly.

'Why of course, Inspector. I'll see if the Directress is available.'

'Thanks a million,' says Christy, hoping his expression doesn't betray the little light that goes off in his mind when he hears that term. Surely it can't be; she'd be much too old.

He's right. The woman who walks in couldn't be more than forty-five. Younger than Dolores Murphy is now, let alone Dolores's Directress.

'Well, hello, Inspector . . .'

'Redmond,' says Christy, offering her his hand. 'Inspector Christy Redmond, Pearse Street Gardaí.'

'And to what do I owe the pleasure, Inspector Redmond?' She shakes his hand limply but does not give him her name.

'And you are?' Christy prompts.

'Oh! Silly me. Gráinne Kelly. I'm the Directress of the college.'

'I didn't realise they still used those feminised titles, Ms Kelly,' Christy says with a little chuckle. 'You know, poetess. Songstress. Executrix. I thought they were considered old-fashioned now—especially on a university campus.'

Gráinne Kelly gives him a stiff smile. Her light brown hair, with subtle rivers of gold that catch the light, looks expensively dyed. It's held back with a black velvet headband studded with pearls. She has a mole above her carefully arched left eyebrow. 'We like to maintain a sense of tradition here,' she says. 'We feel it sets an example to the young women who come here: of solidity and permanence and ties with the past, as well as looking to the future. We strive to nurture intelligent, educated, modern women, but we don't see why the traditions that have stood the test of time for so long ought to be, well, you know, discarded.' She gives a theatrical wave of her hand. Gráinne Kelly speaks like the text of an upscale marketing brochure. 'Would you like some tea, Inspector Redmond? I've just made a pot.'

'That'd be grand, thanks, Ms Kelly.'

'Mrs.'

'Mrs.' He nods. 'Of course.'

'What can I do for you, Inspector?' Gráinne Kelly asks, settling into a salmon velvet armchair and pouring tea from a silver pot. He notices that her collarbones protrude and her wrists are tiny. She has the whitest teeth he has ever seen. And a fat pear-shaped diamond engagement ring.

'Do you take milk? And sugar?'

'A sup of milk and one sugar, thanks very much.'

She pours the milk from a china jug and plops a sugar cube into the cup with a small pair of tongs then looks at him expectantly.

'Well, I've come to inquire about some alumni from the college,' he says.

'Oh, yes? I trust, please God, none of our girls have come to harm?'

'Oh, Janey, not at all. This is a historical matter, you see, Ms—Mrs Kelly.'

A glimmer of relief flickers across her face. The relief that says, *Not my jurisdiction.* 'I see. How historical, exactly, Inspector?'

'Well, it involves two women who graduated from here in the early seventies.'

'Goodness, when I was a small child. That is indeed historical.'

'Yes, very much so. But I did wonder if perhaps the college kept up a connection with its alumni. Social events and so forth. The two women I'm interested in would have been some of the earlier boarders here, I believe, at a time when there were not many women attending the university. One of them even got a PhD. And so, I could be wrong'—he looks up at her, directly, and she gives another quick, forced smile—'but I imagine they would have been, well, celebrated. Looked up to. The sort of women that you might have back for, I don't know, morning teas or whatnot, if you catch my drift, Ms Kelly.'

'Mrs.'

'*Mrs*. Sorry.'

She looks at him searchingly for a few seconds. 'Well, it's true that we do have alumni events. Morning teas, if you like. Dinners. And we have masses in our chapel here. Sure, come and have a look, it's a dear little place.' She stands up and ushers him into a pastel-hued chapel, its roof beams decorated with ornate Celtic knots.

'A lovely place to worship, I'm sure,' says Christy, who has lost his faith on account of the fact that the benevolent God he was brought up to believe in couldn't have allowed anyone to do the things to children he'd seen catalogued in diabolically ordered ring binders. Couldn't have allowed teen drivers to have to be scraped off motorways, nor, more to the point, that deity's own priests to be moved from parish to parish to ruin the lives of even more children. '*God is good*,' Father Fitzgerald used to tell them in mass when Christy was still going. '*No, he's not*,' Christy Redmond began to think. '*He's really not*.' First, he stopped taking communion. Then he just gave up going altogether.

'Well, getting to the point, do either of these names ring a bell for you, Mrs Kelly? Nuala O'Rourke and'—he takes a notepad from his pocket and consults it—'Róisín Downes.' He looks directly into her eyes. And he can see it in her eyes.

She knows. She knows. She knows.

'Let me think,' she says slowly. 'You know, Inspector, I would have to get on to some of my former colleagues who were here during those years. It may be that I have indeed met those two women you mentioned, but I would really need to check my records and speak to the elders. How about I do that? I'm assuming, given this matter is historical in nature, you're not in an awful rush.'

'If you have records that you can check here with me now, I'm happy to wait. It's no bother at all, Mrs Kelly. No bother.'

'Oh, there would be a lot of rummaging through the archives, Inspector.'

'I'm a patient man, Mrs Kelly.'

She looks at him for a moment, pursing her lips. They're painted the colour of new rosebuds. 'Do you have a warrant, Inspector? I can't imagine that you do.'

He looks back at her. 'I didn't come here expecting to need one, Mrs Kelly. I just wanted to ask if anyone knew the whereabouts of Nuala O'Rourke and Róisín Downes.'

'Well, sir, I don't.'

She smooths her skirt and folds her legs to the side, with one ankle folded over the other, like she's having an audience with the Queen. She takes a sip of her tea—more of a loud slurp, which surprises him, given all her carefully choreographed nods to gentility. He hates tea-slurping.

'If that's the way it is to be, I can get a warrant to search the premises, Mrs Kelly,' he says, in a much sterner voice. 'But now, I'm sure you're not wanting that sort of fuss? A shower of gardaí turning the place over?' He looks around. 'Doesn't seem like the sort of impression you'd want to be giving off. Also, if you don't mind me saying, Mrs Kelly, I'm a little confused about why you're bothered about this at all, given that all of this well predates your time here. And nothing is being alleged about the college itself. I'm simply trying to track down a couple of women who might be able to assist me with an investigation. Potential witnesses, like.'

As they're speaking, a message flashes up on his phone from Garda John Barry. 'Excuse me, Mrs Kelly,' he says. Opening the message, he sees that—with exquisite timing—John has sent him a photo of a college alumni event from six years ago. In the centre of a row of women stands a well-groomed older woman with ash-grey hair drawn back in combs and pale blue eyes. The caption reads: *Old girl and PhD pioneer Nuala O'Rourke visits the College to inspire our students, reminding them that they can do anything!* Off to the left-hand side is a woman with light brown shoulder-length hair who is smiling broadly in Nuala's direction. She appears to be mid-clap. She looks delighted. Christy Redmond squints his eyes and enlarges the photograph on his smartphone screen. There, above her left eyebrow, is a mole.

'Okay, Mrs Kelly, we need to stop playing these little games.' He shows her the photo on his phone. 'You seem very pleased to be in Nuala O'Rourke's company there. Perhaps you should search your memory again?'

She stiffens. 'I do remember that visit now. Thank you for refreshing my memory, Inspector. So many faces coming through these doors! She was a most impressive woman, as I remember. I'm just terrible with names.'

'Have you ever spoken to her since?'

'Listen, Inspector, if it is all the same to you, this is beginning to feel like a formal interview. And if that's the case, I'd like to have some legal advice.'

'Well, Mrs Kelly,' Christy says, folding his arms, 'this has certainly escalated.'

'One can't be too careful when one is in a leadership position, responsible for safeguarding young women. It is a big responsibility, and it is one I take very seriously, Inspector.'

'Reputation is always a factor, too, I'd imagine?'

She smiles and rings a little porcelain bell. A woman of Latin American appearance dressed in an old-fashioned maid's uniform arrives.

'Valeria,' Mrs Kelly says, in an exaggerated Spanish accent that sets Christy's teeth on edge, 'be a dear and show Inspector Redmond to the door.'

'Yes, Directress,' says Valeria.

Gráinne Kelly gives him her hand again. It's so limp it sends a shiver down his spine. She breaks into a saccharine smile. 'So pleased to have made your acquaintance, Inspector.'

'You'll be hearing from me, Ms Kelly.'

'Mrs.'

Christy nods and follows Valeria down the corridor. He notices that her shoes are very worn, and she seems to be in pain as she walks.

'Are you Help, Valeria?' he asks her.

Without turning she replies, 'Yes, I am. Why do you ask?'

'Are you okay? Really okay?'

She stops then and looks at him. She appears frightened.

He takes a business card out of his wallet. 'Here, Valeria, you tuck that in your apron. I am an inspector at Pearse Street

Garda Station. You can call me any time. I promise you I'll look after you.'

Valeria nods almost imperceptibly and wipes away a tear. He reaches out to comfort her, but she shakes her head vigorously. 'Please go, Inspector.'

'I understand, Valeria,' he says quietly. 'But don't you lose that card.'

'I don't have the use of a phone,' she whispers, casting an anxious glance down the hall. 'They listen to my calls.'

'I'll sort it,' he says. He pushes through the front door and walks down the steps. Turning back for one last look, he notices a CCTV camera. He waves to it with a big smile, and then heads to his car, repressing the urge to shudder.

—

Back at Pearse Street, he pulls up a swivel chair next to John Barry, who is eating an egg sandwich. 'Janey, would you ever stop eating egg in the office, John? It stinks to high heaven.'

'I do love an egg sambo, Christy. So, how'd you go with that crowd over at the university residence?'

'It's the cleanest place I've been to in a very long time, and yet I feel the need to run a hot bath,' Christy Redmond says. 'Very strange. Odd, pretentious woman running the college, also called Directress, like the woman that enslaved poor Dolores

Murphy and stole her babby. She also got real defensive when I asked her if she knew O'Rourke and Downes. Said she couldn't remember if she'd met them. Classic "I don't recall" shite. And then when I showed her that photo you sent, she says she wants a bleeding lawyer.'

'Well, that's not one bit suspicious at all,' says John Barry, rolling his eyes as he swallows his last bite of egg sandwich.

'Not one single bit,' says Christy Redmond. 'The other thing is, the woman who showed me out was wearing one of them oul' maid's uniforms that Dolores described. I asked if she was Help and she confirmed that she was. So I gave her my card and told her she could call me any time, and she looked that scared. Then she told me she didn't have access to a phone, and that they'd listen on the landline if she made a call on their phone.'

'Christ.'

'Yes. You know, I think this investigation into Dolores and her baby, well, it could just be the start.'

'I think you could be right, Inspector.'

'So how did you go with the Register of Electors?'

'Well, Downes left the country fifteen years ago and hasn't been back since. I did a bit of advanced googling, and it seems like she was at one time in one of their residences in Spain and, at another, she pops up in Massachusetts, then Berkeley. That's where she was last, at least as far as Google is concerned. But that was ten years ago.'

'No death notices?'

'Not that I could find through open sources. I'll get on to the police in California to see if any death has been recorded.'

'Hmm. And what about O'Rourke?'

'Well, she was registered at that house in County Galway for many, many years. And then she drops off. No death recorded either. I did wonder if perhaps she had gone into a care home?'

'Perhaps,' Christy says, 'but listen, she'd only be in her early seventies, so not that old in the scheme of things. And from the looks of that photograph you found from six years ago, she looked well preserved.'

'She did that, Inspector. But that Alzheimer's can strike early. My auntie Margaret got it at fifty-nine.'

'True, that. But let's not get ahead of ourselves. Now, did you have any luck with the Mackie property back in County Meath?'

John Barry shakes his head. 'No, it was sold years ago. Mrs Mackie's dead, too. They had four girls—they're scattered around the area on farms, like. I'm not sure if we'd have much luck with them, though.'

Christy Redmond sighs. Sometimes it seems that all of the doors are closed. 'I'm going to go and get some air and have a think, John. Kate Delaney, Dolores Murphy's niece, mentioned she was going to see if she could track down Clodagh O'Reilly.'

'The Help who moved to Australia? Handy having a journalist on the case, Christy.'

'Well, we don't want to rely on her, but if she did manage to locate Clodagh, we'll see if we can't get the South Australian police to help out. I'm loath to get Kate Delaney too involved. You know her back story, John?'

The garda shakes his head. 'No, sir.'

'She was brutally raped and kidnapped last year. Left to die in a cage under a bridge. Then when things got too hot for the kidnapper, didn't he throw himself off a hotel balcony over in Surfers Paradise?'

'Christ,' says John Barry, whistling through his teeth. 'That's very heavy. To look at her, I'd never have guessed she'd gone through something like that.'

'Indeed, but we just need to tread a bit lightly with her. Dolores has told me that while her niece puts on a brave face, she's not doing so great.'

'Understood, Inspector.'

'Good man. Here, another thing. I want you to go back to that university college. Given who runs it, I imagine it'll have a separate entrance for the Help, right?'

'No doubt.'

'I want you to get a burner phone and go there and watch for a Mexican-looking woman in a maid's uniform to come out. Monday mornings are bin collection day, so I'd say Sunday evening would be your best bet. If her name is Valeria, show her your badge and give her the burner. Tell her it's from me and she's to give me a call if she needs anything. But make sure not to give it to the wrong person. She had long hair pulled back tight in a bun, like, and she walks with a bit of a limp. I'd say she's about five six, slim build. Ever so slightly protruding teeth. She had small silver hoop earrings the day I saw her.'

'No bother, Inspector.'

Christy Redmond walks out of the office and, seeing the usual grim scene in the foyer, thanks the universe for the eleventy-billionth time that he's no longer a general duties garda having to manage all the misery. He exits the station and crosses the road to Trinity College. On one side of the Front Square, some young women are handing out leaflets about the campaign to try to Repeal the Eighth. On the other side, some queer kids have set up a stall with information about legalising gay marriage. He continues to the lawn, where he overhears an animated brunette and her boyfriend arguing over when exactly Martin Amis lost it altogether. Another couple are lying hand in hand on a picnic blanket, looking suspiciously like they may have just enjoyed a spliff. The thing that strikes Christy, as he looks around him, are all the young women. Fizzing with life in all its messy glory. Full of book-smart ideas and righteous anger and never, ever taking a backward step in expressing their opinions.

And Christy Redmond thinks of teenage Dolores in the library. And her baby. And Valeria. And of all the Help, funnelled into servitude by parental ineptitude or negligence or poverty or ignorance. By the vestiges of colonialism and theocracy and men putting the pint before their families. Dolores could have lolled on these lawns. Dolores could have raised her hand to ask questions in lectures. Gingerly at first, no doubt, but as time went on, more confidently. Dolores could have had a boyfriend long before meeting Kevin well into middle age. Dolores could have had a job that wasn't in the typing pool at a bottle factory.

But she didn't. And Christy Redmond is determined to find the people who put an end to that possibility for her—and he is determined to find Dolores's baby.

The evening before bin day, Garda John Barry drives around to the back of the university college. Putting the car into park, he pulls a boxed egg sambo out of his bag; the bins aren't out yet, he notes, meaning he's not too late.

A good hour passes before he hears the rumbling of bin wheels and sees a figure emerging from the college's back entrance and trudging along the driveway. He notices how unkempt it is, compared to the front of the property. John Barry is a keen gardener on his weekends off and so he sees the contrast to the antiseptic feel of the front garden, with its exaggerated clipped conifers and its baskets of flowers. This back entrance is in a bit of a state. He'd love to get out and give it a good weeding.

The figure comes into full view, and she looks Latin American, just as the inspector described. He looks around for CCTV cameras, but there don't seem to be any back here.

Rolling down the car window, he calls out in a soft voice, 'Valeria!' He flashes her his badge through the window and, after a quick glance behind her, the woman scurries to the car.

'Here, this is for you,' he whispers, handing her the burner phone. 'It's from Inspector Christy Redmond from Pearse Street Gardaí. I'm Garda John Barry. You're to use that if you need us. If you go into contacts, you'll see his number and mine. Don't worry, Valeria, we'll make sure you're safe.'

'Santa María. God bless you, John Barry,' she says, her eyes glistening.

'Ah, no bother. Mind yourself, Valeria.'

—

As the garda drives away, Valeria tucks the phone into her apron pocket and continues to carry out her duties. It's not till she has returned to her room at the end of a long hard day that she dares take the burner phone out. She stares at it like it's made of gold.

25

CLODAGH

CLODAGH O'REILLY LIVES in a house made of compacted earth that looks over a valley of proteas and leucadendrons. In the distance, on a clear day, is the shimmer of the sea. She and Danny, her Champion of the World, bought the house an hour out of Adelaide in the golden, grassy hills that meander above the beaches of the Fleurieu Peninsula. This was going to be where they enjoyed their retirement. But Danny died from a sudden heart attack at sixty and so she lives alone, bar the three alpacas who live next door and keep her company. She never did have children in Australia. She and Danny tried for years, but it just never happened.

When she moved here permanently after Danny died, she sold her city runaround and bought a four-wheel drive ute to navigate the white gravel roads lined with grass trees and gums. Her blackish hair is now salt-and-pepper, cut in a square bob that frames her face, which is sun-kissed from years outdoors. She works as an emergency teacher for the schools of the area and makes soy candles that she sells at the Willunga market on a Saturday. Her favourite scent is gardenia. She lost her Ringsend accent a long time ago. She still sounds Irish, but you can't quite place where she's from. Her vowels have softened and her consonants have hardened.

Every morning, she gets up at her time of choosing and selects her beach. Some days it's the tiny, deserted beach at Myponga. Other days, she takes a dip with the Adelaide barristers who have their fancy beach homes at Carrickalinga. Her favourite, Port Willunga, is a bit of a hike from her place, but it's worth it. So pretty. Gentle, aquamarine waves, the water warm and inviting. She lies back, and although at times she is lonely, she feels alive.

It's as far away from the Meath house with its haughty Directress and its endless work and its crappy weather and its drudgery as you could possibly dream.

She still thinks of that other, awful life from time to time. She even thinks of Dolores Murphy occasionally. She noticed a few years back that they had mutual friends from Ringsend on Facebook. But Clodagh O'Reilly has never been much into social media. As a teacher, she has never used her own name. Her profile photograph is a sunset on a beach. She barely posts and has the highest privacy settings. If she's honest with herself, she's only ever used it for spying, or to look at pictures of her nieces and nephews back home. She never sends a friend request to Dolores

Murphy. The memory of her, brief as it is, brings back too many other painful memories. She prefers to think that her life only really started when she and Danny arrived in Australia. They had been one of those couples that her friend Trish said were slightly insufferable, in that they never stopped enjoying one another's company and they often finished each other's sentences. Until Danny's heart gave way and that all came to an end. Now she finds solace in books and the ocean.

One evening, Clodagh O'Reilly arrives home after a day of teaching a pretty ratty lot to hear the phone ringing. Her first thought is that it must be bad news from home; the only people who ring her this late in the day are her family in Ireland, because it's their morning.

She picks up the phone, saying, 'Clodagh speaking.'

'My name is Kate Delaney.'

Clodagh O'Reilly recognises that name. And, if she thinks hard, that voice. She speaks with a clarity that public figures often possess. Who is Kate Delaney again?

'Oh, Jesus Christ, I just realised how I know your name,' Clodagh says, gasping as she recognises the voice of the journalist from that press conference after she came out of hospital. Kate Delaney's the one who was raped and kidnapped. Clodagh remembers the big hunt to find her. The breathless pieces to camera from reporters covering the case on the Hume Highway. It was an altogether desperate business.

Clodagh had followed the news closely, feeling a connection to the woman because she was Irish Australian so the story had captivated her. She was pretty and smart and women like Clodagh around the nation had held their collective breath until she was found. The name *Kate Delaney* had taken on the sort of resonance of Lindy Chamberlain or Madeleine McCann. Two words, in one name, that have so much more meaning imbued in them.

'I'm sorry, that didn't come out the way I meant it,' Clodagh says hastily. 'Kate Delaney. I mean, how do I . . . I know who you are, all right, but I can't imagine why you'd be calling me. I may have forgotten to file my tax return for a couple of years, but that's the most scandalous thing I've done in decades.'

'I'm glad to hear it,' Kate says. 'And actually, my query predates the past few decades.'

Clodagh's heart sinks as she lowers herself onto the stool next to her kitchen bench. 'Oh, yes?'

'Clodagh, I just wanted to ask if you remember my aunt. She was from Ringsend, like you, but you didn't meet her there. Her name's Dolores Murphy.'

Clodagh feels a tightness in her chest, and for a moment she can't respond. 'Has something happened to Dolores?' she manages finally.

'Well, yes and no. But I am talking about the time when you were both—'

'Help?' says Clodagh, her voice rising sharply. She puts the receiver on her lap for a moment. Her ears are ringing. She can hear Kate's faint voice on the other end of the line.

'Clodagh? Clodagh, are you there?'

Clodagh picks up the phone and puts it to her ear again. 'I'm sorry, Kate, that is a part of my life I really don't like to recall. I hope that Dolores is okay, but this is not something I want to talk about.'

On the other end of the line, Kate swallows. Piercing through people's trauma and finding a way to keep them on the phone, finding the right note of empathy, finding the reason why they might want to tell their story, why it's in their interest as well as the public's despite how painful it might be, has always been her forte. But these days she has her own trauma, too. And for close to a year now, when she picks up the phone to get started on an investigation she finds her palms are sweaty and her mouth goes dry—as they did when Clodagh recognised her.

But Dolores. Dolores. Dolores needs her. And they need Clodagh to help them find the Directress.

'I want to say upfront that I'm not here to retraumatise you. I'm not going to ask you about your experiences during that time. But Dolores needs your help.'

'I appreciate that, Kate, but I'm not sure what I can do for her.'

So, Kate explains how Dolores had met Marcus Akenyemi, and how she'd fallen pregnant, and how they'd kept her more or less prisoner during the pregnancy, and how she thought they were supporting her because they looked after her and fed her well, but they were really only looking after the baby. And how they nearly died when they realised the baby was, in their words, 'coloured'. And how they had, nonetheless, taken the baby from her before Dolores even got to hold her. And how Dolores thought that at some point, they might let her see the baby again. But they didn't. And how, like Clodagh, Dolores had run away. And how Dolores had kept her pain to herself for all these years, but when her partner died she decided it was finally time to find her baby.

Clodagh O'Reilly doesn't say anything as Kate recounts Dolores's story. She is quietly weeping through most of it. 'I'm just in bits thinking of poor Dolores going through that,' she says when Kate has finished. Like Mairéad, Clodagh feels the old survivor guilt creeping into her bones and her belly.

'I'm sorry to remind you of it all,' says Kate. 'But we're really struggling to find out where these people are now—and we need to locate them if we're to find the baby.'

'The child would be in, let's see, her thirties, now?' asks Clodagh.

'That's right,' says Kate. 'A bit younger than me.'

'So, if all of this happened after I left the house, how can I help you?'

'I was hoping you might know the name of the Directress.'

Clodagh takes a sharp breath. 'Awful, awful woman.'

She explains that a few years ago, before Danny died, she had what she describes as a 'wee breakdown'. Overwhelmed by memories of her time at the Big House and in Meath, she was no longer able to get up for school in the morning and had to take all of her long-service leave.

'Listen, Kate, did Dolores mention anything to you about Miss Nuala and Miss Róisín?'

'She did, yes.'

There is a long pause on Clodagh's end of the phone.

'I'm sorry, Kate,' she says suddenly. 'I have to go.'

Clodagh O'Reilly holds the phone on her lap for a moment, hearing Kate Delaney's voice saying, 'Please, Clodagh, I really need your help, I promise I'll look after you.' Then she hangs up the phone and switches it off.

She goes and gets a Barossa red from the wine rack under the stairs and pours herself a glass. She drinks it quickly in a way she knows lacks class. But sure, there is no one else to see her now.

She hears that ringing in her ears again. She closes her eyes and there is Miss Róisín, standing behind her in the scullery, whispering in her ear. Clodagh wipes her ear at the memory of Miss Róisín's wet tongue.

'Stop! Jesus, woman, stop!' she says out loud.

She drains her glass and pours another one. And another. She finishes the bottle and stumbles upstairs to her bedroom with the final glass, spilling shiraz on the carpet as she goes.

Miss Róisín is following her up the stairs. She's putting her hand up Clodagh's pinafore.

'No!' Clodagh says aloud. The tears are streaming down her face now. 'No.'

She gets into bed and falls asleep with the glass of wine in her hand, waking to find she's spilled it on her blouse. She takes off the blouse, uses a towel from her ensuite to mop the bottom of the glass, and gets under the blanket in her bra and jeans. She hasn't washed off her foundation or her mascara. Ah, feck it.

That night, she dreams that she's down at Port Willunga. She's slowly easing herself into the water and her pores feel bright. She lies back in the water and washes away what the little voice in her head continued to tell her were her sins. Then, in the moonlight, she sees a fin coming towards her—and suddenly an enormous mouth, bristling with white teeth. The great white looks somehow like the Directress, whom she'd always thought had shark eyes, too. The shark swallows her whole and everything goes black.

—

In the Dublin morning to South Australia's night, Kate Delaney tries Clodagh's number several times, but the call goes straight to message. Clodagh O'Reilly has clearly switched off her phone. Kate wonders if she's done the wrong thing. Should she have left it up to Christy, who is, after all, the professional? Kate just works on instinct and empathy. No one ever taught her how to get someone over the line. She remembers being asked once to give a lecture on how to gain sources' trust and she turned it down on account of the fact that she had no idea. There was no mathematical formula. It just worked out somehow. Which means that in situations like this, she has no go-to method in the bottom of her journalistic drawer. And instinct and empathy amount to a whole lot of nothing when you have a source on the other side of the planet who has switched off her phone. Amount to even less when the person you're calling isn't even a source and you aren't even working as a journalist. You are just trying to help the person in your life who makes everything make sense. Who needs your help and who deserves so much better.

Kate goes downstairs and finds Dolores methodically hanging washing in a complicated Tetris-like arrangement in the hot press. She looks so tired and sad.

'I love you, Dolores,' she says, and gives her aunt a squeeze.

'I love you, too,' says Dolores.

'I want to make it better.'

'I know you do, pet.'

Kate can't bring herself to discuss the aborted call with Clodagh O'Reilly. So, she just clasps her aunt's hand.

'I wonder how the investigation is going,' Dolores says, yawning.

'I'm sure they're doing the best they can.'

Kate notices Dolores's hands are shaking.

—

Clodagh O'Reilly wakes the next morning to find the sun has risen over the valley and burned off a morning mist. On the balcony, some cockatoos are fighting over a deceased lizard, peck-pecking at its eyes. Clodagh opens one of her own eyes, and then the other, to see in the mirrored wardrobe door that the corners of her mouth are stained purple with wine and her teeth are, too.

'The state of you, Clodagh,' she says to herself.

She goes downstairs and makes herself a cup of tea and carries it out onto the deck to sit in the sun and look at her proteas and leucadendrons.

She hears some laughter and sees that some teenage girls who have come to stay with her neighbours are feeding the alpacas from big bales of hay. They're gossiping and laughing in the way that teenage girls do. They see her watching and they're being a bit performative now. They're in that space between girlhood and womanhood—a space where they're comparing notes about hot boys at the same time as cooing childishly at the alpacas they're feeding. All flushed cheeks and slightly wonky black eyeliner and spots covered up with concealer and short shorts and hoodies. Softness and hardness. Clodagh didn't get to have those sorts of teen years. Neither did Dolores, nor any of the other girls who became the Help.

Clodagh feels a stab in her chest at the term. The Help. Those bastards who gave the Directresses and the supervisors their orders and who made the rules for that diabolical structure were out and out misogynists. There was no such thing as male Help. The teenage boys brought up in the Group had their handkerchiefs ironed and their underwear folded. The men were waited on like kings. Clodagh has googled the Group from time to time. She knows that there are still young women being recruited to become the Help. They won't get to run around fields in short shorts and hoodies and feed alpacas and joke about boys.

Fuck the Group. Fuck the Directress. Fuck Miss Róisín.

Clodagh walks inside and looks up the most recent call on her phone. And she rings Kate Delaney.

'Kate speaking,' says a slightly breathless voice on the other end, as if she has had to run for the phone before it rang out.

Still, all these years later, the words are hard for Clodagh to wrap her mouth around.

'I find this very hard to talk about, Kate,' Clodagh says, slowly and deliberately. 'This is the hardest part. I'm disgusted by them. And, I don't know, I think there's some stupid, irrational part of me that thinks that women don't *do this*, you know? That somehow, I must have been to blame for things going in the direction they did. That I must have been complicit. And the complicating factor is that, in a way, I *was* complicit. I went along with it. I didn't know any better. Or maybe I did but didn't know any way out. I was effectively a child; I had no power. And who could I tell? That bleeding Directress? Fat lot of good that would have done.'

'Clodagh, you don't have to explain. I understand.'

'I don't remember ever telling Dolores about it—I mean, my memory is we talked about the whip and that stupid chain they made me wear that had me hobbling with pain, but I didn't tell her about how Miss Róisín would . . .' She trails off.

'It's okay, Clodagh. Really it is.'

'Actually, it's not okay. None of it was okay. How much did Dolores tell you?'

'What do you mean?'

'Well, what did she say that they did to her? You know, the abuse?'

Kate sighs. 'Well, she didn't go into a lot of detail, and to me it seemed like it was definitely sexual abuse, but not of the more serious kind.'

'Well, I can tell you that it *was* serious. It messed me up sexually for years.'

Kate just stays quiet.

'Roísín was a monster,' Clodagh says. 'And so was Nuala.'

'Did Nuala abuse you, too?'

'No. But I saw her with one of the other girls. I'll never scrub the image from my brain. I know she did it to all of them. They both did.'

'I don't know what to say, Clodagh.'

'What is there to say? I'm glad you've got the Gardaí onto those people.'

One of the things she had done before she left the Meath house for good was to rifle through Miss Róisín's handbag to find her driver's licence and write down her full name and date of birth.

'Róisín Margaret Downes, that was her name,' Clodagh says. 'I carried that piece of paper in my purse for years. I don't know what I thought I was going to do with it. But it meant I was able to keep track of her.'

She told Yolanda, the therapist she saw when she had her breakdown, that she'd done this, and they discussed whether it might be a good idea for Clodagh to write to Róisín. But Clodagh was worried that the letter would be seen by someone else, because that was *their* way, and then it would be somehow used against her, and all that emotional labour she'd put into healing would be for nothing.

So she decided, with Yolanda's encouragement, that she would call instead. One of the things she most wanted to know at that time was the name of the Directress, who actively participated in the enslavement of teenage girls and turned a blind eye to serious abuse by Róisín and Nuala.

'I remember one time the Directress walked in on us when we were in bed,' Clodagh says to Kate. 'I could have died of shame.'

'What did the Directress do?' asks Kate.

'She just looked at us with the coldest expression I have ever seen. Those shark eyes of hers. And she said something about how I had to go downstairs and scrub the front steps because they had guests arriving for a conference in the morning. It was ten o'clock at night! But she made me get up. And I just sat there, on the front step, in that horrible second-hand uniform, breaking my heart crying, scrubbing that step like my life depended on it.'

'Oh, Clodagh. I am so sorry.'

'We all are. Anyway, Róisín more or less dropped me after that. I'd see her with other, newer girls from time to time. Except for the very odd time, I'd be in a back room, you know, dusting or something, and there would be no one around, and she'd grab me. And put her tongue in my ear or her hand up my pinafore. And then she'd walk away like nothing had happened. And I'd be thinking, *Did that really happen?* I mean, what the hell was wrong with these people!'

'You must have felt so alone.'

'I did. It was the loneliest I've ever been in my entire life. Even lonelier than after I lost my Danny. And that Directress never mentioned a single word about what she'd seen. Never treated me remotely differently. It made me wonder sometimes was it all a terrible dream. But it wasn't a dream, Kate. I knew it wasn't. So, when I called that house they had in Berkeley where Róisín was living, I put on this posh D4 accent and made up a story about being a family member and how I had some sad news from home and needed to speak to her urgently. And when she got on the line, I told her in no uncertain terms that if she did not give me the name of the Directress, I would write a first-person piece detailing her abuse of me and have it published in the *Irish Times*. That I had journalist contacts there (I didn't) and they had expressed interest in my story. And that I would reveal her full name and where she was living now. And I'd go into all of the mortifying detail of what she did to me, as a teenager, who knew no better, and was in that fecking place because of family circumstance and, well, you know, poverty. I mean, that's the reality, Kate, girls like Dolores and me were there because of poverty. And anyway, I warned her that it would be absolutely fucking devastating for her.'

'You are a tough lady, Clodagh O'Reilly,' says Kate. 'I love it.'

'Well, hardly. I held on to my secret for all those years. The only people I told were my Danny and my therapist, Yolanda. I did nothing to help Dolores, God forgive me, I just abandoned her. And I did nothing to stop any other girl from being tricked into going to that awful place when thinking she was going to a cookery school. What a joke! I should be ashamed of myself for not doing anything.'

'No, you shouldn't,' says Kate. 'These traumas are very, very hard to manage. It's not up to you to be the hero, Clodagh. It's up to them to be better people.'

'Well, fat chance of that ever happening,' says Clodagh. 'But anyway, Róisín was clearly terrified. She told me she'd sue me for libel, that they had access to the best lawyers. I said, "Knock yourself out, sunshine. I'm ready. And I'll find others who'll back me up, too." I may even have mentioned Dolores's name, even though I didn't know for sure what she'd experienced; I only suspected it.'

'Hang on,' says Kate. 'You think Dolores was'—she whispers the word she can no longer bring herself to say out loud—'raped?'

'As I say, I don't really know. But I think it's very possible. Miss Nuala and Miss Róisín were sexually assaulting other girls, including me. And Dolores was so sad and so vulnerable when I met her. I knew that look. So yes, I probably mentioned her to Miss Róisín when I demanded that she tell me the Directress's name. And she did.'

Kate's heart begins to beat faster. 'What was it, Clodagh? Please tell me. It's so important that I know.'

'Oonagh. Oonagh Sullivan. I'll never forget it as long as I live. But here, after getting it, what did I do? A big, fat nothing, Kate. I disappeared back into the mental hole I'd been living in for all those years.'

'Oonagh Sullivan,' repeats Kate. Pulling her laptop across the coffee table, she googles the name. And up she pops. An elderly lady in a nursing home in Donnybrook. Standing next to a politician and bending over to blow out two birthday candles in the shape of a nine and a zero. Long hair piled on top of her head in the way Dolores described. Pigeon chest now shrunken. But there's a steely look in her eyes that would cut glass.

TD Martin O'Donohue visits the veritable Queen of Donnybrook Glades, Mrs Oonagh Sullivan, as she celebrates 90 years young, the caption beneath the photograph in a local newspaper reads. The rest of it is a puff piece about the politician, with no more information about Oonagh Sullivan. But it's her. It's her.

'Thank you so much for telling me what happened, Clodagh. I would say it's a pleasure to speak to you, but under the grim circumstances, well, you know what I mean.'

'Mind yourself, Kate. For all the other reasons you need to mind yourself, too.' Clodagh wants to say more, but dredging up the past has been too exhausting. She can't take on Kate's tragedy as well. At least, not now.

'I will. I promise.'

Kate Delaney hangs up the phone. Pulsing through her body she can feel what the journos call 'story lust'. But this isn't a story. This is Dolores's life. Just as her own ordeal was so much more than a story. *Don't think about that, Kate Delaney,* she tells herself. *You've got the name. Oonagh Sullivan.* She texts Liam.

Hello sweetheart,
I spoke to her. Clodagh. She told me the name of
the Directress.

Wow. Well done you. So what's the name?

Oonagh Sullivan.

Oonagh. No disrespect to all the nice Oonaghs
out there, but I must say it kind of suits what I've
heard of her.

I thought same. The whole thing is so messed up,
Liam. I miss you.

I miss you too, Kater.

I wish you were here to kiss me. And the other things, too. You know I can't say the words.

Ha. No. But yes. Definitely yes. Me too.

She sends him three love heart emojis and he sends her a bunch of kisses. She wishes she could climb on top of him now. Is that inappropriate? she wonders. Probably. Her notion of what's appropriate is so scrambled by years of hearing other people's traumas, not to mention going through her own, that somehow it's not a passion killer. She thinks back to before it all happened, how she'd turn up at his place late at night when she was on a story. And because he was a lawyer and often had to work late himself, he totally got it. He didn't get cranky the way non-journo boyfriends had in the past, jealous of her obsessive focus on her work and not on them. He'd be waiting with some French cheese with slices of pear and a glass of wine, because he knew she loved picking at party food and couldn't stomach big meals.

Kate climbs into bed in her aunt's spare room and wills the night to pass quickly so she can ring Christy Redmond in the morning with the news. Oonagh Sullivan. Donnybrook Glades.

26

DONNYBROOK GLADES

The next day, Kate Delaney wakes at 5.30 am even though she barely slept. She heads downstairs and prepares herself a boiled egg and eats it while leafing through yesterday's *Irish Times.* She forces herself to wait until eight o'clock—an acceptable hour to ring a garda, surely—before ringing the inspector.

'Well, good morning, Kate Delaney,' says Christy Redmond, who is a punctual man, a morning person, and already at his desk. 'I assume, owing to the early hour, that you have news.'

'I got on to Clodagh O'Reilly in South Australia,' says Kate. 'She was also abused by Róisín.'

'I see,' says Christy. 'Not surprising.'

'No, but Christy, this is a far more sordid investigation than we'd thought.'

'What do you mean?'

Kate describes what Clodagh has told her about the penetrative abuse by Róisín and how she saw Nuala abusing another teenage girl.

'These people,' says Christy. 'These awful people. Have you raised this with Dolores? You know we'll need to get her in for another statement if there's more to what O'Rourke did to her.'

'I haven't had the chance yet. I don't know how to, Christy, to be honest.'

'Aye, I can understand that.'

'Róisín's surname is Downes, by the way, middle name Margaret, in case you didn't know.'

'We did, but you're not long behind us,' Christy says. 'Well done, Detective Delaney.'

'Thanks, Inspector. Pretty fucking grim work, though. But here's the thing. Clodagh got up a head of steam a few years ago when she had some sort of breakdown and she contacted Downes. She was in some place in Berkeley in California—one of their residences, or whatever they call them. And anyway, she basically told Downes that if she didn't cough up the name of the Directress, she was going to expose her abuse in the *Irish Times*. So, Downes coughed up the name.'

A smile spreads across Christy Redmond's face, and not just because he's amused at Kate Delaney referring to potential witnesses by their surnames the way gardaí do. 'Did she now? And?'

'Oonagh Sullivan. She celebrated her ninetieth a while back in a care home called Donnybrook Glades. You'll love this: the newspaper caption called her the Queen of Donnybrook Glades.'

'That sounds about right,' says Christy Redmond.

'That's what I thought!'

'I'm so grateful to you for using your Australian connections to get on to her, Kate,' he says. 'And you are very good at this. You'd've made a good garda in another life. But you'll need to rein in the reporter now and leave us to it.'

'I know, and I will, I promise.'

'Thanks again, Kate.'

—

Christy Redmond leans back in his swivel chair and calls out to John Barry on the other side of the felted partition that's covered with their rough mud map of names and places. 'Hey, Johnno. Get your skates on. We've got an appointment in Donnybrook, and I think I'll need back-up for this one.'

'Not the Directress, Christy?'

'The very same.'

'Jaysus.'

—

'That's a hell of a topiary display,' says Christy Redmond as they pull up alongside an elaborately sculpted hedge.

DONNYBROOK GLADES, reads the sign above the double door with a handle shaped like a lion's head. WHO CARES? WE DO!

The foyer is all black-and-white chequerboard tiles, sage velvet furnishings, cascading plants in baskets, pictures of mountain sunsets and religious statues. In one corner is a photograph of a priest with his hands outstretched to a large crowd. Sitting on an overstuffed sofa, long legs clad in tights and knee-high boots, is Kate Delaney.

'No, no, no,' Christy says.

He motions to her to follow him outside to the street, which she reluctantly does.

'Kate, this is a crazy idea, if you don't mind me saying,' Christy says. 'You need to leave.'

As they're talking, a text message flashes up on Christy Redmond's phone. He gasps a little. It's from Valeria at that college with Gráinne Kelly.

Kate sees his open mouth and glances over to surreptitiously read the text.

> Inspector Christy
> Was listening at the door. Hope that not bad.
> She came many time. Noola O'Rourke (? My spelling of Irish names is bad). The Directress is lying. She know her. Have not seen her for few years. She have the mental health issues.

> I think probably so. They whisper about her. Her nerves. She not a nice lady though. Cold hands.
> Valeria

Christy texts his thanks to Valeria and tells her to keep her phone on silent and contact him if she needs anything at all.

He looks up and sees Kate's craned neck. She clasps her hands and gives him a look that's faux-earnest and try-hard nonchalant. He snaps his phone case shut and shakes his head.

She opens her mouth to speak, but he doesn't let her finish.

'Have you ever had anything to do with this crowd?' Christy asks. 'We can't afford to make any mistakes. If they got wind that I was allowing the press to follow me to a potential interview with a key witness in this investigation, I can tell you right now there'd be hell for me to pay. They'd be on to the Commissioner quick smart. There would be complaints to TDs, there would be inquiries. We have to be holier than Hosanna in the highest, Kate. Do you understand how sensitive this is?'

'I'm not here in a press capacity; I'm here as a family member of the complainant,' she says, not sounding very convinced of her own argument.

'Doesn't matter. Not one bit. They'll make something of it. Please, Kate. I'm very grateful to you for finding Oonagh Sullivan for us so quickly. You're good at this, I can see that. But this is a disaster, like. You need to allow us to do our job if there's to be any hope of finding your aunt's baby. You need to let us handle this according to the proper procedure. This Directress sounds like a right piece of work. Doesn't matter if she's a very old lady now; she's been moving in very particular circles all her life and she knows what strings to pull. I need you to help me. And being here right now, that's not helping, Kate.'

'I'm really sorry, Inspector. I just got ahead of myself.' She looks at the ground. 'I haven't felt like this for so long—you know, invested in a story.'

'But it's not a story, Kate. It's your auntie's life. And it's our investigation. Please, *please*, don't be messing with my investigation. Dolores is counting on me. And she's counting on you, too.'

Kate Delaney remembers the feeling that often dawns on you as a journalist: that moment when you realise that although you might think you're at the centre of things, you really, really are not. You're on the periphery. At best, you'll be tolerated. At worst, you are a nuisance. Even if the people you're writing about share a common purpose.

'Okay, I'll head off. Can you at least let me know how you get on?'

Christy Redmond shakes his head. 'Kate, you know I can't do that. I can update Dolores as is appropriate, but I can't give you a blow-by-blow account of my investigation. I'm not risking my job and this case for you.' He sees her face has fallen and, remembering her recent history, he puts his hand on her shoulder. 'The thing is, we're making progress. And that's a very good thing.'

Kate Delaney takes a bus back to Ringsend. And she wishes Liam Carroll was there to hold her hand.

—

At Donnybrook Glades, Garda John Barry is trying to have an extended benign chat with an aged-care worker about the weather. Christy nods and mouths, 'She's gone,' and John mouths, 'Thank Christ.'

'This one's for later, Johnno,' he says, showing John the text message from Valeria and forwarding it to him as he does. 'Thanks for getting that burner over to Valeria.'

'No bother, Inspector.'

Christy turns to the worker, whose name tag reads *Teresa*.

'Hello, Teresa,' he says, looking from the name tag to her face. 'My name's Inspector Christy Redmond, and this is my colleague, Garda John Barry. We're from Pearse Street and we've come to see one of your residents. Is Oonagh Sullivan awake?'

'Ah, well, you're welcome to come and meet her, Inspector, but I don't know how you'll go with her. Mrs Sullivan does be having her . . . challenging behaviours,' Teresa says.

'Does she have the dementia?' Christy asks.

The woman nods. 'It's been very sad watching her go downhill. We used to always say, "There's no flies on Oonagh Sullivan." She's quite—how shall I put it?—formidable.'

Christy Redmond chuckles. 'That does not surprise me, Teresa. I heard she was described as the Queen of Donnybrook Glades.'

'That she was. And still is, really. No one like her. But we all get old, Inspector. Can I ask why you're here?'

'You'll understand we need to keep the details confidential, but it's a historical matter we're looking at, and we think Mrs Sullivan might be able to help us out.'

Teresa's father was a garda, and she respects their work. She's a contractor who comes here three days a week and enjoys her work with the elderly. She doesn't ask any more questions.

'Well, I wish you good luck, Inspector. You'll see when you meet her why you need it.'

Teresa leads Christy and John through a set of double doors and down a long corridor with speckled linoleum and minty walls, the strong smell of bleach not quite masking the faint but persistent whiff of urine. She knocks on a door at the end of the hall. 'Mrs Sullivan, I have some visitors for you,' she says before easing the door open. 'Ah, it looks like she's having a little nap.'

Christy and John stand in the doorway looking in at the Directress, who is lying under a hospital blanket in a yellow fluffy robe, her hair piled on top of her head. Her face is heavily lined, and her body is shrunken, but the architecture of her once-proud features is still visible. There are more than shades of Miss Havisham. She's lying with her face off to the side, her mouth is open, as if in fright. Her claw-like fingers are weighed down with elaborate jewels. Around her neck she wears a small diamond cross. Above her head is a photograph of the Father, and on a little shelf mounted on the opposite wall a statue of the Sacred Heart that glows red. Over near the window are vases of faded synthetic gladioli and lilies.

Teresa turns to the gardaí. 'She doesn't get many visitors these days,' she whispers. 'The family stopped coming. I believe there was a falling-out with the only son. He's gay,' she mouths. 'And she doesn't believe in all that and, well, as you might know, Oonagh's not one for sugarcoating her opinions. I believe at one point she wrote an opinion piece in the paper denouncing his lifestyle. That was it, he's never come since.'

'Awkward,' says Christy.

'Live by the sword, et cetera,' says John.

Teresa walks over to the bed and gives the Directress a little shake. 'Oonagh! Mrs Sullivan! Sure, you have some visitors.'

Oonagh Sullivan stirs and opens her eyes to see Christy Redmond standing over her.

John Barry retreats to a visitor's chair in the corner and opens his notebook.

'Hello, Mrs Sullivan,' says Christy. 'I'm terribly sorry to wake you from your beauty sleep.'

'I'll leave you to it, Inspector,' says Teresa. 'Would you and Garda Barry like a cup of tea?'

'Lovely,' says John. 'White with three sugars.'

'Three sugars? You're a savage,' says Christy. 'I'll just have mine black, thanks, Teresa.'

'Sweet enough, Inspector?' quips Teresa.

'Aye, sweet enough.' He smiles as she lets herself out then returns his attention to the Directress. 'Now, Mrs Sullivan, I'm

Inspector Christy Redmond from Pearse Street, and this is Garda John Barry.'

'Pleased to meet you,' says John, nodding.

Oonagh Sullivan furrows her heavily wrinkled brow and clucks her tongue in her mouth as if in disapproval. She shifts herself up in the bed and reaches down to try to open a drawer in a bedside table, muttering to herself incoherently.

'Do you need some help with that, Mrs Sullivan?' Christy walks over and pulls at the drawer, which is a bit stiff. 'You'll need to get them to fix that for you. It's no use to you if you can't open it yourself.'

Oonagh Sullivan says nothing, just pulls out a glasses case and puts on a pair of spectacles on a long chain. Then she reaches down into the drawer and pulls out a little satin make-up bag. She retrieves a gold compact and an old Chanel lipstick, which she smooths on her lips, smacking them together. She's gone outside the edges of her mouth somewhat, but she seems pleased with what she sees in the compact mirror. Satisfied, she peers down at them through the spectacles but says nothing.

'I suppose you're wondering why we're here, Mrs Sullivan,' says Christy.

Oonagh Sullivan just purses her lips.

'We're here about a historical matter. We think you might be able to help us. You'll remember the Help whose name was Dolores Murphy?'

Oonagh furrows her brow again.

'I'm sure you had a few of them go through there, so I'll refresh your memory, Mrs Sullivan. She was from Ringsend. She had a baby back in 1979. She left the house you ran down in County Meath quite suddenly after that.'

'Up,' says John Barry under his breath. 'Meath is north. Well, north-west, to be precise.'

Christy gives him a look then turns back to Oonagh Sullivan. 'She left the house up in County Meath quite suddenly.'

The Directress looks out the window for a time and then looks back at him.

He can see that she's taking it in. 'Mrs Sullivan, we're here to ask about the baby.'

Oonagh Sullivan shifts herself up in the bed again but still doesn't speak. She just looks at Christy Redmond, then she looks at John Barry, then back to Christy. She opens her mouth and begins to sing in a crackly voice.

'And there she goes, my Ringsend Rose,

In God's garden, there's none rar-rer . . .'

John Barry whistles through his teeth. 'Jay-sus.'

Christy swallows. 'Mrs Sullivan, did you hear what I was asking? I am asking about Dolores Murphy's baby. I'm sure you remember. The father was African. That can't have happened too often back in the seventies. What happened to that baby, Mrs Sullivan? Myself and Garda John Barry here have reason to believe you took that baby without Dolores Murphy's consent?'

Oonagh Sullivan smiles coldly and resumes singing.

'*Sweet seventeen, my seamstress queen,*

She's no bigger, than a thimble.'

Christy Redmond rubs his eyes vigorously. There's something in the chemicals they use to clean this place that's making them water. He's about to ask her again about the baby when the door swings open and a woman bursts in.

'Gardaí?' the woman says, looking from Christy to John like a headmistress. 'I am Helen Byrne,' she says in an officious tone. 'I am the director here at Donnybrook Glades. I must say I am quite shocked that you've taken it upon yourselves to come here and question one of our residents in the dementia ward without seeking permission from me first.'

'With all due respect, Ms Byrne, I am Inspector Christy Redmond from Pearse Street, and I do not require your permission. Your employee Teresa kindly let us in and seemed entirely untroubled about doing so.' Helen Byrne shakes her head and mutters '*That woman*' under her breath. 'But I'm more than happy to let you know why we're here.'

Helen Byrne folds her arms across her chest. She's wearing a medal of Our Lady around her neck, a purple Aran-knit cardigan and orthopaedic shoes. She looks too dowdy, Christy decides, to be one of them. And she's not Help, because she'd never be allowed this level of responsibility if so. But she might not be entirely innocent either.

'Do go on, Inspector.'

'We're here to discuss some historical matters with Mrs Sullivan here, whom we understand to have been the Directress of properties at County Galway and County Meath.'

'Well, that's an awful long time ago, Inspector. Mrs Sullivan's been here for at least twelve years.'

'And that's why we describe the case as historical, Mrs Byrne. But these are serious matters, and that is why it's imperative that we speak to Mrs Sullivan, particularly given her advanced age.'

'Well, I might say, I'd question the ethics of interviewing a dementia patient alone,' Helen Byrne says.

'We're not conducting a formal interview, Mrs Byrne. We're having an informal chat to make an initial assessment of her competency. If we should get to the stage of making things more formal, Mrs Sullivan will be afforded all of her rights under the law.'

Oonagh Sullivan has taken a nail file out of her satin pouch and is methodically filing her nails, then blowing the dust off and examining them, smiling to herself at her handiwork.

'Have you taken your breakfast yet, Oonagh?' Helen Byrne asks her.

Oonagh Sullivan shakes her head.

'I'll make sure they bring you your tray. We have some lovely rashers in for you. And your favourite Clonakilty black pudding.'

Oonagh nods imperiously.

Helen drops her friendly tone as she turns back to Christy Sullivan. 'I'm going to have to make some calls, Inspector. I feel distinctly uncomfortable about this whole situation.'

'You do what you feel is best, Mrs Byrne,' he says. 'But I can assure you, no lines have been crossed here. I should also let you know that we are here in relation to a very serious matter.'

'All the more reason that Mrs Sullivan is treated with the courtesy and dignity she deserves, Inspector.'

John Barry sits in the white plastic chair, putting on his best poker face, but internally he's thinking, *Courtesy and dignity, that's some bleeding joke.*

Christy Redmond raises his eyebrows. 'Courtesy and dignity—or might I say, lack thereof—are the entire reason that we are here, Mrs Byrne. Courtesy and dignity that wasn't granted to others, in the past.'

The Directress stops filing her nails and looks up at him.

'I'm afraid you are going to have to set up a formal interview, in a proper setting,' Helen Byrne says. 'And Mrs Sullivan's family or trusted advisers will arrange for a lawyer to be present. In the meantime, I would ask you both to leave.'

Christy Redmond lets out a long sigh, and John Barry puts his pen and notepad back in his pocket.

Oonagh Sullivan looks from him, to John Barry, to Helen Byrne and back to Christy Redmond again.

'The O'Farrells didn't want her,' Oonagh says suddenly. 'They didn't want to bring a black baby to mass at Merrion.'

Christy Redmond draws a sharp breath. 'The O'Farrells? Which O'Farrells?'

Oonagh Sullivan closes her eyes and pulls the blanket up over her. She makes a shooing motion with her hand as if to say, 'Go away.'

'Please, Mrs Sullivan, which O'Farrells? And who took the baby instead?'

But her eyes remain closed. She shrugs her shoulders and mumbles to herself a little. She turns over in the bed and her peachy lipstick smears on the pillow. She lets out a long sigh. 'You try to do the right thing,' she says sleepily.

Her breathing becomes laboured, and as Christy stands over her, she starts to snore.

'I think that's quite enough, Inspector Redmond,' says Helen Byrne. 'I'll be making some calls. And I'll be having someone make a complaint to the Commissioner. This is no way to treat the elderly.'

'So pleased to make your acquaintance, Mrs Byrne,' says Christy Redmond smoothly. 'Come on, John.'

Garda John Barry gives Helen Byrne a wink as they leave the Directress's room, which he knows will send her spare. She overtakes them and marches ahead down the corridor, no doubt to make her calls.

Teresa walks out of a kitchenette with a tea tray and Christy shrugs, motions towards Helen Byrne, and apologises.

Christy Redmond and John Barry slump into the car.

'The O'Farrells in Merrion parish, Inspector?'

'Aye.'

'I'll get on to that this afternoon.'

'Good man.'

'No bother.'

27

GRÁSTA DÉ

ARRIVING HOME TO Dolores's quiet house in Ringsend, Kate Delaney climbs the stairs to the spare room. She can hear her aunt weeping quietly in the room next door. She's worried about Dolores's mental health—with the grief, the stress of the police investigation, the thoughts of her lost baby, the small matter of almost drowning in despair. And now she knows that it's highly likely Dolores was also sexually assaulted.

Kate's own bad feelings have returned. She throws herself onto the double bed, closing her eyes in an attempt to blot out the flashbacks. Her body hums. She wants Liam so badly. And she's angry at him, in this moment, for leaving her here alone. She lifts up her skirt and sees the now faint scars on her legs from that unspeakable night in Northcote. She hears The Guy's nasal voice in her head. Sees his stupid fingers drumming his steering wheel to Pearl Jam as she cowers, bound and gagged, in the back seat of his pathetic little car. She thinks of the jumpers who lived in the trees that surrounded the Pheasants Nest Bridge and how they'd watched on as she slipped into unconsciousness, starving and alone, but for these ghosts of suicides.

She wants to go and neck a bottle of chardonnay and she goes down to Dolores's fridge in search of wine, but there's none to be had. Which she accepts is a good thing. She doesn't want to become one of those people who drinks alone in the middle of the day. So far, she's managed to keep herself relatively tidy, even through those times when she felt the urge to drive into a tree.

So, she puts on a coat and her trainers, leaves Dolores's terrace and walks down to Sandymount Strand, past the nature reserve, heading to Shellybanks.

The tide is out again and it's a clear, if cold, day. She meanders along the shore, picking up cockle shells, recalling herself in patent leather shoes and frilly socks, running back to Nana to show her grandmother her haul. She turns the cockles over and over in her hand, feeling the little ridges press into her palm. And she sits on the sand, and watches the tide creep slowly in.

She pictures Liam, flailing around in the water, trying to drag her aunt back to safety. And she thinks of why her aunt went out there in the first place. And she knows that if she were Dolores, she'd want to scream at the fucking Directress and fucking Miss Nuala for all the pain they caused her, for taking away her little bundle.

She turns her phone over and over in her hand, thinking. *O'Rourke*, said the message. *Nuala O'Rourke*. Nuala O'Rourke with, Dolores had said, a PhD from UCD. Her journo brain begins to whir. Can't be too many of them. Not in the seventies. Eventually, she snaps open the case and begins to google.

It doesn't take her long to stumble upon that photo of Nuala with Gráinne Kelly. The photo is from a few years ago on an 'Events' page on the website for a women's college at UCD. She clicks back to the homepage. Up pops a dissolving montage of the Barbie Dreamhouse and the young women with apple cheeks and shiny hair and tasteful outfits and the subtle religious references and the hidden away link with a tiny crucifix that tells you this place is 'inspired by the holy principles of the Group'. And there, arms outstretched, is the Father. It's all set to saccharine, uplifting production music. It all looks so great.

'Fuckers,' Kate mutters to herself, thinking of Dolores and all of the Help who keep places like this going.

She looks out at the silvery sea and ponders. Kate has never been a good liar. And she's had it drummed into her that one should never misrepresent oneself when trying to get information out of a source. *But it's not a source, Kate Delaney. And you're not on a story. This is Dolores. This is Dolores's life.*

She thinks again about poor Dolores. And Mammy, who isn't here, and should be. And Pheasants Nest. And The Guy and what he did to her. And the Group. And how they treat women. Even Nuala O'Rourke, her own mind surely addled by her own subjugation and her own, endless, misdeeds. And Kate is filled with sadness and rage. Her eyes fill with tears. And she picks up the phone, sobbing, and she rings that bloody women's college. And she spins them a line, which, well, it's a complete lie, but in this moment, she's so overcome that she almost believes it.

She explains to the very polite receptionist with the clipped D4 tones that she's *terribly sorry but Mammy doesn't have long.* That she's in Australia, in a hospice, and *she's begging to speak with her oldest friend, Nuala O'Rourke.* They lost contact, and *Mammy's dying, and her mind's not with it on the morphine.* Every day it's *Nuala, Nuala, Nuala.* And of course, Kate has no idea where Nuala is, but Mammy had told her that she was at a women's college and Kate noticed on their website that she was *a committed old girl.* Do they have any idea where she's living now? Could they help? *For Mammy's sake?*

'Oh, now, dear, I'm so sorry about your mam,' says the receptionist. 'Let me just look up our records and we'll see what we can find. Nuala, Nuala . . . Ah, yes. Nuala O'Rourke.' The receptionist whispers, 'She's now at a place called Grásta Dé. A, look, well it's a mental health facility down near the water in Blackrock. I'm sure if you give them a call, they can at least advise if Ms O'Rourke is contactable.'

A mental health facility? That tracks. 'Grásta Dé.' *God's grace.* 'Of course,' says Kate, a committed atheist, crossing her fingers behind her back and sniffing, in what she'll later congratulate herself is an Academy Award–winning performance. 'My nana would've said it's a sign. Thank you so much. You're an angel. Mammy will be so grateful.'

She needs to tell Dolores.

It's such a long walk back to Ringsend, though. She pulls out her phone and calls Happy Murphy.

'Happy, I'm at Shellybanks. Would you mind fetching me and driving me home?'

'Jaysus, Shellybanks? You're some sucker for punishment.'

'That's not important. But could you do me a solid and get over here now?'

Happy could. He arrives within minutes and drives her to Dolores's place.

'Can you wait around for a bit, Happy? Dolores's car is in getting fixed so we might need a lift to Blackrock.'

'You're demanding, so you are.'

'Needs must, Happy. Needs must.'

Kate runs upstairs and finds her aunt on her bed. Dolores is staring at the ceiling again. The corners of her mouth are dry. She has one of Kevin's old jumpers wrapped around her. In her hands, she's clutching a tiny lemon cardigan with mother-of-pearl buttons shaped like flowers.

'You know I knitted this for her?' Dolores says as Kate comes and sits on the bed. Dolores is a beautiful knitter, who never drops a stitch. She's always made little jumpers and cardigans and bootees for all the nieces and nephews.

'I told Mammy it was for Bernadette's baby,' she says, referring to one of her older cousins. 'She was due a few months after I came home. Mammy was always so busy she didn't notice I never gave it to Bernadette. I don't know what sort of eejit I thought I was. There was no way they were giving that baby back to me. But I made it to fit size eighteen months, just in case. To give myself time.'

'You kept it all these years?' Kate asks.

'Of course. It's all I have of her. And it's not even hers, all the same. It was just me being a right dope, convincing myself that somehow I'd find her. And I thought with her skin and those big eyes, she'd look beautiful in yellow.'

'I'd say she would have. I wish I'd known her, Dolores. I'm sure with your genes she'd have been great craic to grow up with.'

'My humour and Marcus's looks, can you imagine? I'm sure she's a knockout.' Dolores brushes away a tear that has fallen on the cardigan and clasps Kate's hand.

Kate takes a deep breath.

'Dolores?'

'What's up, pet?'

'I think I know where Nuala is.'

Dolores drops Kate's hand. 'Don't be talking about her. I never want to see that sleveen again.'

'Dolores, I spoke to Clodagh O'Reilly.'

'What? Why didn't you tell me?' Dolores looks angry now.

'I don't know. I was trying to sort things out on my own. Trying not to upset you more than you already are. I'm so worried about you, Dolores.'

Dolores turns her head to look out the window. A crow is on the telephone wire, cocking its head at them.

Kate takes a deep breath.

'Clodagh told me that some pretty awful things happened to her.'

'Well, you know that.'

'No, I mean, things you haven't discussed with me before. Dolores, did Nuala—'

'Stop!' her aunt shouts. Her face is ashen. 'Stop it. Don't say the fecking words.'

'Why didn't you tell the gards about it?'

'Why do you think? Because I'm so mortally embarrassed. Even to this day I can't bear to think on it. It feels like it's *my* fault.'

'It's not your fault.'

Dolores stands and walks over to the window to rest her forehead on the glass. 'I always thought of Marcus as my first time. I wanted him to be my first time.'

'Well, he was.'

'Mostly, yes. But not entirely. I mean, the things she did. Can you imagine a girl in Ireland in the seventies who had no idea about such things? Who has been warned repeatedly that any sex outside of marriage is a mortal sin? Who has been told that she is living a life of celibacy for Our Lord and so is the supervisor who is doing this to her? I remember she had this vanilla-scented soap. You know that sickly sweet smell? And after it, she would wash her hands with this fecking soap. The smell of vanilla makes me sick to this day. I mean, I could have burned alive with the shame.' She begins to bang her head on the windowpane.

Kate runs over to her to pull her away. 'You didn't do this, Dolores. You're not to blame. You weren't to blame any more than I wasn't to blame for what happened to me.'

Dolores turns to look at her. She's so proud of how Kate is managing to carry on despite the terrible things she suffered. And now here she is, consoling her aunt. Dolores needs to be stronger.

'I'm sorry, Kate. I forget sometimes about what you went through. Which is so shite of me.'

'I *want* you to forget. I want everyone to forget. *I* want to forget. I want to be able to sleep again at night. I want to stop punishing Liam. I want to be just, you know, uncomplicatedly happy.'

'We aren't uncomplicated people.'

'I know, and mostly I don't mind. But sometimes it gets so tiring.'

They sit in silence for a while and then Kate tells Dolores that she thinks she knows where Nuala O'Rourke is living—in a clinic for the mentally ill.

'She can't hurt you anymore, Dolores.' Even as Kate says it, she can feel the weight of Christy Redmond's disapproval. He'll be furious that she's getting involved in his case again. But the more she thought about it, out on the grey sand at Shellybanks, the more she felt in her bones that if the inspector got to Nuala O'Rourke first, that would be it. Dolores Murphy would never have the opportunity to confront her abuser.

And while she's not going to tell her aunt to go, she hopes she does decide to, of her own volition.

Dolores shivers. 'Where is she?'

'A place down at Blackrock called Grásta Dé.'

'Grásta Dé? Go away with you. One of Mammy's friends from the Legion of Mary ended up there. She had thirteen, and when her youngest died, that was it. She couldn't cope.'

'Poor woman.'

'So many poor women, Kate. I wonder how long Miss Nuala has been there? I had a keep fit class down behind there—used to go past it all the time.'

'You don't need to call her "Miss" anymore, Dolores.'

'Right you are. I do not. Force of habit.'

Dolores sits up suddenly. 'Where's me fecking shoes?'

Kate holds her breath as her aunt pulls on some socks and shoes and shrugs on a puffer coat. Then Dolores stands in front of the mirror on the back of the door and smears some frosted lipstick onto her chapped lips and gives her cheeks a little pinch. She turns to her niece. 'Well, are you coming with me?'

Kate Delaney smiles. 'You're a tough lady, Dolores Murphy.'

'Apparently I passed it down the line.'

'Howarye, Dolores?' asks Happy gingerly as she makes her way down the narrow staircase with Kate following.

'I'm shite, but I'm good. You know that way?'

'Every day, Dolores, every day.'

—

They pile into Happy's car and drive to Blackrock. The facility is surrounded by a granite wall with a steel-barred gate.

'Shit,' says Kate.

'Where there's a will, there's a way,' says Happy.

'Not necessarily,' says Dolores. 'I mean there's a whole bleeding continent of people starving in Africa. They have a will to find food, but they're still starving.'

'I don't need a lecture, Dolores.'

'Well, don't make stupid comments, Happy.'

'Would you two stop your bloody bickering?' Kate interjects. 'Dolores, look—through the gate. There's a woman going to the garage. I think she's putting out some rubbish.'

'Ah, Jaysus,' says Dolores. 'She'll be the Help.'

'How can you tell?' asks Kate.

'Well, from that ragged pinafore for a start—it's clearly second-hand. And the way she's bowing her head and not looking around in case she makes eye contact with someone. And she's limping a bit; probably wearing one of them barbed chains.'

'Poor woman,' says Kate.

'Again, so many poor women,' says Dolores. 'You stay here.' And she gets out of the car.

Dolores walks over to the gate and waves in her direction. The Help glances around anxiously and then approaches. The two women speak for a few minutes, then the woman looks around again, takes a little notepad and pencil out of her apron pocket and writes something down before thrusting it through the bars and hurrying back inside.

'I don't know what you said there, Dolores, but that looked successful,' says Kate when her aunt returns to the car. 'You should be a journo.'

'We share history,' Dolores says. 'I know a lonely Help when I see one.'

'What did she say?'

'Well, mainly that she is no fan of Miss Nuala. Hates her as much as I do. Wants to leave. Her name is Agnes. I promised I'd try to help her.'

'Jesus,' says Kate. 'I wonder how many of these women are still out there.'

'I'd say a good few,' Dolores says. 'Especially from Latin American countries or places like the Philippines where the Church is still at the centre of everything.'

'I'll bet,' says Kate. 'So what about Nuala O'Rourke?'

'She was there for a while, after she had some sort of episode. Gave Agnes the right creeps. But she's back in the community again now apparently. Living at this address in Merrion.' She unfolds the piece of paper Agnes had given her.

'Go, Agnes,' says Kate. 'Okay, Happy. You know what to do.'

Happy starts the car.

—

Merrion is just up the road from Blackrock and Happy really doesn't need to race over there at quite the speed he does, but he's enjoying the drama of it all, even though he's not really sure what exactly is going on. He'll find out later, and he'll be consumed with rage. All that he does know now is that this has something to do with his sister's hidden history. And he can see from the fierce look in Dolores's eyes that it won't do to be asking too many questions. So he's just decided to be enthusiastic and helpful. Which is what Happy Murphy does best.

He's playing The Smiths' 'This Charming Man' rather loudly and somehow it suits the adrenaline of the occasion, adrenaline which Kate fears may soon fizzle out. Kate and Dolores are sitting in the back of Happy's car, exchanging nervous looks, because they have no real plan. Because Dolores is about to confront the woman who terrified her and abused her as a teenager. Because that woman had a hold over her, even many years after they last clapped eyes on each other. And Dolores doesn't really know what she'll say to her.

They pull up in front of a Georgian terrace: a house not dissimilar to the one a childless couple visited three decades before to pick up Dolores's child. A walnut tree in the front garden surrounded by crocus and daffodil bulbs. A holy cross in the stained-glass panel above the door. Tessellated tiles. The sound of a kettle whistling somewhere inside on a stove and someone slowly and deliberately playing a piano.

Kate and Dolores knock on the front door. They hear the sound of a curtain sharply drawing open above them and see an unfamiliar woman in a twinset and dyed auburn hair that's been set in hot rollers staring down at them.

'Who's there?' a reedy voice calls from the hallway a few moments later.

Kate and Dolores look at each other but say nothing.

They hear mewling and a Siamese kitten bursts out through a cat flap. Kate has never known an owner of a Siamese who wasn't slightly bonkers, so that tracks.

'Pippin! Pippin! You little minx,' says the reedy voice as the door is flung open and a woman scoops up the runaway kitten.

Miss Nuala.

She is tiny. Her arms look like they might snap in half at any moment. She's expensively dressed in a ballet-pink angora wrap knit and cream herringbone trousers. Her now-silver hair is still pulled back in tortoiseshell combs. Around her neck, a very fine gold chain with a crucifix embedded with seed pearls.

She wears pale pink lipstick. Folded under her arm is a copy of *The Times* crossword.

'Hello, dears,' she says, looking from Dolores to Kate and smiling, but not with her eyes. 'How can I help you?'

Dolores Murphy just stares at her, trembling.

'This is my aunt,' Kate says. 'I think you might know her?'

'Is that an Australian accent?' Nuala asks, gaily. 'I don't know any Australians but I am told it is quite lovely there. Daresay I couldn't manage that flight at my age, never mind the heat.'

'Oh, Dolores isn't Australian,' says Kate, a little sharply. 'You'll remember Dolores Murphy, *Miss* Nuala. She's from Ringsend.'

Whatever colour there had been in Nuala O'Rourke's bony cheeks fades.

'Look, I'm not sure how I can help you,' she stammers, and starts to shut the door.

But Dolores has found her steel. She has already jammed her foot in the doorway. She says nothing and just keeps staring at Nuala O'Rourke.

Pippin the kitten, startled by the movement, springs from Nuala's arms.

'Oh, I think you can help us, as it happens,' says Kate, picking up Pippin. 'What did you do with Dolores's baby?'

'Give me back my cat!' says Nuala, snatching the kitten from Kate's grasp.

'Give you back your cat? Your cat? Your bleeding *cat*? What about my baby?!' It's the first thing Dolores has said, and she's incandescent with fury. Kate is proud of her.

'How dare you!' Nuala O'Rourke shrieks. 'I will not be spoken to like that on my own doorstep. Leave this property at once!'

'You will not be spoken to like what, exactly?' Dolores is on a roll now. 'How about a fifteen-year-old who doesn't deserve to be abused?! Do you need me to remind you of the details, *Miss* Nuala? Do you still wash your hands with vanilla-scented soap afterwards? Or how about a powerless teenage girl who doesn't deserve to be enslaved? To spend her days wearing second-hand clothes, cleaning gobs out of hankies and scrubbing floors for no money? Not allowed to make eye contact with men because *she* might tempt *them*? Encouraged to self-harm with a fucking whip and barbed wire? And how *dare* you steal that girl's baby!'

'I will call the Gardaí!' Nuala whispers. 'I will not tolerate this slander!' As she spits out the words, that familiar little hiss on her 's's whistles through her teeth. She sets Kate Delaney's own teeth on edge.

'Too late!' says Dolores. 'Gards already well and truly called. You'll be hearing from them soon enough. And you'll pay for what you did to me, you witch.'

Dolores Murphy turns on her heels and walks away, only to pause after a couple of steps. Walking back to Nuala O'Rourke, who is standing frozen on the front step, Dolores spits in her face. As Nuala O'Rourke slowly wipes her face, Kate Delaney cranes over to her ear. '*Fuck you*,' she says, then marches off down the driveway after her aunt.

Nuala O'Rourke stares after the disappearing car, open-mouthed. Then she smooths her hands over her trousers, fixes the combs in her hair and shuts the door. Inside, she hurries down the polished parquetry to the hallstand and picks up the phone. Upstairs, the curtain draws closed again.

In the car, Happy looks awkward and is staring straight ahead. Dolores is sitting, silently shaking. She's twisting the rings on her fingers. Her knuckles are white. She has the wildest look in her eyes.

Kate goes to say something, but she doesn't know what to say. She puts her head on Dolores's shoulder. 'You're the bravest woman in Ringsend, Dolores Murphy,' she finally whispers.

'Ah, go on with you,' Dolores murmurs, looking out the window.

'I never got to confront the guy who raped me. I was too frightened when I was in his car. And then he left me to die. And then he topped himself, weak bastard. I scream at him in my sleep every night. I dream of doing what you just did.'

Dolores starts to cry. 'I do be forgetting, love.'

'It's okay. We did it together. Whatever happens, she had to live through that moment. She hated that, Dolores.'

'She did, didn't she?' Dolores wipes her eyes and they hold hands.

Kate pulls out her phone and goes to text the inspector to tell him where he might find Miss Nuala, but she's too agitated and doesn't want to deal with being scolded. *Tomorrow, Kate Delaney, call the inspector tomorrow.*

—

The next morning, Inspector Christy Redmond telephones Helen Byrne to arrange a formal interview with Oonagh Sullivan. He's told Mrs Byrne is not available but she will return his call, which she does ninety minutes later.

'I'm terribly sorry, Inspector, but Mrs Sullivan died in her sleep the night before last. And might I say, the shock of two gardaí turning up unannounced in her room can't have helped her old heart. Still, she lived a long and very accomplished life, was a woman of the faith, and she has gone to her maker, please God. And you know, that's all any of us can ask for. The Lord rest her soul.'

'Thank you for informing me,' Christy says in a stiff voice. Hanging up the phone, he throws the pen he's been holding at the wall.

John Barry pops his head around the partition.

'The Directress,' Christy mouths, silently, and draws his finger across his neck.

'Ah, for feck's sake,' says John.

'Make sure you get the details for the funeral. There could be some persons of interest who turn up.'

'Do you think her death is suspicious at all, Inspector?'

'Her dying the very night we turn up? You're dead right I do. I'm going to report this to the Coroner. We need an autopsy and a toxicology report. I've no doubt there will be claims of conscientious objection to post-mortem.'

'Oh, you can bet your house on it.'

Christy Redmond thinks of all the moral compromises Oonagh Sullivan had made on behalf of the Group—the ones he knows about and the ones that, inevitably, he doesn't. And how, for these people, they count for absolute naught. The moment she became a problem for their organisation, they knocked her off. Those wretched people put her out like she was a kipper at the back of the fridge that's past its sell-by date.

—

On the other end of the line, Helen Byrne calmly places the receiver back on the handset and looks up at the man in an expensive overcoat who is standing in her office, his arms folded. He nods, hands her an envelope, and returns to the black Mercedes parked outside. Helen Byrne makes the sign of the cross then calls to the dinner lady to get the residents' lunches ready.

—

Christy goes for a walk up Grafton Street to get some air. The weather has started to turn, and there's a fine mist of rain settling in. He pulls his coat around him and keeps walking through the crowds. He doesn't know where he's going, but he needs to think. As he's doing that, Christy's phone vibrates in his pocket. It's a text message from Kate Delaney.

> Sorry, Inspector, we got to Nuala. You wouldn't be the first cop I beat to a source.
>
> Don't hate me. Dolores needed it. Maybe so did I.
>
> She's in Merrion. Hang on, I'll forward you the address.

'Ah, for Jesus's sake,' Christy mutters to himself. He's too annoyed to reply. Christy Redmond never writes texts when he's cranky. Hotheads don't last long in policing. He calls John Barry instead and tells him to get a car ready. They're going to confront Miss Nuala.

The gardaí arrive at the Merrion terrace a couple of hours later. Christy looks up and sees the drapes abruptly close. Through the door he can hear a cat mewling and a woman crying out, 'Pippin! Pippin!'

The woman comes to the door, straightening her blouse. She tugs at one of her understated earrings and gives them a toothpaste advert smile.

'Well, well,' she trills, when they explain who they are. 'Well.'

'I think you know why we're here,' says John Barry, pulling out his notepad.

Christy shoots him a look.

'I understand you had some visitors yesterday,' the inspector says, studying her face. 'That can't have been an easy conversation.'

She says nothing and they just stare at each other for a few seconds.

'Are we going to do this on your front doorstep, or would you rather do it in privacy inside?' Christy asks.

Miss Nuala O'Rourke glances both ways, and sees one of her elderly neighbours looking at her. 'Okay, then. Come inside. But we shan't be long.'

She ushers them down the parquetry hallway to a little parlour, where she offers them a seat on a stiff and uncomfortable divan with elaborately turned walnut legs and blush-pink velvet upholstery. It's the coldest room Christy Redmond thinks he has ever been in.

She sits across from them in a chinoiserie armchair and folds her feet together in the way women in the Royal Family do. 'I think it's best if I call my solicitor,' she finally says.

'You know, before you do, if it's all the same, you might want to have a think to yourself about how this is all going to play out when we come back here, Nuala,' Christy responds. 'You might want to assess whether helping us at this critical point in our investigation might serve you well down the track.'

She narrows her eyes. 'What do you mean, Inspector?'

'You're facing a decent jail term, Nuala.' He keeps using her name because he can see it's irritating her. 'Assisting in the abduction of a baby from her mammy. Sexual crimes against at least one teenager. Slavery. We've taken Dolores Murphy's statement, but we're certain there are many others. And mind, we'll find them, Nuala. I think you know we will. We've spoken to other Help, too, and they're willing to assist us. There's a sense of momentum building, Nuala.'

'I do not know what you are insinuating,' she says.

'Oh, I think you do, Nuala. I think you do.'

Christy Redmond and John Barry sit there, Christy's arms folded, and both with pursed lips.

'Did ye hear now that the Directress has passed away very suddenly, Nuala?'

Her face goes grey and she goes to say something, but thinks better of it.

'Now correct me if I'm wrong, but it seems that she's the one who cooked up the plan to steal Dolores's baby. And of course, her culpability dies with her. So that leaves you, doesn't it?'

Her eyes dart between them as Pippin springs onto her lap.

'I think we'll both agree that a judge might look kindly on you providing us any information. You know, for mitigation, like? And there is one piece of information that you can give us now that will help. The names of that couple who took the baby.'

'Why on earth would I help a gard who comes to my home peddling lies and slander? Who believes bitter housekeepers with axes to grind? Where is the rule of law in all of this, Inspector? Where is the concept of innocent until proven guilty?'

Christy Redmond notes that Nuala O'Rourke seems awfully sharp for someone with recent experience of the mental health system. He turns to John Barry and sees that John is jotting something down. Great minds.

'Oh, you'll have all of your due process, Nuala. We're just doing our job. I'm just trying to do you, well, a little favour, like. A win-win for both of us in a situation where you stand to lose an awful lot, if you are found guilty. There's nothing you can do about the sex crimes, but you can assist with the matter of the child at least. But it's your picnic, Nuala, you can do as you choose.'

Christy looks at his colleague. 'Come on, John, maybe the lady needs some thinking time.'

'Right so, Inspector.' John puts his notepad and his pen in his top pocket and they both get up off the stiff divan and start to walk down the hall.

'Mulroney,' Nuala stammers after them.

The gardaí turn around.

'Their name was Mulroney. They were in the parish here in Merrion. They took the child when the O'Farrells found out she was . . .' Nuala looks awkward.

'When they found out she was black? Is that what you mean, Nuala?' asks John Barry, who can't help himself.

Nuala O'Rourke says nothing. She has the look in her eye of a person who fears she's been played.

'Now, I've that call to make to my solicitor,' she says. 'If you'll excuse me.'

'Mind yourself, Nuala,' says John Barry with a wink.

Christy Redmond tips his hat and shuts the door behind them.

—

Back at Pearse Street, John Barry is dispatched to search every couple in Dublin with the surname 'Mulroney', while Christy Redmond sits at his desk and furiously scans the PULSE database on his computer, biting his nails as he does. Armed robbery in the Ballymun flats. Methamphetamines haul out near Swords. There's to be a protest on Grafton Street tomorrow afternoon.

He enters the word 'Mulroney', thinking it will be a waste of time. But immediately, up flashes a listing for Wicklow. In a field up near Glenmacnass Waterfall in the Wicklow Mountains, a local garda had been called to an abandoned car on a farmer's property. The car has been traced to a Donal and Maureen Mulroney of Rathfarnham, a retired accountant and his wife. The garda went to the couple's house but found no one home. There are no signs of forced entry, and nothing seems amiss, but the Mulroneys haven't been seen in a couple of weeks. There is a daughter, who has left the country, and the gardaí are trying to track her down.

Christy pauses, re-reads the listing. That's odd, he figures. Retired accountants from Rathfarnham and their wives do not routinely go missing. He checks the database to see if either of them has any priors. Unsurprisingly, there is nothing.

He googles their names, and the search returns an article in the local paper describing a fundraiser held in the parish. In attendance were the Mulroneys and their daughter, Sinéad. Christy enters the name Sinéad Mulroney into the search bar, and a Facebook page pops up. 'Oh, holy mother of God,' he gasps. 'John? Come here.'

John Barry wheels his chair around the partition. Christy Redmond points at a profile picture with a rainbow flag background. The photograph shows an attractive thirty-something woman with caramel skin, Afro curls, large brown eyes, long eyelashes and a level gaze. Christy sits with his hand on his mouth and just points to it, and points to the PULSE entry on his second screen, and wordlessly shakes his head.

'Hoo boy,' says John Barry.

'Get into that Facebook page, Johnno.'

'No bother.'

—

As it happens, it is a bother. Garda John Barry thinks social media is for gobshites. Gardaí have been discouraged from using it, and cautioned that, if they do, they have to be exceedingly careful not to let it compromise their work. Their privacy is at risk and that's not an insubstantial matter when you're on the wrong side of the sorts of people they investigate. John had decided the safest bet was not to open any social media accounts in the first place. Unfortunately, this means that he's terrible at navigating his way through them. The social media companies are notoriously difficult to contact, and when he does manage to get on to someone, they speak to him like he's a moron because he uses the wrong language. He refers to Twitter as Tweeter, now more for effect than anything, because he thinks it's a complete waste of time. When he sits down at his terminal, opens Facebook and types in Sinéad Mulroney's name, to his dismay, she has locked down all of her privacy settings. He can access nothing but the profile photo and a background picture of butterflies. He knows he should just ask one of the younger ones in the office, but he's sick of them making fun of him for being a total Luddite. He decides to go out for an egg sandwich, swallow his pride, and go to the young ones after lunch. But then he has another idea.

—

Kate Delaney feels her phone buzzing in her pocket. Checking the caller ID, she sees it's John Barry.

'Howarye, Kate?' he begins.

'I've been better, John.'

'Listen, I've a favour to ask you, and it's kind of urgent. But it'll help your auntie.'

'You know I'll do anything for Dolores, John.'

John hesitates. 'It's a bit embarrassing.'

'No judgement,' Kate assures him.

The garda heaves a sigh. 'Okay. The truth is, I'm really, really shite at Facebook.'

Kate laughs. 'That's your big confession? I think you're forgiven.'

'No, but it's becoming more and more important in policing, and they just haven't given us the training. On the one hand, they've discouraged us from using it, and I think it's a pile of old bollocks anyway—'

'Ha, it *so* is.'

'—but on the other, we're needing it more and more for finding people. And I just have no idea what the feck I'm doing.'

'Well, John Barry, you have come to the right person, because I pretty much have a PhD in Facebook Stalking.'

'I had a feeling you would. Here's the thing. We think we've found Dolores's daughter.'

'What? Jesus Christ, John,' Kate says. Her heart starts to pound. 'That's burying the lede.'

'But she's got those locked-down privacy settings. And I can't make head nor tail of anything.'

'What's her name, John? Tell me. What's her name?'

'You have to promise me you won't tell the inspector I told you. He'd go off his rocker if he knew.'

'I never, ever betray my sources, John.'

'But this is not a journalist–source relationship,' the garda says doubtfully.

'True, but what I mean is I've had lots of practice in keeping people's secrets.'

'All right. Well, her name is Sinéad Mulroney. She's in her thirties, as you know. And her profile picture shows her with a rainbow—'

'—flag in the background. I see it!' Kate Delaney has already put him on speaker and started searching the name. 'Oh my God, John, she's got Dolores's ridiculously long eyelashes. And Nana's no-bullshit stare. And something about the arch of her eyebrows reminds me of Mammy.' Kate Delaney stares at the photo and starts to sob. 'Oh Jesus, John. It's her. How did you . . .?'

'Never mind that part of it. I just need you to do some of that advanced Facebook stalking and see what you can find. I will tell you one thing: she's from Rathfarnham. Her parents lived across from the Marlay Park. Can you do that for me now, Kate?'

Kate swallows and tries to compose herself. 'Of course I can, John. Of course, of course, of course.'

John Barry thanks her and hangs up and walks back into Pearse Street, taking a bite of his egg sandwich.

Kate Delaney takes a tissue out of her pocket and blows her nose. She looks back at the striking young woman's page—and gasps. *Sinéad Mulroney. One mutual friend.*

28

GLENDALOUGH

KATE STARES AT the screen in disbelief. Even though Kate has lived in Australia since she was in primary school, she and Dolores's long-lost daughter, Kate's first cousin, have a mutual Facebook friend. It's mad.

She clicks on the link. 'Oh, for fuck's sake. Richie Daly.'

In a way, this shouldn't come as a surprise. The King of the Grushys knows pretty much everyone on the Southside. He's a shameless namedropper. He's not a public figure, and yet he has four thousand Facebook friends. Plus there's the Rathfarnham connection; Richie Daly grew up in Ballinteer, which also borders the Marlay Park. He'd undoubtedly know loads of people from Rathfarnham. He probably knew girls who went to school with Sinéad.

She rings him immediately.

'Kate Delaney, how's it goin'?'

'Look, it's a lot. A lot of shit has gone down since I last saw you, Richie.'

'That seems to be the way with you.'

'Yeah, thanks, all the same. Hey, listen, do you know a Sinéad Mulroney?'

'Hmm . . . You'll have to give me some more clues.'

'Well, you're Facebook friends with her.'

'I have a lot of Facebook friends, Kate.'

'So I see, you're a popular boy. Her parents live up by the Marlay Park.'

'Let me have a look,' he says. He puts her on speaker and there's a pause as he checks his Facebook account. 'Oh, yeah, I think she might have been in sixth form with Maeve Doherty, my ex-girlfriend. I met her at a couple of parties. She's a bit, you know, unusual. Or what do they call it, now, like? Neurodivergent?'

Kate sighs and tries not to show her frustration. 'Political correctitude thy name is Daly. Do you know where she is now, Richie?'

'God, I haven't thought of her in years. Maeve's, like, four girlfriends ago. She was a fucking ride, though, if you don't mind me saying.'

'You are incorrigible, Richie. Do you think you could give me Maeve's number?'

'Sure. What's it for? Who is this Sinéad to you?'

'I could tell you, but I'd have to kill you.'

'You're a deadset fuckin' lunatic, so you are.'

'Takes one to know one.'

'Yeah, yeah.'

'I promise I'll fill you in. I just can't at the moment.'

'Okay. Fair play to you, Kate.'

'And to you, Richie. Hey, Richie? I love you, cousin.'

'Don't be a gobshite. I love you, too.'

She hangs up, and a few seconds later her phone chimes with a message. Richie has sent the number. Kate looks up Maeve Doherty's Facebook page to see who she's dealing with. Just as she suspected, she's a Richie Daly ex from central casting. Pastel Ralph Lauren polo shirt with the collar popped. Honey-coloured hair and skin. Definitely doesn't eat carbs after 2 pm.

Kate calls the number. It goes to message, and she leaves a text asking Maeve to call, saying she's Richie's cousin and she'd like to speak to her urgently. Kate just hopes Richie wasn't a dick to her.

That evening, Sinéad Mulroney is in Prague, correcting her English students' tests in the common room of the hostel she's living in. She's beginning to really like this city, and is considering looking for a place of her own. Sinead pays a little more for a single room instead of a bunk in a dormitory, but it's a bit hectic at times, especially when they get in a crowd of Aussie backpackers, who stay up all night singing songs she's never heard before but for which she now knows every word, like

'Khe Sanh' and 'Throw Your Arms Around Me'. And if they're not singing, they're shagging endlessly. They sometimes try to engage her in conversation at breakfast and Sinéad just looks at them blankly and says, 'I'd rather not.' It's not lost on her that she's in her thirties and she's living this life a good decade too late. But no one knows her here, she looks young for her age, so it seems like a good place to navigate this particular, messy, rite of passage.

One of the more performatively loud Australian girls, who seems intent on demonstrating to everyone how worldly and smart she is, insists on flicking the television to BBC World because she is studying media and is, she declares, 'a *complete* news junkie'. Sinéad likes to keep up with things, too, ordinarily, but since she left Dublin, she's been in this sealed bubble away from the rest of the world.

The BBC News music comes on and Sinéad wishes they'd turn it down, but her ears prick up when the presenter's cut-glass accent says, '*And now to Dublin, where the mystery of a car abandoned in the Wicklow Mountains is troubling the Gardaí.*' She looks up and puts her hand to her mouth. There, in a field, is Mam and Dad's Volkswagen.

'Turn it up, turn it up,' she shrieks at the Australians.

Her feet feel like they're going to buckle under her as the news story shows an exterior shot of her house in Rathfarnham and headshots of Mam and Dad.

'Maureen and Donal Mulroney lived a quiet life in the leafy Dublin suburb of Rathfarnham, but no one knows where they are now.

'"You could never meet a more lovely, unassuming couple," says Mrs Meagher, who lives at number four. *"Everyone is really desperately worried about them."'*

A garda comes on the screen next, clearly conducting some sort of press conference. '*We would like to appeal to anyone who knows the whereabouts of Mr and Mrs Mulroney. In particular, we're looking to make contact with their daughter, Sinéad, whom we believe is travelling overseas. Sinéad, if you see this, please make contact with us immediately.*'

A reporter stands in a trench coat and wellingtons with the Glenmacnass Waterfall behind her. '*It's unclear exactly how long Maureen and Donal Mulroney's car has been abandoned here in the Wicklow Mountains. Gardaí are saying that, unfortunately, they suspect foul play. One thing is for certain: this is a case that is confounding authorities. Lorna Kerry, BBC News.*'

Sinéad Mulroney walks from the hostel to the street outside and screams.

—

Maeve Doherty hasn't seen the news story. She calls Kate Delaney back and, in response to Kate's question, explains that she never really knew Sinéad that well, she was a bit of a loner, and that Kate needs to get on to Sinéad's best friend from school, Karen O'Connor.

'Wait, Maeve, before you go, would you mind looking at Sinéad's page and seeing where she is now?' Kate hopes that Maeve won't think this is an intrusion of privacy.

Maeve doesn't. She tells Kate that last night Sinéad posted for the first time in months. It was an evening selfie on that famous bridge—the one in Prague where they filmed the INXS video. She sends Kate a screen grab.

'Thanks a million, Maeve,' says Kate, and she forwards the screen grab to John Barry, who immediately texts back his thanks.

—

Sinéad's best friend, Karen O'Connor, has seen the news story, and has sent Sinéad twenty-three texts and left several increasingly anxious voicemails. Karen is the only person back home who has Sinéad's new number. Sinéad leaves the texts unread and the voicemails unheard. She's in a cab on the way to Václav Havel Airport.

When she gets to the terminal, Sinéad Mulroney finds a quiet spot and rings a Gardaí hotline she finds online.

'I need to get a message to whoever is investigating the disappearance of Donal and Maureen Mulroney,' she tells the operator. 'I'm their daughter, Sinéad. Tell them I'm about to get on a plane to Dublin if they want to meet me at the airport. My plane lands at ten pm.'

—

John Barry hurries to Christy Redmond's desk and says he's managed to track down a selfie that Sinéad posted the night before from the Charles Bridge. 'She's in Prague, Inspector,' he says breathlessly. He doesn't mention Kate Delaney, nor her PhD in Facebook Stalking.

'Good work, John—but I've just had a call to say that she's on a plane,' Christy says. 'We're to meet her at the airport at ten.'

'This is moving fast, Inspector.'

'Aye.'

—

Sinéad Mulroney stares vacantly out the plane window as images of her mam and dad float through her mind. Mam bending down to tie her shoelaces and reassure her that if she practised and practised, one day she'd get it. 'But I'm twelve, Mammy, why can't I do it?' 'Because you are special, Sinéad. You have other gifts.' Dad nudging Mam in the audience as, up on stage, Sinéad spelled 'onomatopoeia' and 'restaurateur'. Mam wiping

Sinéad's tears as she dropped her soft-serve ice cream into the water at the Forty Foot—and then walking all the way back to Dun Laoghaire to get her another one. Mam and Dad taking turns lying with her in her little sleigh bed each night until she was finally soothed to sleep. Mam wiping her hands on her apron. Dad sitting in his chair, tut-tutting at the news presenter's wrong pronunciation on the telly. Or uncharacteristically losing his cool at Superquinn when someone made a racist remark. Their quiet desperation as she begged them to tell her where she really came from. Her creeping feeling now that maybe it shouldn't have mattered. Because Sinéad Mulroney never, not for one day, felt like she wasn't loved. Love didn't seem an adequate word, now, for what Mam and Dad gave her.

She starts crying as she recalls a documentary in which a journalist interviewed a series of adoptees from countries like Romania and the Philippines. And to a person, all of them said that their lives were demonstrably better than they ever could have been were they not adopted, that they adored their adoptive parents and knew they were loved. And yet, and yet, and yet, they wished they weren't adopted. Watching that documentary was the final impetus for the row Sinéad and her parents had that night in Rathfarnham. The row that saw her pack her suitcase and leave.

Why wouldn't they answer her? Clearly something was too painful or too difficult. She can't forget the look in their eyes.

The last look she ever saw in their eyes when she said goodbye. A strange and silent mix of frustration and sorrow and recognition of their moral compromise and, again, always, love.

You know when people you love have gone. You sense their absence, the negative space they once occupied, even if you're not in the same city or the same country. On that plane from Prague to Dublin, Sinéad Mulroney knows that the two people who had never wanted anything as much as they wanted her are gone.

And they are. They're in the coldest depths of Glendalough Upper Lake. Christy Redmond and John Barry won't find them. No one will.

—

The double doors slide open at Dublin Airport's arrivals hall and everywhere there are families. Young couples with toddlers run into their grandparents' arms. Middle-aged parents waving to gap-year backpackers reddened in Australian sun. Families with balloons and banners that say things like WELCOME HOME DARRAGH! Tears and hugs and relief at being Home.

But no one is waiting for Sinéad Mulroney except Inspector Christy Redmond and Garda John Barry, who are craning their necks above the crowd on the lookout for a young woman with caramel skin and curly hair and large brown eyes with ridiculously long eyelashes. They wave politely when they see her emerge, wheeling her suitcase. And Sinéad can't do anything but bury her head in Christy's shoulder and sob.

'Now, now, there, Sinéad. Now, now,' says Christy.

They lead her out to the car and drive to Pearse Street.

'I'm never going to see them again, am I?' she says from the back seat.

And Christy Redmond and John Barry don't have the words to answer.

Christy Redmond is at least in some way relieved to have discovered in the intervening hours from his colleagues at Rathfarnham Garda Station that Maureen and Donal were sighted on CCTV at Dundrum shopping centre, catching the Luas into town, getting their messages at SuperValu in Ballinteer, long after Sinéad was captured on CCTV boarding an EasyJet flight from Dublin to Gatwick. Mrs Meagher at number four had borrowed a cup of sugar from Maureen and the postman had hand-delivered a parcel to Donal. There are no flight records of Sinéad returning to Ireland since. She has flown straight from Prague after seeing the news item on the BBC. She is inconsolably upset. There is nothing to suggest that she is in any way involved in the Mulroneys' disappearance. Christy doesn't think he could have coped with the emotional confusion of finding Dolores's long-lost daughter and discovering that she had murdered her adoptive parents.

The emotional confusion in this case is of a different order. It's hardly like an episode of one of those TV programs where families are reunited and there are tears of joy all round. How exactly does he break it to Sinéad that the reason he became involved in this investigation is not because of the sudden disappearance of her adoptive parents, but because she was stolen from the birth mother who is desperate to find her, and that the parents for whom she is now grieving might have been complicit in the fact she was stolen?

—

In Ringsend the next morning, Kate Delaney is pacing Dolores's tiny living room as her aunt watches the news on RTÉ. Periodically she rushes to the bathroom to vomit, trying to do so quietly so her aunt won't worry.

Why hasn't the inspector called yet? How much longer does she have to keep this secret from her aunt? Dolores had seen the item about Maureen and Donal Mulroney's disappearance in the Wicklow Mountains and the police appeal for Sinéad to call them, but she has no idea that this is in any way connected to her. Kate does, though. She had recognised the name immediately from her Facebook stalking and messaged Richie Daly.

Are Sinéad Mulroney's parents called Donal
and Maureen?

Jesus, Kate, you mean that couple who've gone
missing in the Wicklow Mountains? What are
you involved in?

Never mind, Richie, it's important—can you check her
Facebook account?

There's definitely a Maureen on there. Yep, just found a
photo of them on holiday in Spain. Are you going to tell
me what this is about, Kate?

Christ. I can't now, Richie, but promise I will. Thanks
for your help. X

Abso-fucking-lutely you will.

'That's awful sad,' Dolores says now, as onscreen a journalist reports sombrely that there is still no sign of the missing couple. 'I hope they find them.' She shakes her head and sips her tea. 'They live not far from Annie's place, you know—over near the Marlay Park where I used to take you and Richie to play to give Annie and your mam a break. They don't look like the type to go missing.'

'I guess you never know. I didn't look like the type to go missing, either,' says Kate. 'Dolores, can you please turn the TV off?' She's getting agitated.

'Oh, Kate, how insensitive of me. I'm so sorry.'

Kate runs upstairs. Pete D'Ambrosio, the detective who investigated her case and with whom she became friends after she was found, had told her about his chronic hives that would flare up whenever his PTSD was triggered. The feeling of creeping, tingling, itching. Kate had begun to suffer with the hives, too, though they had settled down since she went to Greece.

Now, sitting in Dolores's spare room waiting for Christy Redmond or John Barry to call, she feels them creeping up her arms, down her neck, all over her back. She lifts her shirt and looks in the mirror. On her back is a network of long angry welts; it looks like she's been whipped. Her pain on behalf of her aunt has somehow manifested itself on her skin. She feels like she wants to tear it off.

Don't get caught in the undertow, Kate Delaney. Run for the wall.

The door bursts open and Dolores walks in. Seeing Kate's back she cries out and puts her hand to her mouth.

'What did you do to yourself, Kate?' she asks. 'Why would you do this?'

'No, Dolores, I didn't do this to myself—it's hives.' And she bolts into the bathroom to be sick again.

When she returns, Dolores is sitting on the bed with her head in her hands. 'It's too much, Kate. I can't bear the waiting anymore. They're never going to find her. I don't know why I ever told anyone, why I did this to myself. I should have just kept it inside. I always lose the people I love. Marcus. Your mammy. Kevin. My baby.'

'I'm here, Dolores,' Kate says. 'And I need you. You're my good-looking auntie.'

Dolores laughs a little through her tears and they sit together on the bed in the box room, hands clasped, until the phone rings. She answers it, listens, then hands the phone to Dolores.

It's Christy Redmond.

'Dolores,' he says, 'I've got someone here who wants to meet you.'

—

At Pearse Street Garda Station the night before, Sinéad Mulroney had sat in an almost catatonic state for the first hour. She wouldn't eat, wouldn't speak, wouldn't make eye contact. Then, as if a switch had been flicked, she came to life. She poured out her story to Christy and John, barely pausing for breath. How and why she had left, the questions she had asked her parents, her guilt now for having asked them, how she'd taken her Irish SIM card out of her phone so they couldn't contact her, how they had been brilliant parents, her absolute mystification at how or why anyone would want to harm them. She pulled out the SIM card she'd kept in her purse and inserted it in her phone, and the three of them listened to all the voicemail messages from Maureen and Donal.

'Please, Sinéad, it's Mam, just come home to us.'

'Please, Sinéad, just let us know that you're safe.'

'Hullo, Sinéad, it's your Daddy here. I want you to know your mammy is out of her mind. (throat clearing) *Your mam and da love you, you know.'*

'Mam here again. You needn't speak to us if you don't want to, just leave a message that you're all right.'

'Mind yourself, Sinéad.'

But then the messages stopped. And there were no other clues as to why the Mulroneys went missing.

John Barry just kept looking at Christy Redmond and Christy Redmond kept looking at John Barry.

'Let me ask you this, Sinéad,' Christy said. 'They never told you any details about your adoption?'

'They said I came from an adoption agency. But I remember when I needed my birth certificate to get a passport, and they didn't have one. They were all flustered about it. And Mam, who never got angry at anyone, snapped at me. I began to wonder if it was one of those dodgy adoptions that the nuns did. You know, where it was all a bit under the table?'

'I do,' said Christy nodding. 'I have seen many of those in my time.'

'Right? So that's what I was beginning to suspect. But I was curious about my heritage—they said I was African, but they didn't know where in Africa I was from. I mean, Africa's a big place. They said they thought my birth mammy was dead. And you know, Mam was an absolutely terrible liar. I never saw her lie about anything. She had very strong morals. Very Catholic, in a good way. And the way she avoided my questions, it just didn't sit well with me. She would look nervously at Dad, and he would change the subject, like. They were the two least fishy people you would ever hope to meet. And yet, when it came to one of the most important things in my life—you know, who am I—they were undeniably fishy. And they just would not answer me, at all. Even when I was raging and screaming at them and begging them to tell me the truth, they just kept their mouths shut. And that's not on. But what about you, Inspector?' She fixed her large eyes on Christy. 'Do *you* know?'

'Sinéad, I'm aware you've had a very rough twenty-four hours, and I'm sure you must be emotionally exhausted. You mentioned earlier that you have in recent years been diagnosed as autistic. Would you like a support person to help you navigate all of this?'

Sinéad shook her head. 'I don't need someone to pass me tissues and patronise me,' she said. 'If there's one thing you should know about high-functioning autistics, it's that all we want is for people to be straight with us. To tell us the truth. We don't cope at all with bullshit. So, please, if there's something I should know, just tell me.'

Christy had sighed and pointed his fingertips together in front of him.

'Very well, Sinéad. The case John and I have been investigating did not start with Maureen and Donal's disappearance. It was launched by your birth mother.'

She looked at him sharply. 'Tell me. Tell me. Tell me.' She could feel what her primary-school teacher used to call the Big Red Angry Beast rising within her. She wanted to upend a chair. 'Tell me!'

'Her name is Dolores Murphy, and she lives here in Dublin, in Ringsend,' Christy said. 'And she wants to meet you. In fact, she's always wanted to meet you. She never wanted to give you up in the first place. You were stolen from her. Not by Maureen and Donal, mind,' he added hastily. 'They weren't the ones to steal you—but we don't know the full circumstances of how they got you. Do you think that you would be open to meeting Dolores, Sinéad?'

And Sinéad Mulroney stared at them, slowly nodding her head.

29

REUNION

THERE ARE SO many loose threads for Christy Redmond and John Barry to tie up.

What about Miss Nuala?

Dolores Murphy will make a full supplementary statement about Nuala O'Rourke's sexual abuse, the gardaí will turn up at Nuala's door and Ireland's most expensive barrister will represent her, claiming she is mentally unfit for trial. The case will draw out for years.

And Miss Róisín?

Despite her advancing years, she's still struggling to keep her hands off earnest American girls doing summer catering courses. Later, she will exercise her right to remain silent and engage one of California's top attorneys to fight extradition when Mairéad O'Riordan and Clodagh O'Reilly make detailed and disturbing allegations of serious sexual abuse against her. When the case hits the news, other Help will come forward and join the case. It too will go on for years.

Where are Donal and Maureen?

In weighted flour sacks, among the weeds and the baby brown trout at the bottom of Upper Glendalough Lake. Their car will be scoured for fingerprints. None will be found. Their case will go down as one of Ireland's most troubling unsolved mysteries.

Who was involved in their disappearance?

Good question. The only clue, found in the centre console of the Mulroneys' car, is a prayer card with a picture of Saint Maria Goretti. Christy Redmond's frustrated superiors inform him that, despite the many statements declaring that the Directress and her underlings were obsessed with the teenage saint, this proves absolutely *feck all*. Every few months for a good few years, Christy Redmond will go to forensics, pull on some white gloves, carefully pull the prayer card out of its plastic pouch, turn it over in his hand and sigh.

How about Valeria?

Positive news on that front. Christy Redmond will secure her release from indentured servitude. She'll end up working for a mate of Christy's in a cafe on the Aran Islands. She'll marry a fisherman. Agnes will be helped to leave the Grásta Dé psychiatric facility and the Group. She'll study for a certificate in aged care.

What will happen to all the other Help?

There will be a worldwide slavery case run out of South America, where the Help were particularly badly treated. Many will die before seeing justice served. Dolores and Mairéad and Clodagh will appear, arms linked, on the cover of the *Irish Times*.

Was the Directress's death a homicide?

Well, of course. But the CCTV at the care home will be 'lost'. Helen Byrne will refuse to cooperate. Ireland's second-most expensive barrister will make an appearance. And Oonagh Sullivan's only son, a performance artist whose work explores the complexity of bondage and discipline culture in lapsed Catholics, will go on to become one of the first men in Ireland to marry his boyfriend. He won't press the matter of foul play.

But before any of that, a mammy and baby who should never have been separated are about to meet for the first time.

—

Dolores Murphy tells Kate she wants to go down to Pearse Street on her own.

'This is my moment, I need it to be mine alone,' she says. 'There will be time for you.'

Kate is frustrated. She's desperate to meet her cousin. She wants to be part of the moment, too. But she sees the fierce look in Dolores's eyes and so doesn't argue. 'I'm here if you need me,' she whispers.

Dolores Murphy is too agitated to get a bus or a taxi, so she just walks all the way. Past the library. Past the church where

Mammy and Daddy were married, and she made her first holy communion, and all the babies were baptised. Past the statue of Our Lady. Past Auntie Maggie's flat, looking down on the dirty Dodder with its bank of swans. Past the pub where Daddy spent the money that should have been for the children's dinners. Over the bridge where the men carry the coffins as a last tribute from the community. Up past the old Christian Brothers school where Happy Murphy wreaked havoc. Past Boland's Mills and past the weird, shiny new tech hub that had sent the housing prices in the area through the roof. Past the queues of buses dropping people into town outside Trinity College. And across the street to Pearse Street Garda Station, where a thirty-five-year-old woman is waiting for her.

Dolores feels like she is walking alongside herself or floating above. In her mind she's rolling down the long grass of the Hill of Tara and tumbling on top of Marcus Akenyemi. Gazing at the stars and singing 'Northern Sky'. The horror of Dr Lonergan's forceps. Seeing her plump little gurgling bundle being weighed by the nurse matron in the corner of the room. The feeling of the hypodermic needle going into her arm. The distant sound of the infant's cries. Holding on to her shrunken belly and her leaking breasts. Walking down Henry Street, checking buggies for biracial babies. Sitting in the typing pool of the bottle factory, daydreaming about what her girl might be learning in school. Getting caught in the undertow at Shellybanks.

Garda John Barry comes out to the foyer and says, 'Howarye, Dolores?' and then says, 'Aw, feck it,' and gives her a hug.

John leads her into the warren of rooms behind the reception desk and stops outside a closed door. He taps on the door and Inspector Christy Redmond emerges.

'Are you all right, Dolores?' he asks.

But Dolores can't speak.

'Ready?'

She takes a breath and nods.

The inspector gestures for her to enter the room.

Dolores steps through the door, and she sees Marcus Akenyemi's large brown eyes and her own ridiculously long eyelashes and the arch of Mary's eyebrow and her mother's level gaze. Her eyes travel down the girl's bare arms and there, on the inside of her elbow, is a birthmark shaped like a strawberry. And she steps forward and takes her girl in her arms and holds her and she says, 'Mammy's here, Mammy's here, Mammy's here, sshhhh, Mammy's here.' And they stand there and just hold each other silently.

How do you make up for a lifetime lost, in a first meeting? You don't. There are just no words to say. It's awkward and it's beautiful and it's sad.

But Sinéad Mulroney and Dolores Murphy are content to sit with it. There's no need to rush now. They have time. They have each other.

—

And that night, Kate Delaney will meet her cousin for the first time. The cousin who passed by her when she was sorting through cockles at Shellybanks. Whose mutual Facebook friend is their other cousin, Richie Daly (who declares the whole thing 'absolutely *mental*'). Who played on the swings in the Marlay Park and collected conkers and caught butterflies. Kate Delaney has trundled past that house in Rathfarnham on the number 16 bus countless times. Just another house, white, semi-detached, with a garden of purple hydrangeas. Looking like all the others, but inside lived a couple with a secret and a child who shared her blood.

That night, Kate dreams of another baby. A baby girl. The dream is so vivid that when she wakes, she reaches out to touch her.

And then she runs to the toilet. And she runs again and again over the next few days. Dolores and Sinéad will hold back her hair at bus stops and the smell of Dolores coming back from one of her 'meetings with Nico' makes Kate turn immediately green. Her breasts are sore and she feels indescribably odd. She hasn't had periods much since the trauma and so she'd stopped thinking about them. But she knows what she's feeling.

She needs to be with Liam Carroll.

'I have to go home,' she tells Dolores and Sinéad, who have barely left each other's sides.

'But this is your home,' says Dolores.

Kate smiles wistfully. 'It's not anymore, Dolores. Would you two think about coming to Australia in a few months?' She puts her hand on her belly. Dolores places her hand on top of Kate's and she looks at her daughter, who smiles.

—

Two weeks later, Kate Delaney is on a runway at Dublin Airport. She presses her face against the plane window and says a silent goodbye to the statues of Our Lady, the startling green fields, the tide slowly creeping in to Shellybanks and, in the airport terminal about to head home to Ringsend, her good-looking auntie and the baby girl she never knew. They're off to start Facebook stalking Akenyemis in Lagos in the hope that Sinéad can make contact with her other people and learn more about who she is and where she came from.

Kate loves this place; this home until you open your mouth, and you find that you somehow don't belong anymore. But it's time to go back to the place where she can make a life again. It won't be perfect. But it will be good. Maybe one day she'll write that novel she never got to start on her Greek island. Or maybe she won't.

—

She hasn't told Liam yet. She wants to surprise him.

Her best friend, Sylvia, meets her at Tullamarine. 'Tiger!' she says, running into Kate's arms. 'Man, you look sick.'

'I hope you mean that as in "fully sick" rather than sick, sick,' Kate says.

'Oh, totally, completely, fully sick.'

Kate has already told Sylvia her news and arranged to stay at her place that night before heading to get her eight-week scan the next afternoon.

Sylvia drives her to the radiographer the next day, regaling her with too much information about episiotomies and mastitis and haemorrhoids.

At the clinic, a no-nonsense radiographer called Nancy applies gel to Kate's tummy and swirls the wand across Kate's abdomen.

And then there she is, on the screen. A little silvery blob. Her baby girl. Liam Carroll's baby girl. A life that almost never happened. A life that could have been extinguished before it started at Pheasants Nest. But wasn't.

'Can you drive me to Liam's?' she asks Sylvia.

'Absolutely, Tiger.'

At Liam's Northcote flat, Kate fishes out the spare key she keeps in the zipped-up compartment of her purse and lets herself in. Her feet are still swollen from the flight, and she takes off her shoes and the cool of the polished concrete soothes her soles.

There, on the bookshelf, is their broken Child of Prague statue. Photos of them standing, windblown, at the Twelve Apostles. Some selfies they took at the Flaggy Shore in Clare. A coin from the Barack Obama Plaza vending machine. Her Gold Walkley. She fetches some dry rice crackers from Liam's pantry, and some ginger ale from his fridge, to try to stave off the nausea.

Then she goes into the bedroom and stretches out on Liam's roughly made bed, which smells like cinnamon. And she waits, until the jet lag overcomes her, and she falls asleep.

At quarter to seven, Liam turns his key in the door. He looks around, sensing a presence. And he walks into his bedroom and finds her, red hair tangled on his pillow, snoring quietly. Her hands are clasped on her chest and underneath them is what looks like a photograph. He tiptoes over and gently takes it from her hand. And there it is, a little silvery blob. His girl. The life that almost never happened. But has.

And he lies down next to her and eases her head into the crook of his arm. And he feels warm.

ACKNOWLEDGEMENTS

I'M NOT QUITE sure how to sum up my gratitude for my beautiful mother, Mary, and her sisters—who sat up with me in their kitchens, late at night and told me their stories. Particularly Anne and Christine, who each have smatterings of Dolores Murphy, and who, like me, wanted her to have those smatterings, so they told me the unvarnished truth about their experiences as young women in an Ireland that has so radically changed. You are like sunshine on my skin, all of you. Including dear Teresa, whom I adored, and is no longer with us, and my dear and gentle godmother, Pauline.

I'm also so thankful for my uncles, who wheeled my pram around Ringsend as a baby and walked me to Shellybanks as a grown-up when I was researching this novel. To Michael, who shared his love of literature with me as a teenager, and who took me down to the Pigeon House Road and Sandymount Strand

and to Shellybanks, and barely paused for breath the whole way, telling me how it was. Boxing the fox, running away from the Christian Brothers, not getting caught in the Cockle Lake by the tides. And Thomas, who got us into that pretty little red lighthouse that punctuates Dublin Bay and introduced me to The La's and sung along to The Smiths and took his time and cared. And Eamonn, who was also called Happy, and no one ever suited a nickname more. And Gerard and Liam, who would do anything for you and know Ringsend inside out. And Patrick, who is better known in those parts than all the rest put together. I'm so far away most of the time, but not in my heart. I love you all.

I am in awe of, and have deep gratitude for, Anne Marie Allen. Anne Marie, like women around the world, had a story not unlike that of Dolores Murphy. The stories those women and their legal representatives tell are horrific. I met Anne Marie through my journalism. These women deserve to be heard. Anne Marie is not just brave, articulate and extremely talented in her own right, she's also one of the loveliest people you would ever hope to meet. I'm so glad to know you, Anne Marie. Thank you for all of your time and your patience with me.

To Claire Harris, Alex McKenzie and all the people who assisted me with 'Purity' for *Four Corners*—without you I would never have met Anne Marie and never got inside the head of the Help and the people from the fictional Group who oppress Dolores. The characters in this book and the religious organisation depicted in it are, of course, entirely made up. But all fiction has threads of truth. All fiction was somehow lived.

To the real Christy, who was such an utter gentleman and who not just talked me through the life of a garda, but even discussed plot points. I am so thankful for your time, Christy. And thank you for letting me borrow your first name, which I love. And to Des, who also generously gave his time speaking about life as a garda, too.

To my cousin Toju and his daughter Éabha, for giving me the perspective of what it's like to grow up Irish–Nigerian. You are both such lovely humans and thank you so much for giving me your time. And to my beautiful cousin Karen, an avid reader who thankfully *didn't* drown at Shellybanks, and who has been my dear friend since we played at the Marlay Park with ribbons in our pigtails. Can't wait to see you again.

Thank you to my agent, Jeanne Ryckmans (who first planted the seed in my mind that Kate Delaney could appear in another book after *Pheasants Nest*), publisher Cate Paterson, and all the people at Allen & Unwin, who have made this book happen and are such professionals and a joy to work with.

Much love to Nick and Rory for again leading me to this process and for holding up the fort when I was in Ireland to research *Shellybanks*. You're owed an overseas trip! Thank you to Rory for making me understand the beauty of neurodiversity, which I really wanted to write about in this book. You are a fine young man and I am so proud to be your mum every single day. And thank you to my beautiful Celeste for coming along on one of my trips to Ireland to be my very proficient teenage research partner. You did such a wonderful job—even coming up with narrative ideas, you clever thing. I'll never forget that time we had together as mother and daughter. Let's do it again.

Thank you to Stephen and Mel and Séamus for putting me up in Ireland, and for your commitment to story and the written and spoken word. Love you.

And lastly, thank you so much to all the readers who embraced *Pheasants Nest* so wholeheartedly and who have now, since you got this far, read *Shellybanks*. In my day job, I frequently go to dark places. And I often say that writing fiction makes me so happy, I feel like I have lemonade in my veins. So, thank you for supporting my work. I can't believe I get to do this.

ALSO FROM ALLEN & UNWIN

PHEASANTS NEST

LOUISE MILLIGAN

A gripping, fast-paced thriller, *Pheasants Nest* is a brilliantly original debut from award-winning journalist Louise Milligan.

Kate Delaney has made the biggest mistake of her life. One impulsive encounter on a girls' night out leaves her kidnapped, bound and in the back of a stranger's car.

As a crime reporter, Kate knows the grim statistics—most abducted women are never found alive. Her terrified boyfriend Liam, and the detectives who rally to find her, lose hope with every hour that passes.

Kate must summon all her courage to stay alive.

'Wry observations of popular culture and Australian foibles . . . I simply didn't want the book to end given the sheer delight of the storytelling.' *The Age*

ISBN 978 1 76147 375 3